JERRY POURNELLE
THE USERS GUIDE TO SMALL COMPUTERS

A BAEN BOOK

For Dan E. MacLean
  and Anton Pietsch
  with thanks.

THE USER'S GUIDE TO SMALL COMPUTERS

All rights reserved including the right of reproduction in whole or in part in any form.

Copyright © 1984 by Jerry Pournelle

All rights reserved, including the right to reproduce this book or portions thereof in any form.

A Baen Book

Baen Enterprises
8-10 W. 36th Street
New York, N.Y. 10018

First Baen printing, October 1984.

ISBN: 0-671-55908-7

Cover art by Robert Tinney

Printed in the United States of America

Distributed by
SIMON & SCHUSTER MASS MERCHANDISE SALES COMPANY
1230 Avenue of the Americas
New York, N.Y. 10020

Praise for America's #1 User

"Jerry Pournelle's 'Users Column' has been one of *BYTE* magazine's most popular columns for years. No matter what the subject, from operating systems to disk drives to software licenses, Jerry states his opinions fully, without compromise, and in a lively colloquial style.

"Jerry's fondness for computers—for his old friend Zeke the Cromemco and for lovely lightweight Adele, who happens to be an Otrona Portable—make his criticism of less appealing machines all the more forceful and credible.

"Letters to Jerry pour in every week from all over the world. No one could copy his style, but everyone agrees that he has not only discovered something essential and attractive in the nature of small computers, but also a vein of human responsiveness to them."

Phil Lemmons, Editor-in-Chief, *BYTE*

"Challenging, articulate, and always opinionated, Jerry Pournelle remains our most controversial computer writer. With machines and software piling up in his wake, Jerry forges onward in the microcomputer revolution, followed by a growing band of energized users. Not content merely to report what's happening from his Chaos Manor viewport, Jerry makes us think about how the wonderful machines will change our lives and shape our future."

Pam Clark,
Editor-in-Chief, *Popular Computing*

TABLE OF CONTENTS

PREFACE: HOW I GOT THIS WAY   vii
PART ONE: GETTING STARTED
    Chapter 1. Writing with Computers   2
    Chapter 2. The Early User's Columns   16

PART TWO: WRITING WITH COMPUTERS
    Chapter 1. The Silverberg Correspondence   52
    Chapter 2. Hardware   57
    Chapter 3. Software   76

PART THREE: EARLY FRIENDS   87
    Chapter 1. Pirates and Operating Systems   89
    Chapter 2. The Great Software Drought   107
    Chapter 3. Languages, Accounts, and Other Madness   128
    Chapter 4. Passing Friends   144

PART FOUR: MOSTLY LANGUAGES
    Chapter 1. The Great Language Debates   158
    Chapter 2. The Debates Continue   177
    Chapter 3. The Debate Goes On   210

PART FIVE: SOME PREDICTIONS   223
    Chapter 1. Here Come the Brains   224
    Chapter 2. The Brains Keep Coming   238

Chapter 3. The Next Five Years in Micro Computing 253
Chapter 4. Can David Survive Goliath in the
          Computer Industry? 266

PART SIX: THE USER GOES POPULAR 271
Chapter 1. The Computer Revolution 272
Chapter 2. The Management Revolution and How
          To Get In On It 282
Chapter 3. The Operating System Jungle 292
Chapter 4. Right Up to the Minute . . . 310
A Few Final Words 331

PREFACE
How I Got This Way

I was one of the earliest writers to use a computer, but I never set out to be a computer expert. I wrote my first computer articles largely to convince the Internal Revenue Service that Ezekial, my friend who happened to be a Z-80 computer, was legitimately deductible. Now, of course, that wouldn't be necessary. Most writers use "word processors," and even the IRS understands their necessity.

It wasn't always that way. I got Zeke in the nearly forgotten days when the most advanced writing tools were self-correcting IBM Selectric typewriters. He cost far more than I could afford, and then came the horrible discovery that although Zeke could do everything I'd bought him for, I wanted him to do a lot of other interesting things—but he needed expensive software I couldn't really afford.

Actually, things were worse than that. Back in the '70s software wasn't a lot less expensive than it is now—but it was sure a lot less reliable. Much of it was totally unusable, yet there were no guarantees whatever. No company would refund your money, and all "warranted" that their software was worthless garbage, utterly without value—unless, of course, you copied it, in which case the software was priceless, and the wretched user who made a backup copy had harmed the publisher irredeemably. That problem remains with us today, of course, but it was even more severe then. That didn't stop Zeke from wanting more software. What was I to do?

I didn't have many alternatives. I could go broke buying programs that usually didn't work; become a pirate and steal my software; or persuade people to give it to me for free. Put that way, the choice seemed clear. Now all I had to do was talk people into giving me the stuff.

That turned out to be easier that I'd have thought. I didn't know much about computers, but I had published a lot of science fact and fiction. I'd done a basic science column for a mass market newspaper, and the advanced science columns for the late lamented *Galaxy Science Fiction*. I knew at least as much about computers as I did about interstellar travel. After all, I *had* a micro computer, and I liked him a lot, even if he did demand expensive software. It shouldn't be that hard to sell a couple of articles about small computers, and once I did that, software publishers might be eager to have Zeke and me review their programs.

The rest was pretty standard marketing. Anyone who makes a living from writing knows you always try the best markets first, and you always study the magazine before submitting anything. *BYTE* was clearly the best computer magazine around, but it was mostly written by computer experts, not writers. I read all the back issues, and decided they might need non-technical articles on *using* micro computers. That, of course, would fit in perfectly with my scheme for acquiring free software. Now all I had to do was convince the *BYTE* editors.

It turned out to be absurdly simple.

I wrote the first column in early 1980. It appeared in the July issue for that year, with the following explanation by editor Chris Morgan:

Editor's Note
The other day we were sitting around the BYTE *offices listening to software and hardware explosions going off around us in the microcomputer world. We wondered, "Who could cover some of the latest developments for us in a funny, frank (and sometimes irascible) style?" The phone rang. It was Jerry Pournelle with an idea for a funny, frank, (and occasionally irascible) series of articles to be presented in* BYTE *on a semi-regular (ie: every two or three months) basis, which would cover the wild microcomputer goings-on at the Pournelle House ("Chaos Manor") in Southern California. We said yes. Herewith the first installment.... CM*

The first three columns came out at irregular intervals. Then one day the phone rang, and one of the junior editors told me my column was overdue, and before I knew it I was writing them every month, and spending hours on the phone with Chris, then with Pamela Clark and Phil Lemmons when Chris Morgan left to become part of the Lotus 1-2-3 team.

The User's Column became a monthly feature, moving from the back pages to the front part of the magazine. It grew in size, too, from 2,500 words quarterly to 7,500 words monthly.

I'm often asked how I find enough to write about. The truth is that I'm overwhelmed. Nearly every month there's a computer fair with announcements of major developments in hardware and software. The legal problems of warranties, licensing agreements, copy protection, copyright, and piracy could generate a column nearly each month. There's an ongoing revolution in computer languages. Prices fall, and capabilities rise. I try to write about all of it, but there's just so much happening in the micro world that even someone who pretends to know everything can't keep up.

Meanwhile, the mail from readers grew from a few pebbles to a monthly landslide—about twenty-five pounds a week, at last count. I enjoy a vast network of eager and unpaid information sources. I hear from people just starting to use computers. I've made a lot of new friends, some of them key computer industry people like Gary Killdall, Bill Godbout, and Adam Osborne. I haven't really become a computer expert, but I hear from a lot of people who are, so the effect is nearly the same.

It can get hectic. Over in one corner of the office there's about six cubic feet of unreviewed software I'm going to get to Real Soon Now. The office extension is so filled with small machines that I've had to store some of them on the floor, and you must step over two computers in order to feed the tropical fish. Every flat surface in the house is covered with computer books and magazines, it is literally true that there is at least one computer in every room of the house except the bathrooms (and that won't last), and the phone rings at any hour of the day or night. I've become the local Post Office's biggest account, and both UPS and Federal Express can find my house blindfolded.

Welcome to Chaos Manor.

PART ONE:
GETTING STARTED

CHAPTER 1
Writing With Computers

This was the first micro-computer article I ever wrote, and chronicles the beginning of my love affair with the little beasts. Most of the questions that puzzled me about getting my first computer are still very relevant. So are the answers I found with the help of my mad friend. Surprisingly few changes have been needed, but where they are, [updates and comments are shown in brackets, like this.] When I wrote this article, I didn't always have the details right, but the principles were true—and I sure was right about the enthusiasm.

"Hey," said my mad friend. "I just got a micro-computer."
That was a year ago. Mac Lean is a retired civil servant who has been involved in everything at one time or another: magic, rockhounding, organic chemistry, electronics, jewelry-making; in his basement sit both offset and letter press, neither used for years after he learned the art of printing; in his attic sits unused professional sewing equipment, enough stagecraft gear to outfit a professional road company, amateur radio gear, and God alone knows what else.
So I paid little attention to his tale of a new micro. A phase, a fad; certainly not anything to change *my* life.
After all, Marilyn Niven, my writing partner's wife, had an Altair which she played with from time to time, but Larry Niven never touched it except to play "Star Trek" and "Hammurabi" and the like. Home computers didn't *do* anything, they merely absorbed time.
Of course I knew that David Gerrold, a fellow science fic-

tion writer, used a tape-controlled Selectric to write his books, and seemed inordinately happy with it; but when I watched him use it I didn't see what it would do for me. David, because of his involvement with "Star Trek," has a lot more correspondence to worry about than I do, and the system seemed better suited to that than to my needs.

Months passed, and two things happened at once. First, I got a very good offer for two books I had written twelve years ago; they were out of print and had reverted. The only problem was they needed a lot of revisions. Every page, nearly every paragraph, needed a touch here, a lick there. It meant they'd have to be retyped from scratch, and I no longer had the manuscripts; I'd have to work from the printed editions.

Wouldn't it, I mused, be marvelous if those books were in some kind of electronically readable form so that I could do the scissors-and-paste job without so much retyping?

Secondly, Computer Power and Light (COMPAL) advertised word processing systems for under $6,000; and another friend, a systems engineer for a large computer company, sent me a copy of the COMPAL ad along with a letter he'd written on his micro computer. He'd written the editor program. It let you change character names, correct spelling, move text around—

COMPAL has a shop a mile from my house. I went by for a demonstration. It took half an hour to get used to the system. My only experiences with computers were from the dark ages: a visit to ILIAC in the 1950s, and some programming in machine language for the IBM 650 in the late 50s. When I was in the aerospace business, computers were black boxes kept in the math sciences department. Programmers magically took your equations and brought you answers. I didn't even know what a "Control" key was.

They showed me. The demonstration went so well that I almost bought the Computer Power and Light system on the spot. It was all so very marvelous: type on a screen, overstrike if you make a mistake, tell the machine the words you don't spell right and let it find them and fix them—incredible.

But what's the use of knowing experts if you don't consult them? I thought of my mad friend Mac Lean.

After a year he hadn't lost interest. Indeed, he spent more and more time with his computer, going for days on end without communicating to human beings. I had wondered why I hadn't seen him very much.

"We can build you something better than that," said he.

"But will it do what they showed me?" I asked.

"Sure. That's Electric Pencil. It's a program."

"They said it would only run on their machine," I told him.

"Nonsense. You can buy that program for other computers. What else do you want the machine to do?"

That, of course, is a key question; and for a rank amateur as I was, it's a hard one to answer. What can these machines do? I knew they could play games, but that was a negative feature: I don't need something else to take up my time. "Taxes," I said. "An accounting system. Something to take care of my books."

"Sure. You may have to do some programming if you want it customized."

Terrifying. But I had mental pictures of doing my writing on the machine, and after all, if they sold text editing programs, surely I could buy a standard accounting system. And the machines would speak **BASIC** and **FORTRAN**, I was assured; neither are difficult languages, they told me.

With **BASIC** and **FORTRAN** I could put my planet design equations (science fiction writers do have some special problems, it seems) and my solar system model and my rocket equations, all of which I then worked on my TI-59 calculator, right into the computer.

So I went through all the various things I thought I might want a computer to do. It was a short list, because, as mentioned, I didn't then know what they *can* do; but I thought it was quite a lot. Keeping track of my files and letters. Inventory of my library. Keeping track of contracts and contract due dates. I kept adding things to the list, expecting Mac Lean to tell me I'd asked for too much.

When I was finished, he said any good micro could do all that and more. So now it was a question of which one. And there were lots of them. How do you choose?

First, we decided against any specialized system; there is a great deal of software floating around, some for sale, some public domain, but you have to have a general-purpose system to use it. If I wanted the machine to do taxes and design planets, I couldn't use a dedicated "word processor."

Moreoever, I had very limited funds, which ruled out the more expensive systems.

I wanted a general purpose system. Because there is so much hardware and software available for it, we decided on the Z-80 CPU and the Altair S-100 bus; perhaps not the most elegant and advanced system around, but reliable; and there are a lot of companies developing new equipment and programs for S-100 systems.

[Note: it was definitely the right choice for 1977. The S-100 bus is still a reasonable option for some people; but there are a lot of other choices now. When I bought my first machine, there were no "integrated systems." Those came later, with the Osborne, and much later, with the IBM PC.]

Mac Lean steered me to Proteus Engineering, a small firm run by Caltech graduate Tony Pietsch, where I got an estimate of what the total would cost. Throughout the procurement process my philosophy has been that I am not in the systems development business. I have no desire to experiment with computers. What I want is a reliable machine that does what I want it to do, and which won't give me problems at 4 AM (my most productive hour). Thus I need consulting engineers to put it all together for me, and who stand ready to maintain the system.

(Not that much maintenance has been needed; but we'll get to that.)

"Be warned," my advisors told me. "Things are not as they seem. You will HAVE PROBLEMS. And when the system does all you expect it to do now, you won't be satisfied, and you'll want it to Do More, and that will cause more problems."

I didn't listen. I was getting A COMPUTER. A machine with more power than the ILIAC had back when I visited that monster. (The ILIAC was at the time the world's most powerful computer.)

I was getting a machine that gave me more computing power than was available to the government a few years ago. It would sit in my office and be all mine. Incredible.

I wrote a check for a retainer.

SYSTEM DESCRIPTION

The system they chose, with my not very informed consent, was a Cromemco Z-80 CPU in the Cromemco "black brick" box. I paid Proteus Engineering the list price for assembled and tested gear. There was also a very reasonable systems integration fee. They bought the kits and built them, with their own modifications, such as a larger fan, and different connectors.

There was considerable discussion of front panels. Like most amateurs, I rather fancied the idea of winking lights, and it was hard to convince me that they cause problems while solving none—unless you are interested in systems development, which I certainly am not. I was talked into the "black brick" and it has been enormously quiet and reliable; but I do miss the winking lights. Sigh.

The memory is four 16K Industrial Microsystems memory boards. A Tarbell cassette board, a VDM, and a VIO board; and an SIO for input/output. I also have two CRT monitor screens, both 15 inches, working through coax switches so that either can connect to VDM or VIO as desired.

[I fancy that either I was carried away by my newly found familiarity with computer jargon, or, like most salespeople who use jargon, I didn't really understand what was going on in my system; in any event, there's no excuse for my writing the above paragraph in a magazine article intended for beginners.

The VDM and VIO boards were memory mapped video boards; that is, they plugged into the computer, and displayed onto the "CRT" monitor screens (which are like TV screens) whatever they found in their part of memory. Memory mapped video is explained in another part of this book. The important thing to realize is that I was dealing with pretty advanced equipment at a time when there wasn't much micro equipment available. The VDM, VIO, and SIO boards took the place of a *terminal*, such as a Qume, or Televideo, or Zenith.]

The disk system is the iCom dual drive 8" floppies. We had some discussion of this; from articles in various magazines I liked the voice-coil type drive systems. Pietsch and Mac Lean pointed out that these were new; they might be excellent, but was I interested in being part of a quality-control testing experiment? The big iComs are heavy enough to use as anchors, and we *know* they're reliable.

On that advice I chose the iComs, and certainly I have no complaints at all. I've never had a glitch from them. Once in a while I get an annoying squeak which iCom says (they were very prompt in putting a knowledgeable engineer on the phone when I called) is harmless—a grounding spring—but it hasn't been bad enough to warrant opening the case and inserting a paper bushing as iCom recommended.

[Sigh. Those iCom drives, like much of the equipment of my original computer, are no longer available. They lasted several years, a long time in the micro business.]

There remained keyboards. I am used to a Selectric typewriter. I absolutely refuse to use a typewriter that puts the quote marks {"} up as a capital number; fiction writers use quotes a LOT. There were, however, not many keyboards available with Selectric layout keytops. Since I was going to get a Diablo for hard copy output I could, of course, use its keyboard (as COMPAL does for their under $6,000 system) but the thing is enormous and there are paper feed problems if you let it sit on your desk.

We compromised. I tried a number of keyboards and ended up with a surplus Memorex, which Proteus converted to serial output and then put through a PROM; now I can throw a switch and my keyboard has TTY or Selectric layout as I choose. I never use the TTY option, but a number of programming-oriented visitors do. I made paper labels to cover the keytops and stuck them on with Scotch tape; amazingly they have held up for months, and Scotch can have a testimonial on the ruggedness and clarity of their tape anytime.

[Mac Lean and I both got surplus Memorex keyboards. They, too, were good at the time, but are long gone now. My Memorex keyboard was replaced by a surplus DEC keyboard, and the DEC has since been replaced by an Archives Computer keyboard. It wasn't that the Memorex or DEC keyboards no longer worked reliably; only that each new one was in turn so much more convenient to use than its predecessor. When micro equipment becomes obsolete, it doesn't cease to do what you bought it for; the owner is seduced by something better . . .]

For output we chose a Diablo 1620. I briefly considered a spinwriter, but those were new and their reliability unknown, while businesses with Diablo told me their printers had never been out of service after several years; and a writer *must* have hard copy exactly on schedule.

The 1620 comes with keyboard, which I thought I would have as a spare. That was a mistake. I have never used the keyboard except to set margins, and the keyboard adds nearly a foot to the overall size of the already monstrous machine. Were I doing it over, I'd get a Diablo without keyboard to save space in my already overcrowded office.

[I still have the Diablo 1620, keyboard and all. It no longer does the volume production work, but it does write all my letters, and it serves as a spare to the NEC Spinwriter that we bought for production printing. I suppose that some day the Diablo will fail, but it shows no signs of quitting as of June 1984.]

That made up the basic system. With all equipment and fees it came to about $12,000; a lot more than I'd planned. I waited anxiously for it. Meanwhile, they put me to work: they handed me the three Osborne publications, *Introductions to Micro-computers*. I got through Volume 0, and glanced at the others; one day I'll read them. [I never have.] They also gave me Brown's *Instant Basic* which is a marvelous book, but mostly useful to those who have a computer and want to learn BASIC. I chafed at the delays . . .

Came the day: SYSTEM INSTALLED!

It came with considerable software which was bought for me. Electric Pencil, FDOS III, and CPM (with millions of programs from the CP/M User's Group). FORTRAN, and of course BASIC.

[FDOS III was an atrocious operating system that came with the iCom disk drives. It no longer exists, thank heaven. CP/M became the standard operating system of the micro computer world. If you'd ever used FDOS, you'd know why.]

It also came with something special: Proteus Engineering's XMON. Of course I had no idea what a monitor does, why you need one, or what horrible problems you can have if you don't have a good one. Fortunately I'll never have to learn. Tony Pietsch's XMON does everything and does it quietly and unobtrusively.

It was only later, visiting others and watching their contortions, that I learned just how good XMON is. I can inspect/insert at any memory location, assign my combination of I/O devices to be either console or list—for example, the 80 character VIO board and CRT can be the "list" device to let me test formats before actually printing on paper—and I can keep the disk directory and systems commands on one screen while writing text in Electric Pencil on the other.

(Actually, XMON can support up to 26 I/O devices *and* 26 format drivers in any combination desired.)

[XMON is another wonder that has since disappeared, although it certainly served its function at the time. In these days of dozens of competing micro computers, it's hard to remember just how primitive everything was when I got my first machine. Alas, some "modern" systems still have not learned the lessons we had to learn five years ago . . .]

Anyway: I had A COMPUTER! Could I write books on it?

USING THE SYSTEM

First I had to learn to use it: I was anxious to get Pencil running, but Mac Lean and Pietsch had me start with some BASIC programs. Keying them into the system and getting them to run forcibly taught me that computers are serious about syntax; there's a vast difference between a semicolon and a colon, and there's no proofreader in the editor's office to catch your goofs.

What I put up was a data base program. It had a convoluted logic, but it did run; the day it worked properly (about a week after I started) we broke out the champagne. Since then I've modified it into non-existence, and learned something about kluges: don't use them. It's easier to start over. Now I'm stuck with variable names and types that don't make sense and slow down my program; fortunately I know enough to rewrite the blasted thing from scratch.

Next, Electric Pencil, the acid test for the system. Data base programs are fine and dandy, but Ezekial (don't all computers have names?) was intended to write books, not do work that I could hire a secretary for. It was time for Electric Pencil.

[Electric Pencil was one of the earliest word processor text editors, and was excellent for its day. It employed "automatic word wrap" at the ends of line; that is, you did not end a line with the "Return" key, but continued to type, and the computer would put the words on the proper lines. Alas, for reasons I have never understood, Electric Pencil used the "Line Feed" key to mark the ends of paragraphs. The big "Return" key didn't do anything useful. The result was that you had to learn whole new typing habits.]

We got Pencil working in an hour. Now I had to use it.

My playing about with BASIC programs had taught me general principles about computer operation, but otherwise I was totally inexperienced. I kept hitting a carriage return at the end of each line. I forgot to hit line-feed at the end of a paragraph.

I shouted. I screamed. I cursed the whole damned system, Hollerith and his ancestors, the unknown Greek who built the Anti-Kythera machine, the inventor of the transistor, and anyone else who had anything to do with loosing these monsters on an unsuspecting world. How could they do this to me? Was it part of some vast conspiracy?

But I was determined. I had too much money in it. Besides, I write science fiction. Other people use these machines. Are they more intelligent than I? Can I afford to *admit* that they are?

Back to work. No carriage-return. Build each paragraph laboriously. Hit line-feed with a shout of triumph when a paragraph is done. It's a slow way to write books, but by damn I will master this monster—

But there were conveniences. Hit the wrong key, and you could simply backspace and strike over it. True, Pencil doesn't recognize the backspace key and you have to use shift-delete, but surely you can learn something that simple. And there are all these other features. Delete to end of line. Delete paragraphs. Insert letters and words. Change names and spelling....

And in a couple of days came the realization: it worked. No more conscious effort, just use the machine.

A week later I tried to use my Selectric II typewriter. The next morning I moved it out to my secretary's desk. It was just too inconvenient.

In other words, I am hooked. The proof came when our agent asked for a screen treatment by the end of the week. Larry and I worked in our customary manner—sit down with lots of coffee and brandy and talk a lot—and I went back and banged the result into the machine. Took a copy to Larry. He came over with his comments. In one afternoon—four hours—we had incorporated his changes, taken the clean ms. and gone over that, put in the rewrite, and got a final draft.

Another time we wrote a 15,000-word novelette in three

days: three days from conception to final draft incorporating all necessary changes.

That was the day Larry decided to try my machine. With no experience whatever he found himself typing in text. True, there was this problem with carriage-return and line-feed, but those are trivial compared to being able to insert and rewrite and get clean copy . . .

And the next day he gave a deposit to Proteus Engineering. Now we'll have identical systems so we can trade disks.

PROBLEMS . . .

There have been a few. First, Pencil is fragile. It wants to accept various control characters. Much of this is due, I am sure, to the keyboard, which has a tendency to give off spurious control characters when too many keys are depressed at once; but some is due to PENCIL itself, which seems unable to recover from goofs, and which is sold without a source so that the experts can't get in and modify it to fit my system and monitor.

It has other problems. When you reach the end of a line the text rearranges itself as it should, but it often drops characters: there is either no buffer, or the line buffer is too small. Without a source there's nothing to be done about it. Maybe we'll have to write our own text editor.

Meanwhile, changing over to DEC keyboards with true n-key rollover should get the spurious control characters out of the system. [It did. All modern systems have "true n-key rollover," meaning that when several keys are depressed at once, the keyboard sends only the signals for depressed keys, not some spurious character made up of a combination of keys. It's still a good idea, though, to test for rollover before buying a terminal or computer. Press a number of keys at the same time and see what happens. If it drives the system crazy, don't buy it.]

When we know exactly what we want for a word processor, we'll have keyboards built and keytops cut with dedicated commands built in; it's obviously easier to hit a key that says "insert line" than to press control and G simultaneously; and it will be easier to teach my secretary how to use it.

For that matter, there's software for sale all the time: if we don't get the text-handler written in time, I'm sure someone will have one to sell complete with source so that the silly glitches (I'm typing fast now and Pencil is dropping letters each time the line rearranges, and that is most annoying) can be cured.

There's another problem: to avoid my having to type in those reverted books that need revising, I want to have my assistant do it; but I have become so dependent on the machine that I need it most of the time, and John can't get at it. I have to find a relatively cheap system that can create Electric Pencil files (or those generated by the new word processor). I can put the simple box in the other room for my assistant's use. It needs no Diablo, and possibly I can make do with letting him save the text on tape, then read it into the master system and back out on disks. This, I freely admit, is a frill, but one worth having, and I'm looking into it now.

But glitches and all, this is so much faster than work on a typewriter that there's no comparison; I estimate that it saves me several months each year; months I can use for travel, or reading, or plain loafing.

Before I got the system, I could, in a good day, turn out ten pages; I have done more, but not often.

The computer lets me turn out words at more than double that rate. It doesn't get in the way of writing: no paper to change, no erasures and strikeovers, no Sno-pake (I used to be an authority on Sno-pake, collecting vintage years); and best of all, every draft is a clean draft—but it's so easy to produce another clean draft that there's no hesitation over rewrite. (It's a common disease with writers: not wanting to mess up a CLEAN DRAFT. The mechanical work of writing is as discouraging as the creative effort.)

On my best day since Ezekial, I did ten pages an *hour* for several hours straight. Marvelous!

That's word processing. What else?

PLANETS AND TAXES AND FILES

It was no trick to get my planet-design and solar system and other scientific programs running. Most I did in BASIC because it's simpler to use (for me); but they're getting translated into FORTRAN because that's simpler to run and considerably quicker (once I fully understand the dreaded FORMAT and COMMON statements).

The troubles came with accounting and taxes.

Everyone advertises a "General Ledger" program. Not one of the blooming things I've seen will work, or, if they do work, will produce anything an accountant would accept unless blind drunk.

For example, one company has a whole line of BASIC programs, each in a book for sale at a price of from $10 to $50. If you buy the expensive "Business System" package they tell you (but not up front where you can see it) that not all the code to get the general ledger programs running is included in the book.

That's all right, though, because you wouldn't want what it produces anyway.

There are very expensive small business accounting systems which presumably work and work well; but if there's anything under $1,000 that works and produces what an accountant would call books, I've yet to see it.

Most produce "special reports" that don't preserve any audit trail, and are no more than a glorified addition system.

So I had to write my own.

My Journal/Ledger program starts with MacKenzie's *Fundamentals of Accounting* and Myer's *Accounting for Non-Accountants;* it is designed to produce journals that look like the journals in those books, and ledgers that look like the ledgers—and which have references to the journal entries.

It turned out to be a lot of hard work, but it was worth it. Moreover, it wasn't much more work than I would have put into doing my taxes—and once done, my taxes took only one day! I simply type in a chart of accounts (ledger page number, ledger page title, segregated so that 0-100 is assets, 101-200 is liabilities, 201-300 is capital, etc.) and then use checkbook stub and credit card receipts to make journal entries in the formats and manner advised by MacKenzie. I don't know any accounting, but the program prints out all the required information, and in the format recommended in the books. Another program posts all that into the ledger entries, a third closes the books and transfers the balances to a profit-and-loss account, and a fourth produces income statements. At all times the journal reference, date, check number if check and credit card type if credit card, are carried with the entry so that even the ledger can be read; in that sense I think my program produces better information than the method recommended by MacKenzie or employed in the Wilmer Bookkeeping Set I used to use.

But whether better or not, it certainly preserves all the information, and it's no work to use. A journal entry consists of a check number (automatically entered if you like) and date; who to; what for; and a ledger page to be debited. The relevant checking account ledger page is automatically credited. When the journal is printed, both the ledger page number and ledger page titles are displayed, indented in the way accountants prefer, with the "who to" and "what for" entries shown as explanation—again in standard accounting format. This can now be posted, (to, say, Southern California Gas Company) and another program will summarize the ledger entries (posting pages 505, 507, 509 to "Utilities," as an example) if you like; and it all happens fast and reliably, with sum of debits and credits checked at each stage, and other tests possible.

Enough enthusiasm for my own programs. I do admit a certain pride in my accounting system, although I wonder why no one else ever did it. My mad friend says it's because programmers are not accountants and accountants are not programmers. That's fine, but I'm neither. I merely pretend to know everything for a living. Mac Lean is also trying to persuade me to sell the business programs I've written, and I suppose I will if I can make it clear that I don't guarantee anything about them: they work for me, and they produce books that accountants understand, but they sure won't teach you to be an accountant, and I haven't the foggiest if they'll work on anything other than CP/M and Microsoft Disk Basic.

[I'm still using my accounting programs. They've been modified many times in the past few years, and for speed were translated into a compiled language. Mine is still the only accounting system that produces books that look like the illustrations in my accounting textbooks.]

I also wrote a file program. It works like a dream: two days to teach my assistant (who'd never seen a computer outside the movies) and another two days for him to enter all the files in the system. Now I can look up any file by file title, subject, category, (data, contract, galley-proof, etc.) and *location*. We can find anything in minutes, even if it has been archived; and I can at any time review what data files I have.

[This was my "Minimum Data Base," which is described in another chapter.]

THE BOTTOM LINE

Would I recommend my system to others? Obviously: I certainly didn't try to talk Larry Niven out of buying one, and he's both friend and partner. Frank Herbert has explored the idea, and so has Joe Haldeman; I expect it won't be long before lots of science fiction writers use computer word processors.

However, for the small businessman or writer (and full-time writers are small business owners whether they know it or not) there are problems. I solved the hairiest by having my system assembled, integrated, and maintained by an engineering consultation firm.

In fact, that's Pournelle's First Law: "If you don't know what you're doing, deal with those who do."

I would also advise all those not utterly familiar with computing systems to do as I did: don't buy the very latest and possibly best, but stick to known reliable equipment. After all, you can write off the cost of the computer over a period of three years (or longer if you prefer); and I expect one day to upgrade and update—but only with hardware known to work. I am not in the systems development business, and have no desire ever to be.

But boy has this thing made it easier to write science fiction.

CHAPTER 2
The Early User's Columns

The First Column
The War on Lousy Documentation

The First User's Column was written in early 1980, and appeared in the July 1980 issue. It began on page 198; it's sometimes hard to remember that in those days that was the back of the book; that issue of BYTE was only 304 pages long! Since that time both the magazine and the column have grown.

Even so, in many ways that column set the tone for the rest. I'm often asked about the "secret" of The User's Column's success. For a long while I wouldn't answer, but I guess I'm secure enough now to Tell All.

For many years, outdoors magazines were some of the most popular periodicals around. They still sell pretty well. The mainstay of the outdoors magazine was the "Me and Joe" article: Me and Joe Went Hunting, Me and Joe Canoed the Feather River, Me and Joe Fished for Grayling in Alaska, etc.

That's the secret. I merely transplanted that kind of article to computer magazines. Instead of Joe, I alternately brought in Ezekial, my friend who happened to be a Z-80; or Dan Mac Lean, my mad friend who got me started in this business.

Thus, the very first User's Column begins...

My mad friend was raving again. "What this world needs," he said, "is some computer reviews by *users*."

"There are a lot of good reviews," I said.

"Yeah, some," he admitted. "But a lot more of them read

like rewrites of the manufacturers 'spec sheets. What I want to see is reviews by people who've really used the stuff."

I thought about that for a while and called *BYTE*. You're looking at the result. This will be a column by and for computer users, and, with rare exceptions, I won't discuss anything I haven't installed and implemented here in Chaos Manor. At Chaos Manor we have computer users ranging from my 9-year-old through a college undergraduate assistant and on up to myself. (Not that I'm the last word in sophistication, but I do sit here and pound this machine a lot; if I can't get something to work, it takes an expert.)

Fair warning, then: the very nature of this column limits its scope. I can't talk about anything I can't run on my machines, nor am I likely to discuss things I have no use for. Fortunately, that latter category is not so limiting as you might suppose. An author is most certainly running a small business, and I have accounting, mail-handling, and filing problems that you wouldn't believe. (Try sorting out data on subjects ranging from solar-power satellites and general relativity on one end, to a concordance of the *chansons du geste* (French poems from the time of Charlemagne) on the other, coming from sources ranging from books and journals to letters from readers.)

The equipment limitations are more severe.

Primarily, I use my friend Ezekial, who happens to be a Cromemco Z-2 with iCom 8-inch soft-sectored floppy disk drives. He talks to me through a Processor Technology VDM memory-mapped video display board, driving a 15-inch Hitachi monitor. However, I can fool him into thinking he's no more than a smart terminal to drive a Novation modem (modulator-demodulator; a device to let computers talk on the telephone). In that case he talks to me through an IMSAI VIO video board on a Sanyo 15-inch monitor, because most of my network contacts prefer a 24 by 80 screen format. Incidentally, the VIO is set up for address hexidecimal B000 in memory-address space and routinely shares memory with the regular Industrial Micro static memory that fills Ezekial from top to bottom. If I turn on the VIO screen I get a picture of what is in memory from B000 to B780, and a weird picture it can be when we're running a long command file . . .

[And *that* was the most readable article in *BYTE* that issue! It just shows how hobbyist-oriented the computer field was in those days. It also shows how proud I was of being able to talk like that.

I soon learned better. For those confused by the above paragraph: I don't blame you. It's actually much simpler than it looks, and later on in the book I'll explain what memory mapped video is, and why you might want to know about it. For the moment, let's get back to the first column.]

Zeke also turns out hard copy on a Diablo 1620 daisy-wheel printer running at 1200 bits/second. The Diablo is easily the most important part of my system, but in my business—writing books and articles—I require good manuscript quality, and the Diablo certainly delivers it reliably and efficiently (if noisily; sometimes it's a bit like being in the same room with a machine gun).

Ezekial's main operating system is CP/M 1.4, although we're putting up version 2.0 Real Soon Now.

In addition to Ezekial, I have a TRS-80 Model I Level II with expansion interface and a full 48 K bytes of memory. The TRS-80 will run 5-inch disks on the TRSDOS or NEWDOS+ disk operating systems. It will also run 8-inch disks on CP/M, and therein lies a tale . . .

[The column went on to discuss the TRS-80 Model I machine, and the wonderful additions to it available from George Gardner's Omikron company.

None of it is relevant now. Omikron still exists and is worth knowing about, but, mercifully, Tandy no longer makes the TRS-80 Model I. The machine was not well designed, and Tandy cut too many corners in order to bring the machine out cheaply. That's a real pity: the TRS-80 Model I had the potential to be that magical computer, the one that starts as a reasonably priced home machine, and can by easy stages be expanded into a full business system. Indeed, the Model I, plus the Omikron Mappers that allowed it to use 8-inch disks, had the *capability* of being a reasonable business system; but due to the design flaws it never had the necessary reliability.

In those days, though, there were few reliable machines that would work right out of the box. The TRS-80 was reasonably cheap, and could be made to do useful work, although the operating system was needlessly complex, and Tandy was far too secretive with the details of what was going on inside the machine. They also sold their add-on equipment, such as disk drives, for outrageously high prices;

the first User's Column recommended a number of alternate sources, including Omikron; all of which, I am pleased to say, did indeed supply more reliable equipment at lower prices than Radio Shack.

Many of the companies I recommended did not advertise in *BYTE*, while Tandy/Radio Shack was an important account. I was a bit nervous about that when I sent in the article; but it excited no comment at all. The *BYTE* editorial staff has never interfered with my column in any way.

The first column also opened the war on bad program documentation, in a review of an interesting data base program called Vulcan.]

Vulcan is a program that falls into a category I call "infuriatingly excellent"; that means it does everything you'd like it to, and perhaps a lot more, but the documentation is plain lousy. Vulcan will let you very quickly and easily structure a complex data base and enter data. You can add to it as you will, including taking files off other data bases. Since Vulcan makes random-access disk files, the data base can be as large as you like.

It's much faster than any other disk-storage data base I've seen, and lets you do really complex things like: find all items with keywords "Solar" OR "Conservation" BUT NOT "Wind" AND NOT "Windmill"; sort by AUTHOR and create a new file; add the PRICE of all those items and INCREASE the price by 12%.

Actually, that wouldn't be a very complicated task for Vulcan, which is as much a language as a program; in fact, Vulcan has a limited BASIC language system built into it. Vulcan can also execute command files (very handy if you have operations to be done at regular, say weekly or monthly, intervals). It will drive both console and hard copy devices. It is really useful.

It will also drive you mad, because Vulcan's author didn't include enough examples in the instructions. We find Vulcan worth the effort, because it is fast and comprehensive, and allows you to change the field structure of the data base at will, or create new data bases selectively out of the master; but we do a lot of pounding on the table and screaming in rage at the documentation.

There's a lot of software like that: infuriatingly better than its competition, but hampered by instructions meaningful only to the software's author. I sometimes think there's a secret school that teaches the black art of writing a document such that the author can prove conclusively that every bit of needed information is contained in the book—but it is guaranteed to be useless to anyone who doesn't already know it to begin with. In fact, I am sure there is such a school, and someday I'm going to find it and put it out of business. Until then, though, we'll have "infuriatingly excellent" software with us and there's not a lot to be done about it.

I believe that was the very first review of Vulcan. Shortly after this review appeared, Vulcan was sold to Ashton-Tate. They rewrote the documentation, making it much better although still not as good as it should have been, and marketed the program under the name dBase-II. Over a hundred thousand copies were sold.

Alas, I never did find that secret school. I have continued to thunder against bad documentation and lack of examples in instructional materials, and I'm told I've had an effect.

THE SECOND COLUMN:
The Language Debates Begin

BYTE conducts a monthly poll of the readership, who vote for their favorite article in the issue. The first User's Column was sufficiently popular that the BYTE staff urged me to continue. The second User's Column won that poll, earning me an extra $100 check.

It also generated a very great deal of mail. The User's Column has always stimulated debates, but probably the most controversial subject is computer languages. That subject was first raised in the second column.

Discussions of computer languages raise strong emotions among programmers. Every language has passionate supporters; when I blundered into the subject, I had no idea of how strong those could be. I learned soon enough.

This was written in the early days of BASIC, when variable names could be only one letter long (A, B, and A$, B$, etc.) and there were few advanced features. Basic programs tended to be a mass of "GO TO" statements, resulting in code that looked like spaghetti. If microcomputers were going to be genuinely useful, there had to be a better approach.

One word of warning: although I do not consider anything said in this column unreasonable, my views on the language question have changed somewhat since this was written. How they've changed, and why, we'll get to in a later section; for now, here are the reactions of a beginning computer user to the problem of learning to program. Note, incidentally, that my determination to remain a user who never writes programs had already vanished before User's Column #2 . . .

It's a typical Sunday afternoon here at Chaos Manor. In one room a dozen kids are playing games on the TRS-80, while here in the office I've been playing about with the "C" programming language after adding a check-writer to my accounting programs. My wife, the only practical member of the family, gently reminds me of my deadlines: galley proofs of a new novel (KING DAVID'S SPACESHIP, Simon and Schuster, for fall publication); two chapters on the latest Niven/Pournelle collaboration (OATH OF FEALTY, Simon and Schuster, Real Soon Now); plus three columns; a speech to a Librarians' convention; and inputs for a NASA study on America's Fifty-year space plan. Some businesspeople worry about cash flow; for authors it's work flow—work comes in bunches, like bananas, and sometimes it seems everything has to be done at once.

So, since it's what we've been doing here lately, I'll talk about computer games and programming languages; a disparate set of topics, but not quite as unconnected as they might seem at first glance.

One of the biggest unsolved problems in the micro field is languages: Which ones are going to be standard? Everyone learns BASIC, of course, because it comes with the machine, and it's a very easy language to learn. Pretty soon, though, you come to the limits of the BASIC supplied with the computer; and now what?

A few years ago there wasn't a lot of choice. You could buy FORTRAN, and perhaps COBOL; you could learn Assembler; but then you were stuck. Moreover, there didn't seem to be any obvious advantages to FORTRAN and COBOL, both of which were not only hard to learn, but also difficult to connect up with the micro. Most of the books on those languages were written with big mainframe machines in mind, and the documentation for the micro versions was, to put it kindly, rather skimpy. Moreover, the user manuals were filled with mysterious references to "logical devices" and other such nonsense, while giving almost no clear examples of how to get programs running on a home computer.

[Although the documentation for micro computer FORTRAN and COBOL has improved somewhat since then, it's still pretty grim. Also, for a number of reasons we'll get to later, I don't recommend FORTRAN and COBOL even if well documented.]

The result was a great expansion of BASICs. What was once a simple teaching language designed largely to let new users become familiar with the way computers think became studded with features. Every time you turned around there was a new BASIC, each one larger than the last, and almost none of them compatible with each other. Whatever portability Basic had enjoyed vanished in a myriad of disk operations, functions, WHILE statements, new input formats, etc., etc., and at the same time the free memory left over after loading Basic got so small that you couldn't handle much data.

The logical end of that process is Microsoft's newest BASIC-80. Understand, it's an excellent BASIC. It has features that, not long ago, the most advanced languages didn't have. It's well documented—at least the commands and functions, which are listed alphabetically, are clearly described. The general information section could be expanded with profit—at present it's written for users who are already more or less familiar with how BASIC operates. There are elaborate procedures for error trapping, and they all work. The editor has been improved. There are procedures (not very well documented) for linking in assembly language subroutines. You can use long variable names such as Personal.data.1 and Personal.data.2 and be certain the program will know they are different variables.

In other words, there's a lot going for it; but it takes up 24K of memory, and it's still BASIC. If you want to understand your program six weeks after you write it, you'll have to put in a lot of Remark statements, every one of which takes up memory space. As with all BASICs, you have to sweat blood to write well-structured code (and if you don't bother, that will come back to haunt you when you want to modify the program). And, like all BASICs, it is S*L*O*W. Fairly simple sorts, even with efficient algorithms, take minutes; disk operations are tedious.

I suspect that Microsoft-80 BASIC is the end of the line; they've carried BASIC about as far as it can go. They've done it very well, but they've also reached the inherent limits of the language; and those limits may not be acceptable.

[This observation has proven surprisingly accurate. There have been marginal improvements in BASIC since then, but nothing radical. Of course the *computers* have improved a lot; they're no longer restricted to 8 bits, and 64K is about the minimum memory size.]

Actually, most programmers have always known that even the best BASIC wasn't good enough; that if you added enough features to make the language useful, you'd end up with a very slow monster that took up far too much memory, and that even if you could tolerate those limits, the language itself forces sloppy thinking and inelegant code. However, knowing the problem didn't make the solution obvious; indeed, it's not obvious yet. We can recognize the limits to BASIC and still not agree on what to do about it.

There seem to be two fundamental paths. One is to start over: to relegate BASIC to its original function as a teaching language, and switch to some other language for serious programming. Many took this path, and came out with microcomputer versions of such languages as "C", APL, ALGOL, LISP, FORTH, STOIC, and PASCAL.

The other way is to "compile" BASIC. One of the first compiled BASICs, BASIC E, is in the public domain; I obtained a fairly decent version with (barely) adequate documentation from the CP/M User's Group two years ago. Then Software Systems brought out an improved BASIC E called CBASIC. It is easy to use and features excellent documentation, some of the best I've ever seen. It has decent file structures; you can not only build either sequential or random-access disk files, but also use sequential operations on random-access files.

There are irritants in CBASIC, particularly with regard to line printer operations. CBASIC has only the "PRINT" and "PRINT USING" commands; there is no "LPRINT." To get hard copy, you must execute a "LINEPRINTER" statement, then one or more "PRINT" statements, then do a "CONSOLE" statement to have the copy sent to the terminal. Every time you do the "CONSOLE" statement, the print buffer empties, and you can get unwanted stuff printed on your hard copy; worse, you can also get unwanted linefeeds, making it tough to format hard copy (although CBASIC does allow you to output characters through a port so that if you are clever enough you can control the lineprinter directly; you could even make a CBASIC program drive a Diablo for reverse printing if you wanted to spend the time writing that program). Another needless limitation is that CBASIC allows a maximum lineprinter width of 133, although a 12 character/inch printer can print lines 158 characters long.

Irritants or no, CBASIC is both well designed and well

documented. It has WHILE; IF-THEN-ELSE (with chaining); long variable names; and logical operations (IF TAX > 0 AND PRICE < MAXIMUM.ACCEPTABLE THEN GOSOB 234 ELSE PRINT "NO GOOD" is a perfectly valid CBASIC expression). It has the CASE (Switch or ON GOTO) statement.

And it saves memory by "compiling." To use CBASIC one creates a program with any editor that makes ASCII files (Electric Pencil programs have to be put through a converter), then turns the CBASIC "compiler" loose on it. What comes out isn't true compilation; the "compiler" strips out remarks and needless line numbers, and compacts the remainder into an intermediate (INT) file; when you want to run the program you must load in a 10K runtime package. The INT file is still interpreted; it is not a machine-language program. You can, though, include scads of remarks, put each statement on a separate line, leave lots of blank space, put in rows of asterisks, indent whole sections of the program, and thus vastly increase program readability without using up memory space. A CBASIC program can be written for legibility.

But it's still BASIC. Because a program *can* be reasonably well structured and self-documenting doesn't mean that it will be; BASIC makes it easy to write incomprehensible code and difficult not to. And CBASIC is VERY SLOW, no faster than Microsoft's BASIC-80 and often slower.

There's another limit. It's very hard to write long programs in CBASIC. This problem is inherent in any compiled language—whether true compilation to machine code, or pseudo-compiling to an INT file. For example: assume I want to add a small feature to my accounting package (which I did in fact write in CBASIC two years ago). I load the source program into the text editor. I add the feature and hook it into the program; since I do sweat blood to write structured code, that's fairly easy. Now I must save the altered source and put it through the compiler. Since it's a long program, the compilation takes many minutes—and toward the end, I get a SYNTAX ERROR message. I've put a comma where it wants a semicolon.

Now I have to load the editor, read in the source, make the change, save, and recompile. Presuming that this time it goes without error, I may have used up half an hour just to change "," to ";"—and I still have no test of the program's *logic*. If I now test for logic and that's not right, I have to start all over again, hoping that this time I don't manage a new syntax error . . .

Thus you can use up a whole afternoon adding something quite simple to a big program. There must be a better way. Why can't someone come up with a language that runs interpretatively like normal BASIC, letting you correct both syntax and logic errors while in an interactive mode; and then allow you to compile the result? While we're at it, let's wish for the compiled program to be in real machine language, code that I could put into ROM's, and moreover that it be *FAST*.

That's the route that Microsoft took. Their BASCOM compiler works just that way with their BASIC-80. It will also compile Microsoft BASIC 4.5, and, with considerable modifications to syntax, programs written in both CBASIC and BASIC E. Moreover, it's a very powerful compiler. It implements almost all the features of BASIC-80, including WHILE, IF-THEN-ELSE, CASE, logicals, string operations, etc. It sounds like the answer to a prayer.

Of course there are problems. Random access disk operations are unbelievably messy, requiring you to learn the dreaded FIELD statement, and worse, a random access file cannot be accessed sequentially. There's considerable overhead burden. For example, this program:

```
10 Print "Hello"
20 END
```

required 9K bytes when compiled into a CP/M COM file; there's obviously a big run-time package built into BASCOM. Worst of all, present Microsoft user contracts require that anyone marketing a program compiled by BASCOM pay a stiff 9% royalty to Microsoft on every copy sold! Since this is about equal to the profit margin of many software houses, it's understandable that there's been no great rush to sell programs employing BASCOM.

But let's assume much of this is fixed. Microsoft has a good reputation for responding to customer suggestions. As an example, at the West Coast Computer Fair I spoke to the Microsoft reps about the lack of a FILES statement (a means of finding out the file names present on disk) in BASCOM; BASIC-80 supported FILES, but not the compiler. Two weeks later I received an updated version of BASCOM, and lo!, the FILES statement had been implemented, along with several features other users had suggested.

At the National Computing Convention, Microsoft reps said they were "rethinking" their contract policy and would probably change it; that change may have been implemented before this sees print. I have also mentioned to them the desirability of allowing sequential access to random files, and they've promised to look into that. [Both these difficulties were fixed shortly after this column appeared in print. I don't know how much effect the column had on Microsoft's decision.]

It's not unreasonable to assume they'll tighten up the overhead code problem. Thus, as I said, let's assume that the major problems of BASCOM are fixed. What will we have?

First, the combination of BASIC-80 and BASCOM is superb for quick and dirty jobs; little special-purpose programs that aren't going to be run very often (possibly only once). For example, I recently wanted to re-format some financial data files. The program had to go open the file, read the data, make a couple of changes, and write the information out in a new format. The only problem was that I also wanted to sort the data before putting it back out, and this had to be done for a *lot* of files. Doing it with interpretive BASIC would take hours and hours; while writing even that simple a program in Assembler would at best use up an afternoon, and might take a lot longer.

The solution was to write it in BASIC-80, test syntax and logic while in interpretive mode, and compile the BASCOM. That took an hour. In another hour I'd reformatted about a hundred files. BASCOM is F*A*S*T, blindingly fast; sorts that take 3.5 minutes in CBASIC are done by BASCOM (using the same algorithm; I just added line numbers to the CBASIC code) in under 20 seconds.

In other words, the combination of BASIC-80 and BASCOM has a *lot* going for it. If I'd written this review a year ago, I'd have concluded that BASIC-80/BASCOM was what the world has been waiting for, and spent the rest of the review suggesting incremental improvements to make it even better.

Now I'm not so sure.

The problem is that when all the improvements are done; when all the bugs are eliminated; when all the new features are added, and the code is tightened and the disk operations simplified—when all that's done, it's still BASIC.

And there are many who believe BASIC is a dead end; that the inherent limits to the language are just too severe for it ever to be acceptable; that incremental improvements actually harm rather than help the field, because they encourage newcomers to stick with BASIC instead of learning something better. My mad friend is convinced of that. So are a number of my associates.

"But," I protested to my mad friend, "I'm interested in *using* computers. I don't *care* about elegance. What I want is something that lets me get the jobs done quickly, and BASIC-80/BASCOM does that...."

"But at a stiff price. How many times have you had to start over with a program because it just wasn't worth the effort to improve one of those BASIC routines? BASIC doesn't let you build software tools. It's like Pidgin English—you can manage to buy dinner and sell copra with Pidgin, but you'll never write Hamlet. Or the Declaration of Independence, or even good laws...."

And the argument starts over and goes on until we get hungry, and at bottom it's all a matter of opinion; and since my space is limited, I'll drop it for the moment. Just now the bottom line is that BASIC-80 and BASCOM work, and if you're willing to accept the inherent limits of BASIC, they're quite splendid; but those limits are severe.

What, then, are the microcomputer user's best alternatives to BASIC? Once again, let me be honest: these are opinions. They're opinions based on considerable user experience, but they're opinions still; and I have found that every known language has passionate supporters, so I am bound to make someone unhappy.

[Little did I know just *how* unhappy some of my readers were going to be. Alas, language discussions arouse *extreme* passions....]

The earliest alternatives to BASIC were FORTRAN and COBOL. These, in my judgment, are languages whose time has long passed. They have little to recommend them, because they have nearly all the limits of compiled BASIC without the advantage of letting you program in interpretive mode before compiling. I've had both for years, and after an initial flurry of enthusiasm for FORTRAN (I never cared at all for COBOL, which may be all right for very large systems, but is plain crippled on micros) they went on the shelf and haven't come off it. Neither FORTRAN nor COBOL lets you write structured code. True, FORTRAN with RATFOR (excellently described in Kernighan and Plauger's book *Software Tools*, Addison-Wesley, 1976) overcomes some of the limits; but to use RATFOR requires *another* compilation stage, so that it can take over an hour to find and correct a trivial error in a fairly simple program. The *Software Tools* approach to programming is excellent, and I strongly recommend the book; but in my judgment the deficiencies of FORTRAN with RATFOR are simply overwhelming, and I can't recommend using them.

Then there's Pascal, which very well may be the wave of the future. Pascal began unfortunately: the first widespread implementation of Pascal for micros was from the University of California at San Diego, and it just didn't work for most users. It wasn't portable, the hooks into the disk operating system were clumsy, there was a built-in editor that was hard to get running properly, and it was *very* slow.

Then came some other Pascals and they too had horrible problems; you had to be really sophisticated to use them. Bugs appeared, and unless you knew an awful lot you couldn't tell whether you'd made a program error or the compiler was at fault. Implementing early Pascals required a constant and fairly complex dialogue between user and publisher.

As a result, many of us lost interest in Pascal. The language looked great in theory, but if you couldn't run it, that hardly mattered.

There are now a lot of Pascals; Pascal for the Apple, Pascal for the TRS-80, Pascal for CP/M; Pascals that pseudo-compile to an INT file the way CBASIC does (Pascal users call the INT file "P-code"); Pascals that truly compile into machine language for 8080, Z-80, 8086, etc. All these look good, and people I respect tell me they run; but since I haven't implemented any of them yet, I can't report on them.

I can say that Pascal has many enthusiasts, and might well be the standard language of the future. Then there's Ada, a Pascal-like language heavily supported by the Department of Defense, which will certainly be around for many years; if I were preparing for a secure career in programming, I'd learn Pascal instantly and keep very close tabs on the progress of Ada.

[That remains good advice. When I wrote that, Ada wasn't completely defined; a committee was still working on it. Now there are working Ada compilers, and the language has both enthusiasts and detractors. Whatever Ada's merits, a knowledge of Ada remains a sure meal ticket, since the Pentagon insists that all new military programs will be written in it.]

Pascal has enthusiasts. So does "C," a programming language developed at Bell Telephone Laboratories. The best (and indeed nearly the only) manual on C is Kernighan and Ritchie, *The C Programming Language*, Prentice-Hall, 1978. This is an excellently written book which anyone at all interested in the C language simply must read. It succeeds in communicating a lot of enthusiasm for C. There are lots of examples of real programs that work. Kernighan, incidentally, is the same Brian Kernighan who co-authored *Software Tools*.

C is nothing like Basic. There are far fewer commands, for one thing. On the other hand, there are a number of conventions. For example, the BASIC command:

For I = 0 TO N-1
NEXT I

would appear in C as:

for (i = 0; i < N; i++)

which looks complex but is, with a bit of experience, quite readable. The "i++" means that i is first to be tested against N, then incremented; the expression could have been written with ++i, which would require that i be incremented *before* the test against N.

[The example, alas, is wrong; which illustrates one of the problems with C. If you don't use it a lot, it's easy to forget some of its rather cryptic conventions.]

Despite (perhaps because of) the numerous time-saving conventions such as ++i, C can be learned by a BASIC user in a couple of weeks. Real facility requires practice; more practice than BASIC precisely because there are many fewer limits in C. Programming with elegance and style takes work—but in C such programs are possible, while BASIC simply won't let you write elegant code.

Of my two C compilers, only one is suitable for those not already familiar with the C language. This is "BDS C," available from Workman & Associates for $125. BDS C comes with a copy of Kernighan and Ritchie and quite extensive documentation on the BDS implementation.

The BDS compiler uses two passes. One might at first think that a disadvantage because of the time required, but in fact it is not: the first pass is done VERY fast, and checks for trivial errors, such as missing semicolons, comments improperly delimited, unmatched parentheses and brackets (C *loves* brackets, braces, and parentheses), and the like. The second pass goes a bit slower but is still much faster than the CBASIC compiler.

Like BASCOM, the compiled C code must be put through a linker, and like Microsoft's, the BDS documentation tells you precisely how to do this. When it's all finished, you have a CP/M command file; and the resulting code is *very* fast. I've not yet been able to benchmark BDS C against a similar BASCOM program, because when you translate from Basic to C you actually restructure the program; but I have two Othello games, one in C and the other compiled by BASCOM, and they seem to run at about the same speed. The C program, however, is about 8K compiled; the BASIC program, performing the same searches and playing at the same level, compiled to over 20K. Other programs doing similar jobs also run in comparable times, and with about the same differences in program size.

Disk operations in BDS C are fairly simple if you understand CP/M, not so simple if you don't—and CP/M's documentation is so notoriously unclear that you'll have to work for a couple of days understanding CP/M before you can write decent disk I/O operations for BDS C. It's worth sharpening up your understanding of CP/M, though, because BDS C lets you do *everything* CP/M will: get the names and *sizes* of files currently on disk, make backups, rename and delete, etc., and it's no more difficult to understand than the "Field" statements in Microsoft BASIC, or the dreaded Format statement in FORTRAN.

String operations in C are more difficult than in BASIC. Actually, they aren't: that is, it's possible to write, in C, all the string functions of Basic (such as LEFT$, etc.), and then call them as needed; and once you have written them, you can use them in any program that needs them—and leave them out if not wanted. And, in fact, that illustrates one of the fundamental differences between BASIC and C: the BASIC language provides a number of functions which you must have present whether you need them or not, and which must be used *exactly* the way BASIC wants them used; while C allows you to leave off functions you don't want, and rewrite those you do to suit your precise requirements.

There is, however, one very severe limit to BDS C: it doesn't support floating point data types. One can use floating point *variables*, because BDS supplies a number of functions which you can call to do floating point arithmetic; but the result is clumsy. If you want to learn the C language, and write games and calendar programs and almost anything that doesn't involve crunching a lot of numbers, BDS C is highly recommended; but it isn't suitable for writing an accounting or financial package.

The other C compiler for micros is the Whitesmith Compiler, available from Lifeboat Associates at $630. This is a full implementation of the standard C described in Kernighan and Ritchie, and is highly regarded by many professionals working with big machines such as the PDP-11; in fact, Whitesmith C was written for big machines and it is only an accident that it could be downscaled for micros. The president of Whitesmith is P.J. Plauger, a fellow science fiction writer and, more important, co-author of *Software Tools*.

Although the Whitesmith Compiler is an excellent professional tool, I cannot recommend it to anyone who doesn't intend to program in C in a big way—and even then I'd recommend buying the BDS C compiler as well. Whitesmith C compiles, eventually, to true ROMable machine code; but it does it by going through an intermediate assembly language called A-Natural. It's slow, and since there's no first pass to find trivial errors, the Whitesmith compiler can grind away for half an hour before reporting a misplaced semicolon. It is certainly not what I'd choose to learn the language with—but I would get it if I were going to market programs written in C.

[Since I wrote this, there have been at least a dozen new implementations of the C programming language for micro computers. There are *lots* of C compilers, some excellent, some not so good. I'm not much of an expert on them.

That's because I've nearly given up the C language, for reasons that will be explained in the chapter on languages. For those who want an 8-bit (ie., *not* for the IBM PC) C compiler to see if they'll like the language, I can still recommend BDS C, which, although not strictly standard, is rather easy to learn, and finds errors very quickly—something highly desirable in a compiler for beginners. Those interested in a more advanced C compiler will have to look to other sources for a recommendation.]

* * *

Then there's LISP, which is a peculiar language. Again, those who like it like it a LOT. It was written in the '50s by Dr. John McCarthy, now director of the Stanford Artificial Intelligence Laboratories (SAIL), and it's extensively used at Stanford and MIT (where McCarthy wrote it).

The Microsoft muLISP-79 is well done—if you like LISP. You may not care for the language. LISP stands for "List Processing," and makes creating highly complex linked lists very easy. It does bit-by-bit arithmetic, meaning that there is no theoretical limit to the precision you can obtain; if you want an exact numerical expansion of, say, 2 to the 55th power, or 87 factorial, you can get them from LISP, and with only about three lines of code for a program—and you'll get the answer faster than you think. LISP is one of the fastest languages I know of, often approaching assembly language programs in speed of operation.

LISP programs are very tight; it's almost impossible to write unstructured code in LISP. It's also very nearly impossible to understand a LISP program, even if you wrote it; at least that's been my experience. You can strain like a gearbox and produce code that runs, and which you understand just at that moment; but hours later it's gibberish. The only thing less comprehensible than a LISP program is one in APL—APL doesn't even use normal letters, but instead requires a special keyboard that can generate strangely bent arrows and other weird symbols. Both LISP and APL programmers delight in writing a whole page of instructions into one line (and you can do it, too, because both languages allow functions to call themselves). They also like to baffle fellow professionals by showing them a line of code and challenging anyone to say what it does.

It's very hard to comment a LISP program—but that's all right, because it isn't traditional for LISP programmers to comment their programs anyway.

In other words, I am not a wild enthusiast for LISP as a "standard" micro language. It's true that one or another LISP variant is used by just about everyone in the Artificial Intelligence field; for certain purposes there's nothing better. But for general purpose programming, LISP and APL are, in my judgment, simply too obscure.

The Microsoft muLISP-79 was written by the Soft Warehouse in Hawaii; I got mine directly from the authors and haven't seen the Microsoft versions (for CP/M and the TRS-80) although they were supposed to be sent weeks ago. I am told that Microsoft has rewritten some of the documentation, which could only improve it. The problem with documenting LISP is that the language is fairly obscure; you need not only a user's manual, but an introduction to LISP itself, which is far more than the muLISP-79 manual claims to be.

The best way to learn LISP is to attend Stanford or MIT and get tutorial instruction from someone already proficient. The next best way is to get access to the MIT Macsyma Consortium computer and run the TEACHLISP programs. There are also a couple of MIT documents which are pretty good introductions. I wish I knew of a good commercial textbook, but I don't. If you want to learn LISP, you've no choice but to play about with it; since muLISP-79 is interactive, that's not so hard to do, and there are some decent examples in the documents supplied. If you like playing with powerful languages, muLISP-79 is recommended—but don't blame me if you don't use it very often after the first wave of enthusiasm.

Which concludes my overview of languages. I haven't mentioned STOIC and FORTH, because they're really a kind of assembler language using the programmer as a parser; they make programming a bit easier, but you've got to be into assembler work before you can use them, and this is, after all, the user's column.

[Needless to say, this generated some strong letters. Let me hasten to say, though, that my examples above were drawn from real experience: I have with my own eyes seen LISP programmers challenge each other to figure out what a line of code can do; and I've seen an awful lot of uncommented LISP programs.

On the other hand, I am now (1984) willing to admit that there's a lot going for the language.

Regarding micro implementations: In addition to muLISP, there is a LISP interpreter called, improbably, "The Stiff Upper LISP"; as micro implementations go, it's pretty good. *No* micro computer LISP is going to do more than give you the flavor of the language; LISP is a memory-hungry beast and wants 4 to 8 megabytes before it really gets useful.

There's a wealth of very useful public domain programs written in LISP, and when micro computers get large enough to make it easy to transfer those programs to personal computers, there will be a minor software revolution. Given present trends, I expect this to happen about 1987.]

So what's the best language to learn? I don't know. I like C. I also like what I've seen of Pascal, assuming the current crop really will run on micros. And despite my misgivings, I still find myself using BASIC-80/BASCOM, particularly for quick and dirty jobs.

It seems certain—to me at least—that Pascal is going to be around a long time, especially what with all that DOD support for the Ada variant. Now that there seem to be some decent Pascal compilers available for micros, we're going to see a lot of software written in Pascal, and those who want to modify their software will have to be familiar with the language.

But there may not be a real conflict between Pascal and C. Both are vastly different from BASIC; different in conception, in terminology, but more important, in the "philosophy" or style of programming employing them. Learning either will help break the Basic habit of sloppy program structure; and having done that, you'll have little trouble learning the other, or indeed any other well-structured language.

And that can't hurt users or programmers.

That column stirred a hornet's nest of comments, particularly from LISP and FORTH enthusiasts. The latter were certainly justified in their unhappiness. That is: FORTH really is a kind of assembly language that uses the programmers as a pre-compiler; but it's a very useful language. We'll see more of it in the chapter on languages.

The real hate mail came from LISP enthusiasts.

THE THIRD USER'S COLUMN
The Language Debate Continues

The third column came quite a long time after the second. It too generated a great deal of mail; enough so that the BYTE *editorial people insisted that the column appear more frequently.*
　A few readers objected to the introductory paragraphs as too chatty and personal for a "professional magazine." Fortunately, most readers disagreed. One letter said that including personal details made my columns seem more like letters from a friend than a magazine article; another compared the columns to a conversation with someone met on an airplane. Certainly more readers liked it than otherwise: this column won second place in the BYTE *poll.*

"Read any good books lately?" asked my mad friend Mac Lean.
　Having just come back from an autograph party for *King David's Spaceship*, and the day before sent off the copy-edited manuscript for the new Niven and Pournelle *Oath of Fealty*, I knew what to say to that. "Haven't had time. But I've *written* some good books lately...."
　"Yeah, well, I wasn't talking about science fiction," said Mac Lean. "I meant good books on computers. I've got a dilly." He held up *PL/I : Structured Programming*, by Joan K. Hughes.
　"Hey, I know her," I said.
　"Well, you tell her for me she's written a really top book. Good index. Clear English. Stand-alone chapters, so you don't have to thumb back and forth to find out what's going on."

"I'll do better than that," I said. "I'll tell my readers."
"Yeah. Sure. When?"
"Uh, Real Soon Now...."

My apologies for being so long about getting this column done, and my thanks to all of you who've written encouraging letters. Things do indeed get hectic here at Chaos Manor, and the last few months have been something to see: books to get done, articles to write; and I built a new wing on the office, which meant moving everything around like Chinese Checkers, which meant that I lost the documentation to half the software sent me for review, which—

I am also, for my sins, Chairman of the Citizens' Advisory Council on National Space Policy, which involves chairing meetings and editing papers and writing summaries and flying to Washington. The result was that for a goodly while there I had no time to play with Ezekial, my friend who happens to be a Z-80; but things are caught up a bit now, and maybe we can get onto a schedule. Just last week I had a surgeon come in and remove the telephone from my ear.

One reason we got caught up was SPELLGUARD.

Every now and then you find programs that do things right, without problems; which have documentation that tells you what to do and how to do it; programs that are a joy to use. SPELLGUARD is like that.

It corrects spelling. That's all it does. It doesn't wash dishes, or set your clock, or do your taxes; but wow! can it correct spelling in standard ASCII text files. It doesn't much care what editor you used to create the files, either.

SPELLGUARD comes with a 20,000-word dictionary. That's just for starters, though. You can add more words: standard words, plurals, different tenses; technical terms; or, if you're a science fiction writer, alien words. You can have more than one dictionary. I find it convenient to have a SPELLGUARD disk for each book I'm writing; that way character names, place names, and special terms (including alien languages) can be added where wanted. As the dictionary grows, SPELLGUARD slows down, which is why I wasn't exact in my remarks about timing.

There are two ways to add words to the dictionary. First, when SPELLGUARD searches your text and finds a word it doesn't know, it offers you the chance to add the word to the dictionary. (You can also ignore the word, or mark it for correction.) Secondly, you can make up a dictionary of your own, or acquire one somewhere, and add that to SPELLGUARD's original. SPELLGUARD comes with programs which will go through and eliminate duplications.

It also comes with an excellent manual. This is about the first program document I've ever seen that needs no improvements at all. The language is clear and concise, every topic is covered, and there's a good table of contents. The document tells you, for instance, that "There is no command in SPELLGUARD to directly delete a word from a dictionary, although the user can accomplish this task by using the command for subtracting dictionaries. Deleting words from a dictionary will be discussed at the end of this section (see Chapter 3.2.e)."

Everything else is just as clear; furthermore, the program prompts make sense. I was able to use SPELLGUARD about five minutes after taking it out of the box.

There are more pleasant surprises. When you run SPELLGUARD, it first gives you a table, telling you how many words it has read, the number and percentage of unique words, the number and percentage that it can't find in the dictionary, and finally a changing column that tells you the percentage of proofreading the program has done (so you know if you've got time to go get a beer...). Note that second item above.

Many and many a year ago, when I was young and impressionable, I fell under the spell of a science fiction writer named A. E. Van Vogt; I certainly never thought Van would someday be a friend, neighbor, and colleague. Van Vogt was (and still is) interested in a rather hard-to-define field of study called General Semantics; and through him I was led to Alfred Count Korzybski and a strange book called *Science and Sanity*. That led me to Wendell Johnson at the University of Iowa. Professor Johnson's interests spanned everything from classical linguistics through speech therapy to General Semantics; a fascinating man and one of the best lecturers I've ever heard.

One of Johnson's research interests was identifying text: how could you tell if an anonymous work had been written by a particular author? Dr. Johnson used a number of quantitative measures, two of the most important being the type/token ratio, and the verb/adjective ratio. Type/token meant the ratio of unique words to total words; verb/adjective is self-explanatory. I remember going nearly blind counting total words and making tables of unique words in, for example, Marlowe's *Duchess of Malfi;* the idea was to find out if Marlow had written any of the Shakespearean plays. (As best we could calculate, he hadn't.)

Now comes SPELLGUARD to give you automatic type/token ratios; and if you really wanted to, you could make up separate verb and adjective dictionaries, thus finding that ratio merely by typing in the text; which, believe me, is a very great deal easier than doing it in teams of two with pencil and paper. I can see how SPELLGUARD, with its very efficient search algorithms, could be useful in a lot of linguistic research projects.

Anyway; if you do any work with text at all, you'll *love* SPELLGUARD.

[SPELLGUARD remains an excellent program; but since I wrote that, I've converted to Oasis System's THE WORD PLUS, which is even better. THE WORD PLUS is faster, has a larger dictionary, and is easier to use. It also costs less.]

SPELLGUARD is a good example of the best modern software: a program that does one thing, does it very well, and has documentation to match. It's easy to use.

Organic Software of Livermore, CA also takes that approach, and has produced two programs that I can recommend even though I'll probably never use them.

The first, DATEBOOK, keeps track of about six months worth of appointments for three people. We had no trouble getting it to run, and it looks to be easy enough to use. The main drawback is that you have to *want* to run it; DATEBOOK takes both disk drives and all of your micro's memory. What I want is "CALENDAR," a program that one day I may have to write; ideally it would come up when I turn on my system, insist that I give it the date (the way Lobo's LDOS operating system does), and then natter at me about what I have to get done. But it's fairly obvious that I can't write *that* program until I have hard disks with multi-megabyte storage.

"CALENDAR" would solve my problem, which is that I forget to look at my appointment book until it's too late. And that does bring up a question: is DATEBOOK really better than a decent appointment book of the kind usually employed by physicians and lawyers? I can't really answer that, but my guess is that I wouldn't buy a computer *just* for that. DATEBOOK has various search patterns, so that you can look for appointment openings of stated lengths, and it will offer you up to nine possible candidates—but you can, after all, do that by glancing at a book, too.

The value of DATEBOOK is that it will keep three people's schedules, and you can work appointments with each other (so that it searches for times when you're both free). It will also search through and find all the appointments you've made with a particular person—something that visual inspection of a book might miss, especially if there are a lot of such entries. And of course DATEBOOK can make hard copy, and update that often. All in all, if I worked in a business where I had lots of appointments and schedules to keep track of, I'd probably use DATEBOOK, but then I'm gadget oriented—and I *have* a computer.

Organic's other interesting program is MILESTONE, and people who need that one will like it a lot. MILESTONE is a PERT-chart generator. It does critical path analysis for jobs with up to 300 tasks; computes milestones (critical events), monthly manpower levels, monthly costs; and in general will handle most of the details we used to have to include in the management plan portion of a research proposal. I sure wish I'd had MILESTONE back when I was president of Pepperdine Research Institute.

MILESTONE isn't easy to use—not because the directions for the *program* aren't clear (they aren't all that good, either; about fair), but because PERT charting and critical path analysis and such like are more arts than science, and not easy jobs. MILESTONE can make them easier, and if I ever again have to generate research proposals, I'll certainly get MILESTONE out.

One of my pet peeves is documentation without examples. I can't imagine why people *do* that: write up instructions on how to use a program, and fail to include specific illustrations of precisely what command you issue and what result that gives. Look: most programmers can't write for sour owl jowls. A lot more have gone to that special school, the one that teaches how to write a document that contains all the information (so you can show it to a supervisor: "See, it was there all the time!"), but written in such a way as to convey zero information to anyone who doesn't *already know* how to do it.

And most computer hackers *hate* to write documents. They've already done the interesting work; they've solved the problem; and telling some mere *user* about the program is just more than they can bear.

All right. It's a sad situation. I concede that it's going to take a lot of time to do something about it. But damn it all! The one thing publishers *can* do is insist on examples.

Let me illustrate. Suppose I am opening MILESTONE after not looking at it for a couple of weeks (as indeed I am). I turn to page 36, and there I find:

"B(egin and E(nd) work
These two values define when the normal working day begins and ends. They must be even hours as defined on a 24 hour clock. Follow the rules for entering integers rather than times."

Now I ask you, what does this mean? I once knew, presumably, but I confess I've forgotten. Listen, all you programmers and publishers out there in computerland! Some of us don't spend all our time thinking about *your* programs; indeed, incredible as it seems, some of us go days on end without even thinking about *computers!*

I suppose we can figure it out. Evidently, MILESTONE isn't going to be much use to a company that begins work at 0930. Start on an even hour, or only PERT by days, weeks, or months (hardly an overwhelming limitation). And I suppose the "rules" for entering integers are that you merely type in the integer, although that's *not* so clear. What *is* clear is that an example would leave no room for doubt; but of course there is no example.

I don't want to be too hard on Organic; MILESTONE in fact comes with a set of example cases. One is Dr. Victor Frankenstein III's PERT for creating a monster. Event One, "Fanatic Desire to Create Life," is a milestone; it has no duration, but you don't start without it. We proceed to Task Two, "Move to ancestral castle," and continue on, searching for Grandfather's notes, hiring a linguist, etc. As it happens, they ran this example as part of a demonstration for me up at the San Francisco Computer Fair, and I can testify that MILESTONE is both fast and accurate: I thought up the need for a linguist to translate the notes. That broke into subtasks: advertise, interview, hire. I watched Burns Van Horne of Organic enter the new tasks. MILESTONE thought for a moment, then rearranged itself, because this became part of the critical path. (Not long ago they sent a revision of MILESTONE, and I notice that my suggested tasks are now in the case study.)

So they have examples, in the sense of worked-out problems for their program; but damn it all, they should have included specific examples all over their manual—and so should every other publisher. Please?

My last column, the one on languages, generated a lot of correspondence (and thanks, all of you who voted it "best of issue..."). Some was predictable: I wasn't sufficiently respectful of LISP, the LISt Processing Language written in 1956 by my friend John McCarthy, and since improved and expanded by McCarthy and my collaborator Marvin Minsky, and used by my friends and associates who wrote ZORK, and—in other words, please, fellows, I don't dislike LISP users.

What I said was that LISP was fine for special purposes, but it wasn't among the candidates for replacing BASIC.

For those offended, my apologies; but I remain unrepentant. LISP may indeed be a great language for professional programmers, as it certainly is for those working in Artificial Intelligence. Furthermore, if you're someplace where you can learn LISP easily—say at MIT or Stanford—then by all means grasp the opportunity.

Most of us, though, don't have that opportunity. Even if you have access to MIT's LISP-teaching programs, even if you have a coach, it's going to take time—lots of time—to learn. The ideal way to learn LISP is to use it; it does have the great feature of being an interactive language (which is BASIC's great advantage). But the LISPs available for micros are very limited (Minsky himself wasn't able to do much with the one I have); and it isn't likely that they'll get better. Not with our present hardware. Comes the revolution, when 32-bit machines with 256 kilobytes of active memory and 50 mega-bytes of disk storage can be bought for $2,000 and change, LISP may then, for all I know, be the best thing available; but not now, unless you have very specialized needs.

There are undoubtedly a large number of programming problems most easily solved by using LISP; but this remains the *User's Column*, directed in large part toward non-professionals who are trying to make their small systems do useful things; and for those readers I just don't recommend LISP. It can be fun to play with, and I'm glad Microsoft published it, but I doubt very seriously that micro computer users will ever do more with LISP than play.

That's my opinion; and I refuse to admit that holding that view is The Sin Against the Holy Ghost, as some of you seem to believe.

But the problem of languages has yet to be solved.

In theory, BASIC is an inadequate language. Listen to the hackers; they'll tell you that BASIC programs "are a maze of GOTO's," or that "You can't do structured programming in BASIC."

But that just ain't true. A good modern BASIC—say Microsoft's BASIC-80, or Software Systems's CBASIC—has DO WHILE, and IF-THEN-ELSE, and CASE, and darned near all the features Pascal has; plus string features that are a *lot* better than any Pascal I've seen; plus decent I/O, which Pascal doesn't have at all. Now true enough, there are problems in BASIC that are easiest to solve with judicious use of GOTO statements, but it's certainly possible to write good BASIC programs without a single GOTO, and even easier to tame the GOTO so it never refers to anything outside a local modular block.

You *can* write top-down structured programs in BASIC. Best of all, you can write the darned thing interactively, testing each step of the way, then test the program logic until it's working; after which you turn it over to Microsoft's BASCOM compiler, and wham!

And for maybe 80% of the jobs you want a micro to do, that's probably the best approach. It's almost certainly the fastest.

So what's wrong with it?

Plenty. First, BASIC still has a fatal flaw: no truly local variables. Passing parameters to a subroutine is darned hard, and controlling side effects (making sure you don't do something you didn't intend) isn't easy. Now, you can reserve I,J,K,L, etc., as indices, and set up "declarations" in remarks up at the top of the program; and with the new cross-reference programs now available you can *usually* find the side effects. Having done that you still have trouble passing parameters; and if the program gets big, so that you'd like to compile it in chunks, you're just out of luck. BASCOM doesn't permit decent chaining of programs, nor does it allow true compilation in parts.

And, in fact, the Microsoft BASCOM is not really the same language as their BASIC-80. In addition to the chaining problems, you can't use computed array sizes, or common statements.

"But," protests the BASIC enthusiast, "that's fixable. In fact, I bet you somebody at Microsoft is working on it right now."

All true. And maybe, one day, they'll really fix the BASIC/BASCOM system up. I'd like to think so, because I find BASIC programs fairly easy to read and write. I expect you'd right now be able to buy a lot of programs in compiled BASIC if it weren't for Microsoft's disastrous policy of demanding royalties for every program compiled with BASCOM. Competition will take care of that; meanwhile, I sure do use BASIC-80 with BASCOM for routine jobs; and a lot of my most useful programs are written in CBASIC.

There's just so much investment in BASIC software! Take Joan Hughes, author of the PL/I book that so impressed Mac Lean. Joan runs Execudata, one of those ubiquitous small systems houses that spring up everywhere. She sells turnkey systems for small businesses. The hardware she favors is Vector Graphics S-100 Bus Z-80 with their "mindless terminal" which is really memory-mapped video. The software comes from all over. The editor is Vector's, and I'm tempted to buy a Vector machine just to get it; it's a lot like Electric Pencil but with most of the bugs out. Other software is written by Execudata or bought commercially. Like all the really classy systems houses, they support everything they sell, and their customers seem more than just satisfied, they're downright enthusiastic. A thoroughly professional operation.

The interesting part is that the author of the best book we've seen on PL/I sells software largely written in CBASIC.

The reason is really given above: Execudata has been around several years. When Joan first started the company, there wasn't a PL/I for micros, and CBASIC was the only BASIC that allowed long variable names (remember the horrible days when variables were "A$" and "B1" and you hadn't the foggiest what they referred to?) and structured concepts. She may change over, now that we have PL/I from Digital Research.

Wonder of wonders (remember, these are the people who

brought you the CP/M manuals) Digital's PL/1 documentation is, if nothing to brag about, at least readable. It's a fairly healthy subset of the ANSI General Purpose (Subset G) PL/I, and it does run.

"Yeah, and so what," asks one of my sane friends. "Who'd use it?" Or: "PL/I is unwieldy and inefficient," says a recent article in another magazine. On the other hand, Mac Lean has spent the last couple of weeks learning it, and he loves it.

Meanwhile, I have—at last!—got not one but two Pascals that run, and I've been wading through Grogono's *Programming in Pascal* as well as reading everything on Pascal I can find.

I can recommend Grogono's book; and for that matter, I can recommend the Pascal/MT+ implementation of Pascal. It works, and unless Mike and Nancy Lehman have turned into liars, which I doubt, Pascal/MT+ is a full implementation of the Standard Pascal, along with a few much-needed extensions.

Their manual is much improved, too: they sent me an early copy, and apparently my anguished screams were too much for them. They've added a number of sections, and, according to Nancy, "That's all because of you. . . ."

I also have the Sorcim Pascal/M up and running. Pascal/M compiles to an intermediate code. It's slower than Pascal/MT+, but it's also more compact—and more portable from machine to machine. It too has extensions to standard Pascal, and I can recommend it.

What I can't recommend is Pascal itself. Not yet, anyway. When I first looked at Pascal several years ago, I thought it the nicest thing I'd ever seen. Now, though, the more I look at Pascal, the more misgivings I have; but I certainly could be wrong, and by next column time I'll know more. Also by then, Mac Lean will have done things with PL/I, and we can do some comparisons.

[I have thoroughly changed my views since I wrote the above; at the same time, I understand why I thought that way. A flood of letters pointed out to me that I had confused the language Pascal with the *implementations* of it available for micros.

They were right, of course; but they were also wrong. That is: what use is it to know that Pascal is a great language, but the only versions of it that run on your own micro aren't any good?

Fortunately, all that has changed. There are some excellent Pascal compilers that work on micro computers (indeed, the latest versions of Pascal MT+, now marketed by Digital Research, is one of them); and the language is more than viable for micro users. And now there's TURBO PASCAL for $49.95!

That's the wonderful thing about these micros. When I wrote the column, what I said was all true. By the time it was published, it was mostly true. Now, only a couple of years later, my observations about Pascal implementations are obsolete.

As Alice said, "Things *flow* here so!"]

Meanwhile, don't throw away your CBASIC; *they've* made some improvements. President Gordon Eubanks says it's a result of my reviews. The needless limit on the lineprinter width has been fixed, and the COMMON and CHAIN features improved. I think the latest version has some other improvements too, but like a brass-plated idiot I've managed to mislay the new manual. Although I've said it before, it's worth mentioning again: the CBASIC documentation is excellent.

Gordon also tells me that by the time this is printed there'll be a new version of CBASIC that allows nested IF statements (fixing one of Joan Hughes's pet complaints), and before the end of the year they'll have parameter passing and local variables, and they're working on speeding it up.

The language situation isn't our only dilemma. Let's face it, our micros are getting obsolete. Now in one sense that's silly: we have available more computing power than the government did ten years ago. The machines work, reliably. So what is this obsolete stuff?

And that's a sensible attitude for users. There's no point in replacing our machines just when we're finally getting good software for them. But that's the problem: we're beginning to see hardware limitations on the new software.

Take SPELLGUARD, for instance: it's a good program. I use it often. But it can't touch *real* spelling programs such as run on the big MIT computers. MIT's Spell (written, incidentally, in LISP) not only finds misspelled words; it shows you the word along with context; shows a menu of words it thinks might have been meant; offers you a chance to put the new word in your permanent dictionary; if that's refused, offers the opportunity to put it in a dictionary kept just for this job; and finally lets you input the proper spelling, which it inserts into the text.

And it does all this at blinding speeds, searching dictionaries of 35 to 50 thousand words.

There ain't no eight-bit machine running floppy disks gonna touch *that* job.

[Even as I wrote that, Wayne Holder was bringing out The Word Plus; by the time my column was published, his program was available, and it did almost everything I described. Isn't the micro world wonderful?]

There are other limits. One big controversy over text editors hinges at bottom on a simple question: do you limit the amount of text you can work on to what can be held in memory (as Pencil does); or do you keep part of it on the disk (as Word Master, WordStar, and Magic Wand do)? If you keep part on disk, you can't conveniently change disks; which can be a serious limit if you're looking to bring in a chunk of an old file, or quickly make a safety copy of something you just can't afford to lose. If you keep it all in memory, not only are you confined to 10,000 words or fewer (with my system, anyway); but you've got real problems if you want windows, and multiple buffers, or if you'd like the machine to do some computing on values in the text.

Obviously I prefer Pencil's limits; I have Wand and WordStar, but I don't use them, Star because it natters at me (when was the last time you wanted to know line and column number every time you typed a letter?) and Wand because of the disk operations. (Word Master, on the other hand, is the best programming editor I know of.) None of the editors available to us, not one of them, can do what I'd really *like* to see. For instance: let me put equations in my text; solve them; and have the answers available as I write. (What I usually do is leave the text on the screen and turn to my programmable TI-59; which is plain silly.)

Yet what I want isn't impossible—for big machines. MIT's MACSYMA can solve very hairy equations, and their EMACS editor is inherently more powerful than anything we can implement on a micro. I haven't seen them combined, but it wouldn't be all that hard to do if you had the memory available.

Anyway. For a few years we'll exploit what we have; but it isn't going to be all that long before Zeke becomes the world's smartest terminal (two memory-mapped screens, a 20 kilobyte PROM monitor to control printing and I/O, etc.), while a new machine does the work. Only—what should the new machine be?

Two years ago everyone would have said, in unison, "the Z-8000." Now we just don't know.

Next, when we get the new machines, what will we use for an operating system?

Again, two years ago everyone who was thinking about the problem would have said, "Unix, of course. What else?" And if we had Unix, which is a fairly complex tree-structured operating system developed by Bell Laboratories, we'd also have answered the language question, since Unix contains a "C" programming language compiler, and indeed is written in C.

Now, again, we just don't know.

What went wrong?

Well, at first, there weren't any reliable Z-8000 chips available. Now that problem's fixed—but there aren't many Z-8000 computers available, are there?

There is one. Onyx has a working Z-8000, with Unix and C, and hard disks, and 128K of memory. They're shipping them as fast as they can make them, and according to their customers I've talked to (half a dozen now) they work and work well.

Meanwhile, there's a serious rival to the Z-8000 and Unix: the dual 8085/8088, working on an S-100 bus, and running Digital Research's operating system that looks a lot like CP/M, and allows you to bring over most of your CP/M files. The 8085/88 won't run Z-80 code, but then neither will the Z-8000. It will execute 8080 code.

Bill Godbout sells an 8085/88 system; and Tony Pietsch, the engineer who built my system, recommends it, along with hard disks and dual-sided double-density floppies to back up the hard disk system. Tony is building a Godbout S-100 system now; there's a chance I'll get one. The Lehmans use a Godbout S-100 8085/88 system for their Pascal/MT+, and they're *very* happy with it; while Sorcim's president Richard Frank says they've got half a dozen of them which they run perpetually, and that you can pitch the Godbout CompuPro box out a second-story window without hurting it.

In other words, Z-8000 with Unix has respectable supporters; and so does 8085/88. Prices aren't quite comparable; the Onyx system costs more, largely because of the Unix software, which aren't cheap. Performance isn't comparable either: the Z-8000 Onyx is *much* faster than the 8085/88 machines. So what happens now?

I don't know. Fortunately, we don't have to do anything just yet. It *may* be that best policy is to skip all the 16-bit machines entirely, and wait for a new generation of 32-bit monsters to come along. Certainly if you're contemplating buying a first system, go ahead and get one: I still recommend S-100 bus and Z-80. You can upgrade to dual-density floppies and hard disks without *too* much risk; but if you want a system to *use* rather than play with, stay conservative and leave systems development to the Tony Pietschs of this world. (Notice that if I get new systems in here, they'll be *in addition* to Zeke; him I don't touch.)

And stand by. Exciting things are happening in micro land.

In 1984, there is still no reasonable system that uses a Z-8000, and my primary micro system is an 8085/8088 Dual Processor from Dr. William Godbout's CompuPro Company. Ezekial, alas, is gone.

My predictions for the future were, surprisingly, about as accurate as anyone's; except that I completely left out the Motorola 68000 chip. Shortly after I wrote this column, Rod Coleman introduced his 68000-based Sage computer, which soon grew into the standard 68000 micro development system. We'll see details on the Sage in a later chapter.

Last-minute flash: Steve Ciarcia, my colleague at BYTE, has brought out a Z-8000 board you can put into your IBM PC. It compiles BASICA for the PC, and makes BASICA potentially an extremely useful production language. More on that in the back of the book; but if you haven't seen it, and you like the IBM PC computer, by all means find out about Steve's "TRUMP CARD" board.

Second flash: Professional BASIC, by Morgan Computing Co., makes BASIC a viable programming language for the IBM PC; while Borland International's TURBO PASCAL has changed the PASCAL world.

Most of this book will be organized more or less by topic rather than by column number; but I did think it reasonable to show just how The Reader's Column began.

PART TWO
WRITING WITH COMPUTERS

CHAPTER 1
The Silverberg Correspondence

*Be not the first by whom the new are tried,
Nor yet the last to lay the old aside.*
Essay on Criticism, Alexander Pope

I recall being taught this maxim by my father at an early age. It's not bad advice. Obviously I didn't take it: I was one of the very first professional writers to use a computer to write my stories and articles.

Ezekial changed my life. He did most of the real work of writing. I never had to retype anything, and I could fiddle with the text until I had *exactly* what I wanted. Computers not only let you write faster, but, by taking the mechanical work out of writing, they let you write *better*. I know of few writers who like to write—we all like to *have written*, but that's a different thing—but computers take so much of the sting out of creative writing that they make it, if not fun, at least comfortable.

My work improved, and I couldn't wait to tell people.

The word got out. The first of my colleagues to succumb was my partner, Larry Niven. Niven took the simple route: he hired Tony Pietsch, who'd built my first system, to install an exact duplicate. Larry solved the maintenance problem as easily: he bought a second machine, which Mrs. Niven could use in her management of his office and literary properties.

That, by the way, is a viable option for professionals who *must* have working computer systems. After all, annual maintenance contracts cost in the neighborhood of 10% of the equipment value; having a second machine as a backup not only provides continuity, but also lets you have the use of two machines. Of course it's not an option most of us choose.

After Larry came Dr. Gregory Benford. Then came the Saturn Encounter, and the flood began.

Because I live near the Jet Propulsion Laboratories which control the Mariner and Voyager spacecraft, my house was often filled with science fiction writers when those marvels encountered Jupiter and Saturn. (Alas, the space explorations were Proxmired, and those days of wonder are gone.)

Many writers saw my computer establishment, liked it, and wanted something like it. Many asked my advice. Then I took Adelle, my Otrona portable computer, to the World Science Fiction Convention in Chicago (Fall, 1982). One of the exhibits was the new Lobo computer, and many writers saw that. Shortly after, there came this letter from Robert Silverberg. While I was preparing an answer, it came to me that I ought to do it "right"; the result was more an article than a letter, but it did answer Silverberg's questions.

I have updated my answer to reflect changes since this was written; the result is my best advice as of Spring, 1984.

Robert Silverberg
Oakland, CA

October 1982

Dear Jerry,

Having provided you without charge with hours of sage advice over the years, I mean to present my bill herewith. Because I'd like about half an hour of your time (and Ezekial's) to give me a brief precis of the sort of stuff I ought to be looking for in a word processor: I have pretty much made up my mind to switch over, in another four or five months. Our conversation last Friday morning was followed by an actual demonstration of the huckster-room machine [the new Lobo] and a TRS, and right now I'm a bit jumbled as I try to sort out the kind of thing I ought to be looking for.

I am not exactly non-mechanical—I drive well enough, I operate video recorders, etc.—and I'm not overly intimidated by what I saw last weekend. I *am* non-mathematical, and am not likely to be using my machine to design worlds or to generate intricate concepts, nor do I care a damn about computer games. So basically what I'm after is a machine I can write fiction on, and perhaps keep certain financial records on; if some extra capacity is there, I won't object, but I don't expect to be using it if a hand calculator will do the job for me. Price is not exactly an object, but since I'm not a hobbyist, I don't need ultra-ultra gadgetry; I'd just as soon spend somewhere between $7K and $10K. Less than that and I suppose I'd end up with junk; more, and I'm probably buying excess capacity.

The trouble is I don't yet speak the language. I know that the things come in three sections, a keyboard, a screen, a printer. I am aware that CP/M is the most widely used way to go. I have heard that I ought to get a screen with the capacity to display a whole manuscript page at once, and that squares with my experience fooling around with a two-paragraph display. I am told, but don't know why, that I ought to have 8-inch disk capacity instead of the smaller size. I want to use a reasonably standard keyboard, so I don't go crazy learning new typing habits after all this time. I want a printer that will fairly quickly turn out copy that looks typewritten, that is, without slashes through the zeroes and other computery manifestations, and I want it to come out on single sheets, not long rolls. And I don't want to stand there feeding in those single sheets one at a time on a 750-page novel—I want to push a button, go away, and find a manuscript when I come back. And how much memory capacity do I need?

What I'd like from you is a two-page rundown of the sort of things that are desirable in a system for a professional writer. (What program do I use? Scripset? WordStar? Which will drive me nuts faster? What significant differences are there?) Figure that you're writing to a very bright Albanian who is trying his best to learn English, but is still just about on the third-grade level. What I'm after is a machine that will make writing easier for me, not one that will push my mind to its limits and expand my horizons. Can you recommend some parameters, and maybe even some specific equipment?

Bob
Robert Silverberg

Jerry Pournelle
Chaos Manor
Hollywood, CA

Dear Bob,

I do indeed thank you for the advice you've given me over the years. I also thank you for this request. Many of my colleagues have asked me what they ought to buy. Your letter, however, is remarkable in that you have given some thought to the questions, making it easy for me to answer.

First, some general principles. Athough as a professional writer you primarily want a "word processor," and being non-mathematical you're sure you're not interested in the number-crunching capability of this machine that will shortly come to live with you, don't close your mind. Computing capability can change one's interests. It's possible that I would have become a theoretical physicist if good pocket calculators had been available in the '40s: it turns out I had indeed correctly understood undergraduate physics, and my terrible grades in the subject were due entirely to my total inability to do elementary arithmetic. I never got the right answers to the physics problems, and gave up in disgust; it was only later (much too late) that I discovered I have a flair for mathematics (provided there's no arithmetic involved . . .)

In any event, a "word processor" is nothing more than a brain-damaged computer. Computers don't know anything, of course; it's only programs that can be "smart." There exist some "word processing machines" which can *only* run text editing and word processing programs; they aren't useful for anything else, which is why I call them brain-damaged.

True, "word processors" have special keys and other conveniences to make learning to use it much faster; but you save a few days at best, while the limitations on the machine are permanent. As a general rule you can assume that any good computer can run any good text editor program—which is to say that a good small computer can be an excellent word processor, while the dedicated word processor cannot easily be turned into a small computer.

Interestingly, there are better text editing programs on small computers than there are on "big" machines like Vaxen; indeed, one widely selling product is a board to adapt a micro chip (Z-80) to run with a Vax (a big minicomputer costing about $100,000) so that you can use WordStar with the Vax!

Once you have your computer, you will wonder what else it can do; and I predict it will not be long before you will use it not only for accounting—small computers are wonderful at tax time—but also for investment calculations. Once you use one of those spread-sheet programs—the kind that lets you set up rows and columns of numbers according to any formula you like, and change all of them by changing any one of them—I guarantee you'll wonder how you ever got along without it.

You will also soon learn that a small computer will handle mailing lists for you. It will keep track of telephone numbers. It can become your card file system, and keep track of all your characters: when born, to whom married, favorite color, and all the other random stuff that makes spear carriers come alive. You can add character names to a dictionary, so that the machine will catch it if you spell someone's name wrong.

The programs to do all this exist already. They won't be cheap, but you won't buy them all at once. The important thing now is to see that the machine you get is capable of running them, without compromising on its ability to do the primary task of "word processing"—which in your case means creative writing.

The books all tell you that in buying a computer one ought first to concentrate on what it does—that is, on software, or programs. That used to be good advice, but nowadays any good general purpose small computer will run such a wide variety of software that it's more important that you feel happy with the machine.

Get one you *like*.

On the other hand, Pournelle's First Law: your computer will do far more than you ever expected it to, and that won't be enough.

With those guidelines in mind, let's look at specific systems.

CHAPTER 2
Hardware

As you note in your letter, computers tend to break into logical chunks: the computer itself, a screen, a keyboard, and a printer. Screen and keyboard are often combined into a beast called a terminal. They need not be, but we won't go into the exceptions just yet. It's also possible to combine computer, screen, and keyboard into a single unit, and we will look at some examples later.

PRINTERS

Meanwhile, let's examine printers.
As of Spring 1984, there are two basic kinds of printer available: "dot matrix" and "impact."
Two others, ink sprayers and laser printers, have highly desirable features, but they're not quite available. For that matter, I'd wait a year or so after the first models come out before buying anything radically new.
Laser printers will change the whole picture when they're generally available; there are even models which can double as your office copier. Alas, I don't expect to buy one for myself before spring of 1985, and thus I can't recommend them to non-experts until at least fourth quarter of that year.
When good laser printers, with sheet feeders based on the mechanism Canon uses in its personal copier, become available, the situation will be quite different from what it is now; but then, nothing ever stands still in micro land. Until

then, you must choose between dot matrix and impact "letter quality."

Dot matrix printers are only marginally practical for professional writers, because the text they produce just doesn't look right. It can be made to look better, but the techniques for producing great-looking text are not yet grafted onto the best editing programs. Dot matrix printers are tempting because they are very fast. Programmers, who need frequent intermediate listouts, find them preferable. Dot matrix printers are also cheap, and those who can't afford impact printers may have no choice; but editors really prefer to read text from an impact "letter quality" printer.

Dot matrix printers improve in quality all the time; even as I write this, they're getting better. The MPI line, for example, has the ability to "double print" so that the output quality, although not as good as that of impact "letter quality," is probably acceptable—particularly for established writers.

The fact remains that editors prefer letter quality printing, and I would not myself ever submit a dot matrix manuscript—which may be blind prejudice on my part, so you'd do well to get a demonstration of the best in dot matrix before buying.

There are a number of impact printers. They all work in a similar manner, namely, that a raised impression of a letter (exactly like that on a typewriter key) is poised with a ribbon between it and the paper, and a small hammer strikes it a blow. The two major kinds of impact printers are "daisy wheel," in which the keys are arranged at the ends of fingerlike rods arrayed in a circle, and "thimble," in which the letters are distributed over the surface of a cylinder.

In either case, the print device—thimble or daisy wheel—is removable, and a wide variety of typefaces and styles can be bought at from ten to twenty dollars each. Thus your fears about slashes through zeros and such like are unfounded; you can get many typefaces you will find aesthetically pleasing, and the output will not only look like typewritten text, it will look better.

So: which is better, daisy wheel or thimble?

I have both; and in my judgment the thimble machine, manufactured by Nippon Electric Company (NEC), is preferable. The NEC Spinwriter is based on newer technology (and better elementary physics) than the Xerox-owned Diablo daisy wheel. Given comparable use, my NEC has needed less service than the Diablo has. The decision is marginal, however. Diablo has a very good service policy, and their service has been excellent. There are more typefaces available in daisy wheels than in thimbles, and my favorite, Bookface Academic, is available only as a daisywheel. However, a more than adequate number of typefaces is available in thimbles, and of course the situation changes all the time.

There are also *slow* impact printers at low prices. I've little experience with them; I think I would go mad if I had to wait all day to get paper copy. Although I do a lot of editing on screen, I still find it easier to do some editing on hard copy—and of course you can't carry your word processor in a briefcase! (Well, there are some computers you can carry in a briefcase, but I can't recommend any of them as your only machine.)

For general purposes output you can't go wrong with either a NEC Spinwriter or a good Diablo printer. I know there are other printers, but not all text editor programs know about all printers; while all the good programs do know about NEC Spinwriter and Diablo. This is important, because if the editor program you like doesn't know about your printer, you will have to hire someone to make the editor talk to the printer, and that can be both expensive and inconvenient.

Some writers have two printers: a fast dot matrix, such as MPI or Epson, to get working copy; and a slow impact printer to do the final submission copy. There are a few problems involved with cables and "printer driver" programs; if you choose to go the "multiple printer" route, be sure that you are dealing with someone who understands what you intend, can show you both printers in operation, and will show you exactly how you switch from one to another.

Your printer will have a friction feed much like a typewriter. That's fine for letters and other stuff that wants single sheets, but not useful if you're trying to print off a novel. Therefore, when you buy your printer, buy a "tractor drive," also known as a "pinfeed." That is a small gadget of metal that will cost an outrageous amount (as much as several hundred dollars for some models). Grumble at the price, but pay it. Then buy your paper in "fanfolds." That is: it isn't a long roll, it's sheets of paper joined together by perforations; you'll soon get used to "busting out" your paper, which is to say, taking that long continuous fanfold and tearing off the sheets.

The fanfold comes in many weights, with and without watermark. It has little pin-feed holes along the sides; the pinfeeds are attached along perforations, and "tearing the ears" off pinfeed paper is one of the simple pleasures for halfwits and authors. Fortunately, you can talk on the telephone (given one of those shoulder rests for the phone) while busting out paper.

You can get pinfeed in multiple sheets separated by carbon, too, and in addition to normal bond, I keep a box of three-part (three sheets of paper, two sheets of carbon) for printing submission drafts. It's a bit harder to bust out because the carbon must be removed, but it saves trips to the Xerox house.

They keep showing me (very expensive) sheet feeders. These are boxes that sit on top of your NEC or Diablo and hold normal bond paper; they're supposed to feed it in one sheet at a time. I have never seen one I would trust to work unattended; while I have gone off to lunch while my Diablo printed 400 pages of a novel on fanfold. I would love to have a reliable sheet feeder; if you ever find one, let me know, because nature arranges that whenever I want to write a letter and print in on letterhead, there's fanfold in my printer, and whenever I'm ready to print a chapter, I've removed the fanfold and tractor so I could feed letterhead through (sheet at a time).

That should take care of the printer, but it doesn't: that is, there's another decision. Do you get a printer with a keyboard on it?

The instant answer to that is "no," because you'll never use that keyboard for much of anything. (Incidentally, that's sad: the Diablo has one of the nicest keyboards I've ever seen. Well-sculpted, keys properly laid out, everything about where you'd want it; but alas, the mechanism to feed paper into it is big, and will get in the way of the screen.) However, there's a problem: if the machine doesn't have a keyboard, how do you set the margins?

That's not trivial. That is: all good text editor and word processor programs can set the margins of your printer, but there will be times when you want to print stuff without using your word processor. Setting the margins without a keyboard requires a small program. Those are available from public domain sources, and *should* be available from the store where you buy the machine.

The disadvantage of the machine with keyboard is that it takes up *room*; a printer is too large anyway, and with keyboard it's a foot wider.

Whatever printer you get, consider a service contract. The printer, being electro-mechanical, is more prone to failure than the computer itself. A service contract will cost you a couple of hundred dollars a year, but without a printer an author is dead in the water.

DISK DRIVES

There are four kinds of disk drives: "hard" or fixed disks; 8 inch floppies; 5¼ inch floppies; and "shirt-pocket" drives, 3+ inches in diameter.

Until recently I wouldn't recommend anything but 8-inch floppy disks as sufficiently reliable for professional work, but that has changed; and indeed, if you can possibly afford one, you'll find a hard disk enormously useful. It's amazing how convenient it is to have 40 (or more) megabytes of text and information on line.

However, you must have at least one floppy disk, and you must get in the habit of saving all your text on floppies as well as on the hard disk. Keeping backup copies is vital; and for an author, it's best to have more than one set of backups, with one copy stored somewhere else. I've always done that with paper copies in case of fire; with computer disk copies it's doubly important.

If you decide on a hard disk, you'll need more information than I can give in this letter; talk to the people where you're buying your computer.

Floppies

Shirt-pocket floppies haven't been out long enough; I don't recommend them just yet. I believe they (along with hard disks) will eventually replace both 8-inch and 5¼ inch disk drives; but not just yet.

Eight inch disks are more reliable than 5¼ inch; they have a much larger capacity; and they are much better engineered. There is also a standard format, so that just about all 8 inch drives can read disks made by all other 8 inch drive systems. The disadvantages are that they are physically much larger (take up a lot more room), and they are noisier since they spin all the time.

Five inch disks only spin when they are in use. They're much smaller, and of course they come standard with nearly all the "packaged" or "all up" machines, such as the IBM PC, Otrona, Kaypro, Eagle, Epson, etc. The reliability has been greatly increased in the past two years. It's still true that if you're going to have a "glitch" it will more likely be on a 5 than an 8; and the 5s are more prone to simple mechanical failures such as broken latches on the disk drive doors.

Details

A "floppy disk" looks something like a phonograph record. It's made of mylar covered with magnetic media—something like a flattened out magnetic tape. Unlike a phonograph, a floppy disk—also known as diskette, or just disk—stores its information in concentric circles, known as tracks; around each track are a series of segments known as sectors. Your disk system will have a special-purpose computer known as a "controller"; the controller knows how to go to each track and sector of the disk, and to either read the information there, or to write information into a particular sector.

The same information density is stored on both the inner and the outer tracks; which means that the information on the inner tracks is packed closer together than the information on the outer tracks. That is, although the outer tracks are longer ("bigger around") than the inner tracks, they have the same number of sectors, and each sector holds the same amount of information.

That information comes in bytes. I won't bother explaining the term's origin. For our purposes, a byte is an alphanumeric character, such as the letter "A", or the symbol @, or the numeral 6. In the old days we stored 128 bytes on each sector of a disk. This is to this day known as "single density." When technology improved, we learned to store more information in a sector, so that we have "double density" and even "quad density" disks. You trade density for reliability, and not long ago the trade wasn't worth making, but now 5 inch double and quad density disk systems (from reliable and experienced makers) are as popular and reliable as the tried and true single-density drives.

In addition, you can get double-sided double-density; in 8

inch drives this means you can store one million bytes—a megabyte—on each disk. To be exact, it's 1.1 million bytes; if you believe the average word in text is six characters (five letters plus a space) then you will be able to store about 130,000 words on a disk. This is pretty close to a full novel.

If you're getting 8 inch drives, I recommend double-sided double density. My own come from CompuPro, and like all CompuPro equipment are utterly reliable. There are also so-called Thinline drives, which take up precisely half the space. Most 8 inch drives are reliable, and, provided that you are dealing with a reputable store that will maintain what they sell, you won't go wrong getting what your computer store likes best.

Incidentally, I strongly advise you to get your equipment from a local area computer store, or else through a local area systems consultant. You can save a lot of money (as much as 20% or so) by dealing with mail-order discount houses; you save the 6% California sales tax simply by ordering out of state. I do NOT, however, recommend that you do that, because if you do have problems with the system, there'll be no one who knows you to turn to.

When we turn to 5¼ inch drives, things get complex. Because they are smaller, they hold less text than 8 inch: double-sided double-density 5¼ inch drives hold about 360,000 bytes (360 Kilobytes, or 360K) per disk. That's about 60,000 words, enough for a novel in the old days, but hardly enough for *Majipoor*, for instance. Most small disks hold a lot less, some less than 100K bytes (16,000 words) per disk. Of course there's no law requiring you to get a whole novel on one disk, and indeed in my early days when I had single-side single-density 8 inch (240 K-bytes per disk) I needed more than one disk per book. However, single-sided single-density small disks hold so ridiculously little text that I recommend you not bother with them. They're also maddeningly S*L*O*W.

Little disks used to have a poor reputation for reliability. That *seems* to have been overcome in the present generation, and I am told that small disks are now as reliable—or nearly so—as 8 inch. I guess I believe that, but when I hear of disk problems, 90% of the time the trouble has been with small disks.

Whereas all 8 inch disk systems (well nearly all of them), including double-sided double density systems, can read single-sided single density (SS SD) disks, there is no standard *format* for small disks. Format refers to the way information is arranged within sector and track, and you don't need to know the details. The important thing is that if you have 8" disks you can exchange disks—text files and *programs*—with anyone else who has 8 inch disks, but with 5¼ inch drives you will probably only be able to exchange disks with someone who has the same kind of computer as you. If what you have bought is not a popular brand of machine, you may be severely limited in the choices of programs you can buy. In the extreme, you may not be able to buy the best text editors.

I still use 8" disks. Of course they're not portable. If you ever intend to take your system anywhere, on trips or to conventions or even extended vacations in another city, then you will have no choice; there are no portable 8 inch systems.

Also, 8" drives spin all the time—this is one reason they're faster than 5¼ inch—which means they make a "white noise" sound. I don't mind it at all, but it is noise. If that would distract you, think about small disks.

SOME SYSTEMS

Just as high fidelity sound systems can be bought as components or as a single unit ("all up"), so can computers. You can buy a whole system, with screen, keyboard, disk drives, and all. Examples are the IBM PC, Eagle, KayPro, Otrona, Corvus Concept, etc. You can also buy different components to be integrated into a single system. In my judgment the very best systems come that way.

You should at least look at the Kaypro line, because their equipment is more than good enough for most purposes, and it's the recommended entry-level system for most new computer users. Kaypro equipment corresponds roughly to the older concept of the Ford or Chevrolet automobiles: not many frills, plenty of reliability, good performance for the cost.

If you build up a system from components—and recall Pournelle's Law, "If you don't know what you're doing, deal with people who do"—you can get a system customized to your particular wants and needs. This is the best way to go for those who can afford it.

If you buy components, you'll have to choose a *terminal* to work with. The terminal consists of a keyboard and a screen, and is the means by which you communicate with your computer. It is sometimes called a console.

You're going to spend a *lot* of time with your terminal, so be certain to get one you like. In fact, the looks and feel of the console is just about the most important single decision factor (after reliability) for a writer. If you don't like the keyboard, if the screen is hard to read, if you find the letters ugly, then you very likely won't want that system. That's one reason for getting a "components" computer: there are a number of choices of console for those, while with an all up system you'll have to take what comes with it. Of course you may very well *love* what comes with an all up, in which case your decision is much easier.

The point is that I can't advise you on terminals. You must go to computer stores and play with the terminals they have. Don't pay any attention to the text editor program or anything else. Concentrate on that terminal.

Does the keyboard feel right? Good touch? Right stiffness in the key springs? (Obviously they'll loosen up as you bang away.) Are the keys in the right place? I prefer a Selectric layout, with the 'single quotes' and "double quotes" over to the right of the semicolon which is in turn to the right of the L key, and I expect you will also; but you can get keyboard layouts in which the quotes are on the top line as SHIFT 2, and I know some writers have become accustomed to that arrangement.

It's also important that your keyboard be able to make all the characters, including some you never saw before, like curly braces and the grave and the squiggle {`}. They don't seem important now, but as you begin to learn your machine you'll find you want them.

Incidentally, it is because of the keyboard that I rule out the IBM Personal Computer; they have inserted an extra key between the Z and the SHIFT which is more than enough to drive me mad. So has DEC (Digital Equipment Company) on their new Personal Computer called "The Rainbow." This misconceived keyboard is in conformity to a "standard" not yet adopted by the ISO (International Standards Organization) and conforms to European practices. As far as I am concerned, they can take it back to Europe.

I am told that you can learn to live with the ISO European keyboard, but I know that if you ever have to type on a normal keyboard after you've learned their screwy layout, you'll have the relearning to do all over again. I can't understand why they did that, and I'm not about to relearn to type just to make some stupid European committee happy.

[I have not changed my sentiments on this. Later I wrote: THAT WRECKED KEYBOARD. . . .

Readers will recall that I am no enthusiast of the key layout on the IBM Personal Computer. They have also reduced the size of the RETURN key and moved it far, far away from the home keys. It's an understatement to say I'm no enthusiast: indeed, I think it is (1) an insult to American touch typists, and (2) an unmitigated disaster. (I'm reminded of the lawyer who sent a telegram saying, "Sir: F— You. Strong letter follows.")

Davis Foulger of New Canaan, Connecticut, who otherwise likes my column, says:

"You're wrong about the keyboard on the IBM Personal Computer . . . I met the engineer who designed it at a conference in New York. He was obviously pained by the criticism of his baby . . . he told me that he had a lot of research to support the assertion that the IBM Personal Computer's keyboard was considerably better than a Selectric keyboard."

There follows a certain amount of irrelevant material condemning the QWERTYUIOP keyboard. It's not that it isn't true: we all know that not only is QWERTYUIOP not optimum for touch typing, but that it was designed that way! That is, when mechanical typewriters first came out, the young ladies using them were able to strike sequences of keys faster than the typewriter could keep up; so the keyboard layout was changed to separate key sequences like "th" and "ou" to slow down the typists. The fact remains that QWERTYUIOP is what most learned on, and while it's easy to learn a new board like the Dvorak, it's nearly impossible to go BACK to a QWERTYUIOP after you've learned a new one.

Then he points out that the IBM PC keyboard has a lot of keys that normal typewriters don't have. Where should they go?

Now I agree that putting on the full ASCII key set is a MUST for a good keyboard, and one of my major criticisms of the Osborne is that it doesn't have the squiggle, grave and curly braces; indeed, the first thing I look at when I see a new computer is the keyboard, and if it's missing some of the keys my enthusiasm wanes rapidly.

But that, too, is irrelevant. My ancient DECWRITER keyboard has the full set of ASCII keys while retaining the Selectric layout including the oversize RETURN and SHIFT keys. Mr. Foulger writes that once one becomes used to the IBM PC keyboard, one finds one's typing becomes much more accurate. "Since the shift key on a Selectric is big, we can be clumsy in reaching for it. As a result, we often are. The PC keyboard forces precision. The shift key is a small target that won't allow the user to make mistakes in reaching for it. As a result, typing improves."

The problem is that I didn't ask IBM to improve my typing. I only wanted a keyboard, not a career.

Comes now Jim Baen. Jim was my editor at *Galaxy* Magazine and later at Ace Books. Somewhere along the line he caught my enthusiasm for small computers, and when the IBM PC came out he bought one of the very first.

He loves it, except for the silly wrecked keyboard. They say you can get used to hanging if you hang long enough, and he could get used to the IBM keyboard—except that he has to go back to the office, where they have normal IBM Selectrics. You can't get used to the PC if you have to use normal machines too.

Jim Baen, however, doesn't give up. He's interested in computer games—one game he's going to publish will be INFERNO, by Larry Niven and Jerry Pournelle—for the IBM PC; and now he's found a programmer who can write software to alter the IBM PC keyboard. The alteration converts the stupid keys between the Z and the SHIFT and the ? and the SHIFT into SHIFT keys. It also converts the ridiculous key that's been put between the home keys and RETURN into a RETURN key. To get the characters that these "extra" keys normally make, you hit ALT and the key. The program's called "Magic Keyboard," from Baen Software, and if you want it you can contact Jim Baen for more information at the address on the copyright page.

Meanwhile, I see from the DEC Personal Computer documentation that it also has software reprogrammable keys, and it's probable that some similar trick can be worked with it. It's a pity that you have to kludge things up that way; you'd have thought that IBM and DEC had people smart enough to quit winners. And one day someone will come out with a properly designed keyboard . . .]

After you've examined the keyboard and sat down to get

the feel of it, look at the display. Do you like it? You're going to be looking at it *a lot.* Is it easy to read? Are you comfortable seated at the screen? Are the letters well formed, and do tails of the descending letters, like y and g and q, actually descend below the line in a pleasing manner? The early KayPro machines had a particularly ugly display character set; now, though, they've gone to a very pleasant one for all their 1984-and-later machines.

How many lines can be displayed, and how long are the lines? I happen to be able to live with 16 lines of 64 characters. A standard manuscript line is 64 characters, so the width limit doesn't bother me, but the 16 lines limit means there's only a paragraph or so on the screen at any given time. Some people don't like that. In my case, though, I put the display on a big 15-inch Hitachi monitor screen located at eye level and 30 inches from my eyes; with my bifocal glasses that arrangement is a godsend.

Most systems give you 24 lines of 80 characters each; plenty enough, since a double-spaced page holds only 25 or 26 lines at most. The best terminals have a 25th "Status" line, and good programs can make use of that line; having it is a worthwhile convenience. A few terminals, such as the Ann Arbor Ambassador, will give you up to 60 lines per screen, and a few others will give you superwide screens (132 characters per line); I've not myself ever seen the need for that, but certainly some might.

By all means try an Ambassador if you can find one on display; I've never seen one. The Corvus Concept, a relatively new machine, has a big display screen, excellent keyboard, pleasant character set, and good editors; the only disadvantage is that the Corvus is not a popular machine, and there's relatively little software for it just now.

You should try at least all these terminals:
IBM 3101
Zenith Z-29
Televideo
Qume

In every case, type something on the keyboard; don't just look at it. If you find yourself making a LOT of mistakes, seriously consider something else; a bad-feeling keyboard, or one with the keys laid out wrong (some have so-called TTY layout, with the quotes up top as a SHIFT-numeral) is not something you must or should endure.

Terminals typically cost between $800 and $1,200. You can save a couple of hundred by buying your terminal through a discount mail order store, but I wouldn't; I'd rather deal with someone I could get at with a baseball bat if something goes wrong. If you deal with a systems consultant, he probably will buy it from a discount house, but he'll know how to get service if there's a problem.

There are a couple of terminals you should *not* try. One comes from a company whose warranty extends for one year from the date of *manufacture* of the equipment—meaning that most of the warranty expired while it was sitting in a warehouse. This outfit has a reputation for delivering equipment DOA. I don't name them because they pay their lawyers more than they do their quality assurance department; but read warranties carefully.

In my judgment you needn't bother with any of the little home computers, like Atari and Commodore. I don't recommend Apple or TRS-80, either, for professional work. You may, after you get your machine, decide to get a games machine for a toy, in which case Apple, Atari, and some of the others are strong contenders; but that's another topic for another letter.

If you find a terminal you love, you're ready to get a computer. If you haven't found a terminal you like, don't despair; there are still "all up" computers.

Let's assume, though, that you like one of the terminals I mentioned above, and you're not interested in portability. Now what?

In that case, your problems are over. Go to a reliable CompuPro Systems Center. Say what terminal you like. Then ask for a full Godbout CompuPro 8085/8088 "Dual Processor" system with a hard disk. Get lots of memory. Have them show you printers. Then write a check. The whole system will be under $10,000, and you'll love it.

What you'll get (besides the terminal) is a box about 24" × 18" × 12" high; this holds the computer, which will be inside on a series of removable cards, called "cards" or "boards." There will be many empty slots that could hold additional boards. The configuration is easily expanded to hold more memory, or to add other nifty features and gadgets as you find out about them. You'll also have a box about 24" × 19" × 7" that holds the disk drives: one hard disk, and either a

5-inch or an 8-inch. The two boxes, plus your terminal, will be connected together by cables. You'll have the terminal you chose. The computer itself can be several feet away from where you put the terminal.

The printer can be as far as 30' away, in another room if you like, although the darned things take just enough attention that I like mine in sight. You'll want a good stand for your printer; they're sold at most computer stores and cost too much, but there's no real substitute.

That's your system. It will come with more than enough programs, including both WordStar and my favorite text editor. There will also be SuperCalc, an excellent spread sheet; and a good data base program that can even be taught to keep accounting books (although you'll do better to get a copy of the accounting program I wrote; it's intended for authors, it works, and it seems to keep the IRS happy).

Avoiding Lemons

First, I recommend the Godbout CompuPro line because Bill Godbout has a reputation for selling well-designed equipment backed by a good quality assurance department; and an awesome reputation for seeing to it that his customers are happy even if a lemon slips out of his factory. I've relied on CompuPro equipment for years (ever since my first Ezekial died), and I've never been disappointed.

Of course there are other companies with good reputations too, and I don't mean to slight them; but I am most familiar with Godbout equipment, and I happen to know Dr. Godbout, and I have to recommend *something* as top of the line. I'll discuss more systems below.

There's a reason for all these warnings about "buy from reputable stores." All electronic equipment, no matter how well made, is subject to "infant mortality"; that is, things burn out in the first few hundred hours of life. This cannot be corrected by quality control, because the failures are the electronic chips—those bug-like little things that contain the equivalent of thousands of vacuum tubes. If a chip fails, there's nothing for it but to replace it. The problem is to figure out which one failed—a task beyond either you or me.

Thus if you get a failure, it's likely to be in the first couple of weeks after you get your system. The remedy is to take the system (boards, if you bought "components") back to whomever you got them from (sometimes it's only one board and it's obvious which one).

Another possibility is to buy only burned-in equipment: for a considerably higher cost, many companies, including CompuPro, will sell you "used" boards that have been run past the time when infant mortality failures typically show up. I leave it to you to decide whether the extra costs are worth it. They are not to me—but I have several working computers. If I were buying my first, I'd pay the extra cost; but then I am utterly dependent on the little beasts.

ALTERNATIVES

First, I don't recommend the TRS-80. If you get a TRS-80 at all, get their "Model Two," which runs CP/M and is a serious machine. I'm not recommending it, though. If I seem down on Tandy, I am: I owned one of their Model One machines, and I could not believe the shoddy workmanship and poor design. It was full of kluges (that's computer jargon for not-so-clever dodges to solve a problem's symptoms). They'd cut corners at every possible opportunity, down to saving 25 cents in parts at the risk of keeping their customers miserable for hours.

In fairness, Tandy will, through their Radio Shack stores, get your equipment running if it breaks down when under warranty; but that's one of the problems. My mad friend used to complain about companies that use their customers as a quality control department: ship it out, and if something goes wrong, have the customer bring it in to be fixed.

Tandy assures me they're doing things right with their new products, such as the 2000, and they do seem well designed and engineered; but I would never buy anything from them in their first model-year. Also, I note they haven't done anything for the people—including me—who bought their first computer products. Nearly all those Model One machines are gathering dust in closets.

Second, I don't recommend any of the home computer systems, including Timex, Apple, Atari, Commodore, Coleco, etc.

Third, there are a *lot* of "all up" systems out there. They carry strange brand names. Most are not made by the companies that sell them; they're merely repackaged machines from someone else. Many of those companies won't be around very long. Some are very nice, and some are questionable.

If you see one that you like, do make certain of one thing: be sure it will either run CP/M or is "IBM PC-compatible"; and don't take anyone's word about the PC compatibility. Get a bunch of computer magazines and find reviews that will tell you exactly what programs the Brand X machines will run. Otherwise, you may find yourself with a computer and no software.

There are still more micro-computer programs for CP/M-80 (8-bit) systems than for anything else, although the "PC-compatible" programs are catching up. Both CP/M and PC compatibility lets you be part of a large community of users. You can buy from a vast pool of programs. If you don't have either CP/M or PC compatibility, you're cut off from that, and often limited to what the manufacturer thinks you should have. Not worth it.

As for what is this mysterious CP/M: it's an "operating system." What it does is tell the computer where on the disk to put stuff, and how to find stuff already written on the disk. It then tells the computer how to chew up this information and display some of it to you.

It should be obvious that there are many ways of storing information on a disk. Suppose the disk has 80 tracks of 28 sectors per track. One way to put information on the disk would be simply to put it on in serial order, filling one track, then going to the next. Ah, but if you didn't fill a track? You'd have to store the information about which sectors were empty and which full.

You might also simply put the information on the disk any old place at all, and each time you end a sector you put at the end a short message, (the computerese term is "pointer") telling where the next chunk of the file begins. That method is known as "linked list."

Anyway, an operating system is a particular scheme for storing information on a disk, and if your disks are standard, then you can probably transfer stuff from your computer to mine, or to any other that runs your operating system. You can also accept programs and files, meaning that you can get hold of a lot of software that you'll want. If you don't have a standard operating system, you'll be able to communicate only with the people who use your something else, and that can be a very limited number.

One last point: the trend now is towards increased compatibility. One route to that is (16-bit) Concurrent CP/M, which will be able to run PC-DOS programs in the near future; Concurrent is being designed so that *it* can run under an established mini-computer operating system known as UNIX. If all goes well, within a couple of years we'll see the micro computing community reunited.

Meanwhile, a good compromise is CP/M 8/16; if you get a CompuPro with hard disk, I recommend 8/16 highly. It's what I have now.

[More on 8/16 in volume Two of this series.]

Portability

Do you want portability? If so, one professional quality choice stands out: the Otrona Attache, which is a genuine desktop machine. It has a full-size keyboard with Selectric style key layout, but it remains truly portable. I can tell you from experience that it looks absolutely gorgeous on a Venice café table. Or in Verona, or Firenze, or Roma. (It has a built-in capability to use European current.)

The Attache has a small screen, adequate when using it in a hotel in Rome, or sitting at Quadri's in Piazza San Marco, but not daily use. However, they sell an *excellent* full-size amber screen, so good that we use it as a monitor here when the Otrona is out in the field.

A monitor, incidentally, isn't a battleship, but a TV set without the TV receiver. They come in green, amber, and black and white, and you takes your pick; I prefer black and white, then amber in that order, while others like green. *De gustibus non est disputandum.*

Get a monitor of convenient size for the place you intend to work. Mine happens to be 15", and I can read my screen from across the room; most people don't want one quite that large, but then most people don't have my eye problems.

I tend to carry my Otrona everywhere, and transfer the text I've written on it to my big machine when I get home. That's fairly easy to do; but in fact, the Otrona is more than adequate as an "only" machine.

The Otrona has 5¼" disks, of course. They're double-sided double-density, 360K per disk. They're more reliable than most little disks. There's also a hard disk for the Otrona. That's not portable; you leave it, along with the monitor, at home base, and transfer the work to it when you come back home. That works very well.

If you do get the Attache, stay with the simple Z-80 8-bit version; don't bother with the "upgrade" to an 8088 to make it "PC-compatible." The "upgrade" doesn't make it PC-compatible at all, and isn't worth the investment.

Almost Portable

Now that the Osborne line is gone, KayPro is the most popular entry-level machine, and deservedly so. They make a full line of equipment, ranging from the lowest cost full computer I'd be willing to recommend up to the KayPro 10 with hard disk.

The KayPro line is "portable" in the sense that there's a handle on the machine, but you'll have arms like an orangutan if you try carrying one far. I'm partial to KayPro stuff; it's reliable and rugged. If you think of the Otrona as an Audi and the KayPro as a Chevrolet (from the days when Chevies were the last word in serviceable reliability) you'll be on the right track.

Indeed, I can recommend KayPro equipment as a first system to anyone; you get a lot of bang for the buck, it's reliable, the resale value is reasonable, and it is far more than adequate to learn on until you know precisely what you want. In practice I find that professional writers graduate to somewhat more aesthetically pleasing equipment, but they keep their KayPro as backup; and, as mentioned, KayPro systems do close up with a handle, so they can be taken to conventions or vacation homes.

Norman Spinrad recently bought a KayPro 10, and he's very happy with it.

PC-Compatible Machines

[Since I wrote this letter, there have been a number of developments in 16-bit PC DOS machines; far too much to cover in this chapter.

In later chapters I'll discuss the IBM PC, and a number of compatibles such as the Eagle. However: for pure word processing, there are, in 1984, few advantages to having PC compatibility. The best word processing software works fine with 8-bit CP/M equipment. Moreover, the KayPro machines can be upgraded to about 80% compatibility with the IBM PC. The CompuPro Dual Processor has the potential for 100% compatibility.

On the other hand, software development for 8-bit machines has slowed to a crawl; the best new stuff is written for 16-bit machines, and most of that is for the IBM PC and PC clones.

Clones worth a writer's time to investigate include the Compaq, the Corona, and the newer versions of Eagle machines. They all work, as does the IBM PC itself. Cost, "feel," and aesthetics should govern here: you're going to be sitting in front of it for a long time.

There are advantages to 16-bit equipment, but CP/M 8-bit systems will be useful for quite a long time, and they cost less.]

* Last minute addition: The Zenith Z-150 is an excellent PC-Clone. Zenith equipment is reliable, and Heath/Zenith has good service and software. You can *still* get parts for 20-year-old Heathkit equipment.

CHAPTER 3
Software

Text Editors

This is obviously the most important program you'll have, so you'll want to select it carefully.

First a small touch of history to reveal possible prejudices. When Larry Niven and I began using computers to write, there were very few text editor programs. We started with one called Electric Pencil, which was about the best available then. It had some major defects.

We also have a program-writing friend, and every time we noticed a defect in Pencil, or wanted a feature that Pencil didn't have, we made notes about it, and our friend—Tony Pietsch—wrote them into a text editor he was designing. The result was a program called Write which Larry and I use, and which I believe is the best *text creation* editor I know of.

I doubt if it is the "best editor"; but then I don't know what that phrase means, since so many people want so many different things. To some, an editor shines if and only if it is very good at generating letters. Others think the major features are the text *formatting* capabilities; this is particularly true for those who use their computers to set camera-ready text for manuals and newsletters and fanzines.

For me, the most important feature of a text editor is that it is *transparent*. By this I mean that it doesn't intrude; that it is as nearly invisible as it can be. It shouldn't tell me things I don't want to know, nor require me to do a lot of fancy fingerwork to accomplish what I want done. I can do without a number of very complex "features" that I probably won't learn to use anyway, if it will do the simple work quickly, quietly, and unobtrusively.

Thus I like Write, which is available for most CP/M computers (but NOT for the IBM PC or PC compatibles). Write may be a little harder to learn than some of the other editors. Not a lot harder; but it will take a day or so to get used to it and to learn enough of its features to be able to do much with it. There are editors—see below—that let you work with them instantly. It has been my experience, though, that the more you learn about them, the less you like them. . . .

Features

Nearly all text editors have a core of basic features. They'll let you move text around (simulate cut and paste). They'll let you insert letters, words, sentences, or paragraphs into existing text. They'll let you correct by typing over the old text, or by (quickly) deleting the old and typing new.

All the editors will "word wrap," which means that as you type to the end of a line, you need not hit carriage return (or manually return the carriage); the editor will automagically jump the cursor (the mark that shows where you're typing) to the beginning of the next line. It will also bring with it the word you're typing. This sounds distracting, but in fact it is not, and you not only quickly get used to it, you soon wonder how you ever lived without it, since you no longer have to interrupt your typing in order to mess with the carriage.

All have these major features; but after that, they differ a lot.

Visible Carriage Returns

One difference seems minor, but to me is not: Does the editor show you "carriage return" characters? That is, in order to tell the printer where to make a new line, the editors insert an actual character, known as "CR" or "carriage return," into the text stream. Most text editors make these invisible: you only know they're there because you see their effect. However, some editors, such as Write, actually put a mark on the screen (usually a little one-letter-wide horizontal arrow). I prefer that, and I've gotten so used to having them that I get unhappy when they're not there. Most editors do not show the carriage return as a visible character; nevertheless, the character is there in your file.

"Core" or Disk Scroller?

There are two fundamental approaches to text editors. They have no standard names, so I've chosen those above: "Core" and "Disk Scroller." Do understand that anyone who hasn't read this essay won't have a clue as to what those terms mean, although anyone familiar with text editors will understand the concepts involved.

A "core" editor keeps all the text it's working on in the computer's main memory. That memory is limited, so the result is that you'll be limited to files of about 36-40K bytes at a time. This corresponds to some 6,000–7,500 words, a bit longer than my typical chapters.

With a "core" editor, you must save off your present disk file (say a chapter) and reload the next, whenever your text gets to be over 6,000 words long. The editor tells you when you're approaching this limit, and nothing happens if you try to pass it, other than that the editor complains and urges you to save your file.

It takes about 20 seconds to save the present file and load a new one (or start a new one).

A "disk scroller," on the other hand, will let you make a file as long as you want, up to the capacity of the disk; with double-sided double-density disks that's a ridiculous length, a whole Majipoor novel if you like. It does this by keeping a disk file "open," and as you write it sort of automatically writes off some of that to the disk. Eventually you save the whole thing into one disk file.

Naturally you can break things up into more than one file if you like, and indeed you'd better.

At first glance, it seems a "disk scroller" would be better, since it allows you to keep your novel in one humungous file. Of course you'd never actually do that, because it would take so very long to go from the beginning to the end of the file (the machine would have to read the whole novel, which could take minutes!). In practice, then, you tend to break the novel up into parts to begin with.

There is one great disadvantage to the "disk scroller" file structure: once you "open" the disk file, you MUST NOT REMOVE THE DISK. Even if you find that the disk is full (and it happens) so there is no room on the disk for your new text, you cannot simply take out the old disk and put in a new; that will produce a fatal error that will LOSE YOUR TEXT. Instead, if you want to save your text, you'll have to make room on the disk by erasing some of the existing files. Presumably you'll have copies . . .

The "core" type of editor, on the other hand, will let you change disks as often as you like. My own editor is a "core" editor, and I have developed the habit of saving all important files twice, once on the file "master" and once on a disk called "backup" or "safety." This takes about twenty seconds, and is a form of insurance I heartily urge.

"Core" editors will also let you input stuff that was on another disk: simply change disks, read in the new stuff, put back your file master, and save it or proceed any other way. "Disk scrollers" make that between difficult and impossible.

Thus, although Mr. David Alexander has chosen an editor for Jack Vance mainly because it is a "disk scroller" and thus will let Jack work on very long files, my own recommendation is just the opposite: other things being equal, I prefer a "core" type of editor because it makes it so easy to make safety copies.

Incidentally, the "core" editors have a "link" mechanism, whereby you tell the end of one file what file follows it, so that you can do all the operations (such as long search-and-replace, printout of the whole novel, etc.) that you could do with a disk scroller. It takes a little more time, but not so very much; while core editors are very fast when it comes to text creation.

EDITORS

I'll try to summarize all the major text editing programs I know. I own and have used most of these.

WordStar: This is easily the most popular word processing program in the microcomputer world. It's fairly easy to learn, and it has been implemented on nearly every conceivable terminal and machine. It comes standard with the Otrona Attache, the Osborne, and a vast number of all-up machines.

I don't like it much.

There are a number of reasons. One is that it's a disk scroller. Of course some say that's a feature rather than a bug.

The main reasons I don't like WordStar, though, have to do with the basic structure of the editor: it uses multiple-keystroke commands to accomplish many simple things. With my editor I strike one key and I am instantly at the end of my text; another takes me instantly to the beginning. WordStar requires you to hit a control-shifted key; wait; then hit another key entirely. It will then (somewhat slowly) take you to the end of text. You go through the same agony to get to the beginning.

WordStar also insists on telling me things I don't want to know. It displays what line and column you are working on at all times; this means that every time you hit a key, a display of row and column up at the top of the screen flickers to show you the new row and column. This alone is enough to drive me mad—and there is NO WAY TO TURN OFF THIS "FEATURE." (Incidentally: I think there are no programmers who are also touch typists, which is why we get monstrosities like this. Programmers, being two-finger key bangers, stare at the keyboard, and haven't any notion of what's going on on-screen while they're typing. I think hunt-and-peckers design all the keyboards, too.)

However: for all its problems, you can work with WordStar, and eventually you'll probably want to learn it. WordStar tends to be almost everyone's *second*-choice editor, and it's available for nearly every computer. A lot of writers—Gary Edmundson, Carolyn Cherryh, and Joe Haldeman all come to mind—prefer it.

Because WordStar is so popular, there are a lot of text processing programs that work in conjunction with it. These include programs to generate indices and tables of contents; footnote handlers; mail list management programs; spelling correction programs; etc. I keep a copy of WordStar just to use these with. The index programs are especially useful.

[Since I wrote this, MicroPro has come out with WordStar 3.3, which is a definite quantum improvement over the older versions. WordStar 3.3 on the IBM PC, especially if you have a hard disk or ever better a "memory disk," is fast, quiet, and easy to use. I still prefer Write for creative writing; but WordStar 3.3 is certainly acceptable.]

NewWord: This is a text editor developed by former employees of MicroPro. It is very similar to WordStar, but it has some new features. Its authors claim that it's "WordStar with the bugs out." NewWord is based on WordStar 3.2, and some of its new features are quite similar to features added by WordStar 3.3.

The NewWord documents are arguably better than WordStar documents. If you like WordStar and you have a chance (such as at a computer show) you'd be well advised to watch for a demonstration of NewWord.

Select: This is the easiest editor to learn I have ever seen. I have sat down and worked with it without ever reading the instructions. You can learn it fast, but it is a severely limited editor, has some very strange "features" that I cannot stand, and I heartily dis-recommend it.

Magic Wand, now known as PeachText: A very popular editor with many excellent features. I had a hand in its original design, although they didn't take all of my advice (and I don't own any part of it). It has a number of good features, and is certainly one of the editors I'd consider if I didn't have Write. It comes with excellent documentation and tutorials on getting it running.

Palantir: Much like Magic Wand, which isn't surprising since it was written by the original author of Magic Wand. A lot of people swear by Palantir. One disadvantage is that it hasn't become very popular, so there aren't too many utilities, such as indexing, written in aid of it. Writers who like Palantir like it a lot. It's another I'd seriously consider if I didn't already have a favorite.

Perfect Writer: An adaptation to micro computers of the EMACS text editor used on big machines at MIT. Versions I've seen have all had bugs. Perfect Writer is a modified "disk scroller" that does the disk access work a lot better than WordStar does. It allows you to "split the screen" so that you can look at more than one file at a time; a feature I wish my editor had (and one which will be added to Write real soon now, I'm told).

It also has a lot of index, footnote, and reference handling features that mine doesn't have.

Alas, it does insist on telling you things you don't want to know. It does that at the bottom of the screen, and the flicker isn't as maddening as WordStar's, but it's there.

I might consider Perfect Writer if I didn't have Write, and there are times when I'm tempted by its index feature and the ability to look at more than one file at a time. However, it has some oddities I don't like at all; that may simply be a matter of what I'm used to.

A few friends who have Perfect Writer like it a lot. Others absolutely hate it.

Spellbinder: This is an editor written by Lexi-soft, an outfit that also sells all up computers known as Lexiwriters. I've little experience with them. Friends on congressional staffs in Washington have one and are very happy, but they have no experience with anything else. I'm told the Lexiwriter is pretty expensive as a package compared to buying the same equipment as components, but I'm not even certain of that.

Spellbinder, though, is an excellent editor, and many writers like it a lot. It has lots of features, is easy enough to use, and easy to learn. You could do a lot worse than Spellbinder. It's another I'd seriously consider using myself.

WordMaster: This is primarily a programmers' editor. It is a disk scroller. It has many very powerful features, but alas, it lacks the essential one, the ability to "word wrap." With WordMaster what you see is what you get: you terminate a line by hitting the Carriage Return key, and if you do not, the line doesn't end.

For years, WordMaster was absolutely the best *programming* editor around, but MicroPro never updated it, and eventually that distinction was lost; so there's little reason for anyone to buy it now. Programs are "line oriented," as opposed to text which is "paragraph oriented." I can't recommend WordMaster for creative writing. It wasn't designed for it. The only major writer I know who uses WordMaster is Gordon Dickson, and he does so because he started with it back when there were very few editors that his equipment could run. He may have changed over by now.

Mince and Final Word

These are both based on the MIT EMACS editor, and are primarily programming editors, although some creative writers swear by them. They both have tons of features. Neither is particularly easy to learn. They're very popular with hackers, but I know of no major writer who uses either for text creation.

VEDIT

This is another programming editor, not really useful for creative writers, but excellent if you write large programs in Pascal or Compiling Basic. It has very powerful macro features (that is, it can do highly complex searches and replaces.)

Comparing Editors

[One way to learn more about text editors is by reading books. I put this review into the August 1983 column; I haven't changed my opinion. Naiman's book is about the best there is.

One of the panels at the West Coast Computer Faire was devoted to text editors and word processing. I'd intended to go to it, but I got trapped in something conflicting. It was conducted by Arthur Naiman. I met him for about one minute before his panel. I'm sorry I missed the panel, because I'm told it was very good. I believe that, because last week I got a copy of Arthur Naiman's new book, *Word Processing Buyer's Guide*, and that's *excellent*.

I would be proud to have written this book. It's clear, objective, and damned thorough. It even has a review of Write, the text editor I use; Naiman read one of my articles and managed to get hold of Tony Pietsch, Write's author, and buy not only Write, but a computer modeled after Ezekial.

I gather from Naiman's book that, like me, he has just about every word processing and text editing program in existence. He even wrote the Sybex *Introduction to WordStar*. Interestingly, Naiman used Write to write the WordStar book. . . .

Naiman uses an interesting point system to evaluate word processing programs; thus you can see *exactly* why he rates the various programs the way he does. This book discusses just about every text editor I know of, plus a lot I had never heard of before reading his book. Anyone contemplating the purchase of a text editor or word processor should run, not walk, to their store and get this book before spending a single dime on word processing software.

Which is still good advice. . .]

BOTTOM LINE

Those are the major editors. For text creation I know of nothing that can beat Write. There are more support programs (indexing, table of contents, footnotes, etc.) for WordStar than any other editor.

Whatever you get, buy a spelling program known as The Word Plus [Version 2.0 arrived yesterday. It's even better.] This terrific package of programs lets you do a lot more than check spelling. It builds special dictionaries (character names and alien words, for instance) that you can use for one book and that book only; it lets you add special words to the main dictionary; builds frequency tables of how often you used a word, and also lists of each unique word in text sorted alphabetically.

AN IDEAL SYSTEM

In April 1984, a reader asked me to describe an ideal system for writing. The following reply appeared in the July 1984 issue of *BYTE*:

Given that I have my choice of almost any system available, obviously I prefer the S-100 system I now use. What I have is a Compupro "boat anchor" box that houses a Z-80 CPU, lots of memory drive, and 8" floppies. It talks to me through a memory-mapped video board that drives a 15" monitor; I talk to it on an Archives keyboard. As soon as Compupro releases its upcoming S-100 video board that emulates the IBM PC display (but will put it up on my 15" monitor) I'll change over to that.

I solve the problem of large storage and quick access to a variety of documents by having a separate S-100 8085/8088 System 8/16 with 40 megabyte hard disk. That system also drives the printer.

You did say "ideal."

You could also build a "dream system" for writers around the Sage IV; we're even looking into the possibility of using a MacIntosh as the terminal for the Sage! The trouble is that just now there's absolutely zero software for the Macintosh; we're waiting for the dust to settle on that. The Sage, though, with a good bit-mapped screen, could be made into a wonderful system.

Obviously not everyone has access to so much equipment.

Writing with computers is so much faster, better, and easier than working with typewriters that it hardly matters what you get, so long as you get a good reliable full service computer, not a game-playing toy. I know writers who love: Zenith Z-100; Apple IIe; Sage; IBM PC; Eagle; Otrona; Osborne; Kaypro; Corvus; Wang; Altos; North Star; Vector Graphic; Epson Qx-10; and one who's devoted to his Exidy Sorcerer.

GET YOUR FEET WET

The most important thing is to take the plunge. Even a mungy computer is better than none at all. If you stay with reputable outfits, and keep in mind the principles I've given above, you won't go wrong: and when you get a computer, you'll find your writing is easier. You'll turn out more text. (Yes, even you, Robert Silverberg!) Moreover, it will be *better*, because every word will be exactly the one you wanted, not the one you were willing to settle for because you didn't want to retype.

Whatever you get, within a month you'll wonder how you got along without it.

PART: THREE
EARLY FRIENDS

To speak of the early years of the computer revolution makes it sound as if the late 70s and early 80s were decades ago; yet so much has happened since then that the time seems longer ago than it was. Until Adam Osborne introduced his Osborne-1, there were no low-cost computer systems. Most computer enthusiasts were hobbyists. Only a very few built their own computers from components—such home-brew systems were rare, and their owners were highly prized—but nearly everyone had to understand what was going on inside the machines.

In those times the most common machines were built around the S-100 bus. "Bus" systems consisted of a large box and a number of removable boards covered with computer chips. The heart of the system was the Central Processing Unit (CPU), which contained the actual micro computer chip. Then there were memory boards, disk controller boards, input/output (I/O) boards, clock boards, etc. Only a few companies offered "single board computers" in which all the necessary functions were put on one circuit board. One of those was David Jackson's Altos Company.

Jackson worked in his garage, and the first Altos computers were hand-built there. Because his idea seemed so simple, it was nearly impossible to get financing; as a result, when his company took off after a couple of years, he still owned a very great deal of it. His original employees—secretary, bookkeeper, etc.—were given stock in lieu of wages. After Altos went public, Jackson's share was, at least on paper, worth three hundred million dollars, and his early employees were also millionaires.

Of course, for every success like Altos there were a dozen failures. Companies sprang up, flourished, withered, and died, all in the space of a few months. Everything changed like dreams. Machine capabilities grew and prices fell even as we watched them.

It was against this background that the early *User's Columns* appeared. There were few experts. We were all learning about these wonderful new machines.

The columns from those days aren't just history and nostalgia. Those were the times when my friends and I raised some fundamental questions that haven't been settled yet: matters such as copy protection, licensing agreements, copyright, and computer piracy. There was considerable speculation on the future: languages, operating systems, new computer chips. Most of these questions are still current. I've done little revising, because little was needed. I have excised some portions that are simply irrelevant, such as reviews of programs and machines no longer available.

The *User's Column* couldn't have been created without two special friends: Ezekial, my friend who happened to be a Z-80 computer, and Dan Mac Lean, my mad friend. You'll see a lot of them in this chapter.

CHAPTER 1
Pirates and Operating Systems

"People do strange things," said my mad friend Mac Lean. "They invent things like the OS-1 operating system."

"You mean it doesn't work?"

"No, it works fine," he said. "And it's about as useful as a chocolate-covered wristwatch. Or maybe a triple hernia. If you like to play with operating systems, and God knows I do, OS-1 will give you hours of delight. But if you want to USE it, you get hours of tedium."

"Why? Isn't it like Unix?"

"Well, yes, it is, sort of."

"But then why isn't OS-1 useful? Everyone likes Unix...."

"Do they? Well, maybe a lot of programmers do. I'm not so sure the users are going to like Unix all that much. Anyway, OS-1 isn't *quite* Unix. It is a tree structured directory system, but there's no mechanism for finding a file in there unless you've kept lists. And you can't even make lists. The 'SET TTY' command will set the screen width, but it won't set the printer width, so you can't even list for hard copy unless you've got a 132-wide printout device. So if you don't remember what's in those directories, you'll never find the files."

"What, never?" I asked.

"Well, hardly ever. The idea is that you can have multiple directories, so a lot of different users can each have their own, right? But floppies are too small for that kind of structure. Look, your utilities occupy most of one disk, and your operating system and its directories take up another disk. On top of that, the OS is so big that you've only got about 32K of RAM left over. That ain't enough to work in. The PL/I compiler can't do much in that. Whitesmith's C compiler won't even start to work. Leor Zolman's [excellent!] BDS C compiler hasn't got room to breathe. What use is a Unix-like system that won't let you compile C programs?"

I still wasn't convinced. "Look," I said. "OS-1 is supposed to have all kinds of nifty features taken from Unix...."

"It almost does," my mad friend said. "The notion behind the Unix system, with pipelines, and all that groovy stuff, is great. Unix treats *everything* like a file, and you can build 'pipelines' from your directory to the device you want the file to go to, or between programs. But OS-1 doesn't do that. Instead, it has pseudo-pipelines, with intermediate file structures. Why do that? Better to use CP/M and a submit program. With OS-1 you just don't have enough RAM, and you have trouble keeping track of where you are, and the command strings are long and tedious if you want to look at other directories. They really tried hard, and you ought to give them an A for effort, but only about a C for usefulness."

"And if we go to 16-bit machines?" I asked. "Such as the 8086? Where we've got plenty of RAM to play with, and hard disks and fast access and...."

He shrugged. "Who knows? But I suspect that if you want a Unix-like system, you might as well have Unix and be done with it. Why compromise with something else?"

And on reflection I have to agree. OS-1 is a heroic effort, but it falls between the cracks.

[And indeed, so have most of the other "almost Unix" systems. Unix, for those who don't know, is a multi-user operating system invented at Bell Labs, and used in many university computer establishments. Until recently there was no version for micro systems: Unix is *very* large (if you buy it for the IBM PC it comes on *15* disks!). It uses a lot of memory.

The Unix question is still very much with us, and very much unsettled; but Mac Lean was right, "almost Unix" systems got nowhere.]

So what *will* be the operating system for future micros? Will we, as a recent editorial said, "get it right the second time"? Or are we stuck with CP/M forever and aye?

Well—first, what does "stuck" mean? For all its problems—

and Lord knows it has plenty—CP/M isn't all that bad, for *users*. Programming hackers really hate it, but true hackers hate almost anything they didn't grow up with. Users don't know some of the inconveniences of CP/M, and worse, most users don't know all the nifty features because of the wretched documentation Digital Research is notorious for; but CP/M *is* fairly easy to learn and use, even for beginners. It gets the job done.

[Digital Research's instruction manuals for CP/M were notoriously dense in the early days. Under constant hammering from reviewers—it was one of the few issues that every computer writer could agree on—Digital made some hefty changes. There are still some problems, as we'll see in later chapters, but they *have* improved. Of course there was a great deal of room for improvement....]

And now that Xerox has adopted CP/M for their much-advertised systems, one conclusion is plain: any popular system of the future will have to be upward compatible with CP/M, because there's just so much good software running under CP/M. Digital Research did us all a good turn by coming up with something *standard* in this field. I remember when we had to use F-DOS....

[The above was one of the first articles in a major computer magazine to pronounce CP/M the micro computer "standard" operating system. Within a few months a dozen more writers said much the same thing; and Lo! CP/M *became* the standard. Prediction? Or cause and effect?]

And then there are the utilities. You don't have to understand CP/M, if someone else does. I've mentioned the CP/M User's Group (CPMUG) before; an outfit that distributes all kinds of nifty utilities, like COPY routines, and FAST which speeds up CP/M 1 4, and such like. The problem with CPMUG is selectivity and updating: there are over 40 disks in the CPMUG library, most filled with junk, useless games, or obsolete versions of programs since updated.

There are other sources of utilities. Various nets distribute all kinds of nifty programs. Modem emulators. Catalog programs. Library routines. You name it. And these get revised all the time. So how can you tell which ones to use?

The answer is, you can't. Comes now Barry Workman, of Workman & Associates. Barry sifts through the CPMUG and other public domain sources, and puts together disks of utilities, which he'll sell for $35.00 each.

"I'll try to put up the most useful CP/M utilities I can find," Workman says. "The latest and fastest copy routines, command line processors, directory programs, a good modem program to use with The Source or Micronet or whatever. Comparators and filters, stuff like that. Ward Christenson's disk catalog utility, which is by itself worth more than the disk if you don't have it."

"How do you select the programs?"

"Mostly I ask people like you what you'd like to have."

The documentation on the Workman disks is adequate, generally better than what was on the CPMUG disks. At least it had better be: Barry, by supplying quantitites of slivovitz which he finds in some unknown place, gets me to go over the stuff for him. I do *not* rewrite it, but I do smooth out some of the ambiguities.

Workman's Utility Disk Two has Ward Christenson's disassembler, some comments from my mad friend on how disassemblers work, and instructions; and some other utilities probably more useful to programmers than users, although again Workman has tried to keep things simple and provide what he thinks will be most useful.

The Workman Utilities are mostly public domain programs, and almost all of them could be obtained by swapping with other people—for that matter, the only copyrighted material on those disks are some documentation files. Workman sells them as a service; nobody's going to get rich at that price. I can't list exactly what's on each of the disks, because that changes according to what Workman thinks is the most useful disk full of stuff he can put together. He does try to send out the latest versions of the various utilities as he gets them. They're worth the price if your time is valuable.

Workman supplies his utilities in a number of disk formats. One, of course, is 8 inch soft sectored, because that's what Ezekial, likes. But of course we have another computer. . . .

LOBO to the Rescue

It was at the West Coast Computer Faire. I was talking to Roger Billings, President of Lobo Drives International, about their hard disks.

"I'm in big trouble," I said.

"Why?"

"Here I am at the Faire. I'll be bringing home a lot of new

software. Automated Simulation has some great new games, like Starfleet Orion. And when I get home my kids are going to kill me, because Ezekial is running fine, but *their* computer isn't. My name is mud if I can't get that TRS-80 going again...."

"What happens?" Roger asked.

"Won't boot. Drives spin, but the system won't come up."

"Hmm. Can we come see you next week?"

"Sure," I said, and promptly forgot the conversation, there being so much to see and do at the Faire. Precisely a week later I was talking on the telephone when the doorbell rang. Here at Chaos Manor that's a big deal. Dogs bark madly and skid on rugs to the door, followed by shouting boys trying to restrain the dogs. Anyone who waits for the door to open is *determined*.

Eventually I got off the phone to find Eliot Lane, Lobo's Product Engineering manager. He had a van outside. "I've come to fix up your TRS-80," he said.

And fix it up he did. The first thing was to replace my Percom disk drives with two new LOBO drives. That turns out to be easy: LOBO drives have the cable connector on the back, where you can get at it wtihout taking out screws (and I wish the Percoms were built that way; it's bloody easy to have one of the power cables come loose inside the drive when you put it together after connecting the data cable). But when we tried booting the system, nothing happened.

Next we installed LOBO's LX-80 expansion interface to replace my TRS-80 interface. My TRS-80 Model One is one of the intermediate versions; in addition to the ribbon cable (with flat booster box) connecting the keyboard to the expansion interface, there's also a round cable—which makes it pretty crowded and hard to get at the RESET button. There's no connection for anything like that on LOBO's LX-80.

"Just ignore it," Eliot said. He proceeded to connect up the LX-80. It didn't work, so we took the TRS-80 keyboard apart, and lo! There was a broken wire in the ribbon cable connecting the two halves of the system together. Eliot soldered jumpers around the broken parts and tried again; and all worked fine.

It still does. We're now running the LOBO LX-80 with LDOS operating system, and both work splendidly. The disk drives are a pair of LOBO 5¼ inch and another pair of LOBO 8"; all four are running at double density, and doing fine, and with this system you can move everything from small disks to big ones and back again, giving you a *lot* of storage.

[The column continues with a long review of the Lobo LX-80 Expansion Interface, an excellent product which vanished when Tandy ceased to sell the TRS-80 Model One computer. Like many after market add-ons for the "Trash 80," the Lobo equipment was much better than the computer it supported.

The column also looks at LDOS, an operating system that was compatible with, and a great improvement over, the wretched Radio Shack TRS-DOS that was supposed to work with the TRS-80. LDOS was clearly superior.

Indeed, LDOS still exists. You can get it for the Lobo Max-80 Computer, and if you have LDOS you can run nearly all the software that was written for the TRS-80 Model One. Some of that software was pretty good; but it's mostly out of date by now.

It's hard to remember that the TRS-80 Model One was once a major system. . . .]

Pirates

"Do you read *BYTE*?" my mad friend asked.

"Stupid question. I *write* for *BYTE*."

"What's that got to do with reading it? Anyway, did you read the editorial on software piracy?" I admitted that I had. "What did you think of it?"

"Didn't think about it a lot—"

"You should. It's dead wrong," Mac Lean said. "Look. Your editor, Chris Morgan, says that software piracy is a major problem—"

"And it really isn't, for users," I mused.

"Well, it's sure going to be," Mac Lean said. "Because look what they're doing. Making programs complicated and uncopyable to 'protect' the publishers. What that really does is make the user's life impossible. Disks are fragile things. I've *got* to have copies of them. Suppose I have a brownout. Ever have that happen to you?"

I nodded. Once we had a power failure while I was copying a disk. It took Mac Lean and a program called SPAT (available on one of the Workman Utility Disks) and a *lot* of work to recover most of what was on either disk.

"And it's worse than that," Mac Lean said. "They worry about pirates, and the result is that the programs are fragile.

They can't recover from mistakes, because instead of error traps they've put in some kind of 'security.' "

And he's right. The more I think about "uncopyable" programs, the more I hate the idea. I sure wouldn't bet any part of my income on something like that—and I'm unlikely ever to recommend an "uncopyable" in this column.

But, then, how do we protect the rights of programmers?

Rights to what? If you mean by that, right to several hundred bucks for a program, why should we? I mean, if people can get that for a program, more power to them, but ye gods, why is it my concern to help publishers get that much? I *want* the price of software to come down.

"But," I mused, "if the price comes down, will we still get good software?"

My mad friend chortled. "Ever meet a true hacker who didn't write software? True, they won't do adequate *documentation*, they never do no matter what you're paying, but try to stop them from writing programs."

And of course he has a point. There's another argument: that software takes a long time to write, maybe months and months or even a year, so doesn't the programmer deserve high prices?

Well, what the hell, it takes me a year or so to write a book, and I don't notice anyone getting any $400 per copy, and as for piracy, I pay taxes to support public institutions whose purpose is to loan out my books for *free*; yet I'm not starving, and neither are my publishers. The average paperback book sells about 50,000 copies, at perhaps $2.75, and makes a little money for the publisher, the distributor, and the author. True, nobody gets rich on that; the money is in best-sellers, which sell a million and more copies.

Or there's the textbook situation. Take Kernighan and Plauger's excellent *Software Tools*, or Grogono's *Programming in Pascal* as examples. They sell for around $15.00, and I suppose they sell 30–40,000 copies. Maybe more. Does anyone seriously contend that it's harder to write a good program than to write a good book? I've done both, and programs are easier, if a bit more tedious; there's more of the equivalent of reading galley proofs (we call it galley slavery) in programming than in writing. But both are hard work.

As for thefts: look, it's really in everyone's interest to bring the price of software down. The more good software—and by good, I mean stuff that's usable by ordinary people to do useful things, programs that are self-instructing and have really good documentation—the more good software available at a reasonable price, the more machines will be sold, and the larger the software market—which is *already* approaching the book-buying market. There are a lot of people in this country, but not very many of them read books; I wouldn't be surprised if the number of computers already sold isn't equal to the number of people who buy hardbound books, and it's a significant fraction of the number who buy paperbacks.

But, pleads the software developer, book publishers don't have to maintain their books; they don't have people telephoning with questions—

Two answers to that: first, if you get the software and its documents are right the first time, you shouldn't be getting those complaints; book publishers don't depend on their customers to be an unpaid quality control department. Secondly—why, the pirates *can't* call in with questions.

So my heart doesn't bleed for the publisher. After all, who steals software? Businesspeople? Nonsense. Try selling a computer system to your local architect and tell him you're furnishing him with stolen programs. Ye gods. No, there are two categories of thieves: hobbyists, and shady systems houses. Let's look at them.

First the hobbyist: this poor joker is typically broke. The computer industry gets every nickel he has; he couldn't pay for what he steals. He probably wouldn't have bought the stolen program anyway, and furthermore, he'll spend the money on something else that's computer-related. Nobody is losing that much money, even in the case of the clubs where they line up and make copy after copy ... because darned few of those present would ever buy $500 programs. They want them to play with, not to sell, and probably not even to use.

What are the alternatives? To preserve those $500 price tags by making the programs unstable? And doggone it, that's precisely what some outfits have done. In an attempt to thwart pirates, they've made their software fragile. I have in mind one data base outfit that has sent me *four separate copies* of their widely advertised program, each supposedly configured just for me; and we have *yet* to make one work. I've given up on them.

Then there's what Mac Lean calls "Levitical Documentation"; the first half of the manual is filled with "Thou Shalt Not" statements, and the licensing agreement is such that you have to be insane to give them your right name. This is professionalism?

Then too: if the software houses did decent documents, they'd make their pile selling those. Adam Osborne got rich giving away programs and selling books. [This was long before Osborne Computers, and even before Adam Osborne sold Osborne Books to McGraw-Hill.] So can anyone else. You just won't convince me that I ought to feel sorry for an outfit that can palm off some wretched document at $30.00, and sell thousands of copies of it at discounts that would set a major publisher's eyes gleaming with greed.

And that's the answer to the systems house pirate, who, if the truth be known, isn't all that great a threat either. True, he does soak up legitimate profits. I know a writer who bought a system from a fly-by-night company, and found that his WordStar and CP/M were pirated. But when he went back to demand satisfaction, the systems house was gone—as, indeed, they usually will be. If they're successful, they *have* to go legitimate eventually; there's just no way to keep their pirate acts secret forever. And if they're not successful, they just haven't stolen that much. (Oh, true, at the hideously inflated prices software publishers charge, the total dollar value is high; but in fact we're talking about fewer than a hundred copies at most, and of those many wouldn't have been sold but could only be given away. Not everyone who takes low-price software will pay a high price for it. . . .)

But if the documentation were useful, with lots of examples, and well written and professionally printed—which, coming with something that sells for hundreds of bucks, damned well *ought* to be that way, even though very few programming documents meet any of those criteria—then even the pirate software houses would have to buy the books.

The answer to software piracy, it seems to me, is about the same as the answer to book piracy: sell decent products at reasonable prices, and write decent documentation for sale at prices competitive with the price of Xeroxing the book. And stop worrying so much about protecting $500 and $600 price tags, because it isn't in the interest of the user community for software prices to stay that high. There are damned few programs worth that much.

* * *

What *is* a program worth? Well, there's a legal maxim: "The value of a thing is what that thing will bring," which is to say that something's worth what people will pay for it.

And you can damn betcha that a program worth $600 had better *work*, and do so with minimum effort, and have decent instructions that can be read by a human being.

And just how many of those are around?

There are a few. My mad friend is ecstatic about Digital Research's PL/I compiler.

"No bugs. It runs. It does what it says it will do."

"How did you learn the language?" I asked.

"Well, you need Digital's documents, of course," he said. "And two or three standard references on PL/I, one of them certainly being the Joan K. Hughes book (*PL/I Programming: A Structured Approach*) that you mentioned last time."

"You do need other reference works, then?"

"Oh, yeah. As usual, Digital has encrypted their documents. But they're up to Digital's usual standards of clarity, meaning that you'll need a Swahili interpreter . . ."

Well, Mac Lean tends to exaggerate. They're not *that* bad. Not quite. It is true that Digital is a company that seems determined never to hire any writers, but what the hell, their documents *are* complete, if confusing.

And Mac Lean remains as enamored of PL/I now as he was six weeks ago, which for him is quite a long time. I think we can safely add Digital's PL/I to the armory of good stuff, programs that work properly and are useful.

PL/I does have difficulties, but everything necessary for rigidly structured code is in the language. The error reports are excellent. It's not as fussy about declarations as Pascal. The language doesn't come out as compact as Pascal, and the programs don't run as fast, but they're easier to write. PL/I forgives quite a few errors.

There are other problems. The Input/Output is confusing, and worse, that's the part that you have to rely on Digital to tell you about. But you can learn it, and having done that, you're safe in programming with PL/I, because Digital is committed to support PL/I compilers for all their operating systems. You'll be able to transport your programs from your present micro to whatever machine—8086, Z-8000, whatever—you eventually replace it with.

Thus, I'll stick my neck out this far: it's worth the time investment—a couple of weeks—to become mildly proficient in PL/I; always assuming that you're going to do some programming of your own, of course. If you're *strictly* a user, though, you're still safe in investing in PL/I programs, since you're probably guaranteed they'll be useful on the next generation of machines.

Digital's PL/I also comes with a really groovy linker and library management routine, allowing you to build up a whole raft of software tools that you can stick into other routines. The method for calling in outside procedures and passing them variables is straightforward, and again preserves maximum portability from machine to machine.

PL/I is a good language for learning structured program concepts; and the Digital implementation is much better than acceptable. Recommended.

[I think I have since changed my view: that is, since I wrote that, I've done very little with PL/I. On the other hand, none of the facts have changed: the language is popular with hackers, and Digital Research has sworn to support it.

I do not myself recommend study of PL/I; at least I haven't followed that advice. . . .]

OUTSIDERS TAKE NOTICE

Shortly after the piracy column appeared, *Infoworld*, at that time edited by John Dvorak and Maggie Canon, ran a guest editorial by Robert Woodhead. Mr. Woodhead cited my column in support of ideas I don't hold. This upset me, but my mad friend pointed out that it showed that others were paying attention to what I said, and it gave me an opportunity to reach a different audience.

Together we prepared this letter, most of which *Infoworld* published:

PIRATES

I don't care what Robert Woodhead may tell you, molesting small children is illegal! Knowledgeable readers will now protest that when Mr. Woodhead wrote in *Infoworld* he didn't say child molesting was legal (and indeed didn't say anything about child molesting at all). All true. What Mr. Woodhead did was say "no matter what Jerry Pournelle (in

BYTE) or software pirates may tell you, the fact of the matter is that software piracy is illegal! It is expressly prohibited by the laws of the United States." I hastened back to my *BYTE* column on software pirates, and lo! I hadn't mentioned legalities at all.

I did have some words to say about the interests of both publishers and consumers. I also spoke of ethics. But anyone who blindly equates ethics with today's jungle of laws where you can get your rights only if you hire slick lawyers (and not always then), is either a lawyer or depraved. Or both.

As a reviewer I have both legal and ethical obligations to take due care to safeguard programs sent me for review, regardless of my opinion of the publisher's licensing agreement; but I don't have to like his policies, and I don't have to say that I do. Similarly for the law: as a citizen I have an obligation to obey the law, but I don't have to like it.

But maybe we ought to look at these laws of the United States.

First, what laws? If software is to be protected by *copyright*, then most of the "licensing agreements" restricting use to one licensed computer are unenforceable. The new copyright law gives authors considerable protection, but it also provides for the public interest. Material protected by copyright law is subject to "fair use" by scholars and certain educational establishments; it is subject to circulation by libraries; under some conditions it can be broadcast by PBS without the author's consent.

As an author I don't necessarily like all of the copyright law provisions, and as an officer of a writers' association I opposed some of them; but that is the law, and if one relies on copyright law for protection, one must abide by all of its provisions; and copyright law can't possibly be construed as restricting use to one licensed computer.

Maybe programs shouldn't be under copyright law. The Author's Guild and a number of other writers' organizations don't want computer programs covered by copyright. Not the machine instructions, anyway. Documentation, being theoretically in a human language (a lot isn't really) is subject to copyright protection; but instructions comprehensible only to a machine probably shouldn't be. It isn't that authors don't want programmers to be protected; it's just that literary copyright law is complex enough now, without adding all this to it.

Item: just what can be protected? There are only so many ways you can do accounting programs, or text formatters. Let's suppose, for example, that two programmers begin with Kernighan and Plauger's *Software Tools*, and each develops a text formatter from it. Suppose further that each takes the book's (excellent!) advice on program structure. Each comes up with a real gonzo program and wants to sell beauceaup copies for moby bucks; so each "copyrights" his program.

Those two programs are likely to be very similar. There are only so many possible ways to accomplish the job. If each sues the other for "copyright infringement," who pays? And what do they both owe to Kernighan and Plauger?

Or take Atari's attempts to gain a monopoly on any computer game employing mazes plus creatures eating small dots. It's in the lawyers' interest to grab everything possible. Is it in the public interest to grant Atari that monopoly?

Because that's what a copyright is. Back in royal times, the English monarchs used to grant monopolies: the exclusive right to trade in salt, for example. Some nations have state monopolies on certain common items—matches as an example—to this day. After the Revolution, the framers intentionally denied the government any broad right to grant monopolies; but the Constitution did give Congress, in Article One, Section 8, the power "to promote the Progress of Science and useful Arts, by securing for limited Times to Authors and Inventors the exclusive Right to their respective Writings and Discoveries." Our legal system has broken down so far that in practice the "exclusive right" belongs only to those with enough resources to hire teams of lawyers; but note what was explicitly said. "To promote the progress of science and useful arts...." In other words, to promote public interest.

So: no matter what Mr. Woodhead tells you, nobody is quite sure what copyright law says about software piracy; nor is there any universal agreement on what it ought to say.

Many software publishers know this. Thus they rely on copyright law to protect their documents, while trying to put the software itself under contract law. They also take a high moral tone. This generates those interesting licensing agreements, in which the vendor warrants nothing, not even that there is media on the disk, while holding the buyer to line after line of restrictions on what he can do with this thing he supposedly bought.

So here we are in the middle of the consumer rebellion, finding that all our efforts to get consumer protection laws were futile. The vendor warrants nothing, denies any implication that his product is useful or merchantable; but at the same time, tries to get you to agree that this unwarranted "product" is valuable. One company has you sign an agreement in which you promise to pay them—on demand—several grand if they ever find a copy with your serial number. Not surprisingly, the agreement also calls for you to pay the lawyers. No matter who "wins" the case, they get theirs.

So: Whatever the law may be, the real question is, what should it be? What's fair? If the vendor won't warrant *anything* about his product, where does he get off taking this high moral tone about his sacred property rights? In my judgment the whole matter is not quite so simple as Mr. Woodhead thinks.

First, what is in the best interests of the computer community? Surely not to keep software prices up at $500 and above. We want competition to drive those prices down to something reasonable. I'll concede the programmer's right to sell his product for whatever the customer is willing to pay. I'll protect his exclusive right to sell what he wrote. But I'm darned if I'll also pay policemen to keep someone else from writing a similar program and selling it cheaper.

Next, what rights should I have if I buy his software? Well, I certainly ought to be able to make backup copies for my own use. Even Mr. Robert J. Woodhead concedes that (although copyright law is not so clear). But what may I do with my copies? Suppose I have two computers: May I run my copies in both machines? The license agreement says no. The license agreement says that the public should pay police and lawyers to prevent the consumer from doing that. But is it really in the public interest that we enforce that?

In fact, how do we do it? I have here three machines, all connected by CP-Net, so that each can access the central disks and certain peripherals. Is this one single computer? Assume so. Now suppose I disconnect Ezekial, my reliable friend who happens to be a Z-80, from the net. Clearly I now have two machines, and in theory at least I must run my fancy program on only on one of them.

But one of my machines is a Godbout 8085/8088, and if I use my wonderful Warp Drive feature, even though I'm running my programs on the 8085, the 8088 is also active! That's two CPU's! Have I violated my license agreement? And for that matter, there's a Z-80 chip in my printer, and another in my terminal, and indeed I've been known to use a Heath H-89 computer (which contains *two* Z-80s!) as a terminal.

Why is it in the public interest to enforce that silly license agreement? (And please don't respond with some talk about the absolute sanctity of contracts. I might agree to some kind of libertarian ideal myself, but in the U.S.A. it has long been established that contracts contrary to the public interest are void. If you don't believe that, look at the laws defining renters' rights.)

I don't think it is in the public interest to enforce most of the license agreements I've seen. I think a software buyer should be able to use his product on any darned machine he wants to, including machines he doesn't even own. That does *not* mean the "owner" should be able to give a copy to his friends, or keep a copy after selling the original secondhand.

But—although I agree it's both illegal and unethical—I'm prepared to argue that giving away programs other than games does a lot less harm than most writers on software piracy would have you believe. I'll go further. If publishers would do decent documents, neatly typeset, written in clear English, giving plenty of examples of the program in use, they could make good money selling them, even to those who stole the programs. They could then sell "User ID Numbers" entitling the holder to program maintenance and updates, no questions asked. Carry that thought far enough and you may get publishers wishing people would steal their software.

In a word, there are other interested parties besides the publisher. There's the programmer, whose interests aren't identical with publishers'. There's the consumer, that poor schmoe who buys the stuff. Sure, I know it takes time and work to write a good program. It takes me a lot of time, years sometimes, to write a book, too. Still, I have to pay taxes to support libraries that lend my books free. I have to concede "fair use" of my stories, and PBS's rights, and other public interest matters.

Even so, I make a good living as a writer. I wish programmers the same opportunities. But as a software user, I want competition to drive the prices down. Actually, in the long run that will be best for programmers. It certainly is for authors: if books cost $100 and up, we'd have damned few readers. And when there's more good software at fair prices, more people invest in computers, expanding the potential market.

I don't condone theft; but so long as products are grossly overpriced, badly documented, and come with no shred of guarantee, there will be software pirates. Moaning about that won't help. What we must do is restructure the law to protect the real interests of all the members of the computer community.

A last note on the piracy issue:

Dr. Colin Mick is a computer and information systems consultant who is also a long-time friend. After the previous materials on software piracy appeared, he sent me his solution to the problem. It's a bit odd, but it makes sense.

Dr. Mick says that publishers ought to sell "authorized user" licenses to anyone who applies. Without the authorized user code, you can't get updates and revisions; with it, you can; and the company ought not inquire how you got the software.

At first this sounds like encouragement to piracy, and it's unlikely to appeal to companies who hope to get several hundred dollars for their programs. However, software prices are coming down rapidly. It will not be many years hence before everything will be under $100. (The price in the first year of release may be higher, but after that it will plummet. This, incidentally, is the price trend of new computer chips: high in the first year or two, falling to dirt—well, sand—cheap thereafter.) When prices get really low, the cost of duplicating and shipping software becomes a critical part of the package price.

Thus I can see a time in the not-too-distant future when the major profits will come from selling documents and updates. The actual machine-readable program will be sort of incidental, and the publisher, while never admitting it, will be pleased as anything if the software is stolen by someone who subsequently buys the documents and an authorized user number.

Creating the program will then be thought of like doing the research for a book: it's impossible to sell the book without doing research, but no one expects to sell his research notes. The money comes from the book itself.

[My predictions about software prices haven't yet happened: programs still cost a lot compared to book prices. However, the trend is toward ever-falling prices, and as machines get more powerful, and languages easier to use, the day will come when software will be written as books are now: by individual authors who do not then go out to start a distribution company, but are content to allow publishers to do that work.]

At the 1984 8th West Coast Computer Faire, I saw a product that is distributed much as Dr. Mick advised, and wrote this review:

PC-WRITE

PC-Write is a full screen text editor that makes use of many special features of the IBM PC computer. I haven't tested PC-Write, but I've seen enough of it to to know it's a pretty good editor—especially for the price.

You can get it for ten dollars, or even for free.

PC-Write is distributed as "Shareware." What this means is that you can buy a copy from the publisher for $10, but that's not the principal means of distribution. Anyone who has a copy is encouraged to give copies to all their friends. The program and its documents are all on disk, so this is quite feasible.

People who get the program and like it are requested to send $75 to Quicksoft, the program's publisher. When you send in the money, you get a printed copy of the document—a marginal improvement over what's on the disk—and an "official registration number." Put the registration number into your copy. Now, when you give copies away, if anyone you've given it to sends in the $75, you'll get $25 sales commission.

Quicksoft's Bob Wallace says they're not doing too badly. A number of people have liked the program enough to register it. He's meanwhile writing new programs to distribute this way.

I don't know whether the "Shareware" concept will catch on. I encourage the trend.

*　*　*

The search for workable solutions to the twin problems of user requirements for backups, and publisher rights to payment, will continue. There are no easy answers.

CHAPTER 2
The Great Software Drought

"It's the great software drought," said my mad friend Mac Lean. "Have you noticed? There's no good new software. Just updates and revisions and new versions of old programs."

[He was right, of course. After the first bloom, we had a dry spell that lasted *weeks* before exciting new programs came out. But I wasn't going to admit defeat....]

"Not true," I protested. "Just yesterday I got Sorcim's SuperCalc—"

"Sure. CP/M version of a year-old Apple program. Good stuff. Useful. Excellent. But not new."

"Hmm. Maybe you're right. Well, at least they're improving old programs. I have an update for Spellguard."

"Aha," said my mad friend. "Tell me, are you still using Spellguard?"

"Yep."

"Thought you had a whole mess of new spelling programs."

"I do. Here's one of them." I held up Microproof. "But I don't use them. Better to stay with Spellguard. Especially now, with its improved dictionary."

Which is true. I suppose it comes as no surprise that I am *very* interested in spelling and editing programs. After all, words are my business—and I am, according to Robert Heinlein, one of the "wurst spellurs" he has ever encountered. I *need* good spelling programs—and I have to use them a *lot*, which means I'm interested in speed and convenience; which is why I stick with Spellguard despite its lack of certain features.

107

Example: in my previous Spellguard review, I said "it corrects spelling." *BYTE*'s editors, in the interests of accuracy, changed that to "finds and marks spelling errors." Other programs, such as Microproof, *correct* spelling errors. All true, but irrelevant. The job to be performed is spelling correction; and Spellguard does that.

[And continued to do so until The Word Plus came along. One of the really nice things about the micro revolution is the way things continue to improve. My review, though, proceeded to take Microproof apart, byte by byte. It was one of the first really negative reviews I'd ever done.

It had an interesting fallout: a few months later, a vastly improved version came to me by Federal Express. Alas, by then Wayne Holder had developed his Word Plus; but apparently I did have a beneficial effect.]

ZEKE's NEW FRIENDS

A few minutes ago, Arthur C. Clarke called me from Sri Lanka. (He lives there. I think the nation has declared him a national treasure; I know that when Robert Heinlein visited him, Dr. Clarke was able to arrange for a Sri Lanka Air Force helicopter to take Robert about the country. . . .)

Arthur had seen some of my computer articles, and what he wanted to know was what everyone nowadays wants to know: What do you buy for a first computer?

Unfortunately, the answer is, "It depends." But let's look at the problem. It's not unrelated to a second difficulty, one I have myself. . . .

I was talking with Ezekial, my friend who happens to be a Cromemco Z-2.

"I'm getting old, boss," he said.

"You were built in 1977!"

"Yeah. In this business, that's *old*. Look, we've written five books and dozens of columns and hundreds of letters. I do all your taxes and accounting. I compile all your programs, in twenty languages. I even play games with you."

"OK, OK, so what do you want?"

"Some rest. A bit of help. Look, I'll make you a deal. I'll help you write books, same as always, but you go get something faster, something new, to do all that compiling and calculating."

"Never thought I'd hear you say it," I said. "Better is the enemy of good enough. And you're plenty good enough!"

"Could use help, boss. Big responsibility, being the only computer around here. Especially now that you're so busy with that Space Council stuff, and the L-5 Society (Plug: if you're interested in helping the space program, join L-5. It's $25 a year to L-5 Society, 1060 E. Elm, Tucson, Az. 85719. Contributions tax deductible within the framework of the law. Secretary this year: Jerry Pournelle.) What happens," (Zeke continued), "if I get sick?"

I thought about it a long time. He's right, of course. He *is* getting old; and he's utterly spoiled me. I can't conceive of writing without a computer. I live in terror that Zeke is going to quit on me. (Actually I don't: he's never given me the slightest cause for alarm. A couple of times in the early days we had glitches that brought Tony Pietsch out (always in the middle of the night; nice chap, Tony), but they always got fixed without having to take Zeke away. But—not long ago something gave out in the disk power supply, keeping Zeke shut down for nearly a week. True, I was out of town at the time, but it could have been a disaster.

I needed a second computer. But what?

In the middle of the dilemma, Adam Osborne sent me his new Osborne 1.

That darned near solved my problem. Osborne's machine is *good*. The first models had some misfeatures, but Adam is an honorable man—and also smart enough not to risk his reputation by sharp practices. They're planning retrofits to take care of all major difficulties and most minor ones.

The worst of these is the shift lock, which is worse than useless. Then, too, with that tiny screen you need smooth vertical scrolling (it already has good horizontal scrolls). There are some other minor annoyances, none all that serious, and as I said, Adam's going to fix them. The new Osborne computers—out by the time this is published—will incorporate the improvements, including true three-key rollover and a decent shift lock, and various other fixes. Those who already bought the machines will be able to get them retrofitted absolutely free. As I said, Adam is an honorable man.

One thing I thought would be a pain turned out not to be. That's the tiny screen. Adam has sent me his larger screen, which you can connect to the Osborne with a cable, but I find I don't use it. The little screen turns out to be just at the right focal distance when I sit at the console; and for someone who, like me, wears bi-focal glasses, that's a real boon.

I carried the Osborne out to Cal Tech's Jet Propulsion Laboratories for the Voyager Two encounter with Saturn. There were over a hundred of the science press corps packed into JPL's Von Karman Center (the press facility). Most had typewriters. One or two had big cumbersome word processors—at least one was a terminal connected through a network to the parent system in New York City. Nobody had anything *near* as convenient as the Osborne, which is quiet, fast responding, and very portable....

Everyone came to look at it. "How can you stand that tiny screen?" asked Eric Burgess, senior science correspondent present. (Eric's the chap who first thought of the message plaque to be attached to the space probes. I was there when he got the idea. But that's another story.) He stared over my shoulder. "It's so small."

"Try it," I invited. I got up to give him my place, and watched as he realized that when you're sitting at the machine you can read it at least as easily as you can a book. Before the encounter was done a dozen science writers were ready to go buy an Osborne.

I also took it to the meeting of the Citizens' Advisory Council on National Space Policy (which I chair), and used it to take notes during the meeting. It was amazing: I was able to type notes and suggestions and ideas into the Osborne without at all disrupting the meeting. The Osborne is quiet and efficient and not at all distracting.

In other words, I like the Osborne. You can't beat it for the price, under $2,000 bucks with over a thousand dollars worth of software. An Osborne and an Epson printer will put you in the computer/word processing business cheaper than anything I can think of, and the Osborne's a real computer, using CP/M and adult software like WordStar and SuperCalc and dBASE II, not a toy.

So. For those who haven't a lot of money to spend and want to get going in computers, I don't hesitate to recommend the Osborne as a first system. However: it is a limited system. It wasn't designed for expansion capabilities, and it's never going to be able to use them. But as a first machine, it has a LOT going for it, and not just the price.

When I first got the Osborne I thought I'd solved one of my problems, which is, how can I have someone entering letters and files and old books while I'm using Ezekial? I certainly am not going to have a multi-user micro, which defeats the whole concept of decentralized computing. One user, one computer; that's the motto.

No, I needed a second machine, with a good text editor. Aha, says I. I'll use the Osborne. Of course the Osborne has only 5¼ inch disks, and Ezekial has 8 inch, but that's all right; the TRS-80 has both 5¼ inch and 8 inch Lobo disks, and those work fine, and under CP/M we can PIP files from the little disks to the big disks. So all we have to do is to take a disk from the Osborne to the TRS-80, and—

Doesn't work. The Osborne disk format is different from the Omikron's format. And, talking to Mike McCulloch of Osborne Associates, I find there's no easy solution to the problem. If there were a "standard" 5¼ inch disk format—as the IBM single density soft-sectored format definitely IS the standard for 8 inch disks—then Osborne would use it. Indeed, when the Osborne crew go to double-density for their disks, they'll use the new IBM 5¼ inch double-density format. But until there IS a standard, they can't employ a standard.

Which means that the only way to get files from the Osborne to Zeke is to send them out the Osborne's serial port. Now the Osborne *has* such ports, both RS-232 and Modem ports, so that's not impossible, and nowadays Osborne will furnish you with software to accomplish the job (well, to accomplish the Osborne end of the job; obviously you'll have to have appropriate software on the other end to catch what the Osborne is pitching).

Moreover, the Osborne format may turn out to *become* the non-existent "standard" for 5¼ inch single-density disks. According to McCulloch, the major software houses have been given copies of the specs as well as an Osborne machine, and have been invited to offer software on disks readable by the Osborne; Adam Osborne has no intention of cutting his users off from the vast marketplace of CP/M software. Just the opposite.

[Alas, no one took them up on that offer, for good reason. The Osborne-1 disk format was needlessly conservative, and held far too little data. As new machines came out, they wanted to increase the capacity of their small disks. Now there are well over *fifty* formats for 5¼" disks. Oh. Well.]

So. By now you get the idea. I recommend the Osborne as a first computer. It's as good an entry level system as I have seen. The only thing that comes close to it are the new IBM and the Heath-Zenith H-89, and both come with only one disk drive and very little software at a price a good bit higher than the Osborne. . . .

I did not, however, recommend the Osborne to Arthur Clarke; and I never seriously considered it as the new machine Zeke wanted me to set up as his assistant. It's not that I don't like the Osborne, and I'll keep mine and use it as a portable for a very long time; but I need more machine than can be bought for $2,000, and so does Arthur Clarke.

"Maybe," I said to my mad friend, "maybe I'll get an H-89. I can get it with CP/M and a printer, and get a company to fit a case for it, and I see advertised a board that will let it talk to 8 inch disks which will solve the problem of communicating with Zeke. I can end up with a portable."

"Good thinking. As long as you think of it as a spare. Your real machine needs a bus."

"True. But for a portable . . . In fact," I said with boyish enthusiasm, "maybe I'll get it as a kit and build it so I can *understand* the machine—"

"Sounds like about as much fun as an appendectomy," said Mac Lean.

I can always count on him to prick any silly bubbles like that.

In the middle of all that came another emergency. Dr. Stefan T. Possony, my long-time friend and associate and collaborator, decided to get a computer. He'd seen Ezekial, and he wanted him. Or one like him.

Not long ago the solution to the problem would have been simple. We'd simply hand money to Tony Pietsch of Proteus, he would produce an updated clone of Ezekial, and all would be well. Unfortunately, Tony's in great demand as a consultant, and has just about gone out of the systems integration business.

So: what to get? For Stefan, and for me.

[I'm not ashamed of the analysis that follows. At the time it made good sense. Now it is interesting only for historical reasons. I haven't cut it because it shows just how wrong one can be when predicting trends. . . .]

It didn't take much research to come to several conclusions. First, a professional system ought to have 8 inch disks. The little disks are fine for entry-level learning systems, but they're just not solid enough—and won't hold enough files—for professional work. Second, the system has to use CP/M. With both Xerox and IBM coming into the field, CP/M is more than a standard, it's a necessity.

[Interesting. Before the IBM came out, the word was that the IBM would use a form of CP/M for its operating system. They tried, too; but when the IBM representatives went to Pebble Beach to talk to Digital Research (CP/M's publisher) they did not get the reception they had expected; the result was pretty unpleasant for Digital.)

Third—the S-100 bus (quiet and built to the IEEE standard if at all possible) is still the most versatile and best all-around small computer system going, and will be for some time. S-100 with a Z-80 CPU is *the* way to go.

"But why not the new IBM?" one of my sane friends asked. "It has a bus. Not the S-100, true, but a bus. And CP/M, and IBM maintenance, and—"

And 5¼ inch floppies, which even with IBM behind them are going to be a problem. Furthermore, as of right now (Fall 1981) the local people selling the IBM know nothing about software availability, although with Microsoft's support I expect that to change by the time you read this.

The IBM may sweep the field; heaven knows it's a handsome enough unit. I learned to write with an IBM typewriter keyboard, and I've found few computer keyboards up to the Selectric—and the new IBM computer keyboard is even nicer. Indeed, I'm thinking seriously of getting an IBM. But for all of IBM's prodigious reputation, they haven't a lot of experience with small computers; and until they gain some, I think I'll wait. Besides, they weren't available back last summer when Stefan wanted his machine.

So what to get? And how to install it long distance? That latter really presented a problem. Possony knows nothing about computers, and there aren't too many off-the-shelf S-100 systems. I could get a Vector; although I've no direct experience with them, people I trust tell me they're excellent.

But then I remembered: I have a good friend, Dr. Colin Mick (Decision Information Services, 399 Sherman Avenue, Palo Alto, CA 94306; 415-327-5797) in the Stanford Area where Dr. Possony lives. A quick phone call, and Colin foolishly volunteered to help Steve. It turned out well. Colin installed a CCS system with Z-19 terminal in Stefan's house. He chose CCS because that's what he has, and he knows some of the CCS design team; the result has been so successful that Colin is now much in demand as a small systems consultant.

Another result is that Possony, already one of the most prolific writers on foreign affairs and international politics in the world, has more than doubled his output. He *loves* his new system; and when you consider that Stefan is a Viennese intellectual who got his Ph.D. the year after I was born, and who has never learned anything about machines, that's quite a statement. It's also a great testimony to Colin's patience and instructional capability.

They got one thing out of it. They're writing a book for first users. Given Colin's understanding of computers, and Stefan's ability to ask penetrating questions, I wouldn't be surprised to see it become the best book ever done on the subject.

So. That was one candidate. CCS seemed a very good system, and certainly a lot of them are being sold.

[CCS, California Computer Systems, is another company that started strong and didn't keep up. Given expert advice the CCS system was quite good; indeed, my son Alex still has a CCS system in excellent condition. It was not, though, a good system for beginners. As I write this, in 1984, I'm told that CCS has asked for protection under the Chapter 11 bankruptcy laws.]

Tony Pietsch, meanwhile, was putting together a Godbout (CompuPro), with the 8085/8088 8-bit/16-bit dual capability. And Richard Frank, of Sorcim, had told me he uses Godbouts for all his development work because he considers them the most rugged and reliable systems available.

I stewed for a while, then called Bill Godbout. The result is that Zeke's big brother is sitting in the next room.

That Godbout CompuPro is built like a Mack truck. You couldn't hurt it with a nine-pound sledge. When it comes to rugged reliability, Godbout is *the* way to go for my money; and Tony says the bus is the quietest he's ever worked with.

What we have is the Godbout (CompuPro) S-100 box, Godbout's disk controller and interfacer board, his 8085/88 CPU as well as the Z-80 CPU (obviously you can't use both at the same time); 128 K of Godbout memory; and his System Support vectored interrupt board. The disk drives are Qume double-sided double-density 8" drives with a Vista box and power supply.

I confess to being a bit worried about double-sided double-density disks. Asking for trouble, I thought; but I was wrong. With the Godbout controller and Qume drives my disks are as quiet as ever were the iComs—and they're *wonderfully* fast.

We're still shaking down the Godbout system. When it's all done and checked out, I intend to get another set of Qumes and install them in Zeke. More on both the Qumes and the Godbout another time.

[We're still using both. The CompuPro Dual Processor system remains the workhorse here at Chaos Manor; and the Qume disk drives haven't given any trouble in three years of hard use.]

So. Zeke has two new friends, the Osborne and the Godbout; and he's about to get new disk drives.

There's more happening here at Chaos Manor. Tony Pietsch's new text editor, Write, is done at last. I'm using it to do this column.

Write is much like Electric Pencil without bugs. It ought to be: back when I started writing with computers, Pencil was the best editor around, and we put together a system to work with it. Unfortunately, Pencil has bugs. One, the tendency to drop letters at the ends of lines, is notorious. Another is a needlessly complex handshaking routine to couple Pencil to the Diablo (that one's so severe we use a special CP/M BIOS reserved just for Pencil). There are other problems, and over the years my partner Larry Niven and I have been making lists of Pencil's faults. We've also made notes on just what we'd like in a text creation editor; features that Pencil never had.

Anton (Tony) Pietsch has been collecting those notes and writing an editor to fit. In these columns and in pieces for *BYTE*'s companion onComputing, I've several times announced that it would be ready "real soon now." I'm happy to say that this time for sure. It's here and it works.

So: what's so good about it?

It depends on what you want an editor for. I make no doubt that some of the really fancy "window" type editors based on the MIT EMACS editor or built around special display boards may be "better" in an abstract sense. Moreover, Micropro's WordMaster remains, in my judgment, the best *programming* editor ever invented.

But for just sitting down and writing I want something as nearly invisible as can be made. I don't want to think about my editor. I don't want it to natter at me about line numbers and column numbers and such. I don't want it drawing funny lines across the screen to mark the ends of pages. I don't want it clicking disks at me, or running out of disk space and giving me no chance to change disks. . . .

And if I want to pull some text in from another disk somewhere, I want to be able to do that. If I want to write some text out onto a safety disk, I want to be able to do that, too. If I want to print out my text onto paper I don't want to have to double-space it on the screen in order to get it double-spaced on the manuscript.

And for heaven's sake, if I fiddle around with a paragraph and snip off words here and add some there I don't want to have to reformat the text! My editor should do that for me, silently, easily, automatically.

And that's what I have in Write. A nearly invisible editor. Add to that a really powerful macro command capability, with loops and global searches and deletes, and an ability to link disk files so that the program treats them as if they were one enormous file—

Add it all up and it's Write, Writers Really Incredible Text Editor. I'm sure I'll have more to say about it another time. Meanwhile, people ask me what I have against WordStar.

The answer is simple. Nothing. Lots of friends use WordStar, and I use it on the Osborne. It's a good editor to run on a terminal. Like all editors on terminals, the scrolling is ugly, but that's not WordStar's fault. Micropro continually works to add features and capabilities, and they've done well.

What they can't do is correct the basic deficiency, which is the two-keystroke command system with delay in between strokes. When I want to delete a line, or scroll, or go from the beginning to the end of the text, I want to do that *right now*. I don't want to hit control-q, then remember that c takes me to the end of the text unless I've hit the space bar in between in which case—

Nor do I want a bunch of prompts and lines and menu items on the screen. OK, so you can suppress those menu descriptions—provided, of course, that you remember all the command items. But you won't. WORDSTAR has too many features. Now that would be all right if you could ignore most of them, but you can't. They take up single-stroke control characters so that there are none left for the functions you want to have happen *fast*. Write's approach is to use the single-strokes for such things as insert/delete toggles, and opening a hole in text for long insertions, and marking blocks of text and moving them, and suchlike; and, much as WordMaster does, have you use the macro command capability for all the really complicated stuff. Write also has the menu available at any time; you can get on screen a whole list of instructions, pages of them if you like. But you don't see them unless you want to. I wish WordStar had taken that approach.

I do recommend WordStar for some purposes. First, it works on most terminals. Because it knows where the ends of pages are, it can do indexing. It formats on screen; what you see is what you get, an intolerable disadvantage when what you want is a simple double-spaced manuscript (who wants his on-*screen* text double-spaced?) but a real boon if you're publishing a newsletter or other matter requiring holes for illustration. It has a good mail-merge utility. If you can use any of those features, WordStar is the only program that has them.

Incidentally, there are a couple of candidates for WordStar's crown, one of them being Mince (acronym for Mince Is Not Complete Emacs) which emulates EMACS, the MIT full-screen editor, and is certainly the best editor if you want to write LISP programs. Mince works on terminals (but not with memory-mapped video; at least I've never been able to get it running on Zeke). Now that the Godbout with the H-19 are up and running, we'll have a more thorough report. But when it comes to creating text, you won't beat Write, Or so say I.

[That was Write 1.4; I'm writing this on Write 1.78, a considerable improvement. Alas, as of Spring 1984 Write doesn't work on the IBM PC; but for 8-bit CP/M 2.2 machines, there's *still* nothing better for text creation. In fact, it's so good that I keep a dedicated Z-80 computer with Archives keyboard that does almost nothing but run my Write programs for text creation. Of course I write a lot more than most people....]

MICRO COMPUTER ALGEBRA

Some time ago, I got a copy of muSIMP/muMATH from the Soft Warehouse. Marketing of these programs has since been taken over by Microsoft, which has probably enhanced the documentation—at least they usually do.

There's nothing quite like muMATH. The basic concept comes from MACSYMA, the symbolic algebra programs continually under development at Massachussetts Institute of Technology's computer laboratories, and which run on the DEC PDP-10. Obviously there is no way to put the full power of a PDP-10 into a micro—although the Godbout 8085/88 comes closer than I would have thought possible a few years ago.

MuMATH consists of a core plus a whole series of auxiliary routines. The programs are written in LISP, but you don't have to know LISP to use them. (It would help, though. Boy would it help.) MuSIMP is another package of routines which will also work with muMATH. Together they will do a surprising lot of useful work. You could, for example, write a VisiCalc in muMATH/muSIMP, and I suspect it would work quite well. There are also examples of how to write a data base using them.

In other words, muMATH/muSIMP have a lot more power than appears on the surface (or, indeed, is hinted at in the advertisements).

Their primary purpose, though, is to do symbolic math. And here I have to confess a fault. When I first got muSIMP/muMATH I tended to compare them to MACSYMA, and of course these programs for the 8080 came up wanting. How could they not? What I should have done was find someone who never had access to MACSYMA and ask what she thought of them, and recently that's what I did.

"Wonderful," said my lovely friend. "I've never even suspected you could do things like that on a computer. How long as this been going on?"

I shrugged.

"You mean I went through three semesters of calculus and did ALL THOSE PROBLEMS while you had a computer program that would do differentiation and integrals? And I mashed through Physics I and II and solved problems with a hand calculator when all that time Ezekial could have done my homework?" By now she was screaming.

"Uh, well—" Under the circumstances I did the only sensible thing a man could do. I hid behind my wife.

But my lovely friend did have a point. True, muSIMP/muMATH are limited in what they can do, but they can do differentiation and integrals and algebra. They can factor and expand polynomials. They can do matrix operations, and simplify equations, and do it all symbolically, the way you'd muck around with the equations using pencil and paper.

The programs aren't perfect. They tend to run out of memory easily. The way to escape that is to set up a kind of sub-program consisting of those elements of muSIMP/muMATH that you need for your particular problem, leaving out all the parts that won't affect what you're doing. For example, you can configure a system that understands trigonometry and complex numbers, but doesn't know that matrices and integrals exist. And so forth.

There are other limits. The documentation isn't exactly encrypted, but it's pretty dense. You really have to want to use the programs to dig your way through that stuff, and as I said earlier, it would help a lot if you understood LISP. The authors of the muSIMP documents plainly do understand LISP, and although they don't expect you to, they keep hoping you will.

Still in all, there's no real competition for muSIMP/muMATH. If you want to do symbolic algebra; if you want to use your computer to help you get through Calculus 102 and Physics 203; then you probably need muSIMP/muMATH.

Recommended for those who need it, with reservations as noted.

[MuSimp and MuMath remain excellent programs. I recommend them highly. Since I wrote the above the TK!Solver programs have been published; they are competition for MuMath They're a bit easier to use, but not as powerful. Those with symbolic algebra problems would be well advised to get a demonstration of MuSimp and MuMath.]

More good news. Microsoft has done it again. They've improved their BASCOM BASIC Compiler.

What they've done is twofold: they've added CHAINING with COMMON, meaning that you can break a program apart into pieces and call in parts, passing variables to each chunk as called. This greatly saves program size, meaning that it saves free memory, meaning that you can run bigger programs with more variables.

Secondly, they've greatly cut down on the runtime package, meaning that the total size of the programs is—or can be—

smaller, and also that larger programs can be compiled and linked.

More good news. They've in part dropped the restrictive licensing provision that made you pay a royalty on any program you sold that had been compiled with BASCOM.

The bad news on that front is that they've dropped the royalty requirement only for the *old* BASCOM; if you want to use the new, with CHAINING and COMMON and smaller runtime package and all that nifty stuff, you still have to pay for each copy you sell. Alas. But I suspect free enterprise will end that; it's only a matter of time.

Meanwhile, the new BASCOM is very nice indeed. Take a trivial example: an old "Star Trek" game I've been playing with. As you might suspect, my "Star Trek" is the *ultimate* game, with invisible Romulans, and shields for the Klingons, and enemy bases, and attacks on Federation bases, and Federation trading ships, and black holes, and—well, you get the idea.

The game was originally written in E-BASIC, a public-domain precursor to Gordon Eubanks' CBASIC. I added to it and translated it into CBASIC, but eventually the program outgrew that. Besides, it was getting awfully slow. What I wanted to do, therefore, was translate it into Microsoft BASIC and compile it; but I couldn't, because the program was just too large. I could break it into pieces for the interpreter, but that was even slower than CBASIC.

Comes new BASCOM and I've done it. Now I have a setup program which invents the game universe and makes the maps; then it calls in another program which processes commands; and every now and then still another program comes in and massages the data. It all works, letting me have a "Star Trek" so complicated that even I am beginning to think it's finished.

Anyway, that's how the new compiler works. On a more serious note, it will compile my tiny data base.

And here I have a problem. Should I review software that I have written? Certainly I have an obligation to tell you it's mine. I try to be objective, but certainly I could overlook flaws in my own programs.

Minimum Data Base grew like Topsy. It started, a long time ago, with a thing called the People's Data Base, by Gupta and others. It was, in fact, the very first program I ever got running. When I bought Zeke, Mac Lean and Tony

Pietsch handed me Debbie (a Microsoft-like BASIC that came with the iCom Disks and, ugh, F-DOS operating system); and they handed me a listing of the People's Data Base.

"Get that running," they ordered.

So I tried. Lord I tried. And I certainly learned that semicolons are not colons, that single quote marks are not double quotes, that BASIC has a *very* precise syntax and improvements are not tolerated; and how to keep my temper well enough that I didn't throw anything heavy at Ezekial.

Eventually I got it running. It wasn't a bad little program; more to the point, it was well-structured, with a main routine and a series of subroutines, some of which themselves called other subroutines. There were no GOTO statements except within subroutines. None of this grasshopper jumping about that so ruins BASIC's reputation.

The program was limited, and soon I ran into the limits. So I began to improve it. The sort was a bubble sort. That wouldn't do, so I put in a shell sort. There were no disk ops. I fixed that. The command menu was processed inefficiently, so I rewrote that, and renamed most of the commands. The "delete entry" system was asinine, and I set up an entirely new way to handle that. And so forth.

Year after year the silly thing grew—and I found I was using it for *everything*. It keeps phone numbers and addresses. It keeps the list of members of the Space Council, and the L-5 Board. When the Boy Scouts go hiking, a "PDATA" (after the old original "People's Data BAse") lets me make lists by meal (what are we eating for Thursday dinner?), or by who is carrying what (who's got Friday's lunch?), and all that. When I do an anthology, a PDATA file keeps track of who has how many shares, what they've been paid, and, when new royalties come in, it calculates what the new payment is and then writes the cover letter, makes mailing labels, and writes the checks.

Versatile. And darned easy to use.

"You ought to sell it," said Barry Workman of Workman Associates. "Let me handle it for you. It won't make you rich, but what do you care? People out there need the program."

"Maybe," said I. "What if—gulp—what if someone reviews it and doesn't like the documentation? I can stand not being thought an elegant programmer, but—"

"Don't worry about it. I learned to use it, didn't I?"

I shrugged. "Also, look, there's very little new in there. True, I didn't steal it from Gupta and the People's Data Base; there probably aren't ten lines of code left from their original. But it's all very straightforward code. Nothing elegant at all."

"That's the value," Workman said. "Look, lots of people want a general purpose DO-ALL program, which is what this is. I notice that when you did all that statistical analysis, you used your PDATA thing—"

"Yeah—"

"And your Christmas cards are on it, and you used to keep your checkbook balance—"

"I don't do that any more. I use a Journal now—"

"Yeah, but you used to," Barry said.

Eventually he wore me down. So. I mention PDATA, a small data base and DO-ALL, available from Workman Associates. If I didn't already have it, I'd probably buy it; I can't conceive of living without it, and I wouldn't have time to write it again.

It IS useful. And it's in both CBASIC and Microsoft BASIC, with the Microsoft version compilable by BASCOM—except that BASCOM will not compile the *general* program because it won't compile anything with arrays defined by variables. PDATA creates data bases and dimensions them according to the number of fields you've specified, but BASCOM wants to know that in advance. This means that you can compile FONES (the telephone program) or NAND (name and address) or any set whose structure you know in advance, but you can't just compile PDATA.

On the other hand, one reason PDATA is so useful is that you can run it interactively in Microsoft MBASIC, and write your own special purpose routines (such as the one that determines what my contributors ought to be paid, given the total royalty). If you know BASIC at all, you can do a lot with PDATA.

So. Useful, yes. But it is not a rival to dBASE II and doesn't claim to be. All it claims to be is a very useful little general purpose data handler that provides a structure to let you mash data. And it will do all the statistics taught in elementary stat courses: sums, averages, standard deviations, medians, means, and correlations between two variables.

I've always liked it, and I'm happy to share it.

[The Pournelle Minimum Data Base, including the source

code to show how it was written, is available from Workman and Associates. It's still pretty useful, because it can be modified so easily for other purposes. I still use it for a lot of stuff. I've modified it into a logbook index program; a program to keep track of anthology payments; a menu planner; and, with extensive modifications, into an accounting system.

(In fact, the real value of the program is the source code; it's modified so easily to serve as the base for other useful programs.)]

QUALITY ASSURANCE . . .

"There may not be a lot of *really new* software," I said to my mad friend, "but there's a lot of good stuff coming out."

"What do you have in mind?" he asked.

"Well, there's Sorcim's SuperCalc. I really like that one. Whatever you'd like to do with scratchpad math, it'll do it, and simply. I've got two different versions, one on 5¼ inch disks for the Osborne, and another on 8 inch for the Godbout. And I love them both."

Which I do. One of the nicest things about SuperCalc is the documentation, which looks a bit formidable when you first open it—there are a lot of pages there—but on inspection it really tells you a lot about how to use the program. Neither I nor my assistants had any difficulty learning to use the program, because not only is there complete program documentation, but good HELP instructions as well.

"But there's no index," my mad friend said. "Mark 'em down. Tell the world. Dammit, there's no excuse for software without indexed documents. . . ."

A sentiment I thoroughly share, but Sorcim has an excuse for this one. SuperCalc is so darned easy to use, once you get the hang of it, that the on-line HELP files, plus the handy-dandy little "AnswerCard" that comes with it, are all you really need; while most of the documentation is a tutorial, not a reference guide. Me, I think I'd have designed the documents slightly differently, with an indexed reference work appended to the tutorial; but that's a mild preference. Certainly you can learn SuperCalc from what they supply.

It's worth learning, too. Like dBase II, and Spellguard, and Write, SuperCalc is destined to become a classic: a program that does what it says it will do, with very little fuss and bother; and the excellent documentation makes it easy to learn.

What SuperCalc does is calculate; it is, of course, a VisiCalc "work-alike," designed to work on 8080/Z-80 CP/M systems. Imagine a big worksheet spread out in rows and columns of cells. Now imagine that into any cell you can enter any darned thing you want: a number, a label such as "Sales Tax" or "horsefeathers," or perhaps a formula such as "the sum of the five cells above this one." Another formula might be "the average of all the cells in the next row" or "the square of the cell above divided by Pi." Finally, imagine that as soon as you enter a number that affects any cells in which you have formulae, the values, no matter how complex, are instantly recalculated and displayed . . .

That's SuperCalc. Not only does it do all the above, but there are really nifty edit features that make it easy to get at the cells you want to work on; and you can save your work into a disk file at any time. I imagine the IRS is going to just hate SuperCalc and all the programs like it; it will now be relatively easy to calculate your taxes in every conceivable way, and choose the one you like best. Nicest part about it, too, is that if you use your computer to do your taxes, it's likely to be deductible; certainly the software is.

SuperCalc is available from Sorcim, a thoroughly professional software company that also supplies the Basic Input Output System (BIOS) for the Godbout 8085 computer; and therein lies an instructive tale.

SuperCalc has an installation program that allows you to tell it what terminal you're using. There are a half-dozen or so terminals SuperCalc likes, plus a few more that it tolerates. One that it likes is the Zenith Z-19, which is good, because that's what I've connected to the new Godbout 8085/88. The Z-19 has a standard 24 lines of 80 columns, plus a special 25th status line which can't be got at without special programming. SuperCalc uses the special programming to give some helpful information.

The Z-19 also has a row of special feature buttons which send an escape sequence—that is, the character "escape" (1B hex) and then a number or letter. SuperCalc catches these and uses them to do nifty things like controlling the cursor and displaying HELP files.

Unfortunately, as I got the package from Sorcim, it *almost* did that. That is, there appeared on the 25th line a message that the "red square" special purpose button was the "HELP" button, and that the "blue square" button would toggle the special shift to turn the numeric keypad into cursor controls; but in fact neither the red nor the blue button did anything at all, while trying to use the shift feature on the numeric keypad produced *weird* results which nothing seemed able to fix.

So now what? I sent a note to Richard Frank, President of Sorcim, and a few days later got a phone call from one of Sorcim's engineers. Other people's Z-19 terminals worked with SuperCalc, so it wasn't the program. A few tests carried out during the phone conversation produced even stranger results: the terminal was operating fine, but the computer wasn't receiving the escape sequences the terminal was generating. Just what was going on?

Eventually we found it. The Godbout BIOS for the 8085 expects one pattern of data and stop bits; the Z-19 sends another. To make it worse, the Z-19, although an excellent terminal in many ways—I recommend it as about as good as you can get just now—has some bugs in its program chips, and those bugs interact with the Sorcim-supplied 8085 BIOS and SuperCalc to generate the strange results I noticed.

If all this seems confusing to you, imagine what *I* thought about it while it was happening to me! Eventually, though, I got my friend and computer consultant Tony Pietsch together with the Sorcim program specialists, and all was fixed nicely. Moreover, Sorcim is putting the problem and its solution into their SuperCalc manual, and notifying Godbout. The moral of this story is that if you insist on a state of the art system—such as the Godbout 8085/88—you'd better be prepared for some unexpected results; but if you deal with reputable companies, you'll eventually get satisfaction.

[Since that time, the CompuPro 8085/8088 Dual Processor has become the mainstay of my computer establishment. Known in the industry as "the boat anchor," the machine is widely used as a development system. When I got it, though, it was still under test. . . .]

Then there are the smaller companies: they want to do right, but they have limited resources. A lot of really good software comes out of such companies, but there are some problems, too.

Example: As a result of my last column, Cornucopia Software has sent me four separate iterations of fixes for

Microproof. Each one had problems, and each time I sent them notes on what they probably ought to do. Lo! They have now managed to take care of nearly all my objections to the program. They've speeded it up enormously, they've overhauled the error-trapping procedures, made it easier to use, and generally fixed things up. Microproof is now reasonably competitive with Spellguard (as the two exist in December 1981; by the time you read this, things could be different, since both companies will be working on their products). Unlike Spellguard, Microproof still doesn't handle dashes very well—the program thinks, for example, that "well—the" as I used it here is a candidate misspelled word—and quotation marks give it problems. There's another difficulty: with Microproof you can correct the word by spelling it properly, after which the program will go through your text file and globally make the changes. What, though, do you do about capitalization? (Mostly you hope you haven't begun any sentences with the word. . . .)

Anyway: it took several iterations, but eventually Cornucopia developed a useful spelling program. A number of other companies have read preliminary reviews, and proceeded to patch things up and send me frantic revisions of their programs.

"So. You're a quality control department," my mad friend said.

"Well, not for everyone. And sometimes it's a fairly complicated situation like the problems with SuperCalc and the Z-19 terminal—"

"Yeah, sure," my mad friend said. "But did you ever stop to think how many software houses routinely use their *paying customers* as their quality control department? Look—how much advance notice software do you get?"

I thought about it. "Not too much. Mostly I get advertised stuff because I write and ask for it. Sometimes an outfit will see a review and ask if I want to see their new product. I try to be fair, but I don't have time to help with development—"

"But you do anyway. Now think about the poor schmoe who buys new software that doesn't quite work. He doesn't know what to do. The license agreements discourage sending anything back for refunds. He doesn't even know how to describe the problem, or maybe he hasn't enough experience with competing programs to know he has a lemon. And meanwhile the publishers keep those $500 price tags—and complain about pirates!"

Unfortunately, my mad friend is right. In fact, things are worse than that. Some companies, like Cornucopia, *try* to fix things when their customers complain, and eventually do things right. There are others that just ignore the complaints. Take the money and run.

And yet. It's certainly to our—the users'—advantage that there be a lot of small software houses springing up. We don't want the field dominated by a few giants with ever-restrictive licensing policies ("Levitical documentation," as my mad friend calls it). We want a lot of competition. Which means, I guess, that those of us who like to try new products had just better get used to being unpaid quality control departments. Sigh.

CHAPTER 3
Languages, Accounts, and Other Madness

LANGUAGES, MON AMOUR ...

There are two new BASIC compilers, and they're both excellent. It's almost an *embarrass de richess* ...

First we have Microsoft's newest BASCOM. I've come to expect good things from Microsoft and I'm not usually disappointed. Remember back when I reviewed the old BASCOM, I complained about their licensing policy that required you to pay royalties to MICROSOFT for every copy of any program you sold that had been compiled with BASCOM? And how I said they'd abandon that someday? Well the good news is that they have indeed abandoned that policy—for the *old* BASCOM.

The bad news is that they've got an even more restrictive licensing policy for the new compiler. Sigh.

More good news, though. The new BASCOM compiler has CHAIN and COMMON, meaning that you can break a program up into chunks so as to conserve space in memory for variables and computations. Moreover, only one run-time package is needed for all this. That is: there's a run-time package that has to be on the disk if you're running any program put together by the new compiler; but only one copy of the run-time program must be present on that disk, even though you may have half a dozen compiled programs.

One major consequence is that the compiled programs are shorter. Not all *that* much shorter, if you count program and run-time package; but the instant you have several compiled programs present, the disk savings mount up. (Of course I chuckle at that; with my new Qume double-sided double-density disk system I have over 2 megabytes of floppy storage available, which means I don't worry so much about disk space. Yet.)

Of course if you use the run-time package, you're liable for the new royalty payments on any software you sell. You could, I guess, sell programs written in Microsoft BASIC and compilable with BASCOM, leaving it to the customer to buy his own copy of BASCOM with run-time package.

And, of course, you can use BASCOM to develop as many programs as you like for yourself. Since BASCOM is *almost* the same language as Microsoft's BASIC-80 interpreter, the result is a very powerful tool: you can run programs interpretatively, squeezing out the syntax errors, then test the program logic, all while having an instant editor available for fix-up. Now, true, it would be a LOT easier if BASIC-80 didn't, infuriatingly, simply dump your program and scrub all its variables whenever you make any program change whatever (even to add a REMARK!); but you can't have everything. (I wish we could, though; and if Microsoft wants to update BASIC-80, I *strongly* suggest that improvement.)

A second major defect of BASCOM is its surprising inability to deal with arrays. The rule with BASCOM is, once dimensioned, always dimensioned. You cannot change dimensions at all. Worse, you can't compute the size of a dimension, even if the compiler has been told everything it would need for the calculation. You can't even use a variable for dimension size. The result is that if you make up a data base program—as I have, see last column for details—you must either re-compile any time you change the data base structure, or you must waste a lot of memory on larger than necessary arrays; neither is very convenient.

Finally, BASIC-80 and BASCOM have a very strange random access file structure—and you cannot access the random files as if they were sequential. Microsoft BASIC stores random files in a packed binary code format that very efficiently uses the disk space; but the files aren't ASCII, and can't be printed by any program not written in Microsoft BASIC, and that can be a pain in the arse.

So: given the defects, what are the alternatives?

One solution might be to turn to Pascal and be done with

it. Why muck with BASIC at all? Compiled Pascal MT+, or INT-file Pascal such as is created with Sorcim's Pascal M or UCSD Pascal, is supposed to be faster, easier to write, more efficient, and inherently better structured than the best BASIC ever written. (I'm not at all convinced; the few tests I've tried show BASIC programs compiled with BASCOM are about as fast as MT+, and *faster* than UCSD Pascal.)

Besides—comes now Digital Research's new CB80 to challenge the whole notion.

CB80 was written by Compiler Systems, which in essence means Gordon Eubanks, the author of CBASIC; and in a real sense CB80 is compiled CBASIC. You can compile all of your CBASIC programs with only minimal changes. Thus CB80 has all the advantages and disadvantages of CBASIC-2.

There are lots of advantages. CBASIC programs are nice to work with. Just for starters, you can redimension arrays as often as you like. You can access random files sequentially, and the file structure is standard ASCII for all files. There's a UCASE (upper case) function, and a nice search function that looks to see if what you want is imbedded in anything else.

Another advantage of CBASIC over Microsoft's BASIC-80 is string space allocation; although CBASIC is a little slower in processing each input line (and slows down more and more as memory fills up), it does its "garbage collection" on the fly, so to speak. BASIC-80, on the other hand, runs at higher speeds until it runs out of string space—after which you find yourself completely locked away from your computer, unable to do any input or output or anything else, for something like one to four minutes while BASIC-80 goes chasing through memory finding old strings the program has been told to forget. Eventually it clears everything up and becomes responsive again, if by then you haven't gotten so furious you've hit the RESET button....

So. CB80 is very nice. But—there's no interpreter. Like Pascal or FORTRAN or PL/I or any of the compiled languages, creating large programs in CB80 takes a lot of time. First you have to create the program on an editor; then you compile it, finding a number of trivial syntax errors which you must fix by loading in your text editor and mashing the source program; then you compile again, then link, then run with the run-time package. By the time you're done, you can use up an afternoon to develop a pretty simple program.

However: because CB80 *is* compiled, and has no line numbers to fool with, you can put in *tons* of remarks, meaning that if you come back to your program in six months you have half a chance of understanding it.

And actually CB80 is better than that.

Now it has labels. Instead of "GOSUB 3680" you can say "GOSUB COUNTIT", or "GOSUB PROCESS.ONE.ITEM." Better yet, you can have *very* complex functions, which you "CALL" and pass parameters to; and the functions use purely local variables that can't affect anything in the program outside.

The functions can take up many lines, and they can be "external"—meaning that the function can be in an entirely different program "module" that gets called in at link time. Multiple line functions can also access and change external variables; and the whole mess can be called by value, as in the statement WHILE FARNUM(FOO) where FARNUM has previously been defined as a function of the variable FOO.

More yet: a multi-line function can have both purely local variables, variables created just for that function (the variable "X" in the function is not the same as the variable "X" in another function or in the main program)—and can *also* affect regular global variables in the rest of your BASIC program. This means you could have a function called "YES" which prints a prompt, gets an input, checks to see if the first letter of that input is either "y" or "Y," and informs the main program.

In other words, CB80 has got pretty darned close to Pascal's Functions and Procedures, and it seems to be a whack of a lot faster than Pascal, too. You could sit down and write a really neat set of "Software Tools"—if you don't know that book by Kernighan and Plauger, you ought to get it; the original was about FORTRAN but now they have one on Pascal, too. You can, with CB80, build a whole library of useful program modules, setting them up in nice orderly blocks to be called in when needed....

That, of course, is the answer to the "no interpreter" problem: build a set of functions that you KNOW will work, and include them into the new programs you write. After a while you'll find that most programming consists of stringing together routines known to be reliable, and once in a while developing a new function to stick into your tool kit.

Although CB80 is marketed by Digital Research and the

manual flies Digital's colors, don't despair: the documentation wasn't really written by Digital, meaning that it's not encrypted and translated into Swahili as much of Digital's documentation is. It *does* have some of the fine hand of the Digital hacker about it; there are, for example, incomprehensible "syntax diagrams" peppered through the text, presented as if they were supposed to mean something; and here and there the sentence density gets completely out of hand. For the most part, though, the CB80 manual is in the really excellent style of the old CBASIC manual: clear, concise, with plenty of examples. You need not be afraid of it.

You might, however, be afraid of CB80's *price*, which is steep, and its *licensing policy*, which is sheer madness: that is, they want a flat $2,000 a year if you're going to compile, link, and market programs using CB80. (The fee applies only to programs you distribute, not to those developed for your own use; still, it's onerous enough.) Again, I suspect competition will bring this down; meanwhile, we can wait....

[A month after I published that, Digital Research announced that they'd dropped licensing fees for selling programs compiled with any program they published. Since then, most companies have followed suit.]

WHICH LANGUAGE NOW?

So. We have increasingly better BASICS, and one of these days we'll get a compiled language as good as CB80 with an interpreter as good as Microsoft's BASIC-80. When that happens, I think FORTRAN and COBOL and even Pascal are going to suffer a sharp drop in popularity.

My mad friend, meanwhile, continues to praise PL/I, which he says is easy to learn and remarkably effective. I confess I haven't had time to write anything but the simplest programs in PL/I, or indeed even time to examine it; but my mad friend is usually fairly reliable in his judgments, and has a very healthy attitude toward computers, namely that they're for him to use, not a new master to control him.

Accounts Comprehensible

Once again I find myself embarrassed: I have to review a program I've written.

I have most of the many computer accouting packages available. Some, I guess, are really swell for what they do; but not one of them, *not one*, looks too useful for me.

I'm a writer. A good part of my life is deductible. It's amazing just how many activities turn out to be income-related research. And it comes as no surprise that the Internal Revenue Service is *very* interested in the records demonstrating that.

And therein lies the problem. Sure, I could hire an accountant. Many of my colleagues do, and a lot of them think I'm crazy when I tell them I keep my own books and make out my own tax returns. And yet, when I begin to question them, I find that I don't work any harder than they do. By the time they've explained everything to their accountant, and turned in all the receipts, and kept all the records and diaries that the accountant wants, they've usually done *more* work than I do; and they pay more taxes, too.

I've always kept my own books; one of the main reasons I let my mad friend talk me into buying Ezekial, my friend who happens to be a Z-80, was the hope that I could computerize my accounting system. Thus I have for *years* eagerly pounced on every new accounting program with eager whinnies of joy . . . and I've been disappointed every time.

Most "accounting" programs don't produce what I would call accounting books. Instead, they offer "special reports." Now understand: I don't know a darned thing about accounting. Everything I think I know came from two books, MacKenzie's *Fundamentals of Accounting* and John N. Myer, *Accounting for Non-Accountants*. Those books explain what accounting is all about—and they give examples. Pictures. Illustrations. Actual examples of Journals and Ledgers, with the funny single, double, and triple lines, the complex scheme of indentations, and the strange check-marks favored by accountants; and so far as I'm concerned, that's what my company's books ought to look like.

Nor am I completely mad; every couple of years I have my boys drift into the local university bookstore and buy all the accounting textbooks they can find, and I look through them; and lo! The textbooks still show that accountants like double and triple lines, and complicated indentations, and. . . .

Yet there's no computer accounting program that I know of that produces books that look like the books in the accounting texts; and since that's the only thing I could understand with my cookbook knowledge of accounting, I had no real choice at all. I had to write programs that DO make Journals and Ledgers that correspond with the examples in the elementary textbooks used in accounting classes.

Which is what I did. My accounting system starts with a simple-minded thing that lets you build a chart of accounts: essentially a list of ledger page names each with a corresponding ledger page number; examples are 501, Postage; 506, Office Supplies; 506.012, Travel Supplies; 523, Business Charitable Contributions; 923, Family Charitable Contributions.

You can add to the chart of accounts at any time, and you can use fractional page numbers, from .001 to .999, if you like, since each ledger page will become a CP/M file title LED-xxx.yyy, as for example LED-506.012.

After you make a chart you use the JOURNAL program to build journals. A journal entry consists of a line revealing to whom you paid (or from whom you received) something; a longer explanation line; an amount; and a series of debits and credits that the program keeps track of (I *HATE* to remember that when you spend money you *credit* cash and *debit* the account you spent it on). The program will not allow you to enter an item that doesn't have equal debits and credits.

You can put stuff into the JOURNAL in any order that you want; there is then a program that will allocate the journal entries by date, so that the journal becomes a chronological record of what you spent for which. It has ways of entering cash, checks (from more than one account if you like; I have two interest-bearing checking accounts and one commercial account, and I need to keep them all straight); a dozen different credit cards; and so forth. It also keeps track of check numbers.

Once you've built a journal you can print it; that will require a printer able to print solid vertical bars (ASCII character 124), since it makes the single, double, and treble lines so loved by accountants.

You can then POST the journal. The POST program takes the journal entries and allocates them among the various ledger pages you created in the chart of accounts. JOURNAL has provision for control accounts. I suppose I had better explain that. Let's say a primary expense category is Postage, and that's the way I intend to report the expenses to the IRS. However, I often find I have to send express mail packets. These ought to be charged to a particular project—in my case, of course, a project is a book. Thus we debit the book account, and credit a controlled account ledger page; we also debit **POSTAGE** and credit cash. When I get income from that particular project the book gets credited, as does "Agented Income," while the bank account and the controlled accounts summary pages get debits; once again the books balance, and I can get some clues about the profitability of any particular book.

Anyway, POST takes care of all that, after which another program prints all those ledgers. Each ledger entry contains a reference to the Journal page and item number, so there is a complete audit trail back and forth; indeed, the whole thing looks exactly like the demonstration items given in Myer's *Accounting for Non-Accountants*, which ought to be no great surprise since that's what the programs were designed to do.

Now note: the programs do not give a lot of "special reports." They don't claim to do a darned thing that isn't covered in the Myer book (which is still in print). They do create books that look like what accounting texts expect, which was all I set out to do.

And since my business gets confused with my family's affairs, I've made it easy to segregate business from family expenditures: cases where the kids come on business trips, and thus have to have their expenses charged to a different account from mine. That sort of thing.

I've used these programs since 1977. Eventually some of my friends asked for copies. Then more. Then I was asked to write up a little manual on how to use the programs, and while I was at it, why not include a brief treatise on what accounting is for and . . .

It was getting out of hand, and one night over the slivovitz Barry Workman got at me with an offer to publish the programs. "After all," he said, "they really are the best accounting programs you know of, aren't they?"

"No. Just the best for the kind of small business I operate. I don't know how good they'd be for an outfit that has lots of accounts receivable and accounts payable, or a big payroll. . . ."

"I use your accounting programs," Barry pointed out. "And so do a number of your friends. Consulting engineers, a couple of freelance salespeople—you know, your programs produce standard ASCII files that can be jiggered up to be the input to much more complicated routines if anyone wants more massaging than your stuff gives them."

And so forth. So eventually I agreed, and now I'm in the embarrassing position of reviewing my own software. All I can say on that score is that I do use the programs; they do work for my kind of small business. They are **NOT** heavy on accounts receivable and accounts payable; they're **FAR** more useful for recording expenses and income in complex ways than they are for controlling monthly billings (writers don't have monthly billings). Given those limits, they are pretty good. They do make books you can read, and that your accountant will recognize. They preserve the audit trail, and they let you have as complex—or as simple—a chart of accounts as you like.

My mad friend tells me that my little treatise on why one keeps books in the first place is the only thing on that subject he's been able to make sense of; but do recall that he's quite mad.

[I still use my accounting system, and it still satisfies the IRS. Barry Workman has managed to find copies of Myer's *Accounting for Non-Accountants* and includes them as part of the package.

Alas, I find that there were *two* editions of Myer's book, and the Second Edition, which is still in print, is nearly worthless. Barry Workman has arranged, therefore, that you get not only a copy of the Second Edition, but a photocopy of the old First Edition; which was, in my judgment, the best introduction to accounting ever written.

I've added a number of auxiliary programs to the package, and over the years I've rewritten the original Journal program to add features. There are lots of good accounting programs available; I can't say mine is best; but it is *still* the only one I know of that produces printouts of books that look like the books in the accounting texts. Sigh.]

Terminal Madness

As if we didn't have enough problems here at Chaos Manor, we had to buy a new terminal the other day.

We've had the Godbout 8085/88 running for a couple of months now. Incidentally, I need a name for that machine; preferably one not too blasphemous. Anyway, we set it up with a Zenith Z-19 terminal, which works all right (except that all three Tony bought had a loosely soldered wire in the horizontal amplifier); but I don't like it. Understand, it's a fine terminal; the dislike is purely personal with me. The keyboard is too close to the screen. I wear bifocal glasses, and I'm torn between moving my head forward and looking down, or moving back and not being able to see the letters at all.

So: what I wanted was a terminal with detached keyboard. Preferably one with a video output on the back so that I can switch the output onto my big 15" Hitachi monitor that sits 29 inches from my head. I also require a really nifty keyboard, one having a good feel and a Selectric key layout.

"Televideo 950," said Bill Godbout when I asked him. "We're converting to Televideo 950s everywhere, and our people really like them."

So. Off I went to look at them at Dick Dickenson's establishment, which seems to be named **COMPU-PLUS** this week. (It began as Computer Components, where my mad friend and I bought our old memo-wreck keyboards and some other surplus equipment; changed to Computer World; changed again to, and I kid you not, "The Place You Go To Buy Computers, Incorporated"; and now has become **COMPU-PLUS**. My son Alex says that next week they'll be Xylophone Computers, but I don't believe that.)

They had a Televideo 950 set up there, and I played about with it, and liked the feel of the keyboard, and the screen was rock steady and easy to read. The letter set looked good. And they had them in stock, and my son Alex needs a terminal for his machine down in San Diego, so if I bought the 950 on the spot he could take the Z-19 away with him.

But there was one other alternative to explore: buy an IBM personal computer and teach it to be a terminal. That would be an expensive solution, but I can forsee a big future for the IBM PC, and just at the moment that's not a problem. So. Off we went to Computerland where they have IBM machines set up and working....

After all, I've worn out three IBM Selectric typewriters. I know that keyboard and its feel and layout, and I love it; and from Greg's *BYTE* review of IBM I could see I liked the graphics and letter set, and they have all the manuals available; meanwhile, Bill Godbout called and said he's sending me a new Godbout disk controller that will handle Qume DT-5 double-sided double-density 5¼ inch disks in IBM-compatible format. So there's everything going for getting an IBM....

Only they've *ruined* the keyboard! What ought to be their strongest point, the thing IBM always excelled at, is their worst misfeature! It took *brains* to do something that awful. No stupid person could have done it.

What IBM did is to put extra keys between the space bar and the SHIFT key. Why, I don't know. They just did. The result is that when you think you've typed, say, a capital T, you get instead /t which isn't useful at all.

There is also no line-feed key; instead they seem to have jiggered up the carriage return key to give BOTH cr and lf when struck. Unfortunately, many programs won't be able to stand that. I suppose there's a way to filter that madness; but there's no help for the SHIFT key being mislocated, nor for the egregious amount of space they put between the home keys and the RETURN key.

So, I may one day buy an IBM, but not until I get over the shock of that ruined keyboard. I've never been so disappointed in my life.

So back to Dick Dickenson's place for a Televideo which we took home with us. Installation was no problem. The documents were absolutely clear, the baud rate switches and other such stuff are on the back and clearly marked, the stop bit settings are simple enough to understand; and Bill Godbout's 8085 BIOS is also clear, so I was able to set up the 950 in no time.

The only thing I didn't like about the 950 was minor: the keyboard cable attaches in *back* of the terminal, so that the cord has to come around the side of the machine. It should attach in front.

So we set it up and turned it on, and it worked first time. Controlled the Godbout perfectly. I played about with it a bit—then I loaded WordMaster.

Blooey.

Why? I wondered. So I experimented some more. And sure enough, any time I sent an ESCAPE character, the terminal went into a different mode, until eventually it got into a block mode where it didn't send anything to the computer at all.

Look through the manual. Nothing on that problem. Try logic. The Televideo 950 uses the ESCAPE key to send an ESCAPE character out; while SHIFT ESCAPE is used to tell the machine, "This is a setup. Don't send out the next character, but execute it as an internal setup instruction." And unfortunately, this particular machine was broken; SHIFT ESCAPE worked fine, but ESCAPE did *both;* that is, sent out the escape character all right, but also executed the next character as an instruction (and sent it out as well). The results were maddening.

So. Back to COMPU-PLUS. "Take it back," I told Dick. "I think I want a DEC VT-100."

"Sure you can have your money back," he says. "But I have a Televideo at home, and we've had that one out there as a demo for a year, and nobody ever had any problems with either of them—"

And it was Saturday, and Alex wanted to go back to San Diego and he needed a terminal and they had three more 950's in stock. . . .

"Okay," I said. "I'll take a different one in exchange. Only this time we try it out here."

"Right," said Dick. "We'll plug it in right here where the demo is. . . ."

So we did. The first one didn't work: couldn't set the proper baud rate. The next one didn't work. Couldn't set something, I forget what. The third one didn't work. Didn't even turn on. And that was surely enough.

So I've got my money back, and I'm using the Z-19 just now. You can conclude anything you want from my ordeal. One lesson for sure: Dick Dickenson's price for a Televideo 950 is about $150 above the discount houses; but when I had a problem, he was right there and ready to take care of it for me. It's worth dealing with established firms with a reputation for good service; or so say I.

WORDS

I have here the biggest software bargain I know of. It's called The Word, and it comes from Oasis Systems.

The Word is a spelling program; but it's also a LOT more. It counts words for you. It makes files of words. It will make a list of each unique word in a text file, and sort it alphabetically. It will also do a list of each word used and the number of times you used it, sorted by frequency of use.

I've used The Word to find strange character names: that is, I'm working on JANISSARIES TWO right now. That story takes place on a planet settled by successive waves of Celts, Minoans, Romans, Franks ... so that the character names tend to be a little strange. They have to be kept consistent with the culture in which they appear.

This is all right for major characters, but what if I'm writing along and I need a minor character name? I grab one of my reference works (such as Robert Graves' *Greek Myths*, or Munro's *Highland Clans and Tartans*) and find a suitable name in the index; and if I'm sensible I make a note of that somewhere. But usually I don't make the note, or can't find it again, and I can't remember where this particular spear carrier appeared when I need to use him (her, it) again....

But with The Word I can simply run it through the spelling program, and the program makes a file of all the words it doesn't recognize. I can now examine that file, and lo! There will be my strange character name.

Then with the FIND program I got from Barry Workman (Utility Disk One) I can go right into the text files and find that word in context. Saves no end of time.

The Word does much more; and it sells for under $100, which is why I say it's the biggest bargain in word-handling software I know of.

Incidentally, I'm still using Spellguard too. The Word, while excellent, isn't quite as convenient for the straight job of spelling checking, particularly at 3 in the morning when I don't want to think about options and toggles and command lines, I want a fully menu-driven program that just does what I ask it to without quibbles; and that's Spellguard. But for really sophisticated word work fully under user control, you just won't beat The Word.

[Since then, Wayne Holder has produced The Word +, which is an even bigger software bargain. I've long since converted to using it for all my spelling work. At my suggestion, he's added several features, and changed some of the instructions; and it's *very* hard to beat, even in 1984. There's nothing close to it for the price.]

THE GREAT BASIC COMPILER DEBATE

I recently received several letters imploring me to choose between Microsoft's BASCOM and Digital Research's CB-80.

Both are, of course, compiling BASICs; the difference is that BASCOM compiles Microsoft's *interpretive* BASIC, while CB-80 compiles CBASIC, which is itself a pseudo-compiled language.

Unfortunately those were no easy letters to answer. As usual, the answer is "it depends."

First, let's establish something: of the two languages, CB-80 is unquestionably the "best" if your criterion is ease of use and ability to write structured programs. CB-80 has "functions" that are indistinguishable in operation from Pascal procedures, calls by label (GOSUB DO-ONE is a perfectly legal statement), and a whole host of features that Microsoft's BASIC simply doesn't support.

When, then, don't I simply recommend CB-80 and be done with it?

It's a bit like Pascal-M *vs.* Pascal-MT+. Microsoft's BASCOM, used in conjunction with Microsoft interpretive BASIC, isn't as fast or as convenient as CB-80; but it's much easier to get your program running because of the *interpretive* feature of the language. With Microsoft BASIC you can write a complex program and run it (slowly) in the interpretive mode. You'll be able immediately to correct all the syntax errors and other trivia; after which you can check the program logic to see that the damned thing really does what you wanted it to do; and only then must you invest the time in actual compilation.

With CB-80 you must write the program; compile it, at which time you'll undoubtedly find a dozen trivial errors; put it back in your editor and fix the trivia; compile again, when you'll find more trivial errors that were masked by the first set of errors; etc. After about four to five iterations of *that* you'll finally be ready to check program logic, which may also drive you crazy because you can't jump around in the program at will the way you can in an interpretive language.

So: what do you want? As for me, I find I do the following: for a quick and dirty program, one I want to get running *right now*, I invariably use Microsoft BASIC; if I'm going to use it very much, I then compile it with BASCOM.

For a program I'm going to take more time with, because it's to be part of my permanent inventory, meaning that it's complex and will need modifications over the years and I'll want lots of comments and a rigid structure, I almost always start with CB-80. That's because CB-80 programs are inherently better structured than BASCOM programs.

Sometimes I'll use Microsoft BASIC to get started, then translate to CB-80 later; but that's rare, because CB-80 has so many nifty features that Microsoft BASIC lacks.

But that's me. I discussed this with my mad friend not long before he died, and he said—not unsurprisingly—that the answer is "none of the above." Mac Lean was enamored of Digital Research's PL-I/80, which is admittedly harder to learn than either of the above BASICs, but which he claimed was far more powerful than either.

And my son Alex, not surprisingly, argues that Pascal is much better; a sentiment shared by Carl Helmers, the former editorial director of *BYTE*.

And if all that's not enough, I can find no end of people to tell you that you must ignore *all* of the above and adopt the "C" Programming Language. This latter is a view for which I have surprisingly friendly sentiment; but the problem is that there is no good C compiler for micro systems. Now true: Leor Zolman's BDS C (available from Lifeboat Associates, and worth the price even if you're only mildly curious about C) is a truly amazing product, well worth the cost; but it isn't the full C language, and the omissions are not trivial. The Whitesmith C compiler is a full C compiler (provided you have 60+ kilobytes of free memory), but it is slower than molasses in January, and has perhaps the worst error reporting features of any language I've ever seen. You can spend *days* trying to get the simplest program running in Whitesmith.

And yet: the C language (and in particular the Whitesmith) compiles to the tightest code of all the higher level languages. It runs fast, and is suitable for operating systems programming—something you certainly can't say for any of the other higher level languages. If there were a really decent C for micro's I'd be inclined to support it; and I'm very much looking forward to the development of a good C for my Godbout 8088.

So: as of this writing I've no definitive advice. If I could buy only one higher level language, I suppose I'd get CB-80; an opinion which I suspect is causing my mad friend to revolve rapidly, since he didn't care much for **BASIC** in any of its guises. The second one I'd buy would be **BDS C**, followed by **BASCOM** and **PL/I-80**. But that's me, and I've different problems from many of you.

I wish I could be more definitive.

CHAPTER 4
Passing Friends

This column, the seventh, marked the end of the first phase of the *User's Column*. By this time, the column was established. It had begun regularly to place highly in the *BYTE* readers' poll, and it generated as much mail as any other feature in the magazine. Other columnists in rival publications began to quote the column, and I was invited to speak at computer shows.

It had all worked as Mac Lean predicted. We had all the free software we ever wanted, we were welcome at computer shows, and we got press releases from major companies.

Then, alas, I had to write this.

Dan Mac Lean, RIP

I often start these columns with a quote from my mad friend. Alas, I'll never be able to do that again. Dan Mac Lean died of cancer in December. He'd known for a good year that he had about a year to live.

My mad friend never published much, but he had a great and beneficial effect on the micro computer world. For one thing, any influence I may have is due to him; he talked me into getting my first machine, held my hand while I learned to use it, and encouraged me to do these columns.

More than that, he was insatiably curious. He examined *everything* in the micro field: programs, hardware, you name it, he'd used it, or knew someone who had; and he had strong opinions.

I suppose he was sometimes wrong, although I don't think

of an instance just now; but because he had strongly held opinions, with good reasons for holding them, he shook up a lot of prejudices. Winning an argument with Mac Lean was possible, but it was never easy; and whether you won or lost, after you discussed a matter with him, you understood it much better than you did when you began.

Mac Lean was an expert software thief: I don't suppose there was a single program in all this world that he hadn't got, somehow. When George Tate first met him, he offered him copies of any programs Ashton-Tate had, on the grounds that if he gave them to him Mac Lean would feel some ethical obligation; and he'd certainly get them, one way or another.

Understand, my mad friend didn't *do* anything unethical with his booty. He never sold anything, and he was reluctant to give programs away, except to people he knew wouldn't have bought them. But he did analyze programs and try to use them, and his views often got into this column. (At the direction of his widow, all of Mac Lean's disks except those containing his own writings have been reformatted; we'll never know precisely what he had on those disks, which is probably just as well.)

He also wrote letters. Lord Almighty, did he write letters. Some of them were hilarious. All were actually serious, and many of his suggestions were taken by major firms. He had a lot more influence than you see on the surface.

Mac Lean worked off and on for the US government, as a consultant to private firms, and as a general information collector. He's helped hundreds of people, and we're all going to miss him. I certainly do.

Mac Lean had talked me into beginning this column, just as he had talked me into getting into the computer revolution. He lived long enough to see computers making a real impact on the world. I'm glad of that

Alas: Dan Mac Lean wasn't the only friend I lost in that period. A couple of months later....

I've been away from my desk for a month, and things are piled higher than you can believe. As a consequence, this column is going to be a bit disorganized (try total mishmash), and I hope you'll all forgive me.

I'm a bit upset anyway. Poor old Ezekial, my friend who

happens to be a Cromemco Z-2, is stacked in the other room, waiting for Noor Singh to come take him over to Tony Pietsch's shop for a complete overhaul. While I was gone, John Carr, our long-suffering associate editor here at Chaos Manor, was working on *Space Viking's Return* when Zeke, with no warning at all, simply died. Fortunately John has been trained to save the text early and often, and little was lost.

I suppose I shouldn't be surprised. Several million words went through Zeke. He was running constantly 18 hours a day for nearly five years, and in all that time he wasn't out of service for more than a week. Moreover, from the description of the problem—he keeps blowing fuses—it may be no more than a blown capacitor in the power supply. Tony is pretty sure he can get Zeke fixed—when he gets time.

But time is very much a problem. Tony is doing Version 1.7 of Write, and he has also put together my *new* Godbout which will have memory-mapped video and the new super-nifty keyboards. I wonder if Zeke, hearing about the new writing machine, simply went away like my old black cat did when the kids brought home a kitten? But that's ridiculous.

Anyway, I'm writing this on The Golem, my big Warp Drive Godbout 8085/8088, using the Televideo 950 terminal, and while it's infinitely easier than using a typewriter or a cheap machine, it's also the first time in five years I've done major work without Zeke.

Of course there are exceptions, since we took the Otrona Attache to Europe, and I had a KayPro II in Chicago; on those, more later.

GOOD GRIEF, ZEKE CAN'T DIE!

That is: not only is Ezekial my friend, and practically a trademark (he gets nearly as much mail as I do), but there's the legal problem.

Consider: I have a ton of software running on Zeke. In theory it is licensed for "a single computer system." If Zeke is gone, have I any right to the software? In theory, I suppose, I should buy it all anew, or pay a license transfer fee. Perhaps, though, if Zeke is still connected to the "system"—that is, there he sits, connected into a single "system net" so that I have met the legal requirements—must he be alive? Can a dead computer be part of a "single computer system"?

Obviously I'm not serious. Or am I? Because somewhere along the line we've got to come up with answers to these questions. What does happen to software when your computer dies? If you sell the machine, who gets the software? And the solution has to be realistic; I suspect that even the chaps who rail loudest against computer pirates have not actually paid twice for their BASIC (or even transferred the license) after they upgraded from a beginner machine to something larger.

As for me, I've come to a decision: there are some user-threatening licensing agreements that I simply will not sign; and I urge all of you to do likewise. As an author I'm hardly going to quarrel with the idea that programmers and their publishers need protection from pirates; but some of them try for too much, and end with imbecile notions. If it's legal for you to loan (or even give, if you don't copy them) my books to a friend, why can't my computers loan programs to each other?

[The next month I was able to report, with some triumph:]

ZEKE LIVES!

Mark Twain had the extraordinary experience of reading his own obituary, after which he said, "Rumors of my death are greatly exaggerated."

Fortunately, Ezekial, my friend who happens to be an ancient Cromemco Z-2, can say the same. After his trip to Tony Pietsch's place, he returned nearly as good as new.

Nearly: a faulty cable managed to short out an input/output board, which in turn rendered one of his buss slots inoperable; and we do have an annoying problem with the B disk drive. Tony says the disk problem could probably be fixed by lowering the entire drive system into a vat of TCE (a dry-cleaning solvent) and agitating it for a couple of hours; in the absence of that, we just live with "PLEASE CLOSE DRIVE DOOR" the first few times we try to access the B drive. The problem goes away after a few minutes' warmup.

Update: last night Zeke died again, clobbering all his disks as he did. Today, in despair, I took apart the old iCom disk system. Lo! I found that there's a bad cable that conveys the 5 volt power; this causes all kinds of weird results, including write operations when the computer is supposed to be reading. Tony Pietsch thinks this is fixable, and thank heaven: I'm just now writing this on the Televideo 950 terminal, and that misplaced DELETE key, plus the obscene BACK TAB key, will soon drive me out of my mind....

I mention Zeke's revival in part because my mail indicates considerable interest in his health, but in fact there's an illustrative lesson here. This ancient machine—he was built some five years ago!—is still plenty good enough for me to write this article with. When I first got Zeke we had dying chip problems and a mysterious gremlin that required exorcism; but after the first couple of months, there just weren't any problems at all. Even now the central machine is in good shape; all our recent problems have been caused by faulty cables.

This seems to be typical: once past the first months, you shouldn't have any problems for several years. Then, all at once, like the wonderful one-horse shay, everything may collapse at once. Actually, the electronics could last for decades; it's mechanical stuff: disk drives, switches, fans, cables and connectors and such, that goes.

The problem is that five years isn't long in the life cycle of a typewriter; but it's an eternity for a microcomputer. By the time you want repairs on your five-year-old equipment, the manufacturer will no longer be making it, and it's likely that none of the technicians will ever have heard of it. This may change when machines begin to sell in hundreds of thousands per model; but just now it seems true enough.

I've no regrets. I've got a lot out of old Zeke, and he may yet last another couple of years; but computer purchasers should be warned: things are moving very fast, and that has consequences.

Meanwhile, I know of only one way to avoid the early ("infant mortality") glitches, and that's to buy "used" equipment: that is, either stuff that's been burned in a lot, like Godbout's rather expensive CSC grade, or literally used equipment if you can find someone reliable to buy it from. (One outfit sends out evaluation hardware with the understanding that they'll swap every month or so: that way they get back a thoroughly tested machine....)

THAT NEW WRITING MACHINE

Of course we have the ideal new writing machine. It's a Godbout Z-80, with Godbout double-sided double-density disks. There's a 16 × 64 memory-mapped video board (see the November column for what that means) playing into a big 15 inch monitor—precisely the setup that I had with Zeke, except that the new Godbout has 1.1 megabytes per disk compared to Ezekial's 240 K.

Best of all, the system boasts the Archive keyboard, which may just be the best keyboard in the industry. It has a sensible key layout, excellent key feel, function keys . . .

There's only one problem. "We" have the new system, but *I* don't have it. They're doing some documentation over in Tony Pietsch's establishment, and he needs the machine (which he set up for me, of course). So I keep getting these reports on how wonderful it will be when I finally get it, and meanwhile I count myself lucky when Zeke is working. Sigh. Real Soon Now. . . .

Alas Poor Ezekial

We sent Ezekial, my old friend who happened to be a Cromemco Z-2, off to the organ banks; he has officially become spare parts for Larry Niven's machine. Like the wonderful one-horse shay, everything went at once. The final problem was the disk system. Zeke used old iCom disks, the kind that had Percom drives with the controller on two boards in the box with the drives and their power supply; and they became unreliable. Spare parts are unobtainable; although those drives were the very best available when we got them, they're from the Dark Ages. To update them would cost more than new Godbouts, and they'd still be slow with very limited storage.

Zeke's bus is too slow, and his old Industrial Micro memory uses too much power. The bottom line, alas, is that it just wasn't worth fixing him up. Noor Singh swears he's going to get him running so that I can donate him to the Los Angeles Science Fantasy Society. The LASFS already owns Altair, the first Niven machine. (That's a little embarrassing, since Altair Niven was officially accepted as a *member* of the club).

There's another possibility. Dan Mac Lean's widow donated Alice, Dan's old Imsai, to the LASFS, and Noor Singh has been hired to get Alice running for the club; it may be that Zeke and Alice (who shamelessly carried on a long-distance affair for years) may yet be united into a single working entity....

Zeke II

Ezekial has departed, but I have consolation: as Noor Singh arrived to remove Zeke, Tony Pietsch delivered Zeke II, which is a state-of-the-art writing machine. That, of course, is the point of all this. I get lots of letters asking my recommendation for "the ideal word processor." My answer usually is, "That depends." However, I've seen nothing better than Zeke II for creative writing.

First: my "ideal" writing system is a computer, not a dedicated word processor. True, there are excellent dedicated word processors on the market, and it's a lot easier to learn to use them than it is to learn to write with a full micro. However, in my judgment, the saving is illusory: it doesn't take *that* much longer to learn a real computer; and then you can tap the power of the software explosion. Most dedicated word processors leave you at the mercy of one company: you get only the software they think you should have.

Consequently, I recommend CP/M systems. Secondly, iron is expensive but silicon is cheap: new computer boards are invented all the time. Get a good S-100 bus system and you can take advantage of the dozens—perhaps hundreds—of firms developing new capabilities for it.

Third, deal with reliable companies with a good track record.

In keeping with these views, Zeke Two consists of a CompuPro S-100 bus and power supply. My friend Bill Grieb continues to swear by the Integrand box which has bus, power supply, disk power supply, and disk drives all built into one handsome wood-grain cabinet, and perhaps he's right. I can only say that the Godbout CompuPro box has never disappointed me. It's built like a Mack Truck, with *two farads* (none of this microfarad stuff!) of power filtration. The only disadvantage is that it's *big*, but I don't mind that. The large size helps keep the components cool.

Inside the box is a CompuPro 6 megaHerz Z-80 Central Processing Unit (CPU), 64K of CompuPro RAM-17, an Interfacer-4, and the CompuPro Disk-One disk controller. That drives a pair of CompuPro 8" double-sided double-density drives at 1.1 megabytes per disk. The Interfacer Four plus the new CBIOS (Customized Basic Input Output System—the thing that tells CP/M about your particular hardware) written by Tony Pietsch allows a number of ways to talk to the system. Tony's CBIOS is now available from CompuPro.

The CBIOS allows you to use either 5¼ inch or 8 inch disks. The Godbout CompuPro controller supports either. It does not run both at once; if you want both on the same system, you will need two different controllers. That, however, is no problem; the Godbout box and BIOS can handle the situation, so that you can transfer files from 8 inch to 5 inch and *vice versa*.

There are disk controllers that will run both 8 inch and 5¼ inch disks; I once asked Bill Godbout why his wouldn't.

"I don't make Muntz TVs, either," he told me.

Interpreted, that means that it's tricky enough running at the speeds his Direct Memory Access (I'll explain that term below) systems use without trying to play games. Bill Godbout once told me, "If the error rate is measurable, it's too high," and his stuff is designed to that philosophy.

I still prefer 8" disk drives, although not as adamantly as I did last year. The 5¼ inch systems are getting more reliable, and running double-sided and double-density they hold quite a lot of information. I do not believe the small disks are as reliable as 8", but many for whom I have respect say they're reliable enough, so my preference is probably pure prejudice; unfortunate, but there it is.

I can also hang a normal terminal on the system, and indeed the same Televideo 950 that drives the Godbout 8085/8088 dual processor can run Zeke II. That, however, is not the normal mode, because we've set Zeke II up mostly as a writing machine. When he's powered up, he comes up in Write, my text editor; and when he's in Write mode, he talks to me through an Ithaca IA 1100 memory-mapped video board. (Memory-mapped video displays what's in a segment of memory; I tried to explain it in the November 1982 *BYTE*).

Tony has modified the Ithaca board to be "write only memory"; that is, you can't read the board's memory, you only see what's displayed on the monitor screen. The board is addressed to the top 1K of memory, and thus overlaps the RAM-17, but they can't interfere with each other.

We took the video chips out of ZEKE I and put them in the Ithaca board, so that the display on my big Hitachi 15" screen is identical to the old Zeke. I continue to use 16 lines of 64 characters to avoid eyestrain. Also, I'm used to it: after all, a standard manuscript has 60-character lines. A page is usually 25 or 26 lines, so I don't see a whole page at once; but I've noticed an unexpected benefit. Having only 16 lines on a screen tends to make me shorten my (usually too long) paragraphs.

We wanted to put in a 24 × 80 "write only memory" board, but we couldn't find one that would work at 6 mhz and had a nice display; if anyone knows of such a beast for the S-100 system, I'd appreciate the information.

Another really nice thing about Zeke II is the keyboard, which comes from an Archive computer. The Archive, incidentally, is the machine Dr. Arthur C. Clarke settled on. His is named "Archie." He got an Archive in part because he could get service for it in Sri Lanka. I'm sure, though, that he fell in love with the keyboard, and if I had to buy an Archive to get this keyboard I probably would. As it happens, Tony was able to obtain three or four of them.

The Archive has great key feel, a good non-electronic "click," and a really nice (Selectric style) key layout. The entire ASCII character set is on board along with arrows on the left side and a numeric key pad on the right.

There aren't any extraneous keys in odd places; and there are a lot of special purpose keys put up where you can get at them without their being in the way. The special purpose keys are really nice in that they make characters with the eighth bit set, so that we can make use of not only the entire range of control characters, but also more than a dozen additional one-stroke commands.

The Archive comes with a printed strip that translates the special function keys into WordStar commands, and I suppose the Archive machine itself takes advantage of those. Since I don't use WordStar, I had some work to do. Figuring out how to make good use of those keys was instructive; more below.

The bottom line is that callous as it may seem, I don't really miss Zeke. This new keyboard is fast and convenient, and the CompuPro disk drives are so much faster than the old iComs that I find myself saving my text far more often. Scrolling is smooth and lightning quick.

I do hope that Noor Singh can make Zeke work again; he's still better than half the junk I see out on the market, and it would be nice if others could get some good from him. Meanwhile, Zeke II is as close to being the "ideal" writing machine as I've ever worked with.

There are a few possible improvements. For one, there's no hard disk; but that's merely a matter of time. Tony has one and is refurbishing the software right now. A hard disk isn't strictly necessary anyway; with Direct Memory Access (DMA) disk controller and double-density disks, saving your text doesn't take very long; and for a writing machine, safety is the number one goal, meaning that you want the machine to make it easy to save early and often. (That's one major advantage of the MIT EMACS editor and its descendants: it can be set to automagically save text even if you don't think of it.)

DMA and high density speed up floppy disk operations something wonderful. Direct Memory Access is literally just that: the disk controller has an on-board microprocessor that can get at your system's memory without going through the regular CPU; that lets it do a faster job of getting stuff from memory and putting it on disk or *vice versa*.

Whether or not there's a hard disk, the ideal writing machine will need fast and reliable floppies. I don't feel really safe until my text is saved off on a disk and the disk has been removed from the machine.

A second limit to Zeke II is there's no "pseudo-disk," i.e. memory that's set up like a disk for fast access. Pseudo-disk ops are nice for spelling checking (as well as compiling and other computer operations). Of course if you have a hard disk you might not want a pseudo-disk as well.

I do have SemiDisk on my dual processor machine, and that would work fine in Zeke II; but CompuPro has announced that they're coming out with a Warp Drive that will work with the Z-80, and since almost everything else in Zeke II is Godbout CompuPro, I thought I'd wait for CompuPro's system. More on Warp Drive and SemiDisk below.

Finally, the Z-80 makes for a vanilla system; more advanced stuff is available. We have here an experimental board from Godbout that runs at *12 megaHerz!* That's *FAST*. However, for a writing machine you don't really need that much speed, and the Z-80 chip has been around long enough to have a track record. Zeke II is as near the state of the art as I'd (now) recommend for a system devoted mostly to text handling.

Terminal Switching

For a while it looked as if I'd be up to my clavicle in keyboards. Although it's possible to make Zeke II run with the 16 × 64 screen as his normal console (as well as when he's running the text editor), there are good reasons to want a 24 × 80 screen when you do programming. At the same time, I have the Televideo 950 nearby because that machine does nearly all our development work, and is also useful for checking spelling and the like.

I sure didn't want a second terminal for Zeke II, so I solved the problem with a "T-Switch" from INMAC. I suppose that requires a bit of explanation.

Computers talk to the outside world in two basic ways: "serial" and "parallel."

Parallel communication sends all the data bits of a single character at the same time. Parallel communication is inherently faster than serial; but it requires many wires (in an 8-bit machine at least ten and generally many more). Parallel is often electrically noisy, and usually more subject to errors induced by stray radio noise.

As an example, Mac Lean used parallel ports to connect his keyboard to Alice the Imsai, and when he began he used a flat ribbon cable. He got a lot of extraneous garbage into his computer. Eventually he converted to a round shielded cable and *most* of the errors vanished.

Centronics printers and other such devices generally use parallel communications. The distance they can be from the computer is limited—15 feet maximum.

The other system is "serial," in which the bits are sent one after another; an eight-bit character thus takes at least ten times as long to send in serial as it would in parallel. (That's not strictly true, but we'll ignore the fine details.)

Your computer has Input/Output "ports" built in as part of its basic structure. Those ports are parallel ports; it takes special hardware to convert from parallel to serial. However, serial signals can be sent further, with less noise. Most letter-quality printers, like the Diablo, and all telephone or modem communications, use the serial method.

There's more than one serial system, but by far the most popular in the micro world is called "RS-232." In theory there's an RS-232 standard; in practice that's *almost* true but not quite. However, it's true enough for T-switches to work.

Suppose you have several serial output devices—say a printer and a modem for communications—and only one RS-232 output port on your computer. Enter the T-Switch, which lets you connect both to the port and switch between them. Obviously only one is active at any given time. Now true, you could accomplish the same result by physically plugging and unplugging cables, but that's hard on the cables as well as darned inconvenient.

I'd only seen the T-Switch in advertisements, but it seemed a good idea; meanwhile, INMAC sent me a catalogue of their equipment for micros. I've ordered stuff from them before, and they're high-priced but speedy and reliable. Anyway, I bought a T-Switch, and the result is that the Televideo 950 can run both Zeke II and the Dual Processor. Actually, things are better than that: Tony has ingeniously set up the BIOS so that even after exiting from Write the Archive keyboard is active, so that I can run Zeke II on the Televideo 950 terminal, but continue to type on my splendid Archive board.

I love it.

[I am still writing on Zeke II; in fact, I'm writing *this* with him. He's not as chatty as Zeke I was, but he's utterly reliable. Meanwhile, Zeke I did achieve his ambition: he and Mac Lean's Alice were united into a single box, and they have lots of new friends to love them.

My wife tells me that one night I'll go to sleep at my keyboard, and awake to find a long message from Mac Lean. I can hardly wait.]

PART FOUR:
MOSTLY LANGUAGES

CHAPTER 1
The Great Language Debates

[From the earliest columns I was involved in animated discussion of which is the "best" computer language. Of course there is no answer to that; but the discussion is not meaningless, particularly for computer users who don't make a career of hacking.

There wasn't a lot of useful software in the early days. There were BIG programs, such as text editors, and dBase II, but computers can do a myriad of little tasks to save you time, if only you can teach the machine to do it. The problem is that you have to write the programs yourself.

Actually, that's not a problem: hacking computer programs can be enormously enjoyable. It's a particularly welcome break from writing. I will not soon forget the afternoons I put into puttering about learning computer languages; my wife asked what I'd been doing, and when I had no answer—I didn't really know what I was doing, mucking about was as good a description as I could come up with—she was furious because I'd wasted so much time.

In fact, though, it turned out to be some of the most valuable work I've ever done: I jumped with both feet into the great computer languages debate, and that proved enormously popular. It has also been controversial.

Aside: "hacking," like many other colorful computerese terms, originated at MIT. The derivation is from an Eastern European expression implying crudity: someone who makes furniture with an axe. However, within much of the computer community, to be a "hacker" was to be skillful, capable of getting the job done without too much concern for theoretical niceties.

I conceived the language debate as a way of informing my readers, particularly users; but it soon became heated because of the attitudes of hackers. Disparaging a computer scientist's favorite language—and more especially a computer science *student's* favorite language—is somewhat less tolerable than telling racial or religious jokes. Nonetheless, the debate remains important to this day.

The language issue has always been an important part of the *User's Column*; but the debate really began to heat up with columns nine and ten, written just after I had gone to the West Coast Computer Faire in 1981. It also became apparent that my editors thought me, uh, well, a person of strong opinions: my columns began to appear with subtitles such as "A Veteran Computer User Voices His Opinions," and graduated from there to things like "Unaccustomed as he is to giving opinions, our veteran user drops a few hints...."

I can't for the life of me see where they got that idea.

The second round of the language debates began calmly enough....

PASCAL, ANYONE?

My son Alex is a senior in computer science at the University of California at San Diego. Since they developed UCSD Pascal there, you will understand that he's become fairly proficient in it.

When we got the Godbout 8085/88 running here, Alex undertook to write some utilities for me, using the Sorcim Pascal-M on the new Godbout machine. Consequently, I had the fascinating experience of watching someone familiar with computers and Pascal, but unfamiliar with CP/M, trying to get programs running. So, as it happens, did Barry Workman, who happened to be over (he's an Assistant Scoutmaster in the Boy Scout troop my younger boys belong to).

There was no problem with Pascal itself. The Sorcim documentation is adequate for that, provided that you're fairly familiar with Pascal.

Hooking to CP/M was another story. Of course Pascal is notoriously deficient in Input/Output to begin with, and it's not so hot in handling strings; but the Sorcim Pascal has implemented a "feature" that sometimes makes things even worse. When Sorcim Pascal looks at a file using the "read line" Pascal command, *it ignores line feeds.*

A story goes with that. ASCII, while nice enough to work with in many respects, has one defect: there's no NEWLINE character. Instead, there are CARRIAGE RETURN and LINE FEED, two separate characters which together give you a NEWLINE. Many programs will insert a line feed when they see a carriage return. Others will not. All have to deal with this somehow. Sorcim Pascal-M solves the problem by ignoring line feeds altogether.

Now this is a Good Thing under certain circumstances, because some text editors (WordMaster, WordStar) put both carriage return and line feed into the text, while others (Electric Pencil, Magic Wand, Write) insert carriage returns only. (To make the confusion more complete, Electric Pencil marks the ends of paragraphs when you hit the line feed key; but the mark it actually inserts in the text is not a line feed, but a carriage return!) In any event, what appear to be identical files can be different, depending on the editor that created them, and what is the poor Pascal programmer to do? So the Sorcim solution is as good as any, except—

Unfortunately, Sorcim has not provided a way to turn this feature off; so that if you want to make an exact copy of a file, you must go through massive contortions to test for whether or not there were line feeds in the original file.

Now the way I intended to learn Pascal was to go through the excellent book *Software Tools in Pascal* by Kernighan and Plauger, and implement all their utilities as I come to them; and alas, one of the first utilities was a COPY utility, and what do I do about the line feed and carriage return problem? Worse, none of that is explained in either Kernighan and Plauger, or in the Pascal-M documentation. (The fact that their read line utility ignores line feeds is told to you; the consequences, and the way to get around it if you want to see if there were line feeds, is not.)

Eventually Alex managed a way around the problem, and after that he turned out programs in rapid-fire order. He'll shortly have written a really good text formatter and printer that will do everything but wash the dishes; the basic program and most of its features work now.

He also got many of the programs from Kernighan and Plauger running, and for good measure, set me up some of the demonstration programs from Peter Grogorno's really excellent *Programming in Pascal* so that *they* work with CP/M. The result is that I can now use Kernighan and Plauger, and Grogorno, as tutorial guides to learning the Pascal language.

And they're really good. I can learn more in a couple of hours of playing about with those books and getting the programs up than I can in a week of reading; and when I'm through, I often have useful utilities as well.

At this point enter Barry Workman. "That's worth something," he said. "There are lots of people who want to learn Pascal and get discouraged because they don't know where to start. You take those programs Alex did, and his notes, and your notes on how to use them and where to start, and the two books, and you've got a complete guide to learning the language."

"Not me," said I. "I write books for a living, and articles for fun, and programs for a hobby, and I'm damned if I'll get into the software publishing business."

"But I'm in the software publishing business," said Barry. "At least by default." (His normal business is consulting on new installations, but he's slowly built up the mail order publishing end as a sideline.) "Let me put that out for you...."

So. Workman offers a package deal on learning Pascal. The disk with Alex's programs (sources and notes), and my notes on what I thought I needed to know, is available with an error analysis package and some other materials, and whether or not it's worth it depends entirely on how badly you want to learn Pascal, and how much of a duffer you are when you begin work. I can truthfully say I wish I'd had the package when I started; it would have saved me a week and perhaps more. But it is not the Earth. You'll still need to work.

SOFTWARE TOOLS

Not too long after Ezekial, my friend who happens to be a Z-80 computer, came to live here at Chaos Manor, my (alas, late) mad friend brought me a book: *Software Tools*, by Brian W. Kernighan and P. J. Plauger (Addison-Wesley). Those were the days when I insisted I was monumentally uninterested in learning to be a programmer. "I only want to *use* the machines," I insisted. "I don't care how programs work."

"You'll want to learn," Mac Lean said. "So here's a painless way to get started. Read it. Hell, you know one of the authors."

It happened that I already admired Bill Plauger's work as a science fiction writer. Even so I was reluctant to get started. Wisely, Mac Lean insisted; one of the many great favors he did for me, and one of the countless reasons I'll continue to miss him for a long time.

Software Tools is one of those books you simply can't get along without if you're serious about learning to program. As Kernighan and Plauger say many times, you learn to write good programs by reading and studying good programs; and they show you a book full of them. The original edition of the book presents RATFOR, "rational FORTRAN"; an attempt to make a good language out of FORTRAN by adding UNTIL, WHILE, CASE, and other requirements of structured programs. Way back in the back of the book they also give you a RATFOR pre-compiler which takes programs using the RATFOR conventions and turns them into reasonable FORTRAN.

The book is full of illustrative programs, and most of them are quite useful. They fit together into a set of "software tools," mostly for text processing, but including a macro expander and other stuff useful for programmers. Their text editor is a bit out of date, but there's a lot in there that I thirsted for the instant I read the book.

There's a problem, though. Although I learned a bit about FORTRAN in the old days ('60s), and have Microsoft FORTRAN for my Z-80, FORTRAN isn't really a very good language for micro computers. Its string handling capabilities are ghastly. There's no BEGIN-END to let you do several things following IF-THEN. The dreaded FORMAT statement doesn't really make sense for today's Input/Output, and FORTRAN was really designed to work with 80-column lines, preferably from cards (so was Pascal; more on that later). The structure of FORTRAN, even with RATFOR, doesn't really encourage writing readable programs. It seemed to me that FORTRAN was a language whose time had passed, and I wasn't willing to invest a lot of time in getting it running properly on Ezekial.

Neither was Mac Lean, and thus I read Kernighan and Plauger but never actually ran their programs. When the CPM Users Group put out the tools on one of their disks, we made an abortive attempt, because this was, after all, back in the dark ages when there weren't many modern languages for micros. You couldn't get C, and the only Pascal was the old version of UCSD (my son Alex who's a senior there pronounces that Scud) Pascal. There was no LISP, WordStar didn't exist, and a micro version of PL/I was only a gleam in Digital Research's eye. There wasn't even an affordable FORTH. As I said, the dark ages. So we seriously considered RATFOR as the language to learn; but we had trouble hooking it into CP/M, and about then we became enamoured of Pascal, there being promised a number of micro versions Real Soon Now. Thus, although I did try to get RATFOR going a couple of times, nothing useful came of it.

That disturbed me, because the idea of "software tools" is a very good one. You take a number of things you want to do, such as finding text patterns in files, archiving files, that sort of thing; build programs to accomplish this in modular blocks; and not only do you have useful programs, but you also have a number of procedures and subroutines and functions you can lift out and put into other programs, either by incorporating the code into the source, or by keeping the "tools" compiled into relocatable machine language for linking in. That way you don't have to reinvent the wheel every month or so.

It all sounded great, especially back then when I had more time to just play around; and every now and then I'd read *Software Tools* with a sigh of regret that I'd never got them running.

That's all changed now.

Comes now Unicorn Systems, which has formed a Software Tools Users' Group, and, more to the point, will sell you the whole box of tools carefully rigged to run with CP/M. They also furnish a lot of documents, including a tutorial.

Unicorn has even put a Unix-like shell around CP/M. For example, if you want to use the "FIND" tool to scan the file "SYSTEM.TXT" for all instances of the word LOBO, you type:

FIND <SYSTEM.TXT LOBO

and all lines in the file SYSTEM.TXT containing the word "LOBO" will appear on the console. Note the <, which indicates input source. If you typed:

FIND <SYSTEM.TXT LOBO >FOO.DAT

then the program would create file FOO.DAT and put the output into that. Very convenient, and there's a whole raft of Unix-like extensions and features built into their shell. It would take most of the column to describe them all.

In addition to the tools and the shell to make CP/M friendlier, you get a spelling program, and of course you get RATFOR, including the source which is written in RATFOR. With the Unicorn package and a FORTRAN compiler you could write a lot of awfully useful programs.

The Unicorn package is a class act: a thick looseleaf binder full of fairly well-organized information, and two plastic boxes containing 15, count them, 15 disks of software tools and sources. Incidentally, their system WILL NOT run on CP/M 1.4; you MUST be using 2.0 or later.

So. A few years ago I'd have been slavering for a chance at something like this, and when at the West Coast Faire Deborah Sherrer, the principal author of most of this stuff, gave me the choice of carrying the package home on an airplane or having it mailed to me, I chose to carry it, bulky as it all was, rather than chance losing it. But, alas, the excitement turned out to be residual; when I got home I didn't do much with it, and haven't yet.

And that's sad. Unicorn has gone to a lot of work to produce something useful, well-packaged, well-documented, and bug-free, and to try to write it up so that beginners can understand it. They succeeded, too. People like them ought to get all the encouragement this profession can give them, and I hope they sell a lot of their packages. Lord knows they're charging no more than a fair price. But—

The problem is that I still think RATFOR and FORTRAN both are languages whose time has passed, especially for micros. Thus, while the Unicorn package plus Kernighan and Plauger are terrific for teaching RATFOR, I can't recommend spending much time learning it. It's outdated.

And so, I fear, are most of the software tools. The Kernighan and Plauger editor beats the daylights out of CP/M's ED, but then what doesn't? ED is only a little better than a Selectric II typewriter. The Software Tools editor was great in its day, but it's line oriented, not full screen, and anyone who's using a line oriented editor in this day and age probably chases down geese to get the makings for fountain pens. Some of the other tools, like FIND, are useful, but ye gods, FIND.COM is a 29K file, and it doesn't run very fast, either. Ditto for most of the other tools: too big, too cumbersome, too slow—and written in the wrong language.

If you really want to use the Software Tools—and they are indeed useful foundations to build on—then you probably want them in a language you speak, not in FORTRAN.

Which brings me to a mild conflict of interest, so I want to make sure you all understand a possible bias on my part.

In my judgment, Unicorn has done a great job, and I really encourage them—but if you want the Software Tools, my recommendation is that you build your own set in Pascal or C. Kernighan and Plauger have put out *Software Tools in Pascal*, a book functionally identical to the original (all the old programs are in it, except, of course, the RATFOR compiler). My son Alex has put together a disk of the first couple of chapters' worth of the programs together with the primitives and inclusion files needed to get the Tools running under either Sorcim Pascal M or Digital Research Pascal MT+. He's added the introductory programs from Peter Grogono's book *Programming in Pascal*, and then he and Barry Workman ganged up to induce me to add my own comments. The result isn't anywhere near as complete as what Unicorn furnishes. If you want *all* the Software Tools to run in Pascal you'll have to type in a number of them yourself; but that's the way I recommend you go, because with the Workman package you learn a language you can build your own tools with.

The Unicorn package, though more complete, leads you toward RATFOR and FORTRAN, which are not ways I'd encourage you to go. On the other hand, Unicorn does give you a nifty CP/M shell you can use to get the feel of Unix, and of course there are all the tools and some interesting extensions already compiled and ready for use. If you do plan to use FORTRAN in future, the Unicorn deal is the best bargain in town.

(Unicorn Systems has since changed its name to CAROUSEL Systems. I don't know why. They continue to offer the Software Tools including sources.)

THE HOLLERITH CARD BLUES

A while back I mentioned that FORTRAN expects its input from 80-column cards. If you use Unicorn's package of Software Tools on text files created by Write, WordStar, or Magic Wand, what the Tools think is a line can cause some pretty strange results. Alas, it's true for many other languages. We will regret the legacy of the Hollerith card for a very long time.

Take Pascal as an example. ISO (International Standards Organization) Pascal has no strings at all. Most implementations put in strings as an extension—but they do it in a way that cripples the language. Pascal M and Pascal MT+ follow the UCSD Pascal system in which the longest string you can have is 255 characters. There's nothing you can do about it, because these Pascal implementations store the string length as a single byte put in front of the string. The Input situation is even worse: micro Pascals can't grab lines longer than 255 characters, and indeed the implementations I'm familiar with truncate line inputs to 80 character lines unless you explicitly tell it differently.

None of this is a problem for text processing if you're using a line oriented editor, each line 80 characters long terminated with a NEWLINE (which in ASCII is also a problem since that's two characters, not one, but we'll leave that for another time). Suppose, however, you want a modern full screen editor, one which leaves the line lengths variable and only marks the ends of paragraphs. One like Write, the editor I use. What now?

Well, of course you can get around that, and Alex shows how in his PASCAL INTRODUCTION PACKAGE. He gives you two ways. Neither is very elegant, but we don't know any elegant methods. One Alex uses is to get your input one character at a time, which works fine but slows things down a lot. The other is a small machine language program that "standardizes" your text files by making a copy with paragraphs broken up into lines of 80 characters or less, using different characters to mark the (artificial) "line ends" from those used to mark paragraph endings. This grabs Write,

Pencil, and Magic Wand files, and runs about as fast as PIP. The various Pascal tools run *much* faster on files passed through this filter, since the programs can now get their input by "lines."

Or you can shelve it all and learn C, or even Digital Research's CB-80 (the compiling version of CBASIC). We've done a few preliminary comparisons of CB80 and Pascal, and they're closer than I expected on both speed and final program code size. We're doing some experiments on that, and we'll have the results in a few weeks.

One reason Alex didn't try CB80 sooner was that CB80 had a ghastly license agreement that required you to pay $2,000 a year, up front before you could sell programs compiled with the language; but they dropped that some time ago.

CB80 has some terrific advantages for text processing, because it can read a "line" of up to 31,000 characters in length, yet you don't have to allocate an enormous buffer to do that. CB80 takes care of that dynamically, so all you must have is enough free memory to put the string in. It then grabs everything up to and including the carriage return, and ignores the line feed character at the end. Now that the licensing of CB80 is rational, I predict a rash of text processing programs using it will come out.

I showed this to Tony Pietsch, and he got another brainstorm; a way to overlay Write so that it will put out text in any format you like, including lines of 64 or 80 characters terminated by a cr-lf (carriage return, line feed) pair. I wouldn't be surprised to have that in a couple of weeks; when Tony gets to working, he works hard.

GOOD STUFF AT LOW COST

The idea of "Software Tools" has wide appeal, and I presume that the Kernighan and Plauger book was responsible for Walt Bilofsky's naming his company "The Software Toolworks". From the address, he's a neighbor, but in fact I never met him until the West Coast Computer Faire.

Bilofsky began by filling a much-needed niche as supplier of programs to the Heath market before converting them to CP/M, and it shows: many of his programs run best with a Z-19 terminal, and some, like his graphics package, won't run without one. (Lately, though, he's gotten heavily into programs for the Osborne.)

Bilofsky sells a wide range of programs, all at low cost (generally under $50.00), and all the ones I've tried are excellent. His ED-A-SKETCH for the Z-19 (and the Osborne), for example, will let you draw and save all kinds of fancy stuff. His PIE Full Screen Editor (also only for the Z-19 terminal), while no Magic Wand or Write, is certainly more than worth the $29.95 he charges. I haven't tried his spelling checker ($49.95 with 50,000 word dictionary equivalent; runs on the Osborne) but if it works as well as his other stuff does it has to be a bargain.

He'll also sell you Eliza, that rather stupid psychiatrist program, for $24.95 (CP/M or Osborne). You'll get tired of Eliza pretty quick, but it is a nice thing to have next time someone asks you to demonstrate your computer at a party.

There are also games (including MYCHESS for the Osborne), and more to the point of this column, languages, including RATFOR for Microsoft FORTRAN (keyed to the Software Tools book); a LISP interpreter; and a C compiler. I somewhat prefer Zolman's BDS C, if for no other reason than the extensive documentation and library utilities that come with the BDS package, but the Software Toolworks program compiles to 8080 assembly language, meaning that you can get in and hand optimize important loops if you need to. It's fast, and I may well end up writing some operating utilities in it.

Things have been a bit hectic here at Chaos Manor, so we haven't had a chance to try all of Bilofsky's programs; but we've tested several, and all work as advertised, and I strongly recommend his philosophy and approach. By all means get his catalog; for sound programs at very reasonable costs, Software Toolworks is hard to beat.

[That remains good advice: Bilofsky's Software Toolworks supplies good stuff at low cost, and no software addict can be without his catalog.]

THEM OLD BDOS BLUES

I suppose I don't have to say that all in all I like CP/M; but there are times when I grow *very* weary of its flaws. It gets particularly annoying when there might be a hardware problem. 'BDOS ERROR ON B: Bad Sector' isn't very informative when you know you can get that message because of any one of a dozen reasons.

I suppose one reason CP/M hasn't annoyed me as much as it does most is that I've always had Tony Pietsch's protective software. Ezekial, for example, has a very large PROM (Programmable Read Only Memory) monitor which looks at everything and has *very* complete diagnostic messages. Thus when I forget and leave Zeke's drive doors open and try to save something, he says, "PLEASE CLOSE DRIVE DOOR," and when I close the doors he goes on as if there'd never been a problem.

Unfortunately, the CBIOS (Customized Basic Input Output System) supplied by Bill Godbout with his 8085/8088 isn't anywhere *near* that friendly, as I found out the other day while doing my taxes. I was entering stuff into my journal, which is a CBASIC program, and my wife called me to dinner. I didn't expect to be long—during tax time at Chaos Manor *everyone* avoids me—so I opened the drive doors and left the Godbout running. When I returned I made some more entries, then tried to save the enlarged file, and like an idiot I used the same file name that I'd used before. And, alas, I hadn't closed the drive doors.

BDOS ERROR ON A: Select Error, it said to me. "Bah," I replied. "It's an open drive door." And unthinkingly I closed the drive door. Whereupon it proceeded to completely clobber my file and thoroughly crash the system.

Fortunately I'd thought of that one long ago when I wrote the Journal program: the actual entries are in files called "JORNL-21" and the like, while the first thing the program tries to write is a summary file called "JRSUM-21" that contains only summary stuff like the number of entries and heading data. It's easy enough to recreate the JRSUM file and thereby save the data in the JORNL file. But it's still infuriating to have to do it.

"You've had it too easy," Tony said. "You're used to my software."

"I know that," I said. "But what do I do *now*?"

"Well, I've done a new CBIOS for the Godbout . . ."

Meaning that open drive doors no longer crash my system. I'm encouraging Tony to send a copy of the new CBIOS to Bill Godbout so others can have that benefit also. I hope he'll do it. The only problem is that he doesn't want to maintain the thing and answer hundreds of questions from users.

He's also taken care of that in Write, Writers Really Incredible Text Editor, which he keeps improving monthly. With Write you can leave the drive doors open, change disks, put in full disks, put in disks with bad media, and WRITE still recovers.

Or tries to. The problem is that Tony can't be responsible for your CBIOS, and if that's not well written, there may not be anything the program can do.

There are only three error messages in CP/M: "Select Error," meaning that the system can't find the drive it's trying to write to; "Bad Sector," meaning that it can't perform whatever operation it's trying to do, like read or write a sector; and "R/O," which means that the directory doesn't match the bit map; that may be because you didn't go control-c after changing disks, but sometimes means either the disk or the directory are full up.

None of them should be fatal. With careful study of CP/M you *ought* to be able to return control to your program. Tony catches stupid errors, such as doors open and the like, in the CBIOS; while the people at Sorcim told him how to let programs recover from other BDOS errors. Unfortunately, most programmers don't know enough about CP/M to do that, and CP/M documentation, including all the books I've seen on the subject, isn't helpful.

The trick—which is NOT supported by Digital Research, and in fact is specifically forbidden in the CP/M documentation—is absurdly simple. In CP/M, location 00 has a jump instruction, and in locations 001 and 002 is the address of the "warm start;" the place in memory you go to do the equivalent of control-c. The Digital Research documents say that this *must* be left unchanged; but in fact, CP/M 1.4 and 2.2 NEVER call that location unless there is a BDOS ERROR.

All of which means that a clever programmer can snatch that warm start location, store it, and put into locations 001 and 002 the address of an error trap routine. On exiting the program you put the warm start address back. If none of this makes any sense to you, don't worry about it; what I'm doing is giving out some underground information for those who can make use of it; and I repeat, this is not supported by Digital, and there are no guarantees that future releases of CP/M (or MP/M) will be compatible with this recovery method.

Also, if your CBIOS is incompetently done, then programmers can't compensate. Alas, there is more than one incompetent **CBIOS** floating around. There are even companies which won't give you the *source* of your CBIOS. If you've been unfortunate to get yours from one of those, you have my sympathy; and my advice, which is to think again before dealing with a company that withholds vital information. The CBIOS matches your particular hardware to the general CP/M operating system, and if it isn't well done—or you can't modify it—then you can be in big trouble.

The potential for error recovery is inherent in CP/M, because the bit map—which tells precisely where the various chunks of your files are hidden—and the directory are right there together, and both are updated quickly and efficiently each time you go control-C, or each time your program makes the appropriate call to accomplish the same thing. Write, for example, does the equivalent of control-C before *every* read or write operation; thus it's always working with an up-to-date bit map, and can cope with changes of disk and the like. (Remember, Tony put Write together from specs furnished by Larry Niven and me; and we're *very* paranoid about losing text, so Write is extremely defensive; and since Larry and I often write with, uh, lots of brandy for the coffee, Write has to be tolerant of operator errors as well.)

But despite the fact that clever programmers can overcome many CP/M flaws, we still have a problem: CP/M, our de facto "standard," has got holes you can drive a truck through. The question before the house is, are they doing anything to fix them? When we get our 16-bit and 32-bit machines, must we endure more **BDOS ERROR ON X. R/O** when we know darned well the disk isn't Read Only because you physically removed the Write Protect mechanism from the disk drive?

CP/M is a good operating system; but there are some improvements needed. We can hope Digital Research will make them. If not—well, think of it as evolution in action. . . .

UTILITIES

I hope CP/M cleans up its act. Meanwhile, I have a temporary solution to some of the problems.

First, if you're not getting the public domain CP/M utilities, either "raw" from the CPM Users Group or "filtered" through someone like Barry Workman, you ought to do something about it.

And more good news: CP/M will give you a reasonably well-formatted directory OR tell you file sizes; it won't do both. You can, however, get XDIR or XD which will. Both have long been available from CPMUG, and Workman furnishes versions for both 1.4 and 2.x on his utility disk one. But there's better news.

Tony Pietsch has just written a real doozy of an XDIR that lets you put in wild card characters (XD *.FOO will list all and only those files with an extension of FOO), optionally allows you to alphabetize by extension (groups all the .ASM files, then the .COM files, etc., with the file names alphabetized within each extension); tells you the number of K each file takes up; tells you what user number is logged on; will show you the directory of ANOTHER USER without your having to log on as that user; tells you how many director entries and how many K remain on that disk; and does it all speedily and efficiently. It's the equivalent of STAT in usefulness and reliability. There's even an XD.DOC file you can call for help. I can't imagine how I got along without it. Tony wrote it for me, Larry, and himself; you can get it and some other stuff from Barry Workman on his Utility Disk Four.

[Workman continues to distribute a number of CP/M utilities, some drawn from public domain, others written for him. Many have been improved since I wrote this.]

M&N'S, AND ARE YOU A COMPILER?

[One of the nicest discoveries at Chaos Manor was the "RAM Drive," a method of fooling your computer into thinking that a lot of memory is a very fast—if somewhat temporary—disk drive. In the early days, there were only two reliable manufacturers of RAM Drive: the Godbout CompuPro system, which used extra memory in an S-100 8085/8088 Dual Processor computer, and required all CompuPro equipment, including the Dual Processor; and Semi-Disk, which made a dedicated board useful *only* as a RAM disk. I had both in my Dual Processor, with the CompuPro Memory Drive labelled a "M:" and the Semi-Disk as "N:".

They sure made life easier.]

I've previously mentioned my Godbout Warp Drive, which

we've designated drive "M," and SemiDisk, which became drive "N." For the few who don't know, these are two different schemes for fooling your computer into thinking that a big block of memory is a disk drive. I doubt that I've sufficiently praised them. Both Godbout's Warp Drive and the SemiDisk system work so well that you don't notice them.

The Godbout system is marginally faster than N drive, and the Godbout memory can be used as RAM for your 8088 when you use your 8085/88 that way; but it requires a Godbout disk controller and an 8085/88 CPU. Meanwhile, SemiDisk is plenty fast enough, and can be used with *any* CP/M 2.2 S-100 bus sytem, no matter what the controller and CPU. And having them can change the way you do things.

There are times when I am willing to take Pascal and stuff the language into a culvert. There are truly times when I completely agree with my late mad friend, who thought Pascal useful for classroom exercises, particularly in places that didn't have computers for the students to work with, but not much use for practical programming. Lately I've been helping my son Alex and his classmates work on the Workman Associates Intro to Pascal package: they're taking standard programs out of standard textbooks, such as Peter Grogono's *Programming in Pascal* and the Kernighan and Plauger classic *Software Tools in Pascal* and getting them to run with the Digital Research Pascal MT+ and the Sorcim Pascal/M compilers. And the job is driving me nuts. Alex and his friends will *earn* every nickel they make.

Pascal really and truly expects the programmer to be a sort of pre-compiler. Consider error messages like "Error number 6: Illegal symbol (possibly missing ',' on line above)," and "Error number 51: ':=' expected." In Pascal MT+ they even show you precisely where this stuff was expected, and usually the compiler is right about the guesses, too.

So why doesn't the compiler simply *supply the needed symbol*? Especially when it found "=" where it expected ":=?" Now it's true that you don't want to depend on the compiler to do your thinking for you. You really ought to go correct the program. But I don't see why it can't give you the exact same error message, plus say "Following assumption implemented:" and show you what it did, then continue with the compilation. That way it would catch nearly all the trivial errors in one pass, and you could then go back and correct them all at once rather than load the editor, add a semicolon, exit the editor, compile until the next trivial error, etc., *ad nauseum.*

We have both M and N drives (on the same machine; if you go PIP M:=N:*.* the result is blindingly fast) and thus the cycle isn't so long for us; after all, the "disk access" times are pretty short, so we're not waiting for the editor or the compiler to load, or the editor to write to disk. I think I would probably have given up on Pascal without them.

It isn't just the trivial errors that make Pascal hard to use. Although the compiler's intolerance for trivial mistakes seems to me a mistake, one assumes that study and practice will overcome that. Nor am I certain precisely what is wrong; but here I'm watching students who've been working with Pascal for four years take hours and hours to debug programs copied from a standard textbook recommended by the compiler writer. That's portability?

I suppose I shouldn't complain. Alex expects to make a lot of money off his Pascal lessons. When he first started working on the concept I wasn't sure it would be worth what Workman said he'd have to charge; but that was before I got involved in helping out. That is: Alex had some exams coming up, so I volunteered to type in a couple of Grogono programs and get them running. They were, after all, simple programs, and all that was needed was to copy them out of a book; an hour or two of typing, and perhaps an hour of debugging. . . .

Hah. Didn't work that way at all. First, even with SemiDisk it took longer than I'd have thought to get rid of all the trivial errors. Then the fun really began. There are more obscure errors and faults in Pascal than you can dream of, even if you spend weeks studying a good introductory text like Grogono's.

For example: "Error number 253: Procedure (or program body) too long. Reduce the size of the procedure and try again."

Search the index in Grogono, Digital's MT+ documentation, and Sorcim's Pascal/M document. Nary a word about this, or at least none I can find. Programs that will compile in MT+ give you error 253 in Pascal/M. Get that fixed, by taking a number of messages that are delivered only once and putting them into a Procedure although it's a bit silly to call a subroutine just to read the instruction messages. Of course the procedure was (trivially) wrong the first couple of times.

Then the random number generator Grogono uses won't work, because he uses the integer 65536. Mike Lehman, who wrote Pascal MT+, told me on the phone to simply change that to 65536.0, thus changing it into a floating point number; but that doesn't work either, because Pascal will not do implicit type conversion, and we needed the MOD (get the remainder) function, and Pascal won't let you do the MOD function unless you're dividing by an integer. . . .

So write a "getremainder" procedure, only that runs into conflicts of variable types, so——

So we wrote a different random number generator, and went through the Grogono program to document where and why we changed variables from integers to reals, and after about three times as much time and work as I'd expected that program is done. There are a lot more like that in the package Alex did; and if you don't know Pascal and intend to learn it, I *strongly* advise you to buy the Workman package: compiler, the Grogono book, the Software tools book, and Alex's lesson disk. That way you won't waste so much time with trivial error hunting, and you can get down to the business of playing with those programs, and modifying them, and using the more useful ones.

And if your time is at all valuable, get either Warp Drive or SemiDisk. The slower your floppies the more dramatic the result, but even with fast disks like Qume DT-8's run by a Godbout controller the time saved adds up fast.

CB80 REVISITED

There is an alternative: Digital Research's CB80, which is compiled CBASIC. Our tests so far show that CB80 is pretty comparable to Pascal MT+ in speed and compactness of code. It's *reasonably* easy to patch in assembly language subroutines in CB80, so that you can optimize loops and stuff that you use all the time. There's a new version with an improved linker that's supposed to make that even simpler; I'll have it in a couple of weeks, and I can report on it then.

Despite my mad friend's misgivings about all forms of BASIC, CB80, in my judgment, remains a real competitor to Pascal and PL/I. It won't write code as fast or as compact as C, but then few higher level languages will; and it's a lot easier to learn than C. I suspect, in fact, that my mad friend would salve his anti-BASIC prejudice by pronouncing that

CB80 isn't "real" BASIC at all, but instead a separate new language.

He'd have a point, too, since CB80 has few of the inherent defects of BASIC. With CB80 you can have truly local variables within functions and procedures, and call them either by label or by value: that is, you can hand the procedure the actual value of the variable it is to work with, letting it create a variable that's local to the procedure so that whatever it does cannot change the "real" variable out in the main program; or you can write the procedure so that it manipulates global variables and affects everything. True, CB80 doesn't name its multi-line functions "procedures;" but they have all the attributes of a Pascal procedure, can be called by name, and in some ways are easier to use.

Bottom line: I'm still thinking about the language problem; I don't think anyone knows which will be—or *should* be—the microcomputer language of the future. But now that CB80 is available without unduly restrictive licensing agreements, I wouldn't count it out.

[Many readers concluded from the above that I really hated the Pascal language. Perhaps they could fairly conclude that; I hadn't intended them to, though. I didn't stuff Pascal into a culvert, I merely said there were times when I felt like it. Oh. Well.]

CHAPTER 2
The Debates Continue

[The next column on the language debates attracted more mail than all my previous columns had. It was rated as the most popular article in that issue (October, 1982) of *BYTE*, and, since back issues of *BYTE* are still sold in some computer stores, I *still* get mail on the subject. I suppose this book will generate more.

In addition, my "Benchmark of Sorts" has become something of a standard test of both languages and machines. It should not be confused with the *"BYTE"* benchmark, which employs a number-sorting algorithm called "Eratosthenes's Sieve;" the *BYTE* Benchmark became popular, but now most programs and many machines are written in such a way as to run that program efficiently. My "Benchmark of Sorts," being based on floating point arithmetical operations, seems more useful as a measure of the practical speed of a machine; but that, I hasten to add, is my view. It has been widely employed.]

The Dangers of Using BASIC
I can practically guarantee some angry letters as a result of this column. Today's question is: Are *all* BASIC programmers brain-damaged, or only some of them? It's a topic of more importance than you think, so we'll sneak up on it.

A BENCHMARK, MORE OR LESS

I'm involved in a couple of computer nets, and one of them has an excellent on-going discussion of the future of small computers. The other night one of my net correspondents mentioned a benchmark he'd used, and the more I thought about it, the better I liked it.

Designing benchmarks is a black art, and one I decline to get too deeply into; but it seems reasonable to have standard ways to compare program speeds. The danger, of course, is in losing one's sense of proportion so that a few seconds in speed difference is promoted into an absolute judgment that one program or language is "better" than another. Obviously, speed is only one of many criteria for determining software worth, particularly when it comes to languages.

Anyway, what my colleague on the net wanted was a program with a minimum of Input-Output (IO). It should spend most of its time in computations, not peripherals. The benchmark he advocated was to create two 10 × 10 matrices and multiply them. I thought about that a while and modified it. What I ended with was a bit more general, in that the size of the matrices isn't fixed, and while I was at it I put in a check sum to be sure the machine got the right answer. The program is given below in both BASIC and Pascal.

After we generated the benchmark program, we ran it for a number of different languages. The results are given in Table One; the programs were all run on the Godbout 8085/8088 Dual Processor with 5 mH. 8085 and 6mH. 8088.

There are some surprises. I'd always thought BASCOM was considerably faster than CB80. Indeed, the first time I ran these tests, I got spurious results that showed just that, and my error is instructive.

My test programs for MBASIC, BASCOM and CB80 are as nearly identical as I can make them. Unfortunately, there's an obscure bug in my present version of CB80: if the first statement in the program is a REM statement AND has a line number, then CB80 cannot compile DECLARATIONS that immediately follow. Obscure or not, that bug stopped me from being able to declare my various indices (in the matrix expression A(I,J), the I & J are *index* variables or indices) as integers; I had to leave them as reals (floating point numbers). This so slowed CB80 that I'm almost ashamed to report the times, which were closer to interpretive MBASIC than BASCOM.

I called Digital Research and got CB80's inventor Gordon Eubanks, and we walked through the program together and discovered the bug, which will be fixed in future CB80 releases.

Meanwhile, if you try to compile this with CB80, eliminate the line number before the first REM statement, and declare I, J, K, L, M, N, as integers. I did, and with integer indices CB80 is as fast as BASCOM.

(Note: I've found a few other ways to foul up CB80 so that it won't compile DECLARATIONS. I've told Digital Research, and I expect they'll be fixed by the time you read this; Gordon Eubanks is as fond of CB80 as most people are of their children, and I doubt he'll allow any flaws to remain long.)

I also compiled the program under two different Pascals and CBASIC86. In the latter case I used CPM86 in my Godbout 8085/8088 Dual Processor. More on CBASIC86 and the Pascals later. Meanwhile, the program run times may be informative.

SPEED VS. CONVENIENCE

"I've already written at length comparing pseudocompiled CBASIC to interpretive MBASIC. Both have strong and weak points. Except for price, though, now that CB80 is available there's little to recommend CBASIC; if you're going to endure the inconvenience of a compiled language, you might as well go on and buy the real thing. CB80 costs a good bit more, but it has many added features, and it's *fast*.

Once of CBASIC's inconveniences is that you can't declare any variables. If you want a variable to be an integer, you must end its name with a % sign. Since CBASIC distinguishes between the variables I and I%, this can make for rather strange bugs in your program. Fortunately they give you a cross reference program; judiciously used that can spot many otherwise obscure errors. If you see a variable named "TRUE" when you've only tested against "TRUE%," you know you're in trouble. If you look at the benchmark times, you'll see that it's worth a *lot* to use integer variables in CBASIC.

[In the past few years, CBASIC has declined in popularity, while Digital Research has continued to improve what used to be called CB80, and is now known as "Compiling CBASIC." There are considerable problems with "Compiling CBASIC," as will be shown below, but it remains a pretty good language for programming; I must confess that most of my useful programs have been written in it. Compiling CBASIC is portable: there are CPM-80, CPM-86, and PC-DOS versions, and all will compile the same source code.

It still has the problem that there is no interpretative version. Bruce Tonkin, whose PBASIC will be described below, swears by Microsoft BASIC and their BASIC Compiler called BASCOM. Fair warning, though: Tonkin is a true hacker, who uses highly sophisticated techniques involving pointers and the like; what he can do is well beyond my capabilities.]

If CBASIC and CB80 have problems, so do the other languages. BASCOM and the Pascals have one very flawed "feature" in common: neither will allow you to input array sizes. Arrays must be dimensioned during compilation. I think Miscrosoft admits that's a bug; the Pascal designers seem to think it's a desirable feature.

That is: in Pascal, you must dimension when you compile. Like Microsoft BASIC, there is no chance to have an array of one size, then later change to a different size. You can dimension a *large* array and then only use part of it, and if your system has plenty of memory, that's the obvious way to do it.

Anyway, it's bad enough as Pascal does it: in order to get times for the different matrix dimensions, I had to change the program source and recompile for each. Inconvenient as this is in Pascal, it's worse for BASCOM, which won't even let you use constants in an array dimension! That is: in Pascal it is legal to say:

m = 20;
n = 20;

and later declare an array of A[1..m, 1..n] of REAL numbers. With Bascom, though, if you say:

m = 20 :
n = 20

and later say DIM A(m,n), the compiler reports a fatal error.

If I had to do a lot of operations involving matrices of varying sizes, I'm sure I'd prefer CB80 to either Pascal or BASCOM just in terms of convenience alone—and CB80 turns out to have some speed advantages, too.

WHAT ARE WE COMPARING, ANYWAY?

Benchmark comparisons of languages are unfair in another way: Do the languages actually do the same thing? That question can be more complex than you thought.

For example, the BASIC source programs used in the test are as nearly identical as I can make them. True, the syntax for DECLARING variables is different in the various languages used: BASCOM and MBASIC want "DEFINT I - N," meaning that *all* variables beginning with the letters I through N (such as "Number" or "Il") will now be considered integers; CB80 (like Pascal) wants an actual declaration variable by variable (ie., INTEGER I, J, K, L, N, N makes those one-letter variables integers, but wouldn't affect a variable called Number or one called Il); and neither CBASIC nor CBASIC86 will let you declare variables at all, except through the inconvenient business of naming them I%, J%, etc. BASCOM won't let you use variables to dimension an array. Within those limits, though, the code stays pretty much the same.

Of course if I were writing the program in either CBASIC or CB80 to begin with, it wouldn't look a lot like the MBASIC/BASCOM program. It would have a lot more white space, and would use functions instead of subroutines. In the interest of fairness, though, I kept the programs as nearly identical as possible.

A Microsoft MBASIC program to multiply matrices.

MAT1.ASC

```
10 REM A PROGRAM TO DO MATRICES
20 DEFINT I- N
25 M = 20 : N = 20
30 INPUT "Number of rows ";M
40 INPUT "Number of columns ";N
50 SUM = 0
55 INPUT "ENTER ANY CHARACTER TO START"; JIVE$
60 GOSUB 150 'DIMENSION
65 PRINT "DIMENSIONED"
70 GOSUB 200 ' FILL A
75 PRINT "A FILLED"
80 GOSUB 280 ' FILL B
85 PRINT "B FILLED"
90 GOSUB 360 ' FILL C
95 PRINT "C FILLED"
100 GOSUB 440 ' MULTIPLY
105 PRINT "MULTIPLIED"
110 GOSUB 540 ' SUM IT UP
120 PRINT "SUM = ";SUM
130 PRINT CHR$(7)
140 GOTO 9999
150 REM DIMENSION
160 DIM A(M,N)
```

```
170 DIM B(N,M)
180 DIM C(M,M)
190 RETURN
200 REM FILL A
210 FOR I = 1 TO M
220 FOR J = 1 TO N
230 A(I,J) = I + J
240 NEXT
250 NEXT
260 RETURN
270 REM ************
280 REM FILL B
290 FOR I = 1 TO M
300 FOR J = 1 TO N
310 B(I,J) = INT((I+J)/J)
320 NEXT
330 NEXT
340 RETURN
350 REM **********
360 REM FILL C
370 FOR I + 1 TO M
380 FOR J + 1 TO N
390 C(I,J) = 0
400 NEXT
410 NEXT
420 RETURN
430 REM **************
440 REM ************ MULTIPLY
450 FOR I = 1 TO M
460 FOR J = 1 TO N
470 FOR K = 1 TO M
480 C(I,J) = C(I,J) + A(I,K)*B(K,J)
490 NEXT
500 NEXT
510 NEXT
520 RETURN
530 REM **************
540 REM *************** SUMMIT
550 FOR I + 1 TO M
560 FOR J = 1 TO N
570 SUM = SUM + C(I,J)
580 NEXT
590 NEXT
600 RETURN
610 REM *************************8
9999 END
```

Listing 2: *A Pascal program to multiply matrices.*

B:MATRIX20.PAS

PROGRAM matrix (input, output);

CONST
  maxsize = 45;
  m = 20;
  n = 20;

VAR
  i,j,k,l : integer;

  A : ARRAY [1 .. m, 1 .. n] OF real;
  B : ARRAY [1 .. n, 1 .. m] OF real;
  C : ARRAY [1 .. m, 1 .. m] OF real;

  Summ : real;

  GUP, BELL : CHAR;

PROCEDURE FILLA;
VAR
  i, j : integer;
BEGIN
  For i := 1 to m DO
    For j := 1 to n DO
      A[i,j] := i + j;
END;

PROCEDURE FILLB;
VAR
  i,j : integer;
BEGIN

  FOR i := 1 to n DO
    For j := 1 to m DO
      B[i,j] := trunc((i + j)/j);
END;

Procedure FILLC;
VAR
  i, j : integer;
BEGIN
  FOR i := 1 to m DO
    FOR j := 1 to m DO
      C[i,j] := O;
END;

```
PROCEDURE matmult ;
 B:MATRIX20.PAS

VAR
  i, j, k : integer;

BEGIN
  FOR i := 1 to m DO
    FOR j := 1 to n DO
      FOR k := 1 to m DO
        C[i,j] := C[i,j,] + A[i,k]*B[k,j]
END;

PROCEDURE summit;

VAR
  i, j : integer;
BEGIN
  FOR i := 1 to m DO
    FOR j := 1 to m DO
      Summ := Summ + C[i,j]
END;

BEGIN (MAIN)

  SUMM := 0;

  Write ('input any darned number to start it.');

  Readln(gup);

  FILLA;
  WRITELN(' A FILLED. ');
  FILLB;
  Writeln(' B filled. ');
  FILIC;
  Writeln(' C filled. ');
  MATMULT;
  Writeln('Multiplied.');
  SUMMIT;
  Writeln('Summ is : ',Summ : 8 );
  BELL := CHR (7);
  WRITELN(BELL);
END.
```

	Time Matrix Size			Code Size (kilobytes)
	10×10	15×15	20×20	
MBASIC	10.4	33	1:14	24+2
MBASIC (no ints)	14.7	45	1:42.4	
CBASIC	13.6	42	1:36	17+1
CBASIC (no ints)	24.2	1:17	3:06.6	17+1
CBASIC86	13.8	43	1:39	18+2
CB/80	3.0	8.8	19.5	8
CB/80 (no ints)	10.4	31.2	1:10	8
Pascal/MT+			16.8	18
Pascal-M	8.6	25.8	58.1	16+1
BASCOM (new BRUN library)			22.0	16+2
BASCOM (no ints)			38.8	
BASCOM (old library)			21.5	16
BASCOM (double precision)			36.4	16+2
SAGE			9.6	

Table 1: *Results of running the matrix multiplication benchmark program in several BASICs and two Pascals. The BASIC program appears in listing 1, and the Pascal program in listing 2.*

Writing the original program in MBASIC was simple. I had it running in about fifteen minutes. Translating to Pascal was a lot more work; I'll get to my thoughts on that later. For the moment let's consider something else: these programs don't *really* do the same thing!

That is: I wasn't interested in testing how long it took to load the programs, nor in how long it took me to tell it the matrix sizes. Thus I wanted to start each from the same place, so I introduced an INPUT statement asking for a dummy variable; as that was input, I started the timer. The original versions of the programs invited you to enter a "number" as a way to start things going. The BASIC programs inputted the variable "JIVE;" since it had no dollar sign, it expected a numerical value. In the Pascal programs, the throwaway variable "gup" was declared to be an integer.

Alas, I tend to forget what I've done in cases like these, and whilst I was timing the program operations, when I saw the prompt "Enter any darned number to start it," I merely hit the RETURN key.

BASIC expects you might do that sometimes: it tells you that's an improper input and invites you to do something else.

The Pascals, however, do *nothing at all!* The system acts as if it has accepted your erroneous input, but in fact it is waiting for you to enter an actual *number*; and it will wait until doomsday if you let it. If you really want to check for illegal input, you have to write your own (rather cumbersome) procedure, whereas BASIC does all that for you.

Of course the simple remedy is to call it JIVE$, and declare "gup" as a CHAR, after which both BASIC and Pascal will accept anything you like including a carriage return; and of course really professional programmers wouldn't make silly mistakes like that. Which brings us to another point. . . .

WHO'S BRAIN-DAMAGED?

Another item that came over the net was a statement by Professor Edsger W. Dijkstra, a Dutch physicist-computer scientist of some fame. Professor Dijkstra is sometimes credited with inventing the whole notion of structured programming; certainly his (about 1960) paper "GOTO Considered Harmful" was very influential in the history of computer science. Many of the notions inherent in top-down structured programming are unquestionably his.

Dijkstra has also published a paper of "unpleasant truths" about computers and computer programs; he says, "Nearly all computing scientists I know well will agree without hesitation to nearly all of [these statements]. Yet we allow the world to behave as if we did not know them. . . ."

Here are a few of his "unpleasant truths:"

"FORTRAN, 'the infantile disorder,' by now twenty years old, is hopelessly inadequate for whatever computer application you have in mind today: it is now too clumsy, too risky, and too expensive to use."

"PL/I—'the fatal disease'—belongs more to the problem set than to the solution set."

"The use of COBOL cripples the mind; its teaching should, therefore, be regarded as a criminal offense."

"APL is a mistake, carried through to perfection. It is the language of the future for the programming techniques of the past: it creates a new generation of coding bums."

And finally:

"It is practically impossible to teach good programming to students that have had a prior exposure to BASIC: as potential programmers they are mentally mutilated beyond hope of regeneration."

Apparently he doesn't like many languages. Since he is said to have been one of Pascal's designers, I suppose he likes it, and we can come back to that. For the moment, let's concentrate on his view that BASIC causes permanent brain damage.

Obviously I don't believe that. Indeed, when first I heard it, it seemed so bizarre that I wondered if Prof. Dijkstra had lost his marbles. On the other hand, he has an excellent reputation for real insights; is there a lesson in this seemingly deranged statement? Why would he have said it?

First, Dijkstra is from the "old" school, from the time when computers were invariably served by High Priests; ordinary mortals did not have access to them. Not only were there no computers, there were no languages "understood of the people" with which to approach them. A businessman might buy a machine, but he still had to hire priests to attend it—until the Dartmouth people with their BASIC language began a real revolution.

There is now another school of thought, one that most *BYTE* readers come from, and almost diametrically opposed to the priesthood notion. We believe that computers are for users. Like the authors of the classic work *Algebra Made Simple*, we believe that "What one fool can do, another can." We tend to prove it, too: despite occasional nasty letters, I continue to believe that the real dynamism in the computer world grows out of *BYTE*-sized hackers and their home machines. Also, we tend to support "distributed computer power;" lots of small machines, each under the control of a single user, rather than time-sharing big machines.

However, the early days of our revolution were pretty rough. The first "distributed" machines had severe memory limits—and BASIC requires memory for REMARK statements. Early BASIC (largely to save memory) used single-letter variables. To save stack space (memory again) we tended to use lots of GOTO. The result was uncommented spaghetti code, incredibly convoluted, which after a few days was incomprehensible even to its authors. Naturally the High Priests were horrified. They should have been.

BASIC has since been much improved, but it certainly remains true that you can write incomprehensible code in BASIC. And so what? You can also write some pretty obscure stuff in Pascal. If you really want to be dense, use LISP or APL. In fact, there's no language that will automatically force you to use good habits—and while the old BASIC languages, implemented on tiny machines, did indeed encourage you to silly excesses, I just don't believe this nonsense about "permanent brain damage."

WHAT DO YOU WANT TO DO, ANYWAY?

The truth of the matter is that there is no one language best for all purposes. If what you need is a quick and dirty program to be run once only and you need the results *right now*, then interpretive BASIC is very likely to be the most powerful tool available—especially if the task involves lots of string and text manipulations. BASIC programs tend to be slow and can be hard to understand, but they can be set up and debugged quite rapidly.

On the other hand, suppose you need a big number crunch program with many calculations and lots of decisions. Suppose further that it will be used for years, and thus will probably need infrequent updating, and you're going to run it every day. It should be obvious that interpretive BASIC is not going to do the job. So—what do we use?

It's precisely here that one's computer "philosophy" becomes important. Dijkstra and his associates would say that the most important thing to do is sit down and analyze your problem. Do a lot of thinking before you do any coding. If you can describe your problem well, you will do a good program: therefore you ought to be a good mathematician, familiar with a variety of problem-solving devices, so that you can come up with elegant and efficient algorithms.

Knowing the proper programming languages, such as Pascal, will help this analytical process, because knowing good languages will force you to think in proper structures.

The result will be a code that is readable and maintainable. It is nearly self-documented. How could it be otherwise?

The other approach is that of the typical micro hacker, who tends to think code before he's really analyzed the problem. He breaks the problem up into chunks and codes this and that, probably testing as he goes, until Lo! the program is suddenly done. Now comes the painful task of documentation, which is done sloppily if at all, and six months later the poor slob hasn't a clue as to how his program works.

Put that way, there's not much choice, is there? And most programming discussions I've seen *do* put it that way. The computer experts speak, and the micro hacker listens all gaga; eventually the poor slob goes away convinced he doesn't know anything. But in the real world, things are often different. To hear the High Priests talk, the mainframe and mini-computer worlds are filled with elegant well-documented programs; but if you believe that, I've got a land deal for you.

Sure, programs *ought* to be written after much thought, and incorporate only elegant self-documenting code; but, well, there wasn't as much time as we thought, and documentation was Ephriam's job only he got a better offer from Wretched House so we had to put Pinhead onto writing it up, I mean the program was finished except for the documents and we needed our best programmers for something else, and——

Then, too, many of the High Priests came out of a worse tradition than you might think. I recall my early days in computerland, programming the IBM 650 RAMAC. There wasn't an assembler: you did it all in "opcodes." There wasn't much memory, except 5,000 10-digit "words" on the drum, and you had to store your code *all over* that silly drum since you couldn't afford to waste the time to let it go a complete revolution between operations. Talk about non-structured code!

So some of the priests got together to design new and better languages, with Pascal one of the major results. It's a nice language, certainly superior to opcodes and assemblers and early BASIC. It may well be that those destined to be professional programmers should begin with Pascal and not learn BASIC at all. There is a problem, though. Before you can do much with Pascal, you have to learn quite a lot about your computer. At a minimum you've got to know how to use an editor to create a source file, and how to invoke the compiler, and how to run your program after it's compiled. You can't just say PRINT 2 + 5 and get an answer, as my 10-year-old did within a few minutes of sitting down at the TRS-80.

Many will give up before they learn enough to use Pascal.

Leave that, though. What annoys me about Pascal is not the language itself, but its enthusiasts. Perhaps Dijkstra had a point to make with his statement about BASIC and brain damage; at least he may have earned the right to say something of that sort. But we hear the minor acolytes of that priesthood echo such sentiments in chorus, and that's another story altogether.

But leave that too. What really drives me wild is when the Pascal enthusiasts try to convince me that the language's bugs are all features.

For example: Pascal MT+ will try to compile, and will run across a statement such as

Summit = Stuff + glop;

which the compiler can't handle. MT+ then reports ":= expected."

Or it will trundle along and suddenly become confused. The compiler then suggests that you ought to have put a ";" at the end of the line above. (It's generally right; alas, Pascal is very picky about those semi-colons, demanding them at the ends of most lines but forbidding them at the ends of others.)

In neither case will the compiler remedy the defect. Sometimes it's able to go on for a while so that it finds more than one error per attempted compilation—but that's by no means assured.

Why is this? I thought I bought a computer to take care of trivial details, and here I'm bean counting. Yet many of the High Priests will solemnly assure you that the compiler *must* work this way, and any attempt to do things any other way is wrong.

Item. The CASE statement, which some languages call "SWITCH;" in BASIC it's generally On . . . GOTO or ON . . . GOSUB. CASE selects among various alternatives. What happens if it gets an alternative you never thought about?

BASIC and most other languages provide for a default, or allow you an ELSE, or otherwise let you deal with the situation. Pascal dumps your program. And believe it or not, the language's designers seem to think that's not a bug, it's a feature. If you get unexpected alternatives, you obviously didn't think things through enough. Go back to Square One and start over. (Hard cheese if you're processing real-time data that won't wait for you to devise a more elegant program....)

(In fact, the lack of an ELSE or OTHERWISE in Pascal's CASE is so keenly felt that most implementations, including Sorcim's Pascal/M and Digital Research's Pascal MT+ have an ELSE as an extension.)

Item: Pascal makes you declare all your variables, and the compiler natters at you in unfriendly tones if you forget. However, it does *not* require you to initialize variables, nor does it do it for you. In my benchmark Pascal program I declared the summation variable Summ, but in an early version of the program I forgot to initialize it to zero. The program compiled and ran. It just didn't give the right answer.

I could go on, citing Pascal's notorious deficiencies in string handling and general IO, but I think I need not pile Pelion on Ossa. My point is that Pascal isn't very convenient; in the modern parlance, it's not really "user-friendly." Depending on who you talk to it may or may not be about as good as we have, but even its friends will generally concede that it could be improved.

Or most of its friends will concede. Alas, some will not; some insist that Pascal's unfriendliness is a feature; that the language is forcing you to think logically, and thus write elegant programs.

WHO NEEDS ELEGANCE

Much of the computer priesthood serves strange gods: not the user, but the ideal known as "elegance." Since no one knows what that means (or perhaps everyone knows, but all know something different), "elegance" often translates as "computer efficiency."

There was, perhaps, a time when that made sense; when computer resources were scarce, and making maximum use of them was a Good Thing. Now, though, hardware prices are falling while capabilities skyrocket, and that goal is questionable at best.

Let me give an example. At the West Coast Computer Faire I saw a new machine using the 68000 chip, and I got into a discussion of it with Carl Helmers, the former editorial director of *BYTE* magazine.

"It uses UCSD P-code as the *operating system*," I said. "That's got to be the most inefficient thing I ever heard of."

"So what?" Carl replied. "The chip is so fast you don't notice."

Now Carl is far more of a Pascal enthusiast than I, but surely he was correct? Once the hardware achieves certain levels, then *more efficient* becomes the enemy of *good enough*. This is especially true in business contexts, where what matters is productivity. In the old days computers were hideously expensive, and companies that bought more computer power than they needed could be in trouble. Unusable computer power was damned expensive.

That's not true now. Every year the price of computer power falls while the cost of programmers rises, and now it's usually cheaper to have too much computer than to have too little and pay for "efficient" programming.

[My reputation as a Pascal hater grew with this article. It was undeserved, as you will see later. I think the Pascal *language* is elegant. However, there were few convenient implementations of it that we could run on our computers.

Correspondents accused me of not knowing the difference between a language and its implementations; I could only reply that I reported on what I had to work with, and I had what was supposed to be the best available.

Some of that is moot now: but it has largely been made so by the introduction of good, low-cost Pascal compilers for micro computers.

The best of that lot (as of Spring, 1984) is Turbo Pascal by Borland International; at $49.95 it's one of the hottest software bargains around.

The columns in those days were not *entirely* devoted to languages; but even when they weren't, the issue crept in.]

CBASIC86

CBASIC86 running on the Godbout 8088 under CP/M-86 was actually *slower* than CBASIC2 on the 8085; yet the 8088 is a 16-bit machine. How can this be?

First, it's obvious that CBASIC86 must be a nearly literal

translation of CBASIC2. It can't possibly be optimized for the 8088.

Second, my engineering genius friend Tony Pietsch points out that given the first point, the 8088 has quite a lot of potential: here a first-cut program is running at speeds comparable to code that's had many programmer-years of work optimizing it for the 8080 family.

Finally, my 8085/8088 didn't cost me very much more than a single processor system, and it *will* run CPM86. I'd never done that before, but it was incredibly easy: insert the CPM86 disk that comes with the Godbout, and hit reset. All the familiar CP/M commands worked. I could read the directory of not only my CP/M86 master in Drive A, but also the CP/M 2.2 disk residing in Drive B.

It was easy enough to PIP the CBASIC86 programs over, then PIP over the program source, and compile. Everything ran the first time, no hitches whatsoever. One of these days I'll get some CPM86 programs that *are* optimized for the 8088 processor, and then I'll have a tame bomb to use. Until then I can use the 8085/8088 with Warp Drive, which I continue to use and love.

Incidentally, the disk operations under CP/M-86 were incredibly slow; but Godbout, at least, supplies the source to the BIOS, and one day I'll optimize it for my disks and controller. I can do that, because you can PIP the BIOS sources from the CP/M-86 disk over to a CP/M-2.2 disk and edit under my regular CP/M editor.

TWO APOLOGIES

As I've mentioned before, I've never learned PL/I. My late mad friend was quite enamoured of the language, and had intended to teach me; but alas his condition didn't permit that.

Unfortunately, in a previous column, I reported from secondary sources that PL/I has no CASE statement. I was wrong, as a number of readers have told me in letters. PL/I does indeed have a CASE statement, called SELECT. The syntax is rather more similar to BASIC's ON ... GOSUB than to Pascal's CASE (tag) OF. Also unlike (standard) Pascal, PL/I provides an OTHERWISE to catch cases the programmer didn't think of.

Secondly: a few months ago, I said that Microsoft BASIC's

random access files were not ASCII, and could not be accessed by the sequential file process. I had good reason to think this, and indeed I spoke with several people in Microsoft's management who told me they'd consider changing the situation.

D. W. McKee, of San Jose, tells me I'm wrong. I quote from his letter:

"Although Microsoft's documentation does not make it clear, it is very possible to use ASCII random files. The procedure is as follows:

"1. Open file as a random file in the normal way. The record length must include comma and " delimiters plus a carriage return and line feed, in addition to the actual data.

"2. Position the pointer to the beginning of the buffer with a GET n, Rec.no.

"3. Print each data element with a print using statement plus a comma between each data element. Appropriate use of the print using format insures that you do not overfill the record length. If you try to write more characters into the record than your record length, an error will be generated. If you are sure that the data cannot overrun the record length, you can use the WRITE statement, which puts the commas in for you, but it also puts " around all strings.

"EG:
OPEN "R", #N, Filenames$
F$ = "#####.##" : F1$ = "####.##"
Comma$ = ","
PRINT # N, USING F$; DATA1; : Print # N, Comma$
Print #N, Using F1$; Data2
PUT # N, Rec.No

Alternative
Write #N, DATA1; DATA2
PUT # N, Rec.No

"4. To read these files, just:
GET # N, Rec.No
INPUT # N, Data1, Data2

"You will note that the FIELD and related string conversion statements are not needed at all.

"These files can be read and edited by WordStar, TYPED by CP/M, etc. I have found this to be a very easy and reliable way to set up files, particularly those involving frequent addition of more records. . . . The first several records can be used for keeping track of how many records are in the file and other similar non-repeating records."

I thank Mr. McKee, who has spent more time studying Microsoft BASIC record structures than I have. Avoiding the dreaded FIELD statement should make life a lot simpler; I only wish I'd been clever enough to figure this out for myself from the Microsoft user documents.

LEARNING BASIC

Predictably there's a flood of books about the computer revolution. I'm adding to it; as I write this, two major publishing houses are bidding for my computer book, and by the time this is printed I'll surely have signed a contract. [I hadn't, but that's beside the point.] Both publishers have expressed one concern: how will my book be different from the flood?

Good question. I'm not sure. But one thing is certain: I will not write a book that starts off talking about the home computer revolution and ends up trying to teach you BASIC; and even if I were fool enough to do that, I'd *certainly* not offer you a book on word processing that contained the program listing of a text editor written in BASIC.

That latter, alas, is what Donald McCunn did in his *WRITE, EDIT, AND PRINT: Word Processing with Personal Computers*. There's a good bit of useful information in the book. He has a decent survey of hardware, and some cogent comments about how machines work and what their limits are. Unfortunately, at $24.95 ($34.95 hardbound) this is, I fear, a book anyone could do without. There may have been a time when a listing of code for a text editor written in Microsoft BASIC would have been useful, but surely that time has passed?

His Word Worker (TM) editor may or may not be useful; the statement numbers run up to 12500 in increments of 5, and I'm not about to type all that into my machine. I will say that the code seems well commented, and if he writes code as well as he writes English it might well work: but ye gods, having done all that, you still have an editor in BASIC; and while I like BASIC for a lot of applications, I think I'd rather chase geese for pens than have to use it to write an editor....

The same author has also done a book called *Computer Programming for the Complete Idiot*. This is a better (and at $6.95 much cheaper) book which *BYTE* readers might consider buying as a gift for business-oriented friends who want to know what the TRS-80 Model I and Microsoft Basic can do. McCunn writes clearly, and as a survey his book has a lot going for it.

As a BASIC instruction manual it falls to the ground, because the various BASIC commands are discussed, not in any logical order, but in the order needed to type in a fairly simple payroll program. I doubt the program itself would be too useful, although I could be wrong about that; but it is used effectively as an example of the kinds of things BASIC can do. The level of sophistication can be gathered from his "chapter" on Debugging Programs. The chapter consists of fewer than 100 lines (about two pages). It ends by telling the reader about TRON and the Break Key.

McCunn's book isn't bad as an illustration of what BASIC can do, but if you want someone to *learn* the language, in my opinion there's only one book: Jerald R. Brown's *INSTANT BASIC*. This first (yellow binding) edition of this collection of mad drawings, corny puns, silly illustrations, and absolutely clear instructions was what Mac Lean handed me when he and Tony Pietsch delivered Ezekial (my first computer). Now there's a second (pink binding) edition, which I presume is improved. Unfortunately, I can't tell; it's simply not possible to recreate the feelings I had when I was first trying to use Ezekial. I do know that everything I'd seen before *INSTANT BASIC* seemed unfriendly and incomprehensible, and what a relief it was to get a book that had been written, not precisely for complete idiots, but for those who knew *nothing* about BASIC.

Understand that the book is completely mad. I particularly recall a rattlesnake crawling across the page saying "I am not a string, so don't thread on me!" Elsewhere it shows how to calculate the speed of a snail in miles per second (which is no bad way to learn about very small numbers....)

If you have friends or relatives with access to a computer and any interest in learning BASIC, I don't believe you could do better than to give them this book and sit them down in front of a machine. (However, if they suffer permanent mental damage, I will not be responsible. I've warned you of Dijkstra's views.)

GO FORTH, YOUNG MAN . . .

Recently I got an angry letter from an Apple enthusiast suggesting that I should retitle this column "CP/M Users" or "S-100 Bus Users." There's justice in that. Just as this moment all my computers are S-100 Bus and CP/M, and I don't write much about things I don't use. However, what I have isn't accidental, either.

Computer capabilities change like dreams. How, then, shall we keep up? Well—we can't. But we can try, and one way is to adopt a motto: "Iron is expensive, but silicon is cheap." That is: get a good standard bus machine, and when new modifications come out you can afford to buy a card every now and then. Of all the readily adaptable machines I've examined, the S-100 Bus variety seems the most versatile and most likely to be in the forefront of the small computer revolution. And do understand that when I give opinions like this, I've discussed them with many others who have a lot of knowledge and experience. E'en so, I may be wrong—indeed, the way things change so in this field, I'm *bound* to be wrong sometimes.

Another reader asks why I ignore FORTH, which has a respectable number of dedicated—dare I say fanatic?—devotees. Alas, I continue to agree with my mad friend: FORTH is not a higher level language at all. Instead, it's a kind of assembly language that uses the programmer as a pre-compiler.

This is not to say that you can't do magnificent things in FORTH, and indeed I'm told that the language is nearly ideal for certain kinds of programs. It's good with graphics, and Atari programmers are enthusiastic about its power for writing games and drawing elaborate maps and displays. (Of course Atari programmers have a heavy incentive to like FORTH: for a long time it was nearly the only powerful language available for their machines.)

The problem is, FORTH is unlike most languages, and thus takes a lot of learning; and until recently you had to invest a good deal of time in the language before you could tell whether it was right for you. That has now changed.

Whether or not you intend to learn FORTH, you can learn a lot from Leo Brodie's new book *STARTING FORTH*.

I very much like this book; indeed, I was given it in San Francisco and idly thumbed through it in the airport bar while waiting for my plane. Next thing I knew I was trapped. I read it while flying home, and then when I got home I continued reading; and when you consider that I'm *not* a FORTH enthusiast, and indeed don't much care for the language, you'll have an idea of how well Brodie writes. I can't imagine why a book about FORTH, illustrated with goofy cartoons of a smooth-talking interpreter, a masked executioner, a tonsured dictionary-writing compiler, a numbers runner, and various monsters would fascinate me; but it did, and indeed kept me reading long after I decided that FORTH was not for me.

If, after reading Brodie you decide you want to *use* FORTH, I'm told that *FORTH ENCYCLOPEDIA* by Mitch Derick and Linda Baker is very good. Note that I do not myself endorse it. The authors gave me the book, and it seems to be written in English; but it's a reference work, not a text, and thus organized in a way that assumes you know more about FORTH than I'm ever likely to. People who do know FORTH seem to like it a lot.

DIRE WARNINGS:

[As the language debates raged on, I received letters. One was full of warnings....]

Mr. Dale Peters of Oklahoma City is a professional programmer who uses COBOL. He wants me to warn micro users away from COBOL before they become ensnared.

I agree with his sentiments, but I wouldn't have thought the warning necessary. However, Mr. Peters says that applications programming schools are still turning out so-called "programmers" who know nothing but COBOL, and that data processing shop managers are beginning to make a serious distinction between COBOL-coders and "real programmers;" which they must do "as the cost of program maintenance gets higher and higher compared to hardware costs."

I suppose I have been naive in thinking COBOL a dying language. If my views have any weight, I agree with Edsger Dijsktra: "Teaching COBOL ought to be regarded as a criminal act...." The language is obsolete, limited in power and scope, and not well implemented on small computers. Most COBOL programs I have seen are hard to understand and harder to maintain. There has to be a better language for almost any application you have in mind.

That letter led to:

Hate Mail

Jeffrey Wade, of Liberty Mutual Insurance Company, writes to inform me that my "little diatribe against COBOL is pure poppycock," and he "thinks my readers ought to know it."

Mr. Wade calls to evidence the fact that "a recent estimate puts the inventory of COBOL programs in the world today at $200 *billion*. In my shop alone, there are 20,000 active COBOL programs. Do you honestly think they'll go away in five years? In your lifetime? In your son's?"

Moreover, COBOL is being updated. It will soon have, according to Wade, "structured programming constructs, Boolean operators, etc." He concludes, "If you're doing business applications which require lots of file processing, you'll be hard pressed to find a better language than my old friend, COBOL."

Perhaps Mr. Wade is right. It's almost certain that COBOL will be around for a while. The question is, is that a positive good or a regrettable evil?

If you want to write self-modifying code, COBOL has a statement that will do that for you. Whether you and, more important, your successor, can understand what you've done is another matter entirely. Meanwhile, structured programming constructs and boolean operators are coming Real Soon Now.

Perhaps, if what you need to do is process inputs from hundreds of terminals—say from a chain of department stores—or you must work with tens of thousands of insurance policies, COBOL is the language of choice. I wouldn't have thought so, but I'm willing to be persuaded.

The one thing you won't persuade me of is that you've much chance of handling the records of 100,000 policy holders on any kind of micro I'm going to see in the next few years.

To put the record straight: *BYTE* calls itself "The Small Systems Journal". I write "The User's Column." Within that context, I cannot and do not recommend COBOL. For larger systems and larger business I would have thought there were better languages, but perhaps I'm wrong.

As to the $200 billion value of all those COBOL programs, I'm reminded of the difference between price and value—or effort and work.

The nature of this column dictates its contents: I have to write about what's been happening here at Chaos Manor. This month we've had two big flaps. One is a frantic effort to clean off my desk so that my wife and I can take a vacation in Europe. She's been planning this trip for a year now. So far I haven't had the heart to tell her that we won't be going alone: I'm taking an Otrona Attache with me.

Anyway, I've been trying to get two books (*CLAN AND CROWN: Janissaries II*, and Volume One of *FUTURE MEN OF WAR*) out the door, dash about to radio and television interview shows to publicize books, answer my mail, and write a couple of chapters of *FOOTFALL*, the next big novel that Niven and I are working on. The usual result of that much activity is that *nothing* gets accomplished, but actually I've done pretty well on everything but the mail.

Meanwhile, flap number two, which has got downright embarrassing: Alex Pournelle's *INTRODUCTION TO PASCAL*.

Alex's INTRO was supposed to be a fairly easy and simple job, requiring a month's work at most. The task was to take some of the teaching programs from Grogono's *Programming in Pascal*, and the fundamental required programs and Input/Output primitives in Kernighan and Plauger's *Software Tools in Pascal*, and get them running under two popular CP/M Pascal compilers. Then he'd write up notes on problems encountered, add a few pages contrasting the two compilers (Sorcim's Pascal/M and Digital Research's Pascal MT+), add a few more pages of tips on using Pascal, and hand it to Barry Workman to publish.

The first draft using Pascal MT+ was done and looked good, and I could honestly say that the materials saved me a *lot* of time when I tried learning Pascal, so I wrote about it. *BYTE*'s pipeline is, after all, pretty long.

Not long enough. The article came out. Orders came in. The INTRO wasn't ready. Now that's not quite accurate: something was ready, but Alex wasn't satisfied with it. He didn't think he was giving people their money's worth. Meanwhile, he'd run into some really colossal problems with the way the compilers handled CP/M files. He could get the teaching programs running, but only through kluges, and he wanted to start over.

Fortunately, the story has a happy ending: the Pascal Intro package has been completely done over, and everyone who bought the old package will get the new one free. Now obviously I'm not a totally disinterested observer; my son wrote this stuff, largely to help me learn—and understand—Pascal. Still, I like to think I can be objective about such things (and do note that I don't own the programs; they belong to Alex). In my judgment, he's done a hell of a job. The package now contains not only the programs, with all the special routines required to get things running smoothly under CP/M, but also a number of essays on typical problems. There's an especially valuable treatment on Pascal Errors and what probably caused them.

THE LANGUAGE DEBATE GOES ON

There are at least two reasons I've given Alex's Pascal INTRODUCTORY PACKAGE as much space as I have. One is obvious: as I said at the beginning, I have to write about what we're doing around here, and Lord knows that has been the major activity, not just this month, but all Summer. There's another and more important reason, namely that it *did* take all Summer.

Pascal is an important language. Nearly every computer publication acts as if it is, and indeed Pascal is a candidate for *the* language of the decade. It is taught to nearly every student at the University of California at San Diego (La Jolla), and UCSD isn't alone in that practice. There are several implementations of Pascal for CP/M, and more are coming.

Alex and his friends are pretty familiar with Pascal—at least with the UCSD implementation of it. Grogono, and Kernighan and Plauger, are very popular, very highly recommended books, usually thought to be the best introductory works on Pascal.

Yet it has taken *months* of work to get these standard textbook programs running and document the differences between what's printed in the textbook and what actually can run on your CP/M system. Moreover, if there's anyone else who has a package that competes with Alex's, we don't know about it, nor do the professional programmers at several large systems houses. We know that, because we tried to find something, *anything*, that might answer some of the problems Alex encountered. We searched through programming manuals line by line. We called programmers. At one point we considered Ouija Boards. None of that was much help. It finally came down to Alex doing just a lot of hard work, finding out what will and will not run, finding compiler bugs and anomalies and glitches, writing them up and trying another approach, until eventually he had things working properly.

Now of course I'm proud of him; but I'm also appalled. If this is a candidate for *the* language of the decade, we may have problems.

IMPLEMENTER BLUES

You'd be amazed at some of the problems Alex ran into. For example: Kernighan and Plauger assume that RECORDS can contain files; and the ISO Standard for Pascal makes the same assumption. MT+ follows the standard. Pascal M, though, like UCSD, will not allow files in records; which makes file-handling complex beyond belief if you want to have several files open at the same time. That situation alone required a number of special procedures and a week's work.

MT+ pattern-finder function POS, which is supposed to find the first instance of a pattern within an array, is not completely reliable. It *usually* works, but that's not good enough; and we didn't have time to map the boundary conditions. Another special routine.

Just getting text, when the routines assume that text files consist of 80-character lines terminated by carriage return and line feed, can be ridiculously complex.

Some bugs are obscure, but thoroughly deadly. Example: in MT+ if you open a comment and forget to close it (that can happen, when you erase lines, or when you nest comments) Pascal MT+ goes away into never-never land; you have to RESET the whole computer to recover. It doesn't report errors, it just hangs up. Incidentally, Pascal has Error #401, Unexpected End of Input, which is supposed to deal with that situation, but it doesn't appear.

Neither Pascal M nor Pascal MT+ manuals explain some vital things like forward declarations: and alas, neither is in the textbooks either. Alex knows about such things, but how will his readers? So he had to add new sections to the teaching aid.

All the implementations—beginning with the UCSD compiler, which everyone has built around—have an annoying defect in string handling. They won't concatenate a single character into a string. They will concatenate chr types (example: chr (26) is control-z, chr(072) is H), but not single variables of type CHAR. Someone ought to fix that....

And on, and on, and on. Sigh.

KERNIGHAN'S LAMENT

My August column spoke of Unicorn Systems' implementation of the Kernighan and Plauger *Software Tools*, and recommended that those who want to do their own programming learn Pascal rather than RATFOR and FORTRAN. Shortly after, I received a letter from Unicorn's Deborah Sherrer.

Unicorn Systems publishes not only the K&P *Tools*, but more importantly what they call a "virtual operating system," that is, a Unix-like shell around CP/M. (See User's Column, AUGUST 1982 *BYTE*.) Mrs. Sherrer says, "The choice of language is not critical to the virtual operating system approach. Had the project been designed *solely* for the micro environment, C or Pascal might have been a more appropriate choice. However, the preprocessor chosen (RATFOR) has proven quite successful in allowing portability between micro and large machine environments. There is no reason why the package could not be available in several languages, though, perhaps with automatic translators between them. We are, in fact, looking into the possibility now and may eventually provide an automatic translator."

I hope they do that. I like their "virtual operating system," because it lets the operating system do a number of the messy things that at the moment you must do inside your programs. One obvious example is file handling: one of the really horrible problems Alex had with implementing the *Software Tools* in Pascal was the different ways that Pascal M and Pascal MT+ handle files; these problems go away if the operating system does this for you, and I am fond of Unicorn Systems' approach to the problem.

Deborah also enclosed a copy of Kernighan's Lament.

In July 1981, Brian Kernighan published Bell Laboratories Computing Science Technical Report #100, entitled "Why Pascal Is Not My Favorite Programming Language." Alex's summary comment is "He doesn't like Pascal because it isn't C." There's some justice to that. The C Programming Language was developed at Bell Labs, and Kernighan (with Dennis M. Ritchie) wrote the standard (and just about the only) book on the language.

There's also a lot of validity to Kernighan's indictments. The question before the house is: Was Kernighan justified in concluding "Pascal, at least in its standard form, is just plain not suitable for serious programming;" and if he was, then what changes must be made in Pascal to make it a "serious programming language?"

Kernighan divides his objections into four major categories:
types and scope
control flow
environment
cosmetics.

His first complaint is universal. Pascal was designed as a "strongly typed" language. What that means in practice is that you cannot mindlessly set a variable of one type equal to a variable of another; the compiler will not let you do that. As Kernighan himself notes, this can be a pretty good thing, since it prevents the common FORTRAN mistake of sending a floating point number off to a subroutine that expects an integer, causing a very hard to find error.

However, in Pascal the size of an array is part of its data type, which is to say that an array dimensioned, say, ten by ten, is not only a different array from one dimensioned ten by fifteen, but a different *kind of animal*, and it's very hard to set one array equal to another. Thus if you want to sort arrays, you have either to set aside a block of memory equal to the very largest array you will ever encounter, then use part of it; or recompile your program every time you have a new array size to worry about. The former method is very wasteful of memory. The latter procedure is at best inconvenient.

His next complaint is against a straw man. That is: there are no string variables in standard Pascal. In the original language there are only arrays of characters, and since each array size is a different *type* it is very messy to compare strings, or set one string equal to another. Kernighan says,

"This botch is the biggest single problem with Pascal. I believe that if it could be fixed, the language would be an order of magnitude more useful." Fortunately, it has been fixed. No actual implementation of Pascal follows the standard. Nearly all CP/M Pascal implementations use the same device, namely that a string is an array of characters with the zero-th element containing the string length. This has the inconvenient result that in most 8-bit machines strings cannot be longer than 255 characters, but it does give you a mechanism for getting the job done.

His next objection is certainly valid: there are no *static* variables in Pascal.

A static variable is one that is retained, but confined inside a particular function or procedure. An example would be the seed with which you call a random number: there is no necessity for the program as a whole to be able to see that seed, but certainly you must keep it around between calls to the random number function.

Alas, Pascal can't do that. When you exit a Pascal function or procedure, all its variables go away. Thus to retain the seed, you would have to make it external to the procedure (and probably global), where it can be seen and interfered with by other parts of the program. This can lead to side effects and bugs thereby generated are among the hardest to find.

And so forth. I'm not going through Kernighan's paper point by point; those interested should get a copy. However, one of his objections requires some discussion.

TERRORIZED BY GOTO?

One real problem of Pascal is that it has no "break" statement; neither is there a "return" from a function or procedure.

This latter is not a bug, it's a feature: that is, the structured programming approach demands that there be a single entrance and a single exit from any part of a program. In Pascal, you "return" from a function or procedure by running off the end of it.

The problem comes when you want a program that goes:
    (PSEUDO-C version)
    while (getnext (stuff)) (

```
IF (something)
   break
rest of while loop.
```

This is harder to implement in Pascal than it might seem. As Kernighan points out, the approach:

```
done := false
while (not done) and (getnext (stuff)) DO
   if something then
      done := true
   else begin
      rest of loop
   end;
```

doesn't work, because in Pascal you cannot force the (not done) to be evaluated before the next call of getnext. Getting around this leads to an extra level of nesting, for you must put the getnext loop inside a WHILE (not done) loop. Pascal enthusiasts would say: "And so what? It's a lot clearer if you make these tests explicitly hierarchical rather than relying on your knowledge of the compiler to see what's done first." They have a point, too. The C programming language (which does guarantee the order of expression evaluations) is popular with computer hackers, but it has a number of fine points that make it hard to use for those who don't work at it a lot; at least I've found that to be true.

Still, the lack of a "BREAK" statement in Pascal can, in more complete situations than the above, lead to some funny-looking code complete with superfluous "bookkeeping" variables. Kernighan goes on to say: "Of course recidivists can use a GOTO and a label (numeric only and it has to be declared) to exit a loop. Otherwise, early exits are a pain, almost always requiring the invention of a boolean variable [a boolean variable is one that takes only two values, true and false] and a certain amount of cunning."

Query: why is using a GOTO and a label so horrible?

Yes, I know; questions like that can get me thrown out of the lodge. We've all been taught that use of GOTO is *always* improper. But is it? In the early days, the GOTO was much abused, so that it was impossible to follow program logic. The code led you into an opaque tangle of spaghetti.

But because something can be abused doesn't mean it has to be abolished. To return to our example, I see nothing at all wrong with:

```
LABEL 99;
begin
while (getnext(stuff)) DO
   if (something) then GOTO 99 (* you're done *)
   else begin
      rest of loop;
   end;
99 :                                    (* exit point *)
   end;
```

I mean, really, how is this different from the BREAK statement? Is it harder to understand? To claim that any use of GOTO is "recidivist" is, in my view, blind prejudice.

THERE'S A NEW C A'COMIN' . . .

I have mixed emotions about the C programming language. On the one hand, I open Kernighan and Ritchie and read a chapter or so, and I think I understand what they're saying; then I go try to write some code in C, and the results are an unmitigated disaster. I think I know what a statement like:
   for (i = 0; i < N; i++) says, although you don't have to be away from the language long to forget; but then comes:
   int n;
   for (n = 0; *s != '\0'; s++)
      n++
   return(n);
and I have to think some more. Whatever else you say about C, it doesn't much resemble English.

These are not fatal objections; as I said, I often find myself tempted to try using C, especially after I've spent a few minutes talking with Leor Zolman; his enthusiasm is catching. Even so, I have never become proficient in the language.

There are a lot of C compilers available.

First, there's Leor's BDS C, available from Workman and Associates. I've written about it many times; the main limit to BDS C is that it hasn't any floating point data types. There are a few other limits, so that you can't—or at least *I* can't—just copy programs out of Kernighan and Ritchie and expect them to run.

There are a surprising number of other C compilers. Dr. James Van Zandt of Nashua, NH has been kind enough to list them all for me:

Small-C: written by Ron Cain, source code published in Dr. Dobbs #45 (May 1980). Small subset of C, excludes structures, multidimensional arrays, floating point, case statements, and other vital stuff. Source and object code available for $17 from The Code Works, Box 550, Goleta, CA 93017.

Small-C Plus: an extension of Cain's Small-C by Kirk Bailey (adds for and do-while loops, switch-case-default, some others). Available for $55 from Alpha Omega Computer Systems, Inc. Box U, Corvallis, OR 97330.

Q/C: Another extension of Small-C, by Jim Colvin (includes for, switch/case, do-while, goto, assignment operators, command line arguments, I/O redirection, etc.) Source (!) and object code available for $95 from The Code Works.

CW/C: A larger extension of Small-C (includes structures, unions, multidimensional arrays, $ifdef, etc.) Object code only available for $75 from The Code Works.

C/80: A subset of C based in part on Small-C, with considerable changes by Walt Bilofsky. Excludes floating point, structures, pointers to pointers, etc. Compiles to 8080 assembly language. Object code only available for $39.95 from The Software Toolworks, 14478 Glorietta Dr., Sherman Oaks, CA 91423.

Infosoft C: An extensive rewrite of Small-C by Richard Roth, described in an article in Dr. Dobbs, November 1981. (Lacks float, goto, &&, etc.). Complex availability: "A runable version for $50 in conjunction with our SAL structured assembler development tool kit listed at $225. Or source may be licensed for an additional $250 when the runable version is licensed." From InfoSoft Systems Inc., 26 Sylvan Road South, Westport, CT 06880

SuperSoft C: They claim this is "most of version 7 Unix standard C." Object code $200, and source code $5000 available from Supersoft Associates, PO Box 1628, Champaign, IL 61820.

Aztec C II: "All C language features except bit fields." Advertised in Dr. Dobbs, March 1982. Object code, assembler, linker available for $195 from Technical Software Systems, Box 55, Shrewsbury, NJ 07701. Compiler without float or long, $135.

tiny-c ONE (interpreter) and tiny-c TWO (compiler): A small language similar to C, described in Dr. Dobbs, May 1980. Interpreter source and object code ($100) and compiler object code ($250) available from tiny c Associates, Box 269, Holmdel, NJ 07733.

Dr. Van Zandt reports: "I've used Small-C, and have started enhancing it. My version compiles at about 220 lines a minute, but it's still slow. I'm looking for a fast compiler that handles floating point, and a matching interpreter for fast debugging. I suspect I'm not alone. Can you help in our search?"

[I wasn't able to help much; and since then a number of other C compilers have come onto the market. I am not a C language expert, or indeed enthusiast; thus I have few strong opinions about which implementation of C is best. For 8-bit machines, the fastest compiler, and probably the most useful version, is still Leor Zolman's **BDS C**, which is available from Workman and Associates. BDS C isn't as complete as some others, but there is an extensive library of utilities, and a vast number of useful programs are available from the BDS C User's Group.

C-80 is also highly recommended by people I respect.]

CHAPTER 3
The Debates Go On

THE LANGUAGES ARTICLE

The languages issue occupied so much space that eventually I did a column with more than half devoted to the subject. The *BYTE* editors decided enough was enough, and pulled that out to form a stand-alone article.

It was quite popular with the readers, and I've updated it to be the bottom line for this part of the book.

The Debate Goes On ...
I've written several large computer programs. The two largest, an accounting package and my "minimum data base" do-all program, were originally written in BASIC. Another large program, my inter-stellar trader game, was written in Pascal. Recently I've had to make extensive revisions in all three of those programs. The results are interesting.

First, I find it impossible to work with BASIC programs. My accounting package, although originally in BASIC, was long ago translated to CBASIC, and from that to CB-80 (also called Compiled CBASIC). The translations make it possible to maintain the programs. If that hadn't been done, I wouldn't even try.

Example: my accounting program doesn't do depreciation, because almost all my accounting is done to satisfy the IRS, and the IRS wants depreciation handled in a rather special way. When I first began using micro computers to keep my books, I wrote what I thought was a simple BASIC program to keep track of depreciation. It didn't have to do much: simply list the item, when it was bought, the useful life, purchase price, amount claimed this year, and cumulative amount claimed over the life of the item. Each year I add new items at the end of the list, then run the program to figure and list out depreciated items.

The program has some checking to do, of course; the last year's claimed amount can't make the cumulative amount claimed be larger than the purchase price. Also, if the item was purchased *this* year, you can't claim a full year's depreciation, and have to pro rate it by the number of months you've used the equipment. Even so, it's a simple program.

It's simple, but this year it took me about as long to update that simple-minded little BASIC program as it did to add new major features to the accounting package. When I get a chance, I'm going to scrap my depreciation program and write it over, probably in CB-80 because it has to handle files, and I've still got some problems doing file handling with CP/M Pascal.

What I'm not going to do is put up with normal BASIC programs, with their line numbers, and cramped printout format, and the primitive text editing capabilities.

With CB-80 it's possible to write structured programs. Moreover, the compiler can be used to catch a lot of bugs. Example: in my minimum data base, there's a procedure to check the size of any entry. This is useful, since entries that are too long can't be printed properly (especially if they're to be printed on a mailing label). The original program got its input by calling a subroutine which both input the data and checked the input length.

Alas, that's silly. If you forget to specify the input length before calling the input subroutine, then the input length is checked against what the program was *last* told the input length should be; and that can cause really boffo problems. I know, because I did forget, not once but several times.

The remedy was simple: use a *function* to get input and check length. Define the function so that you *must* give it a maximum input length as a parameter when you call it. Now if you forget to do that, the compiler will complain.

When I did this, it came to me with blazing clarity that I'd hit on a major secret of good programming practice: let the compiler do much of the work for you. CB-80 is well designed to let you write structured code with good error checking.

However: it doesn't *force* you to write good code. You can still do things the wrong way if you want to. Pascal doesn't force you to write good code either, but it tries harder than CB-80. Marvin Minsky (founder of the MIT Artificial Intelligence Laboratories) once said that Pascal was a voluntarily worn straightjacket. In some ways he's right: one uses Pascal precisely because it won't let you do certain things. This can be annoying when you're writing the program, but it's surely a blessing when, a year later, you haul the thing out and try to remember what you did.

With that for background, let's speculate on the future of computer languages.

Viable Languages

I used to worry about including language discussions in these columns, because probably half my readers don't write programs. However, the mail indicates that this is one of the column's most popular features, and even those who don't write programs find the subject interesting. It is, after all, a matter of some importance: what languages will prevail in the microcomputer field?

No one knows. I have some informed guesses, and I get a lot of feedback from both amateur and expert readers; but I've lost the operator's manual to my crystal ball, so my predictions aren't 100% reliable. For all that, the subject is too important to ignore, and every now and then it's valuable to review just where things are in the field.

Let's set a ground rule. It's obvious that micro computers will continue to grow in capability even as their prices fall. The distinction between microcomputer and minicomputer is already blurred. In the next few years, memory will continue to drop in price while system speeds increase; within two years, one will be able to buy the equivalent of a VAX— the top of the line minicomputer from Digital Equipment Corporation (DEC)—for $6,000 or so, what people now pay for a good micro. This future "micro" will run at 12 to 15 megahertz, and have a half-million to a million bytes of memory; in other words, the micro will in effect have the power of machines that people now pay $75,000 and up for.

What languages will programs for the new generation of "microcomputers" be written in?

The first thing to note is that "efficiency" of the language isn't very important. There's enough computing power, and memory, to make up. True, languages which are *really* slow, or waste great gobs of memory, aren't likely to become popular; but cheeseparing benchmark comparisons won't matter a lot.

Given that, let's look at languages one at a time.

APL

APL, for those who don't know, is an interpreted language (like LISP or BASIC). It makes use of many curious symbols, such as squashed squares and bent arrows. It is very powerful. You can multiply matrices with single command, invert them with another, and do transformations of the results with two more commands. A single line of APL code can do complex arithmetic, logs, trigonometry, and fairly complicated logical operations. Alas, APL has been described, with good reason, as a "write only" language: you're just not likely to understand your program an hour after you've written it. Used interactively, though, it's hard to beat.

I foresee a place for APL in the micro future: it will turn small computers, especially portables, into *very* powerful desk calculators. It will already run on an Osborne-1, I understand that they're working on a version for the Otrona, and I expect that trend to continue. If someone will write a good introductory text, and APL implementers will do good tutorials with lots of examples, it's possible that APL will become quite popular for quick and dirty problem-solving. It won't ever be as popular as BASIC for calculator-like computation, but it will contend with it. I expect to use it that way myself.

There is an excellent APL for the Sage (68000) computer, although, like all APL implementations, it requires special graphics; in the case of the Sage, a special terminal. If APL could ever solve the problem of strange characters and squiggles, it would have a better chance. However, APL purists resist any movement to change the squashed boxes to some reasonably mnemonic English abbreviations, so the language's future remains doubtful.

It's too bad: for quick solutions to numerical problems, it's hard to beat APL for either speed or accuracy.

FORTH and LISP

I expect LISP to absorb FORTH. Not completely, of course, because nothing ever wins completely; but I know of nothing you can do with FORTH that you can't do with LISP, while LISP lets you do a lot that FORTH can't even approach.

FORTH is sometimes used to write operating systems, and was for some time the only powerful language available to Atari programmers. Like LISP, FORTH boasts a number of fanatic adherents. My mad friend used to say that FORTH was a kind of assembly language that used the programmer as a pre-processor.

LISP (List Processing language) was one of the earliest "higher level" computer languages. It was written by John McCarthy in the '50s, and has dominated the Artificial Intelligence (AI) field ever since. It's a very strange language, using peculiar notation, and *lots* of parentheses; but it's very powerful.

The main problems with LISP are (1) it's hard to learn from books, although not so hard to learn if you've access to people who already use it, and (2) it uses memory like mad, so that there haven't been good LISPs for micro computers.

FORTH has some similarities to LISP, but doesn't use as much memory. People I respect have convinced me that LISP is greatly more powerful than FORTH. Having half learned both LISP and FORTH, it's my opinion that they're equally difficult to master; both require a good bit of concentration, and you have to work until something clicks—what the *gestalt* psychologists call "the Aha! experience." They're also rather easy to forget if you don't use them regularly.

Incidentally, those who'd like "a LISP experience" without much investment should get Daniel P. Friedman's *The Little LISPer*. This rather odd book "is a programmed text based on lecture notes from a two-week 'quickie' introduction to LISP for students with no previous programming experience and an admitted dislike for anything quantitative." It has to be experienced to be appreciated; I found myself alternatively fascinated and throwing the book across the room. It certainly shows—not tells, but shows—you a lot about LISP.

As memory gets cheaper, small computers get more powerful, and communications get simpler, I expect many publishers will offer better LISP interpreters (and compilers; LISP is a hybrid, with the possibliity of both interactive—

interpretive mode and compiled mode), as well as more on-line tutorials, so that LISP will be easier to learn. FORTH and LISP users both tend to be fanatics. I'm neither, so it's only an informed guess; but I suspect that as LISPs get more common, LISP will get the bulk of the recruits who would otherwise have gone to FORTH.

[This paragraph was right in its effect, but wrong in much of its analysis.

LISP and FORTH really have little in common. FORTH was developed initially to control telescopes; its major feature is that it is very compact, and has high portability from one machine to another. It is not a memory hog like LISP.

FORTH is about as close to machine language as you can get and still claim to be a "higher level" language. In that sense Mac Lean was right. However, good FORTH programmers can do wonders with it, and often FORTH is the first language available on new machines.

LISP, on the other hand, is very memory hungry: real LISP programmers want 4 to 8 Megabytes. It is an odd language to learn (as is FORTH). It is also extremely powerful for text processing, decision analysis, and highly experimental computer work. There is a wealth of really powerful—and convenient—programs written in LISP that will one day be available when micro computers have enough memory and speed.

LISP is a favorite language in university departments of computer science, and thus gains a lot of recruits: far more than FORTH. In that sense my prediction was correct, even though the analysis was flawed.

COBOL and FORTRAN

Every time I say anything negative about COBOL, I get half a dozen letters reminding me that there are many *billions* of dollars worth of COBOL programs. Surely those won't go away?

I think they will. Not instantly, and I doubt that COBOL will vanish entirely, but I do not see a large place for COBOL in the micro world. If it were going to catch on, it would have by now; and it just hasn't. That, in my judgment, is just as well. COBOL is a language whose time has passed. It doesn't force readable code, it takes experts to maintain large COBOL programs, and it doesn't have most of the features required for structured programming.

It does certain things well. There are built-in commands for sorts and merges and other fairly complex operations. On the other hand, it's not hard to translate well-written COBOL programs into some other language, such as Pascal; while those programs not easily translated are generally almost impossible to maintain. For that matter, you can call some of those splendiferous special routines, such as sort, from inside languages like Modula. . . .

FORTRAN is another language that won't go away entirely, but will, I think, fade into the background. For a while it looked as if FORTRAN, augmented by the RATFOR (RATional FORtran) pre-processor, might stake out a large place in micro-land, but that didn't happen.

FORTRAN is very useful for crunching lots of numbers, and not all that well designed for anything else. You can write complex text-oriented programs in FORTRAN; the original Crowther and Wood Adventure of the Colossal Cave was written in FORTRAN. It wasn't designed for that, though, and FORTRAN. It wasn't designed for that, though, and FORTRAN programmers usually must resort to tricks to make it handle text well.

Because there are so very many COBOL and FORTRAN programs in existence, neither language will die; but as time goes on, most of those programs will be translated into other languages with better structural features, while fewer and fewer programmers will use either language for writing new programs for microcomputers.

If you have heaps and mounds of data, and must do moby number crunching, FORTRAN is still the language of choice; but now that hardware math chips, like the 8087, are available, and implementations of Pascal and Modula that know how to use the math chip, even that advantage is slowly fading.

The C Programming Language

The "C" language was developed at Bell Laboratories. Until recently its fate was totally dependent on the future of the Unix operating system. In the past couple of years, though, CP/M versions of C have appeared. One, Leor Zolman's BDS C Compiler, almost single-handedly made C a formidable contender because so very many useful programs were written in it.

With the development of Unix for large micros—and the vanishing of the distinction between minicomputer and microcomputer—the C language will experience another spurt in popularity. It has long been a favorite with true hackers.

Early implementations of C for micros, such as **BDS C**, had severe limits; now there are lots of C compilers without those limits. In addition, CPM-68K, the CP/M operating system for machines using the 16-bit 68000 processor chip, comes with a C compiler, and new C compilers appear almost weekly, each with additional features or conveniences. There are also a lot of books on C, whereas only two years ago, there was only one. All this attention will undoubtedly stimulate new users to learn something of the C language.

C is popular, and both C and the Unix operating system have fantical supporters. The language is powerful, and is certainly easier to learn than assembly languages.

The drawback is readability. C programs are not self-documenting; one could argue that there ought to be at least one comment for each line of code. Alas, the programs are *almost* readable, and while one is writing C programs, the purpose of each line is quite clear, so that further comments seem silly and are often omitted. Six weeks later the program is nearly incomprehensible.

A second problem with C—at least with the compilers I have been able to work with—is that it generates *very* large programs. For example,

```
/* A Very Simple Program. */
main ()
   {printf ("This is a very simple program.\n");
   }
```

is a program which merely prints the quoted message. (The \n specifies a "newline," ie., carriage return and line feed.)

We compiled it with Lattice C, which is a well regarded C compiler. The program itself is 384 Bytes long. It compiles into 178 bytes of object code. It must be linked to turn it into a command file before it can be run. That produces a program 11008 bytes long. This seems excessive.

When we installed our M-drive (a "silicon disk" program which deludes the computer into believing that extra memory is a *very* fast disk drive), we required a program to format the "memory disk." The program furnished us by

CompuPro was written in Whitesmith C, and was 16K bytes long. Tony Pietsch found this absurd, and wrote a format program in assembly language: it was only 487 bytes long.

There are good reasons for this obesity. The C language was originally intended for use with the Unix operating system, and much of the seemingly excessive code that must be packed into programs compiled in C is there to compensate for the missing Unix. The printf function—formatted printing—is responsible for much of the fatness in the "simple program." We may understand this and still be unhappy at the code size. There may be micro computer implementations which don't generate superfat code, but we haven't come across one.

C has become increasingly popular, and has fanatic supporters. It will certainly survive. However, I don't expect it ever to become a highly popular language, and if I had to bet on its future, I'd say that it will take a respectable niche, after which its growth will be quite slow in comparison to the micro world in general.

Until recently, those interested in learning more about the C language pretty well had to read *The C Programming Language* by Brian Kernighan and Dennis Ritchie. This book was better written than many computer texts, but it wasn't easy reading, and it was never intended for micro computer users.

I have recently received *C Programming Guide*, by Jack Purdom. I found this much clearer than Kernighan and Ritchie. Purdom's book has plenty of illustrative examples, and even compares C programs with similar programs in BASIC. It recognizes that many readers will be using CP/M systems, and explains some of the problems they may encounter. There's a very good discussion of pointers; this is especially welcome, because C makes extensive use of pointers. I recommend this book to anyone interested in learning more about the C language. Read it *before* trying to tackle Kernighan and Ritchie.

I have a large number of C compilers, and hope to do an extensive comparison of them for a future issue.

[I never did make that comparison, because *BYTE* did a splendid comparison article, making mine a work of supererogation.

Since I wrote the above, there have been strong indications that the Unix operating system will, for better or worse, become very important to the micro world. Both Intel, supported by IBM, and Digital Research, supported by AT&T, are working hard on Unix; and the entry of AT&T into the small computer market assures that at least one giant will push Unix hard. Since AT&T—before divestiture—licensed Unix and C to a number of universities for essentially no fee, a whole generation of computer scientists have grown up with Unix and like it. Unix is written in the C language, and indeed the C compiler is an integral part of the Unix system.

There is still some doubt about Unix. It is very large, and it tends to be slow. The IBM PC Unix implementation requires 15 floppy disks. Obviously, one needs lots of memory and a hard disk. In addition, Unix is very flexible; while this is an advantage, it leaves the problem of stability: the wizards at various universities continue to modify it, so that there is no longer any single "Unix" as such; there is Bell Unix, Berkeley Unix, and a number of clones.

AT&T has tremendous resources, and is strongly committed to Unix; this alone will assure that C has a larger place in the micro world than I predicted.]

Pascal and Modula-2

Pascal has been the real success story in micro computing. Last year there were more books published about Pascal than about BASIC. (By books, I mean titles; there were probably more copies sold of BASIC books than Pascal books.)

The Pascal language was devised by Prof. Niklaus Wirth of ETH in Zurich. It was originally intended as a teaching language which would force students to write readable, structured programs, and thus train them to think about programming in a logical way. It generated a number of enthusiastic converts who developed Pascal into a practical language. The structured features caused many program bugs to be caught by the compiler, so that once a program written in Pascal is made to run, it often runs properly without much debugging.

Pascal is now taught in many universities. Some require Pascal proficiency for graduation in any science. There are already Pascal courses in high schools, and that practice is also spreading. Thus the language has a secure place, and is probably second only to BASIC in popularity among micro computer users.

There are some very severe drawbacks to Pascal, particularly as implemented for small computers. The original language had primitive (and not well designed) input/output structures, so that most I/O has to be done through *extensions* to the language. The extensions have not been standardized, which compromises portability. (Portability refers to the ease of getting programs which run on one kind of machine to run on any other.) There are also internal limits to the language. Many of them have been discussed at length in previous columns.

Most of Pascal's deficiencies have been corrected in Niklaus Wirth's newest language called Modula-2. As I write this, we don't have many implementations of Modula-2; but the two potential U.S. publishers of Modula for micros, Volition Systems of San Diego and Logitech of Palo Alto, promise new compilers Real Soon Now. Fortunately, Volition Systems and Logitech are in communication, and seem willing to agree on standard ways of extending Modula. They may set a de facto standard that newer publishers will have to meet, and thus avoid the cacophony of dialects that afflicts Pascal.

My experience has been that Pascal programmers tend to become Modula-2 enthusiasts. Thus much of the excitement and popularity of Pascal may be transferred to Modula-2. There are good reasons for this. Modula-2 is more powerful than Pascal, and a lot easier to use. It is also very easy to translate Pascal programs into Modula-2; 90% or more of the work can be done by a translator program written in Modula-2. Add that Modula is suitable for writing systems programs—I've seen a very powerful operating system written in Modula-2—and it's not hard to predict that Modula-2 will become increasingly more popular as it becomes available.

My own prediction is that Modula will swallow a good chunk of both Pascal and C. So far not many experts join me in that forecast, but I've seen nothing to make me change my views on the matter.

[Two years later I have not changed my view: Modula-2 is the wave of the future, an excellent language with startlingly good features. It has taken longer than I expected to get good Modula-2 compilers on micro systems; but they are beginning to appear.

I personally prefer Modula-2 to any other language: although at the moment I continue to write most of my programs in CB80 or CB86, for lack of a good Modula-2 compiler.]

Ada

The Department of Defense estimates that if all DOD programs were written in a single language, the resulting savings would run to billions of dollars. After long consideration by a number of middle and high level committees, Ada was created to be *the* DOD programming language.

Ada will certainly have a large place in the computer world; any language supported by the Department of Defense would have to. As I've said before, learning to program in Ada is sure-fire job insurance.

Ada was designed by a committee, and it shows: it has *tons* of bells, whistles, features, and gimmicks. This tends to complicate the language, and some computer science experts have professed concern: given the complexity of Ada, how can you verify the language? That is: Can you be sure the compiler is doing all—and only—what you think it will, or can there be mysterious unintended side effects. If one side effect is to launch a missile without permission, all the savings resulting from Ada's creation could literally go up in smoke.

It's very hard to estimate Ada's future in the micro world. There are no full Ada compilers for micro computers, and there aren't likely to be any for a while. I think Ada's future in micro-land depends in large part on just how quickly we get an Ada compiler we can use.

Incidentally, I have just received Augusta, a program that compiles a subset of Ada on the Z-80. It has only just come, so I have been unable to compare it with Janus (which is the other Ada-subset compiler for micro systems). Augusta seems to run, and the manual is written in clear English with numerous examples. It does not support Packages, Multi-tasking, Real numbers, Enumerated types, User defined types and records, or Exception Error Handling. I find the Janus documentation more complete and better organized, but this is impressionistic, not based on detailed objective comparison.

[As my rather sarcastic comments indicated, Augusta wasn't very useful. However, R&R Software continues to expand the capability of their "Janus" Ada, and now expects to have a full Ada compiler for 16-bit machines such as the IBM PC.

Learning Ada is good job insurance. As of summer of 1984 there are no useful programs written in Ada (although the Janus compiler will compile itself, as will at least one other

Ada compiler) and the language has not been optimized, so that programs written in Ada tend to be large and slow. All that will, I am told, change Real Soon Now.

BOTTOM LINE

If I had to pick a single language for future micro computers, it would be Modula-2. That, however, is based on certain expectations about future Modula-2 implementations; just now (Mayday, 1983) I have no Modula-2 for CP/M systems.

[And on Mayday 1984 there wasn't a practical one; but as I write this I have received from Logitech a new version of their Modula compiler for the IBM PC, and Borland International is working hard on a Turbo Modula. It won't be long, I think.]

If I were going to buy and learn one single language of those available today, I'd be hard put to choose. The two I'd consider would be CB-80 and Pascal MT+ with the "Speed Programming Package." Both Pascal-MT+ and CB-80 are expensive; the term "overpriced" is a value judgment I find myself tempted to use. Even so, I like it somewhat better than I do the other Pascal implementations I have.

[I now recommend the Borland International Turbo Pascal implementation. It is fast, it has an integrated editor, and it is cheap.]

Deciding between Pascal and CB-80 isn't easy. Pascal, which also serves as a good introduction to Modula-2, is probably the more valuable to have learned over the long haul; but I find just now that I use CB-80 (and CB-86) more than I use Pascal.

It may be, of course, that I've missed the real contender; that Logo, or Smalltalk, or some such will sweep the field. I don't think that will happen, but it isn't impossible.

The language debate will continue.

PART FIVE:
SOME PREDICTIONS

The late Willy Ley wrote an excellent science column for *Galaxy Science Fiction*. He wasn't replaced after his death until, some years later, I took on the job. A couple of months later, Jim Baen became editor at Galaxy, and one way or another we've worked together ever since.

When Jim and I discussed this book, he recalled one of my earliest *Galaxy* columns. The original was written in 1972 just after I'd attended an annual meeting of the American Association for the Advancement of Science, and was later included in my 1979 book *A Step Farther Out*.

Comments inserted in 1979 are shown in *italics;* 1984 comments appear [in brackets].

CHAPTER 1
Here Come The Brains

Robots are a favorite science fiction theme. Another is the great computer, much smarter than a man, which one way or another takes over the world. Machine intelligence fascinates us.

Comparatively fewer stories deal with enhanced intelligence, mostly because that's very hard work: How do you write about a character who is very much smarter than you are? One theme I've been working on for years involves implants: you take a small transceiver and put it into a human head (or elsewhere in the anatomy if you like), wiring up the output of the receiver into the auditory nerves.

Now you have someone who can communicate by a kind of telepathy; not only with other similarly equipped humans, but with really large computers. In theory, at least, every bit of information known to mankind will be instantly available to this "terminal man."

Dossiers; reference books; dictionaries; encyclopedias; company records; all the data banks of the government; IRS files; any of this can be his for the asking. A detective could get continuous information on the whereabouts of his colleagues, or on the personal habits of the suspect he's questioning. A company president has but to think the question to know about production, sales, and schedules.

There would be more: all the mathematical capability of powerful computers available in real time. Solve integral equations in your head, calculus of finite motion, orbits, stock market projections, all instantly available at a thought.

It is not very far-fetched; in fact, the concept as given above is too tame. There's no real reason to restrict ourselves to the comparatively inefficient input device of the auditory nerve. Why not simply crack the code used by the brain and squirt in the information? More on that later; for now, what I've described could probably be built today. Prosthetic surgeons *already* can wire a hearing aid directly into the auditory nerve.

The only problem would be the language used to communicate with the computer. Voice communication in ordinary English is not yet accomplished—although computers can be taught to recognize a surprisingly large vocabulary. My own computer doesn't have a voice board yet, but it would, I am told, be simple to attach one that would let the machine I'm writing this on recognize some 64 different words and commands.

In fact, it is nearly inevitable that before the end of this century there will be at least some humans equipped with the transplant transceiver I've described.

Unfortunately, it's *very* difficult to think like a man who has a 360/95 in his head. I don't recall too many memorable stories in which the real geniuses were the viewpoint characters, for the obvious reason that the author can't think as would the super-intelligent character. Of the two that impressed me the most, *Flowers For Algernon* (the movie version was called *Charly*) and Ted Sturgeon's "Maturity," the central character lost the genius ability before the story ended.

And if there's a mental hookup to a computer in the future of some of the younger readers—and there probably is—there's another possibility also. A robot can be connected to the central brain, and of course there have been a *lot* of stories on that theme.

The only problem is, the central brain doesn't yet exist. Let's come back to that later.

There's no reason we couldn't build a central brain, but there's another approach: we may be on the way to *real* robots; self-contained, not relying on any kind of link with a central data bank, although able to use one if it's available; very strong; and capable of independent action if not thought.

Again, the mechanics are not complex. The Artificial Intelligence lab at MIT has had some problems trying to build a robot arm as dextrous as a human arm and hand, but given enough money it could be done. What's missing is the brain.

The human brain weighs, on average, about 1.48 kilograms, or 3 ¼ pounds, in the mature male. (Chauvinists may amuse themselves with the fact that female brains run about 10% less in weight; but they're advised to do it privately.) [It was less dangerous to say things like that in 1974.] That little chunk of matter can store some *one million billion* bits of information, which is quite a lot; the best computers don't yet have anything like that capacity, and they're still pretty big.

The computers are getting smaller all the time, though. I recall back in the early '50s visiting the ILIAC at the University of Illinois. ILIAC was at that time the biggest and most powerful computer in the world. Time on it was scheduled months in advance, and was reserved for the Naval Research Laboratories and the Institute for Advanced Studies, and such places. The computer was housed in a former gymnasium and cooled by the world's largest air-conditioner. Three undergraduates with shopping carts were employed full-time, three shifts a day, running around inside ILIAC's innards to replace burned-out vacuum tubes. Every computation was done three times and ILIAC took a majority vote on which was the correct answer—computations were slow, and tubes could burn out while they were going on.

It was an impressive sight. Nowadays, though, I can carry on my belt a TI 59—which is an order of magnitude more powerful than was ILIAC, and a very great deal more reliable.

Every year since the '50s the information storable in a given calculator chip volume has *doubled*; and that trend shows no sign of slowing. So, although the human brain remains, despite all the micro-chip technology, the most efficient data-storage system ever built, electronics is catching up. And the brain is nowhere near as reliable as are the computers of today. Our brain does, though, have the capability for packing a lot of data into a small space and retrieving it quickly.

The brain has another characteristic that's very useful: the information doesn't seem to be stored in any specific place. Karl Lashley, after 30 years of work trying to find the engram—the exact site of any particular memory—gave up. All our memories seem to be stored all over our brains.

That is: Lashley, and now others, train specific reflexes and memory patterns into experimental animals, then extirpate portions of their brains. Take out a chunk here, or a chunk there: surely you'll get the place where the memory is stored if you keep trying, won't you?

No. Short of killing the animal, the memory remains, even when up to 90% of the cortical matter has been removed. Lashley once whimsically told a conference that he'd just demonstrated that learning isn't possible.

The experiment has been duplicated a number of times, and the evidence of human subjects who've had brain damage as a result of accidents confirms it: our various memories are stored, not in one specific place, but in a lot of places; literally, all over our cortices. That's got to be a clue to how the brain works.

A second characteristic of the brain is that it's *fast*. Consider visual stimulation as an example. You see an unexpected object. You generally don't have to stop to think what it is: a hammer, a saucer, a pretty girl, the Top Sergeant, ice cream cone, saber-toothed tiger about to spring, or whatever; you just *know*, and know very quickly.

Yet the brain had to take the impulses from the light pattern on the retina and do something with them. What? Introspection hints that a number of trial and error operations were conducted: "test" patterns were compared with the stimulus object, until there was a close correspondence, and then the "aha!" signal was sent. If, somehow, the "aha!" was sent up for the wrong test pattern, it takes conscious effort to get rid of that and "see" the stimulus as it should be seen.

We're still trying to teach computers to recognize a small number of very precisely drawn patterns, yet yesterday I met a man I hadn't seen for ten years and didn't know well then, and recognized him instantly. Dogs and cats do automatically what we sweat blood to teach computers. If only we could figure out how the brain does it. . . .

A number of neuro-scientists think they've found the proper approach at last. It's only a theory, and it may be all wrong, but there is now a lot of evidence that the human brain works like a hologram. Even if that isn't how *our* internal computer works, a holographic computer could, at least in theory, store information as compactly and retrieve it as rapidly as the human brain, and thus make possible the self-contained robots dear to science fiction.

The first time Dr. David Goodman proposed the holographic brain model to me, I thought he'd lost his mind. Holograms I understood: you take a laser beam and shine part of it onto a photographic plate, while letting the rest fall on an object and be reflected off the object onto the film. The result is a messy interference pattern on the film that, when illuminated with coherent light of the proper frequency, will reproduce an image of the object. Marvelous and all that, but there aren't any laser beams in our heads. It didn't make sense.

Well, of course it does make sense. There's no certainty that holography is the actual mechanism for memory storage in human beings, but we *can* show the mechanism the brain might use to do it that way. First, though, let's look at some of the characteristics of holograms.

They've been around a long time, to begin with, and they don't need lasers. Lasers are merely a rather convenient (if you're rich enough to afford them) source of very coherent light. If you don't have a laser, a monochromatic filter will do the job nicely, or you can use a slit, or both.

A coherent light beam differs from ordinary light in the same way that a platoon of soldiers marching in step differs from a mob running onto the field after the football game. The light is all the same frequency (marching in step) and going in the same direction (parallel rays). Using any source of coherent light to make a hologram of a single point gives you a familiar enough thing: a Fresnel lens, which looks like a mess of concentric circles. Holography was around as "lenseless photography" back before WW II.

As soon as you have several points, the neat appearance vanishes, of course. A hologram of something complicated, such as several chessmen or a group of toy soldiers, is just a smeared film with strange patterns on it.

Incidentally, you can buy holograms from Edmund Scientific or a number of other sources, and they're fascinating things. I've even seen one of a watch with a magnifying glass in front of it. Because the whole image, from many viewpoints, is stored in the hologram, you can move your head around until you see the watch *through* the image of the magnifying glass—and then you can read the time. Otherwise the watch numerals are too small to see.

Hmm. Our mental images have the property of viewpoint changes; we can recall them from a number of different angles.

Another interesting property of holograms is that any significant part of the photographic plate contains the *whole* picture. If you want to give a friend a copy of your hologram, simply snip it in half; then you've both got one. He can do the same thing, of course, and so can the guy he gave his to. Eventually, when it gets small enough, the images become fuzzy; acuity and detail have been lost, but the whole image is still there.

That sounds suspiciously like the results Lashley got with his brain experiments, and also like reports from soldiers with severe brain tissue losses: fuzzy memories, but all of them still there. (I'll come back to that point and deal with aphasias and the like in a moment.)

Holograms can also be used as *recognition filters*. Let us take a hologram of the word "Truth" for example, and view a page of print through it. Because the hologram is blurry, we can't read the text: BUT, if the word "truth" is on that page, whether it's standing alone or embedded in a longer word, you will see a very bright spot of light at the point where the word will be found when you remove the filter.

The printed word can be quite different from the one used to make the hologram, by the way. Different type fonts can be employed, and the letters can be different sizes. The spot of light won't be as bright or as sharp if the hologram was made from a type font different from the image examined, but it will still be there, because it's the *pattern* that's important.

The Post Office is working on mail-sorting through use of this technique. Computers can be taught to recognize patterns this way. The police find it interesting too: you can set up a gadget to watch the freeways and scream when it sees a 1964 Buick, but ignore everything else; or examine licence plates for a particular number.

There's another possibllity. Cataracts are caused by cloudy lenses. If you could just manage to make a hologram of the cataracted lens, you could, at least in theory, give the sufferer a pair of glasses that would compensate for his cataracts.

That technique isn't in the very near future, but it looks promising.

You'll have noticed that this property of holograms sounds a bit like the brain's pattern-search when confronted with an unfamiliar object. A large number of test patterns can be examined "through" a hologram of the stimulus object, and one will stand out.

Brain physiologists have found another property of the brain that's similar to a holographic computer. The brain appears to perform a Fourier transform on data presented to it; and holograms can be transmitted through Fourier-transform messages.

A Fourier transform is a mathematical operation that takes a complex wave form, pattern, signals, or what have you, and breaks it down into a somewhat longer, but precisely structured, signal of simpler frequencies. If you have a very squiggly line, for example, it can be turned into a string of numbers and transmitted that way, then be reconstructed exactly. The brain appears to make this kind of transformation of data.

Once a message (or image, or memory) is in Fourier format, it's easy systematically to compare it with other messages, because it is patterned into a string of information; you have only to go through those whose first term is the same as your unknown, ignoring all the millions of others; and then find those with similar second terms, etc., until you've located either the proper matching stored item, or one very close to it. If our memories are stored either in Fourier format or in a manner easily converted to that, we've a mechanism for the remarkable ability we have to recognize objects so swiftly.

So. It would be convenient if the brain could manufacture holograms; but can it, and does it?

It *can*: that is, we can show a mechanism it could use to do it. Whether it does or not isn't known, but there don't appear to be any experiments that absolutely rule out the theory.

There are rythmic pulses in the brain that radiate from a small area: it's a bit like watching ripples from a stone thrown into a pond. Waves or ripples of neurons firing at precise frequencies spread through the cerebrum. These, of course, correspond to the "laser" or coherent light source of a hologram. Beat them against incoming impulses and you get an electrical/neuron-firing analog of a hologram.

Just as you can store thousands of holograms on a single photographic plate by using different frequencies of coherent light for each one, so could the brain store millions of billions of bits of information by using a number of different frequencies and sources of "coherent" neuron impulses.

That model also makes something else a bit less puzzling; selective loss of memory. Older people often retain very sharp memories for long-past events, while losing the ability to remember more recent things; perhaps they're losing the ability to come up with new coherent reference standards. Some amnesiacs recall nearly everything in great detail, yet can't remember specific blocks of their life: the loss or scrambling of certain "reference standards" would tend to cause *en bloc* memory losses without affecting other memories at all.

Aphasias are often caused by specific brain-structure damage. I have met a man who can write anything he likes, including all his early memories; but he can't talk. A brain injury caused him to "forget" how. It's terribly frustrating, of course. It's also hard to explain, but if the brain uses holographic codes for information storage, then the encoder/decoder must survive for that information to be recovered. A sufficiently selective injury might well destroy one decoder while leaving another intact.

In other words, the model fits a great deal of known data. Farther than that no one can go. The brain *could* use holograms.

Not very long ago, Ted Sturgeon, A. E. van Vogt, and I were invited to speak to the Los Angeles Cryonics Society. That's the outfit that arranges to have people quick-frozen and stored at the temperature of liquid nitrogen in the hopes that someday they can be revived in a time when technology is sufficiently advanced to be able to cure whatever it was that killed them to begin with.

I chose to give my talk on the holographic brain model. The implications weren't very encouraging for the Cryonics Society.

If the brain uses holographic computer methods, then the information storage is probably *dynamic*, not static; and even if a frozen man could be revived, since the electrical impulses would have been stopped, he'd have no memories, and thus no personality. If the holographic brain model is a true picture, it's goodbye to that particular form of immortality.

On the other hand, whether our own brains use holograms or not, holographic computers almost undoubtedly will work; and the holographic information storage technique offers us a way to construct those independent robots that figure so large in science fiction stories. Either way, it looks as if the big brains may be coming before the turn of the century.

The above was written in 1974. It needed surprisingly little revision—none, in fact, except to foreshadow the next part. Since 1974, though, there have been some exciting developments. Most of them came to light at the 1976 meeting of the American Association for the Advancement of Science, and were reported in my column "Science and Man's Future: Prognosis Magnificient!" from which the following has been derived. JEP 1979

Studies of how we think—and of how machines might do so—continue. Take biofeedback. The results are uncanny, and they're just beginning. Barbara Brown, the Veteran's Administration Hospital physiologist whose book *New Mind, New Body* began much of the current interest in biofeedback, is now convinced that there's nothing the eastern yogas can do that you can't teach yourself in weeks to months. Think about that for a moment: heart rate, breathing, relaxation, muscle tension, glandular responses—every one of them subject to your own will. Dr. Brown is convinced of it.

The results are pouring in, and not just from her VA hospital in Sepulveda, either. Ulcers cured, neuroses conquered, irrational fears and hatreds brought under conscious control, and all without mysticism. When I put it to Dr. Brown that there was already far more objective evidence for the validity of the new psycho-physiological theories than there ever has been for Freudian psychoanalysis, she enthusiastically agreed.

One does want to be careful. There are many charlatans in the biofeedback business; some sell equipment, others claim to be "teachers." The field is just too new to have many standards, in either equipment or personnel, and the potential buyer should be wary. However, there is definite evidence, hard data, to indicate that you can, with patience (but far less than yoga demands) learn to control many allergies, indigestion, shyness, fear of crowds, stage fright, and muscular spasmodic pain; and that's got to be good news.

After I left the AAAS meeting in Boston I wandered the streets of New York between editorial appointments. On the streets and avenues around Times Square I found an amazing sight. (No, not *that*; after all, I live not far from Hollywood and thus am rather hard to shock.)

Every store window was filled with calculators. Not merely "four function" glorified arithmetic machines, but real calculators with scientific powers-of-ten notation, trig, logs, statistical functions, and the rest. Programmable calculators for under $300. (*Since that was written programmables have fallen in price; you can get a good one with all scientific functions for $50 now, while the equivalent of my SR-50 now sells for $12.95 in discount houses. JEP.*)

Presumably there's a market for the machines: which means that we may, in a few years, have a large population of people who really do use numbers in their everyday lives. That could have a profound impact on our society. Might we even hope for some rational decision-making?

John R. McCarthy of the Stanford University Artificial Intelligence Laboratories certainly hopes so. McCarthy is sometimes called "the western Marvin Minsky." He foresees home computer systems in the next decade. OK, that's not surprising; they're available now. (*Since* that *was written, the home computer market has boomed beyond anyone's prediction; in less than two years home computers have become well-nigh ubiquitous, and everyone knows someone who has one or is getting one. I even have one; I'm writing this on it. JEP*) McCarthy envisions something a great deal more significant, though: information utilities.

There is no technological reason why every reader could not, right now, have access to all the computing power he or she needs. Not wants—what's needed is more than what's wanted, simply because most people don't realize just what these gadgets can do. Start with the simple things like financial records, with the machine reminding you of bills to be paid and asking if you want to pay them—then doing it if so instructed. At the end of the year it flawlessly and painlessly computes your income tax for you.

Well, so what? We can live without all that, and we might

worry a bit about privacy if we didn't have physical control over the data records and such. Science fiction stories have for years assumed computer-controlled houses, with temperatures, cooking, menus, grocery orders, etc., all taken care of by electronics; but we can live without it.

Still, it would be convenient. (*More than I knew when I wrote that; I don't see how I could get along without my computer, which does much of that, now that I'm used to it. JEP*)

But what of publishing? McCarthy sees the end of the publishing business as we know it. If you want to publish a book, you type it into the computer terminal in your home; edit the text to suit yourself; and for a small fee put the resulting book into the central information utility data banks.

(*So far I have described how I now, only two years after I wrote the above, prepare my own books. The difference is that after I have them composed on the TV-like screen, and edited to my satisfaction—a computer-controlled typewriter puts in onto paper, which is mailed to New York, edited again, and given to someone to type into electronically readable form for typesetting. Obviously that stage will be eliminated soon; why can I not send a tape and be done with it? Incidentally, the new newspaper known as the NY Trib has no typewriters or paper at all: reporters and rewrite persons work on a TV screen, editors call that up to their screens, and when done the text goes directly to composing without ever being on paper at all. JEP*)

Once a book is in the central utility data banks, those who want to read it can call it up to their TV screen; a royalty goes from their bank account to the author's; where is the need for printer or publisher? Of course some will still want *books* that you can feel and carry around; but a great deal of publishing can be as described above, and for that matter there's no reason why your home terminal cannot make at reasonable cost a hard copy of anything you really want to keep.

Few publishers own printing plants; most hire that done. What publishers provide is editorial services and distribution. The latter function will largely vanish: the information utility does that job. There remain editorial services.

With such a plethora of books as might appear given the above—after all, the only cost to "publish" a book would be to have it typed, plus a rather nominal fee to the utility for storing it—critics and editors will probably grow in importance. "Recommended and edited by Jim Baen," or "A Frederik Pohl Selection" would take on new significance, and one assumes that these editors would continue to work with authors since they'd hardly recommend a book they didn't like (and some authors might even admit that a good editor can help a book). "Big Name" authors would probably have little to worry about, with their readers sending in standing orders for their works; new writers would probably have to get a "name critic" to review their stuff.

OK; still not all that new for veteran science fiction readers; but did you catch the time scale? The equipment, *all* of it, exists *now*. The telephone net to link nearly everyone in the U.S. with the information utilities exists *now*. Computer electronics costs are plummeting. McCarthy's home terminal can be with us in the next five years, with the information utility fully developed in ten to fifteen.

In fact, the only obstacle is entreprenurial: the equipment and technology exist at affordable costs. It takes only someone to organize it.

But—in twenty years we may not need the home terminals except as backup. Dr. Adam Reed of Rockefeller University has a new scheme: direct computer to brain hookups.

Ten years: Dr Reed believes that within ten years we will have cracked the code that the brain uses for information processing and storage. Once that's done, information can be fed directly into the brain's central processing unit without going through such comparatively slow peripheral equipment as eyes and ears. You need not read a book: the computer can squirt the book's contents directly into your mind.

Of course it won't be the same experience: that is, when I read *War and Peace* there was more than a transfer of information. There were also emotional responses. Those would be lacking in the direct information-acquisition experience. Thus there will probably remain a few nuts who read, just as TV hasn't quite eliminated literacy in the U.S.; but it may well be that within your lifetime the normal method of acquiring information, particularly of grasping the content of dull books that everyone wants to have read but no one wants to read, will be through computers.

This means a complete restructuring of our education system, and perhaps it is high time; yet I have met few teachers who have thought about the new capability at all, and there is no one I know of planning for the time when we do not have to sit in classrooms for the first twenty years of our lives.

There will always be a need for education, of course; for those who can teach their pupils to *use* the information available to them; and who will teach them to be civilized (although that latter may not be a function of schools, and certainly is only indifferently performed in large areas just now.)

Incidentally: Reed believes that each of us has a different code; not all brains use the same information processing symbols. Thus each of us would need a computer that has been taught to use *our* coding system. That is no bar, of course; the computer system need not be very expensive, and probably won't be, at least not after a few years. (One speculation: if each of us uses a different coding system, then true telepathy would be rare—and far more common among identical twins than among others. All of which seems to echo experience.)

And the implications of all this are staggering. In the near future—in *your lifetimes*, most of you—there will be those who, having obtained an implant, will quite literally know everything known to the human race. (This assumes that the information utilities will also exist; but those seem inevitable.) Want a multiple-regression equation linking weather, gasoline consumption, electricity generation, ship keels laid, the price of wheat futures, and the number of wall posters in Peking? Merely think the question and wait; it shouldn't be long before you have it.

Because, according to Reed, the implanted transceivers I have used in various stories (*High Justice, Exiles to Glory*, etc.) are perfectly workable—but I may have been too conservative. Certainly though we will have implants that "talk" to you, feeding information directly to auditory and optic nerves; in fact we have them, crudely, now, and use them to make the blind see and the deaf hear. So far have we come in the past few years. In the not distant future we shall do more for the handicapped than was ever thought possible. The "Bionic Man," shorn of some of the more impossible touches that violate the laws of thermodynamics, may become reality in this century.

But go further: when the coding system is completely known, a human personality can be "recorded;" and if the cloning experiments prove out, the personality can be transcribed into a younger edition of the same person: know what you have learned at fifty, or eighty, and put that into a body aged 25.

Far out? Science fiction? No. There's a very real possibility that it can happen to some of you; a very small possibility that it might happen to me.

It's getting hard for science fiction writers to keep up: even we are getting future shock. But it's all for real, you know.

It can all happen. The Big Brains are coming.

[The evidence for holographic data storage in the brain is ambiguous. Dr. Marvin Minsky, Donner Professor of Technology at MIT and a thorough expert on both human and artificial intelligence, doesn't accept it, and I gather that the theory is a bit out of favor.

It remains *possible* but less likely than when I reported it. On the other hand, the small implanted transceivers described above have become even more likely; they may exist before the turn of the century.]

CHAPTER 2
The Brains Keep Coming

In the early 1980s Jim Baen was editor at Ace Books. He missed the monthly grind of *Galaxy Science Fiction* and eventually invented a magazine that looked like a book. It bore the unlikely name *Destinies*, which made it sound like a "metaphysics" publication; but it was arguably the best science fiction magazine in existence during its life.

Given the years Jim and I had worked together at *Galaxy*, it was probably inevitable that I would become the science editor and columnist for *Destinies;* and in due time I produced this essay.

I've just finished reading my 1974 essay "Here Come The Brains" (included in my book *A Step Farther Out*, Ace 1979, and if you read this column you *must* want that book....) and I find that when I refurbished that essay in spring of '79 I had to insert about a dozen interpolated comments. The Big Brain Revolution procedes apace as I predicted—except that it's somewhat ahead of schedule.

Consider: I wrote that essay on what was then one of the best tools available to a writer, an IBM Selectric II typewriter. The 1979 revisions weren't done on a typewriter at all. Instead, I used a home computer system, in which the text appears on a glass TV-like screen and can easily be edited in various ways. In fact, one doesn't bother with things like a carriage return at the ends of lines: the computer figures that out and wraps the words around for you. You just type, and mark the ends of paragraphs, and let the machine take care of the other trivial details.

But for this essay I'm working with something considerably in advance of my home system. Oh, true, I'm physically banging away on my normal keyboard (which looks suspiciously like a Selectric keyboard; one's fingers get used to certain patterns) but in fact my computer is taking a rest. I've got it fooled into thinking it's no more than a rather smart terminal, and the actual text storage and editing is being done on the other side of the continent in New Jersey. Moreover, as I write this I'm in nearly instant communication with a number of computer experts not shy about letting me know if I've made a mistake. (Actually, it's a rather upsetting experience to know that a dozen or more people may be looking over your shoulder, and normally I wouldn't write under those circumstances; but it is amusing to use an experimental information exchange brain for *this* column, and it may even be that useful suggestions will come from someone in, say, Seattle, or at Stanford.)

Now, true, my impromptu "consultants" for this article consist of a random selection of people mad enough to be up and logged onto a computer at this ghastly hour; but it need not be that way. I could have invited several people to watch and make comments, and it would have worked the same way.

And there's one look into the future: the nearly unlimited conference with instant feedback. Of course it's possible now and certainly will be simple in the future to restrict one's audience to those invited; the public features are peculiar to the system I'm working with, not inherent in the long-range use of a big brain. This happens to be a commercial system which has invited several users to try it out (I suspect in part to see if we'd be interested in paying for the service) and not all the bells and whistles are installed. Still, it's more than enough to give an idea of how it works.

Then, too, a few months ago Larry and I were shown around MIT's Artificial Intelligence Laboratories, and got to see some of their *very* large brains in operation; and they are impressive indeed.

Anway, given all this new computing experience that has suddenly come my way, it seemed reasonable to devote a column to the present and future state of the Big Brains....

* * *

But first, perhaps we ought to look at the "little brains" available to anyone—and realize that not long ago these micro computers now aggressively sold by firms like Radio Shack and the Heath Company would have been considered very powerful machines indeed. In fact, my home micro in its own right has considerably more computational power than the best computers envisioned by Robert Heinlein in his future history series—and he was one of the most accurate predictors of the future that we had.

Recall what his best computers were doing? Andrew Jackson "Slipstick" Libby, a young genius with total recall who'd memorized the log tables, was able to do the machine's job, which mostly consisted of multiplying numbers and solving simple algebraic equations. No human alive could keep up with my computer, which can patiently rattle off complicated equations full of natural logs and fractional exponents.

And I've often told the story of my 1954 visit to ILIAC, then the world's largest and most expensive machine, which couldn't even match a good modern hand calculator, much less an inexpensive (under $1000 in 1979 dollars) home micro. There's a lot of computational power available in the "little" brains; enough to make several business revolutions fairly certain, and we'll return to that subject.

Moreover, the *big* brains are more and more available to the general public. In the '60s there were a number of commercial firms which offered access to big machines; that idea died because it was too early, but now I see new ads for nets that for $100 hookup and a few bucks an hour will connect you to a big machine similar to the MIT system, and I predict a great future for that business. By the time this gets into print I expect there will be two or three nets; before this essay gets collected into book form there will be a LOT of them, probably including Ma Bell who may find it profitable to give away the computer time to encourage you to use your phone more.

So what good is all that?

A lot. And the effects will change your life, some in subtle ways, some fairly dramatic.

First, the text editor itself. Although there are some bugs in these programs (MIT's fanciest text editor sort of grew, and to the extent it was designed at all was intended for people fairly sophisticated in the use of computers rather than naive users) the fact is that even the worst of them beat the daylights out of a Selectric II. Consider: one major secret of success in professional writing is that the public rarely sees a first draft. The best way to do good writing is to rewrite. Sometimes to rewrite a *lot*. But that takes mechanical work. There's nothing fun about bashing the keys of a typewriter, and it's even less amusing to take a nice clean draft and start tearing it apart. The psychological block against smearing ink on a pretty, new copy fresh back from the typist is Alps-sized.

But if you know that a clean copy can be obtained in seconds ... and that you needn't retype anything other than the changes themselves ... then rewriting becomes easy.

Computers can take all the mechanical work out of writing. They can go further than that. They can automatically check spelling, and ask if you really meant "thrity" or "seperate." It won't be long before programs to correct grammar will be available.

That's text creation. What of publishing?

The publishing industry as we know it is inevitably doomed. I've described this before, but it can't hurt to repeat it: once the big brains become easily available to everyone, "publishing" will consist of writing your book and depositing it in a central information utility. Those wanting to read it simply ask for it; their credit card information is already on file as part of their access to the big computer. The book appears on their screen and their account is charged for the service. A royalty is simultaneously credited to the author's account.

This could be done now, but it won't happen for a few years. At the moment, books are more convenient: you can carry a book around with you, from room to room or even out of the house, while to read via computer requires you to stay next to the terminal. However they'll soon improve the terminals. There's no reason you couldn't have a handy flat screen, not a lot bigger or heavier than a book, something easily held in your lap, with controls for "turning pages" backward or forward. The first ones will have a cable running to a wall jack, but later improvements can let your pocket terminal communicate wirelessly via satellite, giving all the handiness of a book—and the convenience of carrying a whole library.

Now publishing by computer has problems. One severe difficulty will be piracy—but then piracy is already a problem in these days of cheap copying machines and offset presses. As far as I can tell there are no "show stopper" problems associated with using computers for most information exchange.

Another industry that will be greatly affected by cheap Big Brains is education. For example: MIT has a program called MACSYMA, short for Symbolic Algebra, which literally lets you play about with systems of equations, do substitutions, change variables, put in trial values, integrate, differentiate, get numerical answers—all without having to worry about mistakes in your arithmetic. MACSYMA is capable of very high-powered operations, such as expanding Taylor series, doing Fourrier transforms, and mucking around with functions of complex variables—but it is also simple to use. Mrs. Ellen Lewis Golden, one of the MIT Mathlab staff, was amused to find that her seven-year-old son had plugged in every mathematical fact he'd been taught and solemnly reported that MACSYMA got a grade of 100.

If something like that had been available when I was an undergraduate, I may well have become a theoretical physicist. I never had much trouble understanding the *concepts* of modern physics, but when it actually came to crunching the numbers to produce a result tallying with the answer in the back of the book I had a notable lack of success. Since I couldn't be *sure* I understood what I was doing—the only real check was whether you got the right answer—there seemed nothing for it but to go into a field in which I got better grades. It wasn't for years that I learned that my mistakes were truly trivial, things like multiplying wrong or dropping decimal places, or even silly late-night mistakes in addition. By then it was too late.

Five years from now that won't happen to anyone. Within five years every student (well, every student in an up-to-date university) will have access to enough computing power to generate the right answers provided the student has asked the right questions. The dropped decimal and the inadvertent change of sign are on their way out as eliminators of hard-science majors. I can't think that will be detrimental to our future.

Beyond that, what? First, let's set some ground rules. I can't possibly cover the entire subject of the electronics revolution. I can't consider all the implications of the big brains in simulations: of such sophisticated modeling that you really can do "thought experiments" with new chemical and physical processes and get meaningful results; but it's clear that such modeling and the resulting proliferation of formerly-too-expensive experiments will have a fairly profound effect on the knowledge explosion.

For this column I want primarily to look at the effect of big brains as they become increasingly available to the general public. Even that's a tall order.

After all—what are computers used for now? Games, mostly, isn't it? Do the people who buy them actually do anything but play "Star Trek"?

Yes: true, for the first couple of years all the magazines intended for the home computer user were largely filled with articles about and programs for playing games (and usually damned dull games at that) but that's no longer true. Now the average issue of *BYTE* is likely to be devoted to accounting systems, or basic robotics. There are still games in plenty, but even in that field it's interesting to watch progress: from "guess a number" and primitive versions of hangman to Othello and Chess . . . and then beyond board games entirely, to things you can't do without either a computer or a large crew of referees.

As for example ZORK, a fine madness in which one goes exploring a dungeon, gathers treasures, solves puzzles, maps large areas, escapes death (or even gets resurrected if need be!). In ZORK and its predecessor ADVENTURE and other games of that ilk, the machine knows where you can get to from where you are, and tells you what you see when you do certain things. A typical ZORK command might be "Go north," and the reponse might be "You have come to a long winding corridor, dimly lit with torches. At the far end you see six elves kneeling to shoot dice. From their conversation you learn they are dicing to determine which one will kill you."

Now what earthly use is a thing like that (beyond having fun with it)?

Well, number one, in order to make the game interesting the implementers have had to invent something fairly sophisticated: a parser, which actually takes simple English and does a fair job of interpreting it into something the computer can deal with. And that is, when you stop to think of it, no small feat—and as applicable to a business computing system, or a device for controlling industrial processes, as to a game.

Second, the ZORK and ADVENUTRE type of games have in them a map: at any given point in the game there are a number of things you can do, and your alternatives change as you move through the dungeon; moreover, you may have removed objects from a particular room so that the next time you visit it your alternatives are not at all those you had the last time through.

Generalize that: doesn't it sound like a pretty sophisticated "programmed learning" device? Change the script from dice-throwing elves to "Force = mass times acceleration," and the response you give from "Go north and get sword" to an attempt to explain what $F = MA$ means—and you're on the way to a teaching program. With a little work you can set things up so that a good teacher, knowing nothing about computers and programs, would be able to design a course and put the proper concepts into it.

The implications for education are obvious. A great deal of learning requires nothing more than a very patient teacher. I can think of few humans as patient as a computer....

Now programmed learning has to be done carefully; there are a lot of subjects not amenable to it. But some things simply must be learned (taxonomy, syntax, things of that ilk) and they're as dull to the teacher as the student; computers are ideal teachers in many such instances. Mrs. Pournelle has found that her classroom computer has sufficient fascination that many of her students will play educational games by the hour—the same students whose span of attention is usually measureable in seconds.

And for that matter, need we dismiss the fun aspects of ZORK quite so quickly? These games are not dull (I found ZORK a trap into which I put altogether too much time) and solving one can take longer than reading a novel. In fact, the adventure-oriented game may well become a rival to the adventure novel, and Larry Niven and I are seriously considering designing such an adventure to be implemented by the computer geniuses for sale to the computer-owning public. An enthusiastic blurb for one of my recent books said "You will live the life of the JANISSARIES ..."; the computer adventure would make that very nearly true.

* * *

So far we've talked about "Big Brains" and computers as if they were black boxes; and in one sense that's the proper way to think about them. As these things become more advanced there's less and less need to understand what goes on inside them. Indeed, when I first bought mine I was determined not to know.

That resolution faded when I discovered one of the major problems with these machines: the people who understand them simply cannot talk intelligently to the people who don't. As a result there are all kinds of nasty surprises waiting for the naive user. In simple self-defense I had to delve into the theory of modern computers ... and once inside the black box my insatiable curiosity took over.

Once you know what's happening inside the computer it becomes a lot easier to predict their future: not only to see that it will not be long before you and I will be able to afford a system with nearly all the capabilities of MIT's Big Brain, but to *know* that development is inevitable.

Thus I'm going to take a minor excursion into how these things work, but do understand: the brain revolution does not depend on a general public understanding of the machines, nor does it depend on the computer scientists learning how to write. If it did, I'd say the revolution is a long way off indeed; but as I hope to show in a few paragraphs, that problem is going to solve itself.

The first thing you learn about modern computers is that they're *small*. The working heart of my fairly advanced home micro is an eletronic chip about three inches long by one wide. The rest of my system, taking up about four cubic feet for the computer itself and another three for the disk drives, is auxilliary equipment: power supplies and motors and memory boards and the like, and all of it could be considerably compressed if necessary, since a great deal of it is empty space to promote cooling air flow.

Because they're small, these machines are *fast*. In the early days of computers it seemed ridiculous to worry about the physical size of the machines: after all, the information moved about inside them at the speed of light, and what's a foot or so at that speed? But as larger and more complex computers were contemplated that path length became increasingly important until it was critical, and if the Large Scale Integrated circuit (LSI) hadn't been developed the really big brains would have been impossible.

LSI technology also made the machines cheap: the central processing unit chip in my computer can be bought in quantities for under twenty dollars. The recent popularity of home computers has also brought down the price of the other chips: while last year memory was in the order of $1600 for 64,000 "bytes" (don't worry about it; a byte can be thought of as an alpha-numeric character like the number 8 or the letter a or the symbol *) you can now buy 64,000 bytes for under $500—and the price, as well as the size of the memory chips, continues to plummet.

About that number 64,000. It's fairly critical to micro computers, because it's the number of memory cells the central processing unit—the tiny brain chip that does all the work—can directly address. Actually the number isn't 64,000, but 65,536, which is two to the 16th power. "Micro" computers are 8-bit machines and employ two-word addresses, and once again I'll explain before I lose someone.

A computer is a two-state device: that is, deep in the machine's heart there is nothing more complicated than an ability to detect whether a particular chunk of the computer's memory contains a zero or a one. (Incidentally, although there are a number of science fiction novels that deal with the marvel wrought by the invention of a three-state or multi-state machine using a logic more complex than the zero,one logic of present devices, don't believe them: with a two-state machine you can simulate any degree of multi-state logic.) For reasons we won't go into here, a single cell's worth of information is called a "bit," and at the risk of boring some of my computer-familiar readers, let me say it another way: one "bit" of information consists of no more and no less than knowing whether a particular memory location holds a zero or a one. (Purists will know that there's nothing sacred about zero and one; I could as easily use "true or false" or "red or green" or any other pair of mutually exclusive terms.)

A single bit of information generally isn't very useful. (Although it *could* be: is the switch that controls an ICBM launch open or closed?) Computers therefore collect the bits into larger chunks which are sometimes called "words." Micro computers use words that are 8 bits long. Now it is obvious that the number of different "things" an eight-bit word can distinguish between is two to the eighth, i.e., 256. (I know;

for some of you it isn't obvious, but in the interest of getting on with this you'll simply have to take my word for it.)

Each memory cell of a micro will hold one 8-bit "word." Since there are 26 letters in the alphabet, (double that to distinguish between lower case and capitals), and ten digits (0 through 9), each word of micro memory can hold the binary equivalent of one alpha-numeric character. Actually, in addition to the letters and numbers a standard character set includes punctuation marks and also some "special" characters such as "carriage return" and "delete," used to control devices like automatic typewriters; even with all those we only come up to 128 distinct characters, which is two to the seventh. For a number of reasons, a seven-bit machine would be highly inconvenient, so the central computer chip is designed to handle the next larger number.

The capability to deal with eight-bit words is designed into the central processing chip, an LSI which contains the equivalent of thousands of transistors and vacuum tubes. Also built-in to the microprocessor chip is an ability to use two words as a memory address—which is why you can't (without a number of programming tricks) put more than 65,536 memory cells in a micro.

Now that's a fairly large number, but it's not all *that* big: for example it's only about 11,000 words of standard English text, which means that if you want to work on something larger (like a novel) you have to have some other means of storing the information because you can't keep all of it in the computer's memory. There are a number of mass storage devices adapted to the home computer market. At the moment the most common is a simple tape cassette. More convenient is a "floppy disk," which looks a bit like a phonograph record sprayed with the dull brown magnetic coating of a cassette tape. Floppies can hold some 256,000 alpha-numeric characters and feed that information into the computer at many thousands of characters a second. More convenient still is the "hard disk," which by using a very rigid magnetic disk can squeeze several millions of words into a package smaller than a cubic foot, and can pick up or put down information at blinding speed—for example, a good hard disk system can copy this entire article onto disk quicker than I can read the four-word message saying that it has made the copy.

And the point of all this is that there are two major differences between micro computers and the really big brains: the big machines process bigger "words" (some use 16-bit words and some 32-bit words) and thus address far more memory as well as process a lot more information per cycle; and the big machines have hard disks. Those differences are rapidly vanishing. There is already a reliable hard disk for home computers selling for under $5000, and that price will fall; while a number of electronic suppliers are designing 16- and 32-bit chips suitable for small systems. In addition, there are a lot of new techniques for making memory cheaper. The result is that well before the end of the 1980s you and I will be able to afford machines with all the computing power now available to MIT's big brains.

That doesn't mean that we will automatically be able to do everything the big systems can do. Hardware isn't everything. Left to itself, a big computer won't do anything more than a small one (or indeed anything at all). That's one of the things that happened to the earlier commercial attempts to sell time on big machines: the customers just didn't know what to do with them.

Computers are extremely stupid. All they really know how to do is twiddle bits at incredible speeds. Their usefulness comes when someone figures out how to take a gadget that can add ones and zeros and turn that capability into, say, a text editor like the one I'm writing this on.

One way someone might do that would be to build a program specific to a particular processor. The CPU (Central Processing Unit, the "brain") has what's called an "instruction set," which is a list of its capabilities and the command the machine has to get in order to make it do that. A typical instruction might be "load the accumulator with the character stored in the memory location you'll find in your H,L register." Another might be "subtract one from the number now in the accumulator." Each such operation is commanded by a code number. When I first got involved with computers back in the '50s all programming was like that: you figured out what tiny specific operations the machine had to perform in order to get the result you wanted. (I was trying to make it invert a matrix, and it took three of us all summer to write the program.)

There are two problems with this kind of programming.

It's hard to do, and it is highly specific to the particular machine; a program that runs on one computer won't run on another. Fortunately, though, once good machines were developed the people who really knew computers invented programs that would understand much higher languages: that is, there are now programming languages in which the way you tell the machine to invert a matrix is to say "INVERT MATRIX." A special program translates that instruction into the tiny specific operations needed for the particular machine you're running at the time; and the same program will run on more than one kind of computer.

And that has started a new revolution that WILL result in general distribution of the kinds of capabilities now found only in places like MIT and Stanford and the University of California.

At the moment computer science is in a transition state. The people who tend the big brains (particularly the grad students in universities) tend to be computer hackers; people intimately acquainted with the gory details of the machines; who know how to get inside the system and twiddle bits. Thus when they design higher-level languages they often build in a lot of their specialized knowledge, and that makes the higher-level languages harder to understand than they need be. In addition, although I know of no necessary reason why people really expert in computer science can't write plain English, the fact is that the ability to communicate with computers and other computer hackers almost guarantees an inability to communicate with the balance of humanity; thus there is a great disparity between what the machines can do and the ability to teach non specialists how to use them.

But that will inevitably vanish. On the professional level, big companies like IBM and Honeywell are well aware that user-oriented documentation is perhaps their chief stumbling block to increased sales, and are willing to pay large salaries to people who can eliminate the problem; and as I'm fond of saying to one of the MIT hackers, English isn't *that* much harder to learn than LISP (a computer language popular at MIT and Stanford and incomprehensible to mere mortals). Secondly, the widespread availability of small machines has spawned a new generation of computer owners who, because the micros started with hobbyist kits, had no choice but to learn something of the machine's innards, but who are really more interested in *using* their machines than in twiddling bits inside them. They too will help fill the gap between computer scientist and the general public.

But finally and most important, the machines themselves are becoming large enough to support *really* high-level languages. In fairness to the computer hackers, for many years even the best machines were so limited that a complex program had to be very cleverly designed; really sophisticated techniques were required to get both the editing program and a decent amount of text into, say, 16,000 words of memory, and make the whole thing run fast enough to be useful. And of course the more sophisticated the program, the less likely it is to be comprehensible to the untrained—and the more likely it is to have unexpected quirks which the programmer knows how to avoid but which he didn't remember to tell the naive user. Now, though, with cheap memory and fast machines so easily available, the sophistication can go into the "translator" programs, so that the user can work with truly high-level languages; in other words, to work in languages that automatically explain what the program is doing in terms comprehensible to people who haven't a clue as to what's going on inside the machine.

And that will take us into a really incredible era: a time when a very large part of the population will have instantly available not merely information, but the capability of doing things with it.

Example: last year my work load got so great that I had to hire an assistant. I learned to my horror that government has made things so complicated that you need a fair chunk of an employee's time just to keep the records and fill out the forms necessary to employ someone. In fact, I'm not at all sure I'm joking when I say that one major reason for high unemployment is that the average person contemplating going into business simply cannot figure out how legally to hire anyone.

But my computer came to the rescue; and I note that most computer magazines now advertise programs to handle taxes and accounting systems and payroll forms and such like.

It won't be long before the average citizen has as much

computing power as the government; some of the disparity between citizen and government will be eliminated.

Information networks will spring into existence. Some will be frivolous: perhaps electronic fanzines (something like that already exists); but others can be quite serious. National organizations with near-instant communications between members are not only practical but inevitable; the effects on our domestic politics should be interesting.

The information collecting capabilities are formidable. I will not soon forget the afternoon when John McCarthy of the Stanford Artificial Intelligence Laboratories plugged his hand-carried terminal into the telephone on my desk, called Stanford, and asked for "hot news on fusion power;" the result was a precis of a number of items, including some from sources you'd never think to look at. I wish I had access to something like that every time I have to do a particularly hairy research article.

Fire departments can have instantly available data about the composition and flammability of every structure in their protection area, along with the precise location of water supplies and gas and power shut-offs. Court records can make sense. Legal research becomes greatly simplified—and available to all of us, not merely to lawyers.

And of course the potential for abuse is obvious. Big computers make collecting dossiers on nearly everyone quite simple; Congress has already had to deal with that. But the big machines also make *really* secure codes quite practical; we already know how to use "trapdoor" functions that let you encipher whatever you'd like—letters, your diary, records of illegal bets, anything you choose—in a way that even the most powerful machines available to government can't break. The advantages are not all to government.

There are some real dangers to widespread access to knowledge. When really powerful machines plus good chemistry simulation programs are widely distributed, there's nothing to prevent some whacko from inventing a new explosive through computer experiments. We can all think of other deviant activities the big machines may facilitate. The brain revolution is hardly an unmixed blessing.

But like it or not, the djinn is out of the bottle. The brain revolution snuck up on us; very few science fiction writers have dealt with a society much like ours in which really sophisticated machines are universally available—but that's what we're getting. The big brains are not only coming, they're here.

CHAPTER 3
The Next Five Years in Micro Computing

In Spring of 1983, the National Computing Convention (NCC) was held in Anaheim. I was invited to be one of the principal speakers. As it happens, I shared the platform with Dr. Adam Osborne; it was the last big computer show that Osborne Computer Company attended. By fall, OCC was in Chapter 11.

The Anaheim NCC was chiefly remembered for The Inferno: there were more exhibits than the Convention Center could hold, so the NCC authorities caused large tents to be erected in the parking lot; latecomers to NCC were put in them. I would have supposed that anyone could predict what would happen to a translucent tent erected in Southern California in June; but then I live here. Apparently the convention authorities were shocked to discover that their air conditioning systems were simply overwhelmed. The temperature inside those tents shot up past uncomfortable to unbearable.

One good thing came of it: Bill Godbout's CompuPro exhibit was in The Inferno. His exhibitors, mostly young ladies, tended to melt, but they loyally stayed on. They were obviously in worse shape than the computers. I measured the input temperature to a CompuPro boat anchor at something over 100° F. The machine never exhibited a glitch, which is more than I can say for his staff.

Anaheim is just close enough to my home that I didn't take a hotel room, which was a mistake: I dashed down for my speech, got caught in traffic, and eventually found the convention center parking lots full. I was very nearly late for my speech, so I took a chance and parked in an illegal spot. Sure enough, they towed my car.

It wasn't an auspicious beginning; but the speech went well enough.

THE NEXT FIVE YEARS IN MICROCOMPUTERS
JERRY POURNELLE

(Based on a presentation given at the 1983 NCC, Anaheim, May 1983; Dr. Adam Osborne was the other speaker at the presentation.)

I've told this story before, but it's worth repeating. In 1954 I was invited to Champagne/Urbana to see the ILIAC. ILIAC at that time was the world's most powerful computer. Housed in a gymnasium, it was supported by the world's largest air conditioning system.

ILIAC was a vacuum tube machine. Two undergraduates had the singular job of rushing about inside ILIAC with shopping carts full of tubes; when one burned out, they'd replace it. It did all its calculations three times and took a majority vote on the answer, because a tube might burn out while it was making a calculation.

For all that, time was scheduled on ILIAC months in advance; it really was the world's most powerful machine.

The TI-59 programmable scientific calculator is considerably more powerful than ILIAC was.

That development took thirty years, but technology always accelerates. Barring nuclear war, there should be nearly as much change in computers in the next ten years as there was in the preceding thirty.

When you try to predict trends, you're usually too far out over the short run, and too conservative over the long haul. Still, we can see where the computer revolution is taking us: by the year 2000, anyone in the West who seriously wants to can get the answer to any question, the answer to which is known or calculable.

That's a pretty strange world, but it's nearly inevitable. Micros will contribute to that world: they'll be the link between the big machines and the ordinary citizen. Having stepped that far out, let's get closer to home and look ahead five years.

PREDICT WHAT FOR WHOM?

Just What Micro Industry Do We Mean?
When the micro world first started, it was all one community: hobbyists. The last time NCC was held in Anaheim, all the micro computers—ALL OF THEM, software, hardware, support people, the whole works— were hidden away in one back room at the Disneyland Hotel.

Like pariahs. As if AFIPS (American Federation of Information Processing Societies, which sponsors NCC) was ashamed of us.

This year's NCC is dominated by micro computers. The old High Priests of the computer industry may still dislike us, but they can't ignore us.

In those days, hobbyists dominated the micro world. If you weren't a hobbyist, if you were just a user like me, you were not only rare, you had no choice but to team up with one of the wizards. You didn't just walk into a store and buy a computer system. Good equipment was put together, often from kits.

That's all changed now. One of the people who changed it was Adam Osborne, who packaged a working system with enough software to make it useful, and sold the whole works, machine, software, and all, for about half what anybody else charged for a comparable package.

That's one of the currents in the micro stream. Another is represented by Bill Godbout and his CompuPro team. They sell advanced equipment. CompuPro machines are widely used for software development, but you still have to know something about micro computers, or have consultants who do, in order to take full advantage of the CompuPro line.

Another trend is represented by Apple's Lisa: not really all that advanced, maybe even overpriced when you consider what's inside the machine; but sold to a market that's interested in the convenience. Lisa doesn't really compete with Osborne or CompuPro; as far as I can see, Lisa is cutting into a market that's used to paying a lot more than $10,000 for machinery. This is the computer as executive perk.

Clearly, then, trends will affect the Godbouts and the Osbornes quite differently, and those two won't be the whole story either. Micro processors are going to appear in all sorts of ways that won't be recognizable as computers. Home appliances, cars, television sets, home security systems, games, and a lot more—all those industries will be affected.

In other words, there's no such thing as "the" future of the micro computer industry; it's a bit like asking someone in 1950 to talk about the future of the transistor. We can only look at broad trends.

Adam Osborne is interested in the mass market, and predicts that most micros will, in the next few years, be sold to people who don't want *computers* at all. They only want machines that do things.

He may be right—although, given the trends toward making "computer literacy" the new buzz words, and requiring an understanding of computers for graduation from college—and perhaps even high school—one could argue that Osborne has misread the trend. In any event, I'll stay mostly with the things that look and act like computers.

TECHNOLOGY

Hardware

We can sum up the hardware trend in one sentence: more capability for less money. That trend will accelerate.

Memory

The price of memory has fallen every year. When I first bought Ezekial, my late friend who happened to be a Z-80, 16K of high quality (Industrial Micro) static memory cost well over $500. That's $31.25/K. Today, top quality static memory (CompuPro) costs $995 for 128K, or $7.77/K. Dynamic memory has become more reliable, and it's a lot cheaper. This month's *BYTE* advertises deals such as 256K for $795, or $3.10/K.

I can do even better than that. I have a MACROTEC dynamic board: a full megabyte, for $1,983 list. That works out to $1.94/K. These are advertised retail quantity one prices.

The next generation in memory requires some new technology; it won't be enough to simply glue a batch of the 64K chips together. However, there's absolutely no reason to suppose the new technology won't be forthcoming, either from here or from Japan. Thus we can in confidence say:

Five years from now, memory will cost no more than 15% of what it does now. The smallest machines will have a full megabyte; most will have a lot more. Ten megabyte micro computers will be common.

ROMS and languages and programs and monitors.
ROMS will be cheaper, too, so that it will be easy to have ROM software as part of a computer package. Instead of programs on disks, machines will have their operating system, text editor, and other commonly used stuff built in, the way BASIC was built in to the old TRS-80 Model I.

Use of ROMS as a means for distributing software may cut down a lot on piracy.

EROMs (Erasable Read Only Memory) will let you do things like reconfigure the keyboard, and otherwise customize the system. You do that once and forget it.

Mass Storage.
I've titled this section "mass storage" rather than Disk Drives. I think floppy disks will be with us in five years, but they may largely be relegated to their original purpose of transferring information from one machine to another, rather than as a mass storage device.

Incidentally, my engineering advisors predict that in five years, both the 8 inch and the 5¼ inch floppy disks will be a dying breed; they'll be replaced by some kind of hard disk, possibly the cartridge winchesters, and one of the vest-pocket disk systems. The vest-pocket (3¼ to 3½ inch) disks would already have made great inroads into the 5¼ inch market if the industry could agree on some kind of standards.

Note the trend in disks. Ezekial's disk system—2 drives, controller, interface, and cables—cost $2,000 for 241 × 2 = 482K of storage, or $4.15/K. This month's *BYTE* advertises CompuPro double-sided quad density disks with controller at $1,595; for that you get 2.2 megabytes, 2,200K, or $0.73/K.

The trend in hard disks is just as dramatic. Five years ago, you couldn't afford hard disks. Now, George Morrow will sell you 16 Megabytes formatted, with controller, for $1,595; that's 0.099, less than a dime, per K.

Of course there are other mass storage devices. We have bubble memory, battery-backed memory, streaming tapes, disk cartridges, and such like. We don't need to know precisely what we'll be using five years from now. We can, however, be sure that it won't cost more than a nickle a K, and will probably be a lot less; and that it will be fast.

Five years from now, it won't be worthwhile building a micro with less than ten megabytes of mass storage.

CPU

There's an interesting race going on: which chip will dominate the next few years? The leading contenders are the 8086 and its successors, vs. the 68000. The Z-8000 seems to have dropped out of contention. The 16032 is a dark horse, with very interesting chip architecture.

Most analysts believe that the 8086, followed by the upward compatible 2-86, possibly followed by more upward compatible successors, and the 68000 are the chips to watch. Which one you ought to go with is a financially important decision, but it's not crucial to our analysis.

We're pushing out to the limits of VLSI technology, but there are bound to be breakthroughs. If we only assume CPU complexities will go up by a factor of two while the price is cut in half, we get a four-fold increase in bang for the buck.

Linking

The main problem with Ethernet is that it's expensive. That won't last. I don't mean that the hardware for Ethernet itself will necessarily fall in price, although that's very likely; I do mean that hardware for linking computers together into networks will be made steadily more available.

Some engineers think the RS-232 system, carried to its full potential, will be more than sufficient. Others reject that. Few, however, believe we won't have reliable, fast, and low-cost inter-system communications hardware well before 1988.

For example, I fully expect one day to talk to my editor in New York while we both have text on our screens. I'll use a light pen, or something similar, to mark my text, and my editor will see the same thing happen on her screen, but we won't have to give up our voice communications to do that. The limiting factor here isn't computer technology, it's the phone company.

Other stuff

Pournelle's Law: Iron is expensive, but silicon is cheap.

Modem hardware, memory management units, system support, math chips, voice recognition units, and all that paraphernalia, will get cheaper and more plentiful.

The trend in printer equipment isn't quite as dramatic. In 1978 I paid about $3,000 for a good letter-quality printer. I'd have to pay about $2,000 today, and I'd be surprised if I didn't have to pay at least $1,000, possibly $1,500, in 1988.

Impact printers require a good bit of machined metal, and that gets more, not less expensive. The cost of chips has dropped enough that printers can be smarter and still be less expensive, but there's a minimum that mechanical equipment isn't likely to fall below.

However: machines that are a combination of laser printer and copy machine are available this year for about $15,000 in quantity one, and about $7,000 in quantity 1,000. The usual trend is for this year's quantity 1,000 price to be next year's quantity one price. Within five years, laser printers that will also be your office copy machine will be available for no more than letter-quality printers cost today. This will give us amazing capabilities for producing camera-ready copy, complete with variable type faces and excellent graphics.

Bottom Line on Hardware

Hardware costs less for more capability. Total systems costs are coming down.

In 1977, Ezekial, my first Z-80 machine, cost about $12,000 including software, systems intergration, letter-quality printer, modem, cables, and a maintenance contract. He was a very advanced machine for his time.

In 1983, Zeke II cost about $8,500. In speed and other capabilities, Zeke II is at least twice as powerful as Zeke I was. It's three times as fast, has a 1200 Baud Modem, twice as much memory, and almost ten times as much disk storage. It has more and better software. Yet it costs only 75% as much.

If all I wanted was enough equipment for word processing, I could save even more by getting an Osborne, their communications pack, and a tolerable printer. I'd still end up with as much system as Zeke ever was, all for $3,500 or so. That's 30% of what I paid for Zeke, but the same capability.

That trend will obviously continue. In five years, you should be able to get a full business quality system for what home computers cost now; while microcomputers that will do nearly all that the $100,000 minicomputers can do will be available for under $10,000. Notice that I'm using real dollars, with no adjustments for inflation.

SOFTWARE

The general statement is simple: software is going to be cheaper, more universal, and easier to use.

For instance, right here at this show Epson America is showing some pretty radical software: it's Chris Rutkowski's VALDOCS system, which in effect uses the text editor as an operation system.

The VALDOCS concept is certainly headed in the right direction. You turn on the machine and it comes up in the text editor. You want to call a friend, you push a couple of keys and you're in communications, either by voice (by picking up your phone) or computer-to-computer. You want to see today's schedule, you push another button. You can get a printout of your next week's appointments. Another button uses your computer as a desk calculator.

In theory, you don't have to refer to the documentation; you find out how to use VALDOCS with on-line HELP.

That's where software is going. It isn't there yet, because (in my judgment) the Z-80 isn't fast or powerful enough to support all that work with tolerable speeds. No matter. The hardware exists. I think it would be easy to get VALDOCS working like a striped ape on a machine like the Eagle 1600, for example, with its hard disk and fast screen.

There are other trend-setting programs on display out there. Lotus 1-2-3 is moving in the right direction. So is VisiOn. Richard Frank's people at Sorcim haven't yet integrated SuperWriter and SuperCalc, but that's only a matter of time.

There are also the voice-controlled systems, and of course there's Apple's Lisa.

They're all headed in the same direction: making very complex programs easy to use. They integrate the computer directly into people's lives, and make it accessible to people who aren't interested in learning CP/M and BASIC; this trend will accelerate.

Prices will inevitably fall: as the market base expands, it will be possible to make large profits from moderately priced software. Books, after all, sell for under $25, but there's no shortage of people willing to write them, and some of us make a fair living writing books. Software development will be the same.

As software prices fall, support levels will fall: documents will be better, there will be more and better on-line HELP features, and the need for expensive people to answer telephones will disappear. Companies that can't do it right the first time won't survive.

Programming languages are getting more accessible, and a *lot* of people will learn to program. A few years ago, hardware was available, and some people took advantage of it, to start new companies. The result was Altos, and Apple, and some other outfits you've heard of.

A number of well-known software houses started the same way.

That will happen again and again over the next five years, as development-quality systems become available at popular prices. Languages are falling in price: I've recently been told of a BASIC compiler for less than $100. JRT Pascal isn't likely to be the only high level language for under $50.

As micros become more powerful, imagination and program design gets more important than the ability to write efficient code. If you can make your program easy to use, who cares how elegant it is? Not very long ago, what was important was the ability to do fantastic tricks in assembly language, but when memory gets cheap, it's not worth paying computer wizards to write memory-efficient code.

Even now, what's really important is the ability to describe needed programs—to write what my mad friend Mac Lean called a *metalanguage description* of a program. Coding VisiCalc so that it would run on an Apple was really brilliant work; writing the same program in Pascal to run on the Sage 68000 is a student exercise.

There are some other discontinuities just around the corner. For example, within the next five years, probably a lot sooner than that, someone is going to build what amounts to a LISP machine for micro prices. There's a *lot* of software written in LISP: text editors, spelling programs, that sort of thing, and also a lot of teaching programs. A lot of artificial intelligence people will suddenly be able to write programs with a potential market of tens of thousands of copies.

The educational potential of computers hasn't even been touched. In my judgment, it's better that kids program computers than that the computer programs the kids; I've never been wildly fond of so-called programmed learning. On the other hand, the use of computer *games* to teach valuable lessons has hardly been exploited at all. There's potential for a billion-dollar industry in educational software, but first it has to be created.

LIMITS

Will Micros Really Rival Minis?
Answer: yes.

There are some definite hardware limits to micro computers. There's only so much you can do with a single chip before you run into fundamental problems. Those limits won't matter, though, because of parallel processing. Concurrent CP/M-86 is just now catching on; when people realize just what you can do with concurrent processing, it will really take off.

Example: the VALDOCS program I mentioned earlier tries to do everything by overlays. When you call the scheduler, or the address book, it saves off your text automatically. It effectively logs you out of the editor, and you're limited by the speed of your disk drives.

With concurrent processing you won't have to do that, and programs to accomplish all that VALDOCS does, and more, won't be hard to write, especially if you have a language like Modula-2 to write them in.

A few years ago, those of us who like peering into the future said that the trend was toward "one user, one CPU." We believed that multi-user systems were swimming against the current.

Now I think it's clear: we're headed not just for "One User, One CPU," but several CPU's for each user. We haven't even begun to wring out the potential of parallel processing.

The kind of multi-user system I see coming gives each user several CPU chips connected through a bus and capable of doing concurrent processing; quite a lot of memory; a terminal; and some kind of disk drive, quite possibly a small Winchester. His operating system will allow concurrent processing, so that he can appear to be several "virtual terminals;" one of those terminals has his text editor, another has scheduler and card file box, another is connected to an electronic mail network.

Locally he'll be connected to other users through a network that allows him to share use of a laser printer and a really big hard disk with tape backup.

The only difference between what I've described and a VAX is that the micro system will be a lot easier to use, and it will be cheap.

The trend, then, is clear: micros will get more like minis at the same time their prices are falling, while higher level languages will be more widely available and cheaper.

That's significant, because the trend will be toward portability and modularity. It won't be necessary to start over when writing a new program. Programmers can bring over a number of modules intact, and just write new stuff. They'll also be able to *understand* their programs.

Meanwhile, there'll be a trend toward making graphics available to a wider and wider group of programmers. You won't have to be a wizard in order to write decent graphics. Some languages, like Modula-2, really lend themselves to this, and I expect in the next couple of years to see Modula graphics modules offered for sale to programmers. There are graphics statements in many BASIC languages right now. The Otrona has them, and the Zenith Z-100 even has color statements in its BASIC.

All this will make graphics available to the business and educational programmer as well as to the gamer.

GAMES

Speaking of games: Larry Niven and I are at this moment writing a game around our book *Inferno*. I notice that Infocom, the company that markets ZORK and various other script-driven interactive games, has sufficient cash flow to take out really big ads now.

We can expect to see a lot more of this, and gaming rights will become as important to authors as their foreign rights. If you couple video disks to interactive games, you get a possibility of a whole new entertainment form, a story in which the reader can participate. I notice that's already happening in certain comics books, where you're instructed to turn to different pages depending on your decision at various points in the story.

Video disks, languages like PILOT, and new cheap fast processors can create a new entertainment field. I'm not sure when it will happen, but it can't be too long before you can buy a video disk and game cartridge that lets you be the central character in a *Star Wars* adventure, and when it comes time to fly your ship, or shoot the bad guys, you actually control the ship and the gun turrets: combining interactive fiction with an arcade-type game.

Misc.

So far I haven't even said anything about new languages, or trends toward programs like PEARL and The Last One, so-called Program-Writing programs. Both trends will continue, of course. Computer-assisted programming is one of the goals of the artificial intelligence community. This too will contribute to the software explosion, driving it to the logical limit: if you can describe what a program does, you can write the program.

I do not think we will reach that limit in five years; but we will have moved a surprisingly long way toward it.

Voice Recognition and Speech Synthesis
Talking Computers.

I've seen some spectacular things done in this field, but I don't really have a good feel for how quickly it will develop. Certainly the hardware will be available. It already is. The difficulty is in devising crash-proof software. That's going to depend a lot on the AI community, and predicting the state of AI is a risky business. They're always going to have a breakthrough Real Soon Now.

Then they get one, and things change rapidly.

Specifics

I'll make a few guesses based on the above analysis.

I'll make a guess that there's a 50% probability that by 1988, Dr. Osborne's company will be selling machines that talk and listen. The odds are 4 to 1 that CompuPro will have such machines.

Interactive fiction and script-driven games will be a significant part of the entertainment industry. Old line firms like Doubleday and Ballantine and Random House will publish and distribute these games, and they'll be sold in B. Dalton bookstores.

Word processing systems will outsell typewriters.

The Telephone Company will offer information utility service.

Information utilities will be a lot easier to access, and will make available a lot more data. We won't quite be to the point where anyone who wants to can get the answer to any question, but we'll be approaching it.

Someone will begin to worry about the kinds of information available, and will want to restrict such things as the formula for mustard gas, and how to make botulin toxin. A lot of lawyers will get rich arguing about this.

The ability to ask questions and know where to find information will be at least as important as memorizing facts, and some educational theorists will notice that. Lord knows what kind of crazy fad that will start. There's no predicting what a Ph.D. in education can dream up.

Within five years we'll see computers included as part of television sets. When you buy a TV, you'll get the computer.

There will be a noticeable trend toward "The Electronic Cottage": more people working at home with communications by computer. They'll go to the office perhaps one day a week.

Finally: about five years ago, John McCarthy of Stanford bought a Heathkit color television. The intention was to have a robot build the television set.

As of this year, the robot hasn't even been able to open the box.

Within five years, John's robot will certainly have opened the box and removed the components. I doubt that it will have built the set—but I won't give long odds.

[My NCC speech was later published in *BYTE*; shortly after it came out, a reader wrote to tell me that about 80% of what I had predicted had already happened. Alas, he was right; I had been insufficiently bold.

Still, the essay remains a good description of trends.]

CHAPTER 4
Can David Survive Goliath In The Computer Industry?

This appeared in the January 1984 column. I still believe it.

Survival
I'm writing this in early October. Just at the moment, in obvious reaction to the Osborne disaster, both computer and mainstream magazines are full of articles and editorials about "the great shake-out" in the micro industry. A number of companies are said to be in trouble, and "experts" are predicting that we've reached a new age in micros, one in which only the giants like IBM can survive.

I don't believe that.

I suppose the micro industry will be dominated by the giants—but there's plenty of room for the others. In U.S. business as a whole, about 10% of all sales are made by companies with a gross income of less than half a million dollars. There are some 5 million of them. Another 35% of all sales are made by the 520,625 companies with gross sales of $500,000 to $25 million. At the other end of the spectrum, a bit less than half of all sales are made by the 2,355 companies with gross income of $100 million or more.

That's all U.S. business, from steel rails to books to coffee spoons. The computer industry is skewed a bit more toward smaller companies. I think it will stay that way, because the micro world changes like dreams, and smaller, leaner companies, with fewer links in the decision chain, can respond faster to changes in technology.

The giants look to big sales—hundreds of thousands of copies of nearly identical units. While they're setting up to do that, the small, adaptable, fast-moving outfits get their innings.

Example: there's a persistent rumor that **IBM** has developed a small, portable computer based on the iA-186 central processing unit (CPU) chip. The problem is that Intel isn't producing the chips fast enough. They've had to put their customers on allocation.

IBM can't work that way. However, if you really want a 186 computer, Slicer will be glad to sell you one. It comes without frills. There's no case, and no power supply, but it works. Jim Hudson and I are doing an article on the Slicer, which is a good buy for technically sophisticated users. My point, though, is that Slicer can make profits on their machine, even though they'll never have any large share of the micro computer market.

[The Slicer remains a great "hacker's special" way to get in on the 1-86 chip; but it comes "no-frills," meaning that there's no case and no power supply. You better *really* like hacking up hardware before you buy one. If you do, though, it's a good deal.]

Another example: I first met Rod Coleman at the West Coast Computer Faire. Forty days before the Faire, his Sage Computer company was destroyed by a disastrous fire. Rod was standing there with his three working machines. None had a hard disk; he'd show you melted fragments and refer to them as "our well-burned-in disk drive." In less than a year, Sage went to a million dollars' annual business; I recently got an announcement that they'd had a million-dollar month; and they haven't stopped growing. Their Sage IV may well be the best 68,000-chip computer on the market.

Yet another example: even as Osborne was getting into trouble, KayPro was growing by leaps and bounds. The reasons for that are complex, and indeed KayPro couldn't possibly be doing as well as it does if Osborne hadn't led the way; but it does show that small, well-made and well-thought-out *systems* can thrive. The KayPro 10 is the first portable machine to use a hard disk. Other innovations are coming.

[Since then, KayPro has pretty well taken over the entry-level market. They make really good first machines.]

A final example. Bill Godbout just threw a big party to celebrate the tenth anniversary of CompuPro. Here's a company with a reputation for armor-plated high technology hardware. They very nearly dominate the development systems market. Now they're trying to expand their market share by selling easy-to-use business systems.

Last time I looked, CompuPro had made 2% of the micro market. That doesn't sound like much—but if you look at CompuPro's actual dollar income, they've been doing business at a steadily rising rate. Most accountants would sell their livers for that kind of profitability.

At the height of the Osborne boom, they were shipping somewhere around 8,000 computers a month. That generated sales in the order of $100 million a year. That may not be big by IBM standards, but it's not peanuts, and made Osborne one of the Big Ones in the micro field.

There are 5.5 million U.S. companies, and just about every one of them will spend $2,000 a year on micro computers. There are at least a million people who spend a thousand a year on personal computer products, and I'd be greatly surprised if that number didn't hit ten million in the next few years. One half of one percent of that is $105 million—Osborne's peak income.

Look at it another way. Assume sales are distributed by company size roughly the way they are in U.S. business as a whole.

Of $20 billion total sales, ten giants will get half. The other half will support a thousand companies with average sales of ten million dollars, which in practice is more likely to be 900 smaller outfits and fifty large ones. Even so, there's plenty of room.

This isn't to say that things won't get tricky. They always are when you're up against large resources. The big boys can survive mistakes that bankrupt small companies. They can afford to lose money setting up store outlets and service centers. They can also afford to advertise.

The smaller outfits have some advantages too. They don't have to tool up for big production runs, and their decision structures are leaner, so they can track new technology better. They may not have in-house service organizations, but as the industry matures there'll be more and more trained technicians. Some will stay independent; others will work for service companies like Xerox, which is rapidly becoming something like a cross between AAMCO and Tuneup Masters, only for micros. Parts outfits will spring up. Somebody's going to get rich out of stocking spare parts, repair kits, and instruction sheets.

It may happen that someday all the really exciting developments in the computer field will come from the research labs set up by the giants; but that hasn't happened yet, and I don't really think it will. In fact, I see small computers as the great equalizers. I think they're going to change the structure of business in this country, not just for the micro business, but for everyone, making it much easier for small outfits to compete with the giants; but that's a topic for another column.

PART SIX:
THE USER GOES POPULAR

My first computer article was in the *BYTE* companion magazine onComputing. That magazine didn't last long, but the *BYTE* publishers continued to work on producing something that would appeal to the general computer user as well as the *BYTE* readership (who tend to be semi-fanatics). Eventually they came up with *Popular Computing*.

At first I had little to do with *Popular*. I had enough work at *BYTE*. Then Pamela Clark, who had been my editor at *BYTE*, moved to *Popular* as Editor-in-chief. I had always liked working with Pam, so when she asked if I could do a new column for her in addition to the *BYTE* piece, it wasn't hard to decide.

The *BYTE* columns tend to ramble through a great many subjects. The shorter *Popular* columns are supposed to focus on one topic. Of course very little at Chaos Manor goes as it is supposed to. . . .

CHAPTER 1
The Computer Revolution

I've just returned to Chaos Manor from COMDEX, the big winter computer dealer-and-product show in Las Vegas. The show was enormous: 80,000 attended, with nearly 1,500 exhibits, almost all devoted to micro computers. It's obvious that the micro computer revolution is doing well. We've had a few casualties, like Osborne and the Texas Instruments TI-99 series, but you can't expect victory without a few losses. The setbacks have been at the edges of the movement; the main body is going strong. The war is well ahead of schedule.

This may sound overly dramatic. I don't think it is. The micro revolution will transform society in ways more fundamental than ever did the automobile or television.

You Shall Know The Truth . . .
Before the end of this century, big computers will be linked together in networks of staggering complexity. Micro computers will give everyone access to these nets. By the year 2000, anyone in western civilization who seriously wants to will be able to get the answer to any question, as long as the answer is known or calculable.

Computer people like to communicate with each other. Even if they're too shy to meet face to face, they can communicate through their machines, and they do. Computer networks are commercially valuable; but they'll happen even if no one tries to develop them. They'll develop even if governments try to suppress them.

Imagine a thousand computer freaks within the government, each able to send instant messages to thousands of friends. Now try to imagine Watergate staying covered up for long.

When Poland invaded itself, the first thing the soldiers did was shut down the telephones. Free flowing communications are anathema to tyrants. If the computer revolution proceeds, closed societies are endangered. If you want total control of your population, you not only must keep your people from talking freely with outsiders, you also have to keep them from communicating with each other.

The Soviet Union controls typewriters; a grocery clerk was recenty sent to the gulag for five years for possession of an unlicensed mimeograph machine. Underground works of literature are painstakingly copied by typewriter and carbon paper. Comes the computer—and does that floppy disk hold the latest Five-Year Plan or a forbidden novel by Solzhenitsyn—or the one disguised as the other?

Closed societies cannot endure widespread use of computers. They have no choice but to keep these machines under strict control. They must suppress the micro revolution.

Armies March On Their Micros . . .

Suppressing the micro doesn't work either. Consider the Falkland Islands incident, or the Israeli incursion into Lebanon; both proved that military power depends on more than blood, sweat, toil, and tears. You need good soldiers; but you also need high technology equipment. In particular, you need good computers.

During World War II, when the British, Germans, or Russians had motor equipment problems, they had to send for experts to fix their trucks and tanks. The Americans didn't usually bother. They'd grown up with cars and trucks; common soldiers knew about spark plugs and distributors and carburetors.

The result is a dilemma for tyrants. Suppress the micro computer, and lose your military power; or embrace it, and lose control of the nation.

Thus, I may be a bit whimsical at times; but underneath I'm deadly serious. The micro computer revolution will do more to make the world an open society than any previous invention.

What Do You Mean, Revolution?

We've had computers for many years, but it's only recently that they sparked a real revolution. So long as the machines were confined to experts; so long as they were barricaded behind doors, fenced off in corporate computers centers, guarded by white-coated high priests, they were in the service of the establishments, not the revolutionaries. Then came the micros.

At first, micro computers were confined to hobbyists, who were the pioneers and rangers of the micro revolution. Those were the days of teletype machines, when paper tape was the only medium for exchanging programs, and it took an hour to load BASIC into a computer that had no more than 10,000 bytes of memory. In those times, big computer companies ignored micros, which couldn't possibly be a threat to their High Priest-dominated professions. Even after the micros had moved well beyond that first stage, the big outfits considered us poor relations.

In 1980 the National Computer Convention—a trade fair put on by the non-profit American Federation of Information Processing Societies—was held in the Anaheim Convention Center. AFIPS didn't want to have anything to do with micro computers, and tried to exclude them entirely. Eventually they relented, but banished us to the back room of the Disneyland Hotel a mile away. The *real* show was the big mainframe and mini computers. At least that's what they thought.

In those days, micro owners had great difficulties exchanging programs, because no two systems had the same disk formats. Ezekial, my late friend who happened to be a Z-80, began with a (horrible) disk system called "FDOS." David Gerrold, a fellow science fiction writer, had a North Star. Gordon Dickson, another colleague, had CDOS. Each of these disk operating systems would work only with specific hardware. We couldn't possibly exchange programs, or even read each other's text files.

Then came CP/M. It may not have been the *best* disk operating system for micros, but it had one tremendous advantage: it would work with a very wide variety of hardware. Suddenly the micro community could communicate. We had a standard. The micro revolution was born.

So What Was So Revolutionary?

Prior to CP/M (Control Process/Micro), the computer world was chopped up into a myraid of tiny communities. It had ever been thus in the world of big mainframes and mini computers. IBM machines couldn't exchange programs or files with Control Data and Univac machines, nor could they communicate with Digital Equipment and Data General mini computers. Each major computer firm had its own operating system. Each manufacturer tried to fence off its customers from the rest of the computer world.

In the mainframe and mini worlds, payroll and accounting programs cost $100,000 to buy, and $25,000 a year to maintain; businesses risked their corporate lives when they bought (or more likely, leased) computers. More than one business vanished as a result of choosing the wrong company—for once you chose, you were stuck. You couldn't change, because you'd lose all that you'd put into program development.

Reverberations of those days are with us yet, as we'll see.

Some Real Differences

In the micro world after CP/M, things were *very* different. In the first place, even the most expensive programs were ridiculously cheap by minicomputer standards. True, most micro programs didn't do all that the big mini programs did—but a surprising number of them could do quite a lot. In particular, they could handle payrolls and accounting—and they could do word processing and text editing. Indeed, microcomputer text editing programs have always been at least as good, and sometimes better, than the editors found on mainframes and minis; and they don't cost very much.

The most expensive computer available in 1979 wasn't really much more useful to a creative writer than was my Ezekial with Electric Pencil. Micro users got in the habit of expecting a lot of computing power for not very much money.

Secondly, micro people liked to communicate, and to swap programs. They didn't want to be fenced off into small communities the way minicomputer people had been.

Examples abound. The North Star disk operating system was at least as fast, convenient, and easy to use as CP/M. However, in an effort to isolate its customers, North Star chose not to implement that system for anything but North Star hardware. If they hadn't done that, their operating system might have won out over CP/M; but they did, and North Star had to come up with ways to make their machines run CP/M lest the company vanish.

When Tandy brought out their (long since abandoned) TRS-80 Model One, they made two serious mistakes. The first was doing the hardware on the cheap and using their customers as the company's quality control department. The second was offering a proprietary operating system, TRS-DOS, which was deliberately made incompatible with CP/M. They went even further. Their Radio Shack marketing arm was forbidden to sell "foreign" (i.e. non-Tandy published) programs for their machines.

Texas Instruments did much the same thing with their (recently abandoned) TI-99 series. They wouldn't publish the internal specs for the machines, and far from encouraging independent programmers, they put severe obstacles in their way.

Their experiences should be studied by all the newcomers to the micro field.

Then Came Osborne

CP/M became a de facto micro standard, but you still had to learn a lot about small computers in order to get one and use it. Adam Osborne put together a complete computer system, with two disk drives, memory, keyboard, and screen, packaged them together with some of the best available software, and sold the whole bundle for a reasonable price. He included enough documents to allow intelligent people who'd never heard of a computer to get the whole thing operating in a couple of days at most.

The result was phenomenal. True enough: the computer was ugly, awkward in size, and had a pretty terrible keyboard. The disk drives didn't hold very much data. The thing was too heavy to be portable, and the screen was too small (unless, like me, you wore bi-focal glasses and could sit right up against it). No matter. The machines sold phenomenally well; so well that a number of big companies suddenly realized there was gold in that there market. Imitators sprang up.

The micro revolution gained hundreds of thousands of new recruits. For a few glorious months it looked as if we'd won without a battle.

Big Blue Counterattacks

There had long been rumors that IBM was going to enter the micro market. Finally they did, with a machine technologically advanced over most of the popular micros of the time (although nowhere near the actual state of the art). Those of us who'd thought about the situation weren't at all surprised to learn that the IBM machine wouldn't run *any* of the existing micro software.

We weren't surprised to learn they had a new operating system, either.

The IBM machine is based on a 16-bit (more or less) CPU (Central Processing Unit, or "brain"), while all the earlier micros were built around 8-bit CPUs. Now certainly the 16-bit machines are potentially faster and more powerful than the older machines; most micro companies, though, had been slow to introduce them, because they were concerned that their previous customers would be able to salvage something from their previous investments in micro equipment. At the very least they ought to be able to transfer their data files, such as employee records and corporate accounting books, from the older machines to the new.

IBM, though, didn't have any previous micro customers. Moreover, they had a long history of (1) isolating their customers from the non-IBM world, and (2) not caring much about making their new systems compatible with their older ones. They thus had little incentive to worry about the micro community, and they didn't. Although Digital Research had CP/M-86, which allowed easy transfer of data files from 8-bit to 16-bit systems, IBM chose to go with something new, called PC-DOS (for the PC). PC-DOS began nearly identical to a more generic operating system called MS-DOS; but within months the two drifted apart, and they've been getting less and less compatible ever since.

The result wasn't pleasant. CP/M had nearly united the micro community; IBM's entry split it again.

That's not permanent. At the recent COMDEX show there were literally dozens of new small computers. Nearly every one of them is very proud of being "PC-Compatible." Indeed, the very beer and coffee at the show seemed to be "PC-Compatible."

At COMDEX Tandy introduced a new machine, the Model 2000. It's faster than the IBM PC—but it uses the MS-DOS operating system. Moreover, Tandy is carefully publishing details of the machine's hardware and software requirements. They're even thinking of stocking non-Radio Shack programs in Radio Shack stores. Indeed, at the press conference where they introduced the Model 2000 you would never have guessed that TRS-DOS ever existed. . . .

Disturbing Rumors
It looks, then, as if the internal divisions are ending in favor of IBM PC-DOS as the new de facto standard. Alas, things are not so simple—yet.

First, although IBM chose the Intel 8086 family of computer chips, there are other 16-bit CPU chips that are about as good (and some say much better). In particular there's the Motorola 68000 which Apple favors. Although the 68000 isn't likely to eliminate the 8086 and its follow-ons, Apple will continue to hold a good-sized share of the micro market, so that particular division seems permanent.

Second, all is not settled in the world of PC compatibility. Although PC DOS, particularly PC-DOS 2.0 and later, is a viable operating system at least as good as CP/M, it's not much advanced over the CP/M we had in 1980. However, Digital Research has brought out Concurrent CP/M-86, which has the ability to make your IBM Personal Computer think you are four different users. This can have great advantages: suppose you're writing a paper, and want to do some calculations, and while you're doing those you find you have to look up a phone number. Under PC-DOS you'd have to save off your text onto a disk, then bring in a calculator program; save the calculator program; and bring in your address file; then reload the calculator; and when finished with the calculations, go back to the text editor.

All that's possible, but tedious. Under Concurrent CP/M, you can run all these jobs at the same time, switching back and forth between them as required. This is a powerful improvement over PC DOS.

Furthermore, Concurrent CP/M knows how to run PC-DOS programs. Naturally it can run CP/M-86 programs, and transfer CP/M-80 data files from 8-bit machines.

There's a persistent rumor that IBM will abandon PC-DOS in favor of Concurrent. This comes from so many sources that I'm inclined to believe it. It would be nice if true, since it would tend to reunite the micro community.

There's another rumor: that IBM intends this only as an

intermediate stage; that they're planning to move to a proprietary operating system and fence off their customers from the rest of the micro world.

I think IBM is too smart to do that. It would be a drastic mistake. True, they'd create some divisions in the micro community—but perhaps not so great a division as they think. Micro users are getting smarter; surely even newcomers can see the disadvantages to being isolated, and thus at the mercy of Big Blue? But if they do try it, we must resist.

The Shakeout Blues
Getting into the micro revolution is expensive. Not as expensive as it once was; Ezekial cost nearly $12,000 in 1978, while you can get a better machine now for under $3,000. Still, there's little you can do with the home computers (under $1,000); seriously getting into the micro world costs money.

That creates a problem in public confidence. If the micro revolution is winning, what happened to Osborne? Wasn't he one of the early leaders? If he can be driven out of business, who can't be? Perhaps it's best to stay with IBM, even if they want to stifle the micro revolution by making Microland look like the land of the mini computers.

Nonsense.

Certainly Osborne collapsed; and of the dozens and dozens of new companies I saw at COMDEX, each with yet another copy of the PC, I do not expect three-quarters to be at the show two years from now. So what?

The Osborne owners haven't been ruined. The machine remains a good machine—and the Xerox Americare service organization has moved in to provide repair service contracts for Osbornes. True, it would be better not to have an orphan—but how much better? Before you decide that IBM is the only safe purchase, recall that for the price of a fully equipped PC without software, you could have bought *two* Osbornes.

Moreover, for every company that goes under, there are others that thrive. Apple, Hewlett-Packard, Godbout-CompuPro, Tandy are all companies that have been around for ten years and more.

One needn't retreat into the arms of IBM in order to enter the micro world.

The Onrushing Train

There's another force for communications.

In the early days of the computer revolution, important programs for micros had to be written in assembly language. This isn't easy. It takes special training and a lot of concentration. Moreover, assembly language produces programs that run ONLY on a specific kind of machine. Such programs can't easily be transferred from one machine to another; often they can't be moved at all. Even so, in the early days the programmers generally had no choice if they wanted to write large and complex programs, because the micros of that era were badly limited in speed and memory.

That's all changed.

Now the machines are large enough that we can program in higher level (i.e. more like English) languages, such as Pascal. Moreover, languages are getting much easier to use. It might take as much as a year to learn assembly language programming well enough to write something as complicated as a text editor—and less than six months to learn how to do it with a structured language like Modula-2.

Programs written in high level languages are easily transferred from one machine to another.

In the old days of mainframe and mini computers, the computer cost a great deal. It was vitally important to use the machine efficiently. That took programmer time, and ran the cost of programs out of sight.

Today, the most expensive micro costs a lot less than a year's worth of a good programmer's time. However, so long as the machines can talk to each other, a programmer can work knowing that there's a huge market base. He need not charge the earth for his work, because he expects to sell many copies.

As the base expands, the cost of software goes down, and the features you can include in programs goes up. As I write this, there isn't yet as large a market for programs as there is for books, but the program market potential is growing. By the end of the decade there may well be as many computer owners as there are book buyers.

The cost of programs will approach the cost of reference books. Meanwhile, programming languages will improve, and so will the machines, so that it will be as easy—and as difficult—to write a new computer program as it is to write a book.

When that day comes, the computer revolution will be self-sustaining.

May it come soon.

In Times To Come

In the future, we'll tackle the operating system jungle, examining in detail just what is the difference between CP/M, PC-DOS, MS-DOS, and Apple DOS; look at programming languages and why you ought to know about them; and talk about which computer shows to go to and which to avoid.

Stay tuned. The Computer Revolution needs you.

CHAPTER 2
The Management Revolution and How To Get In On It

Just prior to World War II, James Burnham proclaimed *The Managerial Revolution* in a book now universally accepted as one of the most important of its decade. Burnham showed that the divorce between ownership and management would bring about profound changes in society.

A recent Research Institute of America (RIA) *Personal Report for the Executive* warns managers and executives that new computer techniques are going to make even more fundamental changes in the nature of business management.

The report says that "in the years immediately ahead, computerization will spread more rapidly than electricity did at the beginning of the century." The micro will bring about a fundamental transformation of the ways we do business. It is clear that "the vast access to knowledge and quick decision making that the computer bestows will allow fewer managers to exercise far more control than is presently feasible."

RIA then asks, should the aspiring manager try to become a computer expert? They conclude no; that "ease of use seems to be developing as fast as computer capability." Thus the challenge is not to use the computer, but to figure out what it is you want it to do.

That analysis is largely correct, but the advice is fundamentally flawed. Sure, you can wait for the coming "easy software;" but those who do will miss out on many advantages of the micro revolution. You don't need to be a computer *expert*, but there's much you should learn now.

The Computer Establishment

For many years, computers were hidden inside laboratories and attended by white-coated high priests. Ordinary people weren't allowed to get near them. One had to have special talents and be blessed by the gods to approach a computer.

Then came the micro to prove all that was nonsense. Ordinary people found they could use computers in their daily work. Some large computer facility managers welcomed the micro revolution, and worked to make their establishments mesh smoothly with the smaller machines. Other high priests haven't given up, though. They've just changed tactics.

One delaying tactic is "User Friendliness."

Our Machine is SIMPLE to Use

A recent series of radio and television commercials features two business people. One is reading from a computer system manual, and bewilderedly mutters things like "operating system" and "DOS 2.0;" the other is whistling merrily as he does fantastic things with his "user friendly" computer system.

At the Spring 1983 COMDEX computer show in Georgia a year ago, the Eagle Computer Company made much of how easy it is to get their computer running "within five minutes of taking it out of the box." The Epson QX-10 computer is sold with a special ("breathtakingly sensible") keyboard and VALDOCS software; the company's advertisements stress how easy it is to use the computer without knowing anything about it.

Apple computer's Lisa machine uses "icons": these are pictorial representations of tasks. Instead of typing "ERA THATFILE.TXT," you make an arrow on the screen point to a picture of a file folder with the correct name, then move the arrow to a picture of a waste basket; then press a button, and the file is "thrown away." Why should you learn a technical term like "ERASE"?

A recent spate of articles drives these points home. "Software is not easy to use," one writer tells us in BYTE. "Stand up and shout, 'My software is not easy to use, and I am not a dummy.' There, I bet you feel a lot better."

Samuel Dean, for 15 years a lawyer but now chairman of the board of Select Information Systems, goes further. In a recent article he decries programs that want commands. Dean asks us to imagine a restaurant in which there are no menus; you merely tell the waiter what you want, and he'll bring it. "Imagine a command-driven restaurant," Dean writes. "Then mourn for it when it fails because no one knows what to order." Software, we're told, is like that: "Users don't want to be able to order anything they can imagine. . . . They only want to get the job done. Open-ended, command-driven software is dead."

It may all be true, but it's not obvious to me.

The Terminology Tradition

The doctors at Menningers' tell a story to the patients. It seems a motorist had a flat tire outside the fence at the state mental hospital. As the motorist changed the tire, a patient watched from within. The motorist removed the five lug nuts holding on the wheel and laid them in a hub cap; tripped; and the nuts rolled down into a storm drain, where they were lost forever. It was getting dark.

The patient inside spoke up. "Look, take one nut off each wheel and use them. That gives you at least three on each wheel, plenty enough to get you to a parts store."

"Hey, thanks," the motorist said. "That's a good idea. Tell me, why is somebody as smart as you in there?"

"I'm in here for being crazy, not for being stupid."

Computer users aren't stupid, either.

Users do have a problem. The machines are very new, but they're part of an old industry. Traditions have developed and hardened, particularly in terminology. Some of the traditions make sense. Many don't but we seem to be stuck with them.

I'm reminded of the early days of the space program: not only had most of the experiments with rockets been done in Germany, but a large part of the U.S. rocket development team was composed of German refugees. The result was that we all said "Brenschloss" rather than "burnout," and while few went so far as to say "Sauerstoff" instead of oxygen, there were plenty of Germanic terms. You either learned them or got out of the space business.

Small computers were developed in the United States, so we haven't had to learn a foreign tongue; but we might as well have. Take for example the terms "TTY" and "CRT." Both are firmly embedded into micro terminology, and indeed you can't learn the CP/M operating system without knowing them; yet their use is purely traditional, stemming from a time when the only cheap device for communicating with your micro was a teletype (TTY), and only the wealthy could afford a "glass screen," otherwise known as a CRT (cathode ray tube: a term that itself dates from before scientists understood electrons and vacuum tubes).

Early micro users didn't mind learning a specialized terminology; indeed, there was a certain pride to having a jargon incomprehensible to the rest of the world. Moreover, while *using* computers is not complex and doesn't require high-tech skills, designing them certainly is and does, and there has always been a reasonably close affinity between the real technocrats and the rest of us—which means those who proclaim the good news of the micro revolution must learn quite a lot of high-tech language.

The problem comes when we try to translate computer terminology into ordinary English. It's seldom easy, and often it's not well done. One reason the job is done badly is that far too many engineers, programmers, and computer writers assume that computer users aren't just uninformed, but stupid. They talk down to their audience; worse, they assume that their readers will never understand, so there's no point in *really* trying to explain what's going on.

That fits in perfectly with the High Priests' counter-attack. Only the priesthood can *really* understand; users should wait for the priests to bring them user-friendliness.

Why Not English?

Science fiction writers have been telling us about computers for years. The best SF writers read a lot of technical literature and have friends among the technological elite; even so, few science fiction stories prior to 1960 had an accurate picture of the computer world. Most saw future computers as enormous and expensive, accessible only to highly trained experts.

There were exceptions, though. Poul Anderson foresaw widespread use of computers small enough to install in space ships, yet complex enough to have human personalities. So did Isaac Asimov.

Walter M. Miller, Jr. (who now uses a micro) predicted the desk-sized "Abominable Autoscribe," which took English dictation from the Abbot of St. Leibowitz and translated it into Latin, although, alas, the computer was flawed and produced only ancient Salvonic.

The interesting point is that all these machines were easy to use because they were commanded through ordinary English. There was no "menu" of functions. One told the computer what one wanted, and it either did it, or explained why it couldn't.

That's what I call user-friendly.

However, we don't have such machines yet. The artificial intelligence people are at work, but it will be a while before we get them. I do suspect it will happen a lot quicker than Mr. Dean thinks. In the meantime, we have to deal with what we have, which unfortunately includes primitive command structures such as:

A> PIP A:=B:*.TXT[V]

as well as unreadable documents, undocumented "features," and just plain bugs.

Working With What We Have

Mr. Norman Dean is concerned about "the first-time user, the scared, irritable novice who for the first time must not only work with a computer but do something useful with it."

That's a fair description of me a few years ago. I doubt I will ever forget the night that my engineer friend Tony Pietsch brought me my first machine: a Z-80 that had cost more than I could afford. Tony had installed only one program, a complicated beast called a monitor that would allow you to examine any spot in the machine's memory, put instructions and data into memory, and do other such arcane systems-oriented tasks. There wasn't a stick of useful software, not even BASIC. "There it is," Tony said. "Have fun."

I could have strangled him. There wasn't a thing I could do with that machine. Fortunately, we got Electric Pencil, an early text editor, running within a day or so.

Pencil wasn't all that easy to learn. When I first started, I wasn't at all sure that I'd ever prefer an expensive lump of steel and silicon to my self-correcting Selectric typewriter. Within a week, though, I knew better; and within a month I'd taken the typewriter out of my office. It has never returned.

My *BYTE* column is entitled "The User's Column," and emphasizes what you can do with these machines. I don't know much about how they work, and I'm not very interested in learning. I'm not only ignorant of those details, I'm determined to remain that way.

Ignorant, yes; but I'm not stupid.

In a recent BYTE article Sam Edwards, co-author of the PFS:WRITE and other PFS software, gives two possible sign-off messages from computer systems. One is:

"END OF SESSION."

The other gives a whole bunch of statistics, including connect time, disk accesses, keystrokes, disk updates, characters displayed, etc., as well as the message "END OF SESSION." He says, "If you find yourself enchanted by the latter sign-off, read no further. You are a hacker, and this article is not written for you."

Nonsense.

I'm no hacker, but I do know that information is useful. Not always useful, of course; but often enough. Sometimes I don't know enough to make use of information that's offered me: but that's hardly a reason to throw information away. Maybe there's nothing useful I can do with the knowledge that my last session with the machine used 456 disk accesses; but maybe I just can't do anything *yet*. Perhaps tomorrow I'll learn. Meanwhile, how am I harmed by knowing?

When They're Perfect———>

Some day, small computers will be as easy to use as those I gave my characters in the novel *The Mote In God's Eye*. Until then, though, I have work to do. Like Mr. Norman Dean, I need to make the machine do something useful. Unlike him, though, I don't think my chances are improved by crippling the machine's capabilities.

The hard fact is that computers are to the competitive business environment what the six-shooter was (in legend at least) to the American Southwest: the great equalizer. A badly educated but intelligent and diligent man or woman with a small computer can be as productive as the most skilled typist or comptometer operator; indeed, can be more valuable to a firm than the other two combined.

It isn't just skilled trades that the small computer will affect. The MBA degree has assumed an unnatural importance in the business world. A great many of the "management skills" taught in the MBA program turn out to be nothing more than information organization—something a small computer can do quite well. You only need to know how.

Getting Started

The "Simplify even if you cripple it" school bases their argument on the bewilderment of the first time user. Now indeed, they have a point. A person first facing "A>" with no hint as to what it all means or what to do about it must surely be tempted to say, "It's obviously very complicated. I can't learn that."

The temptation is even more severe if a computer wizard says "You're right. Half a mo', I'll fix it so you'll never see 'A>' again," and proceeds to make the system "user friendly" by setting up a special menu of easy-to-use commands.

Well, why not? It gets the job done, doesn't it?

Not necessarily.

The Real Revolution

What they're offering is fairy gold. It's as if the Ford company decided to install a new set of "user friendly" controls in their cars. Why should you have to learn about brake pedals and steering wheels? Out with them! There have to be easier ways! Of course you'll never be able to drive anything but a Ford....

Similarly, the Epson Company will give you **VALDOCS** to protect you from the horrors of CP/M's A>, and add their "breathtakingly sensible HASCI keyboard" that doesn't have some of the standard keys you'll need to operate other computers—or for that matter, that you'll need to run better software than the limited and very slow **VALDOCS** program system.

Learn **VALDOCS** and you'll know nothing but **VALDOCS**—and you'll be forever dependent on that program and its updates.

Interestingly, Epson has recently taken to advertising that they'll also supply you with the CP/M operating system, and have begun to talk about the many features of their machine (it's a good machine, and there are a lot of them) instead of concentrating on how simple the little beast is to use. Perhaps they've caught on?

I'm not sure what "computer literacy" is. If it means the ability to sit down at any microcomputer and within hours to days be able to do useful work with it, then I'm all for it: but you won't learn that kind of computer literacy if they've crippled your machine in order to make it "user friendly."

Computers have been around for a long time, but the *real*

computer revolution came not when the small machines became available, but when most of those machines could talk to each other; when programs written for one kind of small computer would run on a whole lot of *other* computers.

It's that ability to use anyone else's software that makes the micro computer the great intellectual equalizer, so powerful that perhaps it can compensate for the disastrous state of our public education system. Lord knows *something* had better do so.

Now true enough: even crippled these machines are useful. True again, "A>" can be frightening. Indeed, it's no bad thing to make it simpler for beginners to get started—but it's senseless to be so protective that we don't tell beginners there's work involved in joining the computer revolution. It's not as much work as learning to talk, or even to read; it is comparable to learning to drive a car.

Why shouldn't it be? Sure, you can play games, and even do useful work like type manuscripts, without having to cope with the dreaded A>; but if you wait for the computer wizards to make the systems "user friendly," you'll find that someone who didn't wait has gone far ahead of you.

The truth is that it takes no more than a couple of days to cope with A> and PIP A:=B:*.*[v] and "User Numbers" and DOS 2.0 and much of the other arcana; and once you've done that, you're not limited to one system.

Horror Stories

Far too many new computer users are deliberately harming the micro revolution. They do it by demanding what they think is "user friendliness." What they get is crippled machinery. The manufacturer, or a software publisher, despairs of simplifying the instructions to take care of every possible misunderstanding. Instead, he eliminates features—or never tells the user about them.

Take Eagle Computer as an example. The Eagle 1600 is a wonderful computer, superior in nearly every way to the IBM PC: but you'd never guess that from the Eagle's documents. They tell you how to get their text processor, Eagle Writer, and their spread sheet Eagle Calc up and running in short minutes; but to keep it simple, there they stop. You'll not discover from their documents that the Eagle can do a lot more.

Eagle is revising their documents. They didn't *intend* to

keep their users ignorant. The same can't be said for many other companies. Some of them *want* you to be stuck with their simple way of doing simple things, lest you discover the real world of micro computing, and outgrow their system.

Tales of Triumph

My friend Eleanor was a typical liberal arts major. The only job she could find was a low-paid clerical position in a medium-sized business office. It soon became obvious to her that most of the work in her department could be done by a small computer.

Eleanor got an Osborne computer—all she could afford— and a data base program called dBase-II. Both the program and the computer were more than adequate for the job, but I have never heard anyone accuse either of being "user friendly." It took work to get dBase running, and she had to cope with the dreaded A> and PIP and all the rest.

Once she learned, though, she found a dozen programs that could do useful things for the company. She talked them into buying a more powerful machine that would run them. Eleanor now has a professional position as office manager. She makes more money, and doesn't work as hard.

One teaching-hospital physician I know devised a simple way to analyze experimental data with a CompuPro machine. He had to learn BASIC to do his analyses. Then he had to learn to use the machine as a word processor. The result was worth it: so far, five publications he'd never have gotten out.

Other examples abound.

The Moral

The moral of this story is obvious. Don't wait for the High Priests. Specifically, take the tales of "user friendliness" with a good teaspoon of salt. The High Priests would just love to convince you that computers are really very complicated, and you're not bright enough to do more than the simplest things until the experts are through massaging them. Don't believe that.

Second, don't fall for the line that says, "With our machines, you will instantly know all about computers without doing any work." That's nonsense. Certainly you should avoid sloppy documents and software full of user-hostile messages; but you should also be prepared for a few hours of skull sweat. Becoming really computer-literate takes work. Fortunately, after the first hurdles, it's mostly fun.

Third, learn in stages. Don't decide you'll learn assembly language programming as your first assignment. Start with first things, such as just what that A> signifies, and the difference between the "program level" and the "operating system level." Learn how to make copies of your valuable software and files. Then proceed.

Work systematically. It will take a little longer, but the results will be worth it.

The RIA report is certainly correct: computers have had very little impact on management compared to what's coming in the near future. Big changes are coming. One day we'll all be able to use the machines without knowing anything about them. Real Soon Now.

Until then, there's no magic formula, no one program or machine that will do everything—but many programs can do a lot. They're not very user friendly—but they'll get the job done. We'll talk about a number of them in future issues.

It takes a little work to join the micro revolution, but the rewards can be high.

CHAPTER 3
The Operating System Jungle

In the old days before the micro revolution, different kinds of computers didn't talk to each other. If you had an IBM, you used IBM software; if you had Digital Equipment, you were stuck with what DEC (or the DEC User's Group) offered. Usually each computer user had to develop his own customized programs, which often cost tens of thousands of dollars, and had to be maintained by full-time professional programmers. How could it be otherwise? There were never more than a few hundred copies of any one kind of computer.

Micros changed that. Thousands were sold. Because of the large potential market, programmers could afford to develop elaborate general purpose programs for sale at, if not reasonable, at least not outrageous prices. It has always been important for the micro revolution that our machines be able to exchange programs and data.

Unfortunately, a bewildering jungle of "operating systems" threatens to divide the micro community. Fighting this menace requires some understanding of operating systems: what they are, and why they're important.

The next two columns will take a hard and critical look at the operating system jungle. We'll also explain some of the stranger terms, like "patching the DOS," and what it means to boot a system.

Before BASIC

Micro computers are built around a single chip called the Central Processing Unit (CPU), or "brain." The chip designers build into it an "instruction set"—a list of commands it can respond to. These instructions are quite technical.

Typical instructions might be: "store the number found in register A in the memory location found in registers H & L;" "go to the location found in register B for your next instruction;" or "put the value you find in port 6 into register A." Those are, of course, the English translations; the actual instructions would be no more than a series of 0's and 1's, and might look like 10101101; that's called *binary* and 10101101 is a *binary number*.

It's obvious that most users aren't going to program in binary. For that matter, most aren't going to work in any kind of machine language, but even the machine language programmers don't want to work in binary, so one of the first programs that gets written for a new microcomputer is a thing called a "monitor." (To add to the confusion, the computer's glass TV-like screen is often called a "monitor" also, but it has nothing to do with the monitor *program*.)

Monitors

A monitor is a program that listens for input, such as letters and numbers typed from a keyboard, or a file from a cassette tape; does something with that input, such as display it on a screen, or store it in memory; and handles output. It also lets you go to various memory locations and inspect or change what's there, and do other low-level but vital control operations. In the early days when most micros were in the hands of hobbyists, integrated or "all up" computers didn't exist; a micro consisted of a box of electronics. It was up to you to communicate with it. There were a number of devices for doing this, including teletype (TTY) machines, but the most common method was with a terminal. Computers don't automatically know how to talk to a terminal; they do that through the monitor program. In those days monitor programs were very important, and good ones were passed around from one user to another. You still can't live without one.

Operating Systems

Fortunately, in today's micro the monitor comes as part of an "operating system," which is a kind of "super monitor." The operating system translates commands, such as SAVE 36 FOO.DAT (meaning write 36 "pages" of memory into a disk file entitled **FOO.DAT**) into language the machine can understand. The most visible function of a micro's operating system (OS) is disk control, so operating systems are often called the "DOS" (Disk Operating System) even though the OS contains a monitor program and does a good bit more than just tell the machine how to save and recover data on disks.

The first practical micro computers used the 8080 CPU chip. The computers wouldn't have been much use without some way to store programs and data, so the hobbyists turned to floppy disks because they were cheap. Alas, floppies hadn't been designed for that purpose at all; they'd been designed to transfer information from one big computer to another. One of the first things the hobbyists had to choose, then, was a "disk format."

The disk "format" refers to the way that information is put onto the disk: how many concentric tracks, how many chunks—called sectors—each track is carved into, and how many characters—called bytes—will be put into each sector. In those days there weren't many different kinds of floppy disks, and one, the 8-inch single-sided single-density "IBM Format" stood out as something very near to being a standard.

Given a format, there are still a lot of ways to pack information onto a disk. Wherever you put it, you'll need a catalogue of what's on the disk: this is called a directory.

An operating system tells the computer where on the disk to look for the directory, and how to find the programs listed in that directory. There are many ways to do that, and at one time more than a dozen such ways were employed.

Then Came CP/M

Then as if by magic appeared Dr. Gary Kildall's Digital Research Incorporated with an operating system known as CP/M (Control Program/Micro). CP/M was a bit complicated, but it worked, with *many* different computers. For the first time, people who owned a Cromemco computer could exchange disks with people who owned an **IMSAI**.

There were other operating systems. One, North Star, that was as good as CP/M; but North Star tried to keep their operating system out of non-North Star machines. They hoped thereby to sell more hardware, but the plan backfired. CP/M became the standard for 8-bit micros.

The Joys of File Transfer

File transfer was simple under CP/M. In most cases, you could simply write your file to a disk and hand it to a friend; even though he had a different kind of machine, he could read your disk.

Note that there are two fundamentally different kinds of files: *data files*, and *command files*. Data files are such things as lists of names and addresses; the text of this article; a source program written in BASIC, or indeed any *source* program. Command files are just that: programs intended to be run by the computer, as for example *compiled* BASIC programs. Humans can't read them. It is usually much easier to transfer data files than command files, and once you have transferred a command file, you can't be *sure* that it will run on the new machine.

However, if both machines run the CP/M operating system, there is a very good chance they will run each other's programs. This is one of the powerful attractions of CP/M systems, and the major reason why CP/M became the standard operating system for micro computers based on the 8080 chip, and later for Z-80 systems. The Z-80 is an improved chip that is *upward compatible* with the 8080.

Upward compatible is a term that can apply to either hardware or software. In this case it means that the Z-80 can run all programs that will run on an 8080; but since the Z-80 accepts some instructions unknown to the 8080, not all Z-80 programs will run on an 8080.

A Thing Of Shreds and Patches

CP/M had flaws. Many were discovered by users, who also discovered the fixes for them. Hobbyists in those days often circulated the fixes, which took the form of "patches" to CP/M.

"Patching" is done with the CP/M debugging utility known as DDT (which stands for Dynamic Debugging Tool, but the initials came before the name). The original DDT was developed by the New England Model Railroad Club to help get their model trains running under control of a microcomputer. Although DDT is a program, it works as if it were an operating system complete with monitor. A program to be "patched" is read into the computer under DDT; the entries in certain memory locations are changed; and the changed memory image is saved on disk. Patching sounds complex, but in fact it is not very difficult once one is familiar with both DDT and CP/M. Most users rely on dealers to install patches to programs. That may be wise, depending on the dealer; it certainly does no harm for the user to understand what's going on.

As more flaws and remedies were found, CP/M went through several versions, from the original CP/M 1.3 and 1.4 to 2.2, which is now standard; only a few very stubborn hobbyists hang onto the 1.4. Each version was a distinct improvement over the last.

Each was also upward compatible with the last, which was a Good Thing and tended to keep the micro community united, because all our old programs would run under the new operating system. Alas, when Digital Research brought out CP/M 3.0, which is now known as CP/M +, they did *not* keep it strictly upward compatible with 2.2, and a number of programs got left behind. This wasn't good, and CP/M + has never really caught on. Many users, including me, never bothered to install it. Why take the effort only to find that your favorite programs no longer work?

Upward compatibility, of machines, software, and operating systems, is clearly desirable for users. Of course the people who want to sell you all new products to replace your old ones will have another story; but upward compatibility unites the micro community. That's important, because the more potential customers there are for new software, the more the software developers will be willing to invest in making it nifty.

Incidentally, you will often see a letter after CP/M 2.2, such as 2.2j; this refers to a particular version developed by a computer manufacturer or software house. In theory, at least, all letter versions of CP/M 2.2 can read each other's disks and run each other's programs.

Alas, although the operating systems are compatible, the *disk formats* are not. Although there are only a few 8-inch disk formats, and all 8-inch CP/M systems can read the so-called IBM single-sided single-density format, there are more than *fifty* different 5 ¼″ disk formats, most of which cannot read each other's disks even though the disks were made with the same operating system. Sigh.

Slowly, though, software houses are developing programs like Uniform, which translate from one disk format to another, reuniting the micro community.

The Others

In addition to CP/M, a few other operating systems have survived from the early days.

Like North Star, CDOS is a good example of a bad market strategy. In the early days, Cromemco had a good start in the micro world. Ezekial, my friend who happened to be a Z-80 computer, was a Cromemco. Unfortunately, the company wasn't satisfied with having excellent equipment: they wanted to isolate their users from the rest of the micro world. They did this through a proprietary operating system called CDOS.

That didn't work. CDOS never really caught on. I know few who use it, and I suspect the attempt to impose it has harmed Cromemco's computer sales.

You may hear of TPM. It is supposed to be 100% upward compatible with CP/M. I've only seen it work with the Epson QX-10. TPM documents are hard to get and not easy to read once you have them. It's unlikely to catch on.

Enhancements?

There is one CP/M improvement that's 100% compatible with plain or "vanilla" CP/M. Interestingly enough, it's free.

ZCPR is a public-domain program that substitutes for a PART of CP/M. It takes advantage of the special instructions available on the Z-80, and thus works only with computers that have a Z-80 CPU. It has a number of interesting and convenient features.

ZCPR will never catch on with the general user community, but some micro enthusiasts fanatically approve it. Installing ZCPR requires some knowledge of CP/M; in particular, you must know how to patch the operating system.

ZCPR is available from the CP/M User Group, or through Workman and Associates.

The Unix Clones

Unix is an operating system developed at Bell Labs. It uses a *lot* of memory. There were a few attempts to put Unix on 8-bit micros, but they were not useful; the amazing thing is that it could be done at all. The Unix operating system and its imitators such as OS-1 and Xenix are best discussed when we take up the world of 16-bit computers. We'll also look at Turbodos there.

The Winner

Although some rivals survived, CP/M dominated the world of the 8080 and Z-80 machines. There were sporadic raids and intrusions, such as Tandy's attempt to introduce a new operating system called TRS-DOS for its ill-fated TRS-80 Model One computers, but after a while even Tandy went over to CP/M. Incidentally, a greatly modified and much improved version of TRS-DOS survives under the name L-DOS. It is a perfectly good operating system, but it has never had wide popularity. For all practical purposes, CP/M's victory in the 8080/Z-80 world was complete.

ENTER THE APPLE

Although the 8080 chip began the micro revolution, another soon became popular: the 6502, which was the CPU chosen by Wozniak and Jobs for the Apple. The Apple Computer was one of the first "all up" systems: that is, instead of a box of electronics which you had to connect to a terminal, the Apple came with a keyboard, and a way to attach it to your television.

Naturally the Apple people had their own operating system (they could hardly help it), called Apple DOS. It is the only successful example of a micro computer company isolating their users from the rest of the micro world. Neither the operating system nor the disk format resemble anything on other computers.

The CP/M operating system was intended for a variety of different machines, and was therefore totally contained on the CP/M disk. All a machine had to do was to read Track 0, Sector 0 into memory location 0, and go to location 0 for further instructions. CP/M then told it how to read the rest of the CP/M operating system, and where in memory to put it. This is known as *booting* the system. The term comes from the proverb about "pulling yourself up by your bootstraps." When you first "bring up" a computer using the CP/M operating system, it performs a "cold boot," meaning that it reads in everything and starts over. From time to time CP/M may perform a "warm boot"; in this case the computer reads in a *part* of the CP/M operating system. KayPro computers actually announce "Warm Boot!" when they perform that operation.

The Apple must also be "booted." Apple's DOS was intended only for Apples, and Apple DOS was contained in part on the disk, and in part in a Read Only Memory (ROM) chip that was an actual part of the Apple computer. Some people use the term "firmware" to designate programs contained in ROM, as opposed to "software" which comes on a disk or on tape. Apple DOS was part software and part firmware.

Apple and Apple DOS thoroughly dominated that section of the market. Indeed, Apple's only significant competition was Franklin and a few others who competed by copying the Apple DOS, both software and firmware, in its entirety. From time to time Apple would upgrade the DOS—in some cases the upgrade did little more than fix notorious bugs—and there are now a number of versions of Apple DOS, all supposed to be upward compatible with their predecessors. Alas, they aren't; we have programs that no longer work with the latest Apple DOS. Most, however, do. Apple charged quite a bit for their upgrades; in some cases their commercial practices were more reminiscent of Caligula than Albert Schweitzer.

APPLE CP/M CARDS

Apple DOS is not compatible with any other operating system whatever (other than the exact copies marketed by Franklin and some Asian pirates). Thus it's not possible to transfer programs from the Apple to another kind of micro.

However, it is possible to turn an Apple (Apple II or IIe) into another kind of micro. What happens is that you put in a card containing a Z-80 CPU chip, memory, and a different ROM. This actually makes the Apple computer a mere terminal for the Z-80. Then you put a CP/M disk into the drive and boot it.

The ROM tells the Z-80 chip to read Track 0, Sector 0 into memory location 0, and then go there for the first instruction; lo, you have CP/M running. Alas, the Apple *disk format* is sufficiently strange as to make it difficult to transfer programs and files to and from the Apple, but it can be done, and some outfits sell CP/M utilities for Apple computers.

We have tried several of these CPU cards for Apples. Most of them work, but some are better than others. I currently recommend the Applicard from Personal Computer Products as the best we've worked with. This afternoon I learned that Digital Research has just completed an Apple Gold Card, which does the same job.

UCSD PASCAL

In addition to Apple DOS and CP/M there is one other important operating system for Apple (and other computers): UCSD Pascal. As the name implies, this is primarily intended for use with programs written in the computer language Pascal; but it is much more than that. Quite a bit of good business software was developed for this so-called "P-system." It was also one of the first operating systems for micros that allowed the reliable use of hard disks.

Like CP/M, UCSD Pascal (P-system) requires an additional card for the Apple. Once installed, the machine actually ceases to be an Apple, and while running under P-system it won't run standard Apple DOS programs. You can, however, always go back to Apple DOS by disabling the P-system card.

P-system is a complete DOS, with a unique disk file system, and a command structure much different from CP/M, but similar to that of a number of big machines. We will see P-system again when we discuss 16-bit micro computers.

Although a number of experienced users, including Carl Helmers, the founding editorial director of *BYTE* Magazine, remain enthusiastic boosters of UCSD operating system, P-system is not the mainstream of the computer community, and the number of UCSD P-system users has not kept pace with the growth of the micro revolution.

The Vanished World

For the first few years of the micro revolution, all the machines used 8-bit CPU's. There were only a few operating systems, and CP/M was dominant among serious users. Then new technology brought in 16-bit machines, and everything changed. The unity of the micro community was shattered. Some companies want to keep the micro world divided.

The battle of the operating systems continues. At stake are billions of dollars. The outcome is important: if the micro community is carved into segments that can't communicate, we all lose.

Now we'll look at the current situation, and try to see where the micro revolution is going.

Just as we thought that CP/M and Apple DOS would unify the micro computer world, technology struck again. We moved into the world of 16-bit computers. Many observers expected history to repeat itself: one, or at most two operating systems would dominate. So far it hasn't quite worked that way. Worse, as we'll see presently, the operating system jungle even affects hardware design.

First out with a popular 16-bit machines was TI with its 99 series. TI, like many others, was too greedy. It tried to isolate its customers from the rest of the micro world. Software would only be developed internally. The result was that outside developers ignored the machine. The TI-99 eventually vanished.

One candidate standard was the UCSD Pascal operating system. Known as P-system, it had the merit of theoretical portability among many different kinds of computers. There were many Apple installations. The same P-system programs can in theory run with either 8-bit or 16-bit computers. There is a large P-system user's group (USUS), and P-system is the standard operating system furnished with advanced machines such as Sage. Given all these advantages, one might expect P-system to be a powerful unifying force.

There are several reasons why it hasn't been. First, the 8-bit P-system was extremely hardware dependent. It took expertise to get it running with new disk formats. Then P-system itself fragmented into versions. There remain P-system islands—Apple P-system with several hundred thousand users is much the largest—but most remain essentially incompatible with each other. P-system survives, but barring radical new developments, it will be outside the mainstream.

Then Came IBM

The really major event in 16-bit history was the appearance of the IBM Personal Computer. There were faster, better designed, and more advanced machines available, but no one could match IBM's marketing techniques. The magic initials quickly moved to dominate the 16-bit field. So many were sold that everyone wanted to be compatible with it.

MS-DOS replaced CP/M—but not entirely. The micro world was fragmented.

Every computer writer has heard a dozen stories about why IBM didn't use CP/M from Digital Research. They can't all be true. Whatever the reason, IBM turned to Microsoft of Seattle to supply the operating system for the PC. Microsoft, in turn, bought the program from a small outfit called Seattle Engineering.

In the beginning, MS-DOS (for Microsoft Disk Operating System) was identical with PC-DOS. MS-DOS had remarkable internal similarities to the older 8-bit CP/M 1.4; unlike CP/M 2.2, the first versions of MS-DOS had no provision for user numbers or subordinate directories. This made it very inconvenient when used on systems with large capacity hard disks. MS-DOS had a few features not in CP/M 1.4, but was nothing really new. Like CP/M-86 (the 16-bit version of CP/M), MS-DOS was an improvement over what micro users were accustomed to, but not a radical innovation. Although CPM-86 was available, it was expensive, and PC-DOS sold eight times as many copies as CP/M for the IBM PC. Programs to transfer files from PC-DOS to CP/M-86 (and vice versa) evolved slowly, but the two systems were otherwise incompatible.

As time passed, PC-DOS evolved incremental improvements. Versions 2.0 and later have additional new features. The most notable is subordinate disk directories for added convenience when using large fixed disk systems.

MS-DOS also evolved—and did not stay identical to PC-DOS. The differences are, so far, minor but not trivial.

Because PC-DOS and MS-DOS were so much alike, you might think that the 16-bit world could be unified with fairly little effort; but operating systems compatibility isn't as forgiving as it sounds.

Are We Compatible?

The IBM PC sold extremely well. A lot of people wrote software for it—so much that it makes sense to divide 16-bit hardware and software into two classes: compatible with the IBM PC, and not compatible.

Although that makes sense, it's not as simple as it sounds. There are many kinds of incompatibility.

The simplest form of compatibility is disk file organization: can a given machine read disks made by the IBM PC? Fortunately, this is no longer so important: there are now several programs that will transform disk files from one format to another—even from 8-bit CP/M to 16-bit PC-DOS. It's not always a trivial task, but anyone determined enough can get the files into the PC, or from it to another machine.

This is all right for data files—address lists, text, ledgers, etc. Program compatibility is another matter. Many programs that run fine on the PC won't work on other machines. The usual reason for this is "hardware dependence": the program's writer has made use of features exclusive to the PC. The most common source of incompatibility comes when the program writes to the screen.

The MS-DOS/PC-DOS operating system, like all operating systems, has standard ways to get information from the keyboard and send it to the screen. However, screens have a variety of features—blinking characters, half shade, bold face, etc. Some machines have these features and some don't. The operating system does not make provision for easy use of every possible feature. Many programmers study the machine's hardware until they find fast and simple ways to display data. They bypass the operating system to use features specific to the PC. Since other machines don't do things the same way, the programs won't work on them. Two of the best known hardware dependent programs are Lotus 1-2-3 and Flight Simulator.

Software engineers are thus faced with a dilemma. The more machines their software will run on, the fewer special features of the machine can be used. In general, software that uses special features looks better, is easier to use, and sells better. Since there are so many IBM PC's out there, the temptation is to write software dependent on its peculiarities.

That gives hardware designers their own dilemma. Customers are sophisticated: they know that machines without software aren't much use. If there isn't a lot of software for a machine, it won't sell very well; if it hasn't sold very well, the market base isn't large enough to tempt software developers to write for it. The temptation, then, is to imitate IBM as closely as possible. On the other hand, there have been considerable improvements in machine technology since IBM designed the PC. Should one, then, use the latest technology—or "design down" to the PC's poorer performance levels?

Thus we have two operating systems, MS-DOS and PC-DOS, that, while similar, run different programs on their respective machines. Rather than unity, we have fragmentation of a new order. If that were the only fragmentation in the 16-bit world we might learn to cope, but technology continues to advance. The lack of operating system standards limits the development of both software and hardware.

A Better Way?

The real crunch is coming up now. Microcomputer technology has taken some real jumps in the past year. It is possible to design machines with stunning capabilities, and it is clearly absurd to accept the limits imposed by IBM compatibility.

When micros first came out, memory was extremely expensive. Operating systems had to be *small*, which meant they couldn't do very much. This was the major reason why CP/M was so very limited.

Memory is now cheap, and new computer chips can make use of a great deal more of it; yet, because PC-DOS is still only an update of CP/M 1.4, it remains very limited in its capabilities.

Programmers are forced to reinvent the wheel. If you want the machine to do arithmetic, a program has to be written for that. If you want it to draw lines, or do music, or pass the results of one program along to another, or sort text files, or work with several different kinds of printers, you have to write programs for each task.

Many programmers build up a library of useful subprograms—usually called "utilities"—which they can incorporate into new efforts. Since every programmer has an idea of how best to accomplish each job, these are all different, and one programmer can't use another's utilities. There's a lot of duplication of effort.

There's a better way: put more into the operating system.

For example: suppose you're writing a letter, and you need to do some calculations. Why must you exit the program in order to add up the expense account? Indeed, this is so inconvenient that many users—including me—keep a desk calculator near the computer. Clearly your computer knows how to calculate; why can't it do it while you're writing a letter?

One way would be to write a desk calculator program into the text editor. Another would be to put the calculator into the operating system. Then *any* program could call it.

I can think of a whole raft of stuff that ought to be in the

operating system, available to any program that wants to call it. Some features stand out:
- Desk Calculator
- Random Access Filer
  - Address book
  - Calendar
- File Sorter
- Graph and Chart Maker
  - Bar Graphs
  - Pie Graphs
  - Line Graphs
  - Convert one kind of graph to another.
- Let the output of one program be the input to another.
- Copy a file
- Archive a file

Although there are plans to add some of these features to PC-DOS, it will still be a quick fix. What's really needed is to rethink the situation and start over.

Where Do We Go From Here?
Apple Computer's Macintosh is an example of what could be done with a new start. It's still limited, but certainly a step in the right direction. The MacOperating System is a full 64 K-bytes of Read Only Memory (ROM), and has provisions for text editing functions, drawing lines and shapes, and displaying parts of several different programs at the same time. This latter capability is accomplished by segmenting the display screen into areas called "windows."

Mac was brought out with much fanfare and little software, but a number of software developers are hard at work. The Mac operating system is highly advanced, and is supposed to allow programmers easily to make use of Mac's advanced features. Apple has shown that micros need not be saddled with oversimplified operating systems.

At the same time, they've produced yet another fissure in the microcomputer community. Macintosh uses a highly specialized disk format. It's unlikely that any software developed for Mac will run on non-Apple machines. Apple has bet heavily that the machine will be so attractive that its users won't care about their isolation.

Meanwhile, Digital Research has produced a new operating system called Concurrent CP/M. Like the Macintosh it has windows. It also has the ability to let the computer run several programs at the same time (as the Macintosh is said to do). This is called "multi-tasking," and is what "concurrency" means. The next version of Concurrent is supposed to contain provisions for running PC-DOS programs as well. If so, Concurrent will go a long way toward uniting a major part of the micro universe.

There Are Still Problems
The IBM PC and its clones are built around the Intel 8088 chip. Apple's Macintosh uses the Motorola 68000. Both chips have advantages, but of course each has a different instruction set. Programs written for the 68000 can't run on the 8088 without modification. Beyond the 8088 lies a whole family of Intel chips, each more powerful than the last. Programs for the 68000 won't run on them, either.

However, as computers get more powerful, they are able to use higher levels of programming languages. As the "level" of a language rises, it gets less and less dependent on specific machines. BASIC, for example, is a moderately high level language; many BASIC statements (such as PRINT "FOO") accomplish the same thing no matter what machine they're running on.

The first generation of microcomputers was too slow and too limited to run complicated programs written in higher level languages. The next generation will be different. Powerful languages like Pascal, Modula-2, C, LISP, FORTH, Ada, and others will make programming much simpler, and should make programs more "portable" i.e., able to run with little or no modification on many different kinds of machines.

Unification Through Unix?
There's still a problem. Concurrent CP/M (CCP/M) can bring aboard MS-DOS and PC-DOS—but we're still working with highly limited operating systems. CC/PM can access a desk calculator, file utilities, address book, etc., without abandoning the job you're working on, but those are still separate programs. They're not built into the operating system and callable by any program.

There's a second limitation: CCP/M is a single user system. Even after CP/M had nearly united the non-Apple micro world, there were sporadic attempts to introduce something new. One, TurboDOS, was a multi-user system that enjoyed brief popularity, but never reached more than a few thousand installations.

Until recently the lack of multi-user operating systems was no loss. Older microcomputers simply weren't powerful enough to support multiple users. They're getting there now, though, and the advantages of allowing a number of users to access each other's large data bases, and pass work back and forth as it's completed, are fairly high.

Quite a few computer people believe we'll need a multitasking multi-user operating system, with a full set of utilities such as I have described above. Moreover, it should work on a wide variety of machines.

There is such a system. It's called Unix.

Unix was developed at Bell Laboratories, and is employed in a great number of university computer systems. Unix generates strong feelings: most programmers either love it or hate it. Beginners generally hate it; Unix has command features almost guaranteed to drive you mad until you learn about them. The more experience one has with Unix, the better liked it becomes—but that transition generally takes months. Most users won't spend the time needed to love Unix.

Unix is a very flexible system. It's easily modified to accommodate new commands and even new command structures. The resulting structure is called a "shell." Unix enthusiasts often say that it's a trivial exercise to put a "user-friendly shell" around Unix. On the other hand, I have never met anyone who had actually seen that done.

Unix is very large; if you get the system for the IBM PC, it comes on 15 disks. You'd have to have a hard disk to make use of Unix, and even then it would be pretty slow on a micro.

The micro community is deeply divided over the future of Unix. Dr. William Godbout, whose CompuPro computers are used by many top-rated software developers, firmly believes that Unix is the wave of the future. "Memory is coming down in price, and the new CPU chips can access up to a gigabyte. We can put most of Unix into half a megabyte of ROM. That way it will be fast, and always available." He estimates that by the time we need it, the hardware costs of providing Unix on ROM will be under $200.

Other system developers believe that Unix is the wave of the past. "Too big, too slow, and too hard to use," says Sage

Computer's president, Rod Coleman. "Trying to use Unix is like playing the game Adventure. We'll have full megabyte operating systems, and maybe a lot of it will be in ROM, but it won't be Unix."

If Not Unix, What?

A lot of micro experts don't much care for Unix but believe we'll be forced to it for lack of anything else. Microcomputers of the future will almost certainly have a multiuser multitasking (concurrent) operating system; it will be big, and at least as useful as Macintosh's OS; and it should be sufficiently portable to unite a large part of the micro community.

Anything less concedes most of the market to IBM.

There's also the problem of what IBM will do. It has announced it's going to have a "windows" program, but hasn't said what it is. Some experts believe IBM will adopt Digital Research's Concurrent CP/M. That would have the merit of preserving all the existing software. Under this plan, IBM would encourage DRI to make CCP/M run under Unix.

Secondly, IBM itself could bring out Unix. PC-DOS programs would run under IBM Unix. New programs would ignore PC-DOS.

Finally, there are persistent rumors that IBM is developing a proprietary operating system, one it might not license to competitors. This would permanently divide the micro world. Every company that has tried isolating its micro customers has regretted it—but none of them were as big as IBM.

No one knows what Big Blue is up to. IBM is one of the few large companies able to keep secrets. My guess, based on slender evidence, is that IBM will support Digital Research's Concurrent while continuing to experiment with Unix, and that it hasn't made a longer range decision.

The Dark Horses

There are two more things to consider. One, AT&T has just moved into the minicomputer field. All the AT&T machines use Unix-V. It's obvious there will be microcomputers to complement the line, and that they'll use the Unix system too.

AT&T is large enough to compete with IBM. The company

has little marketing experience, but it can survive a lot of mistakes. AT&T entry into the field is a powerful blow for Unix—and AT&T is known to be working closely with Digital Research. That combination can have major influence.

Finally, Niklaus Wirth is said to have designed a new operating system around his Modula-2 language. Modula-2 is aptly described as "modernized Pascal."

Modula-2 already operates in a specialized programming environment, something like a cross between P-system and the Macintosh operating system. Wirth has had a number of years to think about the future of personal computers since his Pascal language became widely accepted through its own merits without big advertising campaigns. His Lilith, a computer built in Europe to his specifications, has many advanced features, and is an extremely powerful programming tool. Programmers who try the Wirth operating systems hate to go back to anything else. An operating system based on Modula-2 would have many highly attractive features. A number of hardware firms, including CompuPro, Corvus, and Sage, have expressed interest in adapting the Modula-2 system for their machines.

The micro world still has room for new and brilliant ideas. An operating system would herald a flood of useful new software. Continued failure to adopt a standard operating system—even one less than optimum—benefits only very large companies like IBM. It's vital that something be done, so that we can get on with the computer revolution.

Last minute: Unix continues to forge ahead, but in Fall 1984 there will be Modula-2 for the Sage, and by 1985 a TURBO modula for the IBM PC. These could change the world.

CHAPTER 4
Right Up To The Minute . . .

The User's Column changed and evolved, although I like to think it kept its original flavor. In spring of 1984, *BYTE*'s Editor-in-chief Phil Lemmons decided to change the name. For several years there had been some good natured rivalry between Steve Ciarcia and me: Steve's column, Ciarcia's Circuit Cellar, was for years the unquestionably most popular feature in the magazine, but now it appeared I might have caught him. (And might not; it's comparing apples and bananas anyway, since Steve's column is hardware and hacker oriented.) In any event, Phil Lemmons thought there was an attractive symmetry between Ciarcia's Circuit Cellar, which is indeed in a cellar (and is incredibly neat and orderly), and Computing At Chaos Manor.

Mrs. Pournelle likes to deny that our house deserves the appellation "Chaos Manor." Everyone who visits us knows better.

To show what the column has become, this is the latest; I'm sending in the column and this manuscript at the same time. *BYTE* had space problems, so this is more complete than the column!

COMPUTING AT CHAOS MANOR

The Phone Company Strikes Back
I've just come back from COMDEX Winter in the Los Angeles Exposition Center where I got to play with the new AT&T computers.

Like, Wow!

When AT&T announced a computer line, there was a bit of panic on Wall Street; after they announced their prices, the excitement died away. Too expensive. Who's worried about a computer line whose lowest cost item is a $9950 desk top? How can that affect the micro world? That's what many Wall Street analysts said, anyway.

Dream on.

I don't own any computer stocks—the conflict of interest is obvious—but if I did, I'd give that analysis a lot of thought. People, that AT&T desk top computer is one hell of a machine.

True: just now, as I saw it, with little application software, it's not much of a threat to anyone; but give it time, and there'll be a different story. The AT&T 3B2/300 desktop provides an awful lot of bang for the buck. If I seriously wanted into the software business, I'd buy a 3B2 development system and get to work polishing up my skills in the C programming language; and I'd expect to get rich from it.

AT&T quotes a four-week delivery time on the 3B2/300 desktop. With half a megabyte of memory (plus 32K of ROM for bootstrapping and housekeeping) it costs $9,950 "with standard industry discounts available." For that you get the basic machine built around the 32000 microprocessor chip, one 5¼ inch floppy, a Quantum 10K hard disk, two RS-232 ports, a dumb terminal, and the Unix System V operating system extended with a number of popular Unix utilities such as YALOE and YACC (Yet Another Line Oriented Editor, and Yet Another Compiler Compiler), and the Vi editor from Berkeley Unix.

The WE 32000 chip is a true 32-bit processor; it corresponds somewhat to the National Semiconductor 32032, or the Motorola 68020. It's also capable of 8- and 16-bit operations. Moreover, AT&T is committed to heavy-duty silicon support of the system: at the moment, the WE 32000 system has an external Memory Management Unit (MMU) and other external support chips. The whole system is designed to interface with Unix. AT&T plans in future to combine the CPU, MMU, and other support into a single chip, thus increasing both speed and reliability; they say the new chips will be upward compatible with the present 32000 systems.

As I write this, memory for the 3B2 is $2,400 per megabyte. AT&T makes their own 256K memory chips, and bundles them in clusters to make one meg boards no larger than a paperback book. Alas, I didn't think to photograph one of their boards next to one of my paperbacks to illustrate the point, but a megabyte is about 166,000 English words: the AT&T memory board could hold all the words in one of my novels and have room to spare.

You'd undoubtedly want a full megabyte of memory for a development system, and indeed, to handle full Unix you'll probably need two; so the base price for a real world development system is more like $14,500. We'd also want to upgrade the disk to at least 40 megabytes: that's $2,000 more. Finally, AT&T will sell you a wonderful terminal with a bit-mapped screen and its own We 32000 processor to run it; that's an additional $5,000, so our development system costs $22K; hardly cheap.

However: we now have all we need. For an additional $500 per user (less if we want to use less expensive terminals), we can add up to 15 more users. The system is full multi-tasking multi-user Unix: we can let each of our terminals run more than one job. I saw 20 simultaneous jobs running on the 3B2/300, and that didn't seem to slow it down much.

The Death Star Connection

One of the strangest sights I ever saw was the AT&T "Death Star" logo on an IBM PC; but there it was. You can use the PC as a terminal for the 3B2/300. AT&T, in connection with Locus, a small but highly competent Santa Monica software house, has worked out the hardware and software to network the 3B2 with the PC. What we saw running at Comdex used a 3-Com Ethernet Board in the PC and the regular 3B2 Ethernet board; but the software will work just as well with Omninet or (at lower speed, of course) with a straight RS-232 connection. That means we could connect up a Corvus Concept, or any other machine that supports Omninet; or, if we want to write the interface driver, any machine with an RS-232 interface.

This gives the 3B2 a lot of flexibility. Even with all terminals and the networking and throwing in a good printer, we're under $30,000 for a ten-user system with full Unix.

There's more, though.

Opening Windows

What I saw running on that 3B2 wasn't any ordinary Unix: this Unix had windows, and a mouse, and while it didn't yet have icons it had nearly all the capabilities you expect from

Apple's Lisa, only this was loaded down with multiple users and was still *fast*. Yet more: using that marvelous bit-mapped screen you can run programs under the debugger, and see the program output in one window, the debugger in another, and the source code in a third—while having one or two other applications programs running along in still more windows. The debugger lets you insert break points, step the program along line by line through the source code, get the contents of the registers, i.e., it offers all the features you'd expect from a good debugging utility. I'm told it's an outgrowth of the "BLIT" windowing Unix prototype, but has a lot more capability.

The debugging system takes advantage of the speed and power of the WE 32000 in the terminal. Windowing is managed about the way you'd expect, with pull-down menus, and the ability to change window size and shape, and shuffle the windows to put the one you like on top; all this is done with the mouse in much the same way that Wirth's Modula Operating System works. I suppose I shouldn't be surprised, since most of these concepts have previously appeared at the Xerox Palo Alto Research Center (PARC); the whole micro community owes Xerox a vote of thanks for acting as the software R&D center for the industry. I can't imagine why they don't market some of the goodies they've developed, instead of exporting them to their competitors, but they've sure helped us all.

In any event, if there's something more powerful than the 3B2/300 for software development at anything like the cost, I haven't seen it.

The 3B2/300 weighs about 30 pounds, and is roughly the same size and shape as an IBM XT. Its innards are certainly no more complex than an XT's. If the introductory quantity one price is $9,950, what will the quantity one hundred price be a year from now? Ditto with memory: that $2,400/megabyte is quantity one today; I expect it to fall by half within two years.

Do They Know The Territory?

Every publication from computer magazines to *The Wall Street Journal* has speculated that AT&T knows a lot about computers, but they don't now how to market. How could The Phone Company learn that? This is, after all, the hated Ma Bell. . . .

So, naturally, when I got a chance to interview AT&T Vice President of Technology Division John Scanlon, even though it wasn't very original of me I figured I'd get that one out of the way. "Great R&D," said I, "but can AT&T handle marketing?"

"We seem to have done a good job of creating a demand for Unix," he said.

Which is true enough. Moreover, I notice that even IBM is supporting Unix, both directly and through Intel which is developing Unix for the Intel iAPX-286 chip.

"We already have Unix for our machines. Just turn on the switch: it comes up in Unix, with most of the features and utilities that programmers want. Who else can offer that at our prices?"

Maybe some others, particularly if you count Unix clones such as Charles River Data Systems, thought I, but I didn't want to argue with him.

"And we're not through. Right now a full Unix system really needs two megabytes, but we're getting it smaller. We're 90% to getting Unix tamed. After all, we've used Unix inside Bell for years to provide turnkey systems for our internal use. We do accounting, and telephone control, and billing, and we can develop new Unix shells for each application."

There's a lot to that. If some outside company had been supplying Ma Bell with office computers for accounting, billing, word processing, and all the mundane tasks one uses computers for, we'd think it a highly experienced company. AT&T has in fact been using a lot of its own equipment for years; it just didn't show outside their system. They've got more user-service experience that we usually give them credit for.

"But," I asked, "have you really tamed Unix? It takes a Unix wizard to keep the system going—at least it does everywhere I know."

"We have to get the size down," Scanlon told me. "At $4,800 for two megabytes—and you need that now—Unix is too expensive for the mass market. But we'll get it there, and when we do, we'll get it matched to silicon. Maybe in a few years we'll have Unix on a chip."

Ridiculous, thought I.

Then I remembered where I was.

I was sitting in a carpeted office that looked much like an

expensive executive suite. I'd reached it by going through expensively furnished lounge and reception areas. Of course; AT&T can afford lavish offices—except this wasn't any lavish office. This was in a bay of the Los Angeles Exposition Center. AT&T not only had the largest exhibit area I've ever seen at *any* computer show: they had taken an even *larger* area, closed it to the public, and lavishly furnished it for the convenience of their dealers, executives, and the press.

Out in their exhibit area there were about 100—and I do not say this for exaggeration—about 100 young men and women in dark suits, the most neatly uniformed and well-groomed corps of show people in my memory. Many were extremely polite, plenty of social skills, but knew nothing whatever about computers.

If throwing money—or people—at a problem will solve it, AT&T will never have any difficulties. Of course that doesn't often work—

But then it began to sink in. Along with all the well-scrubbed young ladies in stockings and heels and pinstripe suits and little neckties, and the young men in identical plumage—in among those were mixed real working software engineers, and even a sprinkling of true wizards from Bell Labs. As a matter of fact, it was easy to spot the real hackers: the programmers all read *BYTE* and knew exactly who I was, while the press relations people had never heard of me but tried to pretend that they had.

I don't have to ask if Bell Labs understands transistors. For reasons too complicated to explain, I have framed on my wall a one-dollar bill signed by Dr. William Shockley: it's a tiny part of the Nobel Prize he received for inventing the transistor while he was at Bell Labs.

The Phone Company never did lack for scientists and engineers. AT&T won't have problems in that department. They have been one of the few companies that plan for decades ahead.

If That's Not Enough

They also have some brilliant management, beginning with Jack Scanlon, who understands this business pretty darned well. We sat in a lavish office suite surrounded by the trappings of corporate power: but Scanlon talks like any true hacker. He reminded me of a lot of the sharper micro people I know: there was that same breadth of knowledge about the field, familiarity with every intimate detail of his own product, obvious pride in the company's achievements—

He gets particularly excited about what they can do with silicon, and the next generation of chips. "Every year we can double the number of transistors we can put on a chip. The guys who design those chips have to do something with all those transistors. We're seeing a whole new renaissance in silicon architecture. The difference between hardware and software is vanishing...."

And more. On software, and computer languages: "Language is the wrong way to look at it. Step back a few steps. Watch that guy at his desk. What does he want the machine to do? He knows he can do more than one thing at a time. He has to worry about a lot of things at once. What I want is fundamental building blocks he can throw together fast. This guy wants spelling and maybe a spread sheet, another fellow needs a data base.... Building blocks. Once we know the concepts we don't have to worry about languages. We can even put them in silicon.

"Obviously we're going to support the popular languages, C and Pascal and Ada and Modula, but the real goal is to see what people want the machines to do for them."

That sounds a lot like marketing smarts to me.

Sure: AT&T will make marketing mistakes. They are used to figuring out what they think people need and providing it whether it's wanted or not. It will take considerable effort to modify that attitude.

Consider: here they spent more than I've ever seen *any* company spend at *any* computer show: this to bring their products to a dinky little COMDEX that I wouldn't have bothered to go across town to see if AT&T hadn't been there. The press corps was the smallest for any show I've been to since the '70s. Having brought their machine to the tiniest pond they could find, they still didn't have a good mechanism for getting people to their press conference. The COMDEX show staff were even telling people it had been cancelled; if I didn't have a nasty suspicious nature so that I checked with AT&T myself, I'd have missed it.

Just before COMDEX, I received three phone calls, two letters, and a telegram reminding me that I could have an interview with John Scanlon. When I discovered I was missing their press conference—they had it in the Bonaventure Hotel, a mile from the show—an AT&T expediting officer put me in a cab to get me there. They sure paid attention to their press relations: but with what result? Apple sent *far* less to get Macintosh on the cover of every magazine in the country. I've yet to see real coverage of the AT&T market entry.

On the other hand, they can afford to make mistakes. When I said that at AT&T's lavish press luncheon, some of the computer press people said, "Yeah, and they got started early."

Maybe; but that 3B2 is one heck of a machine. It's state of the art, and it's available *now*. Of course it's not a retail system. They intend just now to sell to system developers and "value adders" who'll package it into full systems that will inevitably cost quite a lot. Retailers needn't worry just yet.

However: where else can you get a Unix development system that you can also use for your general purpose computing at that price? And certainly the Phone Company knows how to build rugged, reliable equipment. I wonder what the 3B2/300 will cost next year?

Of course we haven't heard the last from the micro world either. AT&T's machines are still positioned for maximum effect in the minicomputer world, and if they have a year to develop before they impact micros, so do first class micro computer outfits like Sage and CompuPro. The race isn't anywhere near decided.

Whatever happens, the micro industry had better think hard about AT&T. They're sure to have an impact as big as IBM's. AT&T is big, they're here to stay—and they've got some damned impressive machinery.

Big Mac

I've been sitting here bringing up Macwrite, and while swapping disks back and forth on my Macintosh I thought about the contrast with the AT&T system and Unix. It takes a couple of minutes to get the Macintosh ready to run a simple text editor, for me that's far too big a waste of time, especially when the only editor available is Macwrite.

In other words: I'm nowhere near as impressed with the Macintosh as everyone else seems to be.

I know I'm in trouble for saying that. I've already experienced what happens when one is less than enthusiastic about Macintosh: the Mactribesmen descend in force with fire and sword. You must overlook all the Mac's faults, for after all, they're only temporary. Everything will be fixed....

If IBM or AT&T had come out with a machine that had a single disk drive, no control or escape keys, non-standard interface between keyboard system, proprietary operating system, limited memory, closed architecture with no possible access to the machine's innards, disk formats totally incompatible with anything else in the micro community, no languages except Microsoft BASIC (and plenty of bugs in that), and absolutely no applications software, the micro community would have screamed bloody murder. Apple has done precisely that, and everyone applauds.

I'm sorry, but I don't. As I write this, the Macintosh is a wonderful toy; but it's not very much more.

Now, it certainly is fascinating. I know no one who has a Mac who wants to sell it. When it was my turn with the Mac that Dr. Hyson and I own between us, he parted with it reluctantly, and I can certainly see why. The machine is fun.

It just isn't very useful, because there's no application software. Indeed, there's less than we thought, because Microsoft's Multiplan, which we bought with the Mac, is no longer being delivered; the dealers have just been told to take it off the shelf. We have not yet been told why, or what Microsoft will do about our copy (which we paid full retail for, as we did with the Mac itself).

The Creator

In fact, the ONLY application software for Mac that's actually on the market is Bruce Tonkin's "The Creator" data base. "The Creator" is a kind of personal filing system, and there are versions for nearly every micro computer I know of. The data files created by it can be transferred among all these systems—except, of course, for the Macintosh, which sits in lonely isolation.

For the price—$35.00 postpaid, 30-day money-back guarantee—"The Creator" is one of the best values in micro land. I recommend it for nearly any machine; but especially for the Macintosh, since it lets you do *something* useful with the machine.

The Macintosh version of The Creator is written in Microsoft BASIC. It doesn't use the Macmouse, because MacMicrosoft BASIC is too full of bugs to allow that. Instead, Bruce takes all input from the keyboard, and formats it himself; of necessity he has to treat the Mac as a glass teletype, ignoring all its splendid Macfeatures such as quickdraw, because there's no way to get at them.

Tonkin writes many of his programs in his "PBASIC," which is a pre-processor for Microsoft BASIC that works somewhat as the RATFOR precompiler works for standard FORTRAN. PBASIC lets you do structured code, and handles most of the housekeeping for you. I've reviewed it before, and I still recommend it; Bruce has written some impressive software in PBASIC. The output of the PBASIC "compiler" is legal Microsoft BASIC: you can then truly compile that with Microsoft's Bascom to get tight, fast code that's very portable from machine to machine.

Alas, though, it won't work on the Macintosh, because Macwrite won't let you build large enough source code files to make it worth porting PBASIC over to the Mac.

For The Rest Of Us?

I've lived in Hollywood for some years, and I've grown familiar with the typical Tinseltown deal. A producer goes to a star and says: "I've got a great script and your favorite director. Sure would like to have you in the picture." Then he goes to the director. "I've got a star and a script, and the star sure wants you—" Then to the writer; and finally to the money people. When it's all finished, everything he's said is retroactively true.

Similarly: Macintosh is going to sell like hotcakes because of all that wonderful applications software. Now you can't do much with software on the Mac, because there's too little memory, and it takes anywhere from five to as many as 40 [!] disk swaps to copy a macdisk; but it's all right, because there will be a second disk drive, and a hard disk, and other excellent hardware after market add-ons to fit on the Mac's "virtual slot;" and after that the software will be easy to write. Software houses are going to work very hard to write applications software for the Mac because there's such a huge market, since they're selling an awful lot of Macs. Hardware houses will do macadd-ons because there's so much software. Etc.

It can certainly be made into retroactive truth. By the time this comes out, I expect it will be. Some of those Hollywood deals fall flat, though: it all depends on how quickly they can be put together before everyone in the industry catches on. Meanwhile, right now the Mac is mostly useful for people with special requirements, such as advertising layouts with text, or producing memos with graphics.

It sure is fun, though.

The EDP Manager's Blues

The most important effect of the microcomputer revolution has been the explosion of new and useful *interactive* software. Prior to micros there were no decent text editors. Spread sheets did not exist. Data base programs were expensive and complex.

You couldn't just sit down and *use* a computer. The machines were very expensive, and had to be kept in use. Only experts actually worked with computers. Would-be users had to tell an expert precisely what was wanted, but they had little idea of what computers could do for them.

The micro changed all that. Anyone could play with a computer. The interaction produced an explosion of software. That created new problems for managers of Electronic Data Processing (EDP) departments of large companies.

For example: a company vice president buys a micro computer and plays with one of the spread sheet programs. Soon he can see a dozen ways this can help him, so he calls in his EDP manager. "I want our sales reports set up like that," he says. "That way I can change things and see how they affect the forecast."

The EDP manager just shakes his head. "We don't have programs that can do that."

"Why not? Hell, write one."

The EDP manager looks reluctant. "It would be pretty expensive," he says. "At least a hundred thousand dollars."

It's easy to see what the vice president is now thinking. He paid only a few thousand for his whole setup, computer and all, and his expert tells him that machines costing half a million a year and up can't do what his desk-top micro can. He's not likely to be receptive when the EDP shop asks for a larger budget.

It's all true, too. You can buy a micro computer with a much better text editor than anything available on big mainframes or mini computers, and while the big machines can process *enormous* financial models and highly complex simulations, there aren't many interactive tools like SuperCalc available.

An example may illustrate. My long-time friend and editor Jim Baen recently took over the publishing and distibution of much of the Simon & Schuster/Pocket Books science fiction line. The first thing he did was put the sales history of each book into a data base on his IBM PC. Then he manipulated various factors with a spread sheet program. Within a few days he knew precisely how to treat each book. Simon & Schuster had much larger computers—but none of their editors ever had the kind of decision information that Jim has.

The irony is that Jim took all his data from computer printouts and keyed it in by hand. There was no way that the Simon & Schuster/Pocket computer system could talk to a micro—nor could their programs organize the data into spread sheet format for interactive experimentation.

Big computers are not necessarily best. The utility of a computer depends on the software, and there's far more *user* software for micros than for larger machines.

There's No Secret
What happened is simple enough. Great programs can come about in a number of ways. Probably the best programs come when a gifted programmer gets a great idea, and has both the time and the computer facilities to work on it.

Prior to micros this didn't happen often. As with any profession, most programmers aren't highly original. When one did have a great idea, it was hard to persuade the employer to spare him from his other work, much less give him time on an expensive machine. Even if all that happened, the machines weren't very available. It wasn't your machine, to use any hour of the day or night. You couldn't idly doodle with it. You'd have to explain your idea in detail—and suppose it hadn't jelled? Wayne Holder's excellent The Word Plus didn't start off to be a spelling program at all.

The combination of bright people, time off to work on good ideas, and lots of machine time to do it with didn't happen very often before micros.

A sometimes successful way to develop good programs is through software engineering teams. Most software for the mini and mainframe worlds is written this way. Teamwork has its problems. The method is clearly expensive. It still works best when the team members have lots of interactive machine time.

The team approach won't be financed unless there's a good prospective return on the investment.

In the mainframe or mini world, outside developers (people independent of the equipment's manufacturer) are not likely to sell many copies of a new program unless it's *very* successful. Often they can't sell more than a few hundred—sometimes no more than a dozen—copies. Each copy will have to sell at a high price. If it's not to be sold, but only used internally, it will have to be terribly important in order to justify the development costs.

Winds of Change

The micro revolution changed all that. Suddenly there was an enormous customer base. Programs might sell hundreds of thousand of copies. Investing large sums in program development made sense.

Equally important, creative programmers now had the computer resources to develop their ideas. Wayne Ratliffe developed Vulcan, which became dBase-II. Michael Shrayer wrote Electric Pencil. Wayne Holder produced The Word Plus. Richard Frank, Paul McQuestin, and others wrote Pascal/M, then SuperCalc. VisiCalc was responsible for a vastly renewed interest in Apple computers.

The larger the market base, the more likely outside developers are to produce innovative software. The lesson is clear: it's vital that the micro world remain as unified as possible. That's especially true for the "fifty dwarves:" companies other than IBM and AT&T. As Ben Franklin said after the Declaration of Independence, "We must all hang together, or we shall most assuredly all hang separately." Attempts to divide the micro world into small, secure fiefdoms aid no one but the giants.

Cataloging

For some years now I've used Ward Christenson's public domain disk catalog program. Lately, though, I've been importuned to try a new one called Eureka! from Mendocino Software. Eureka! has a number of advantages, including the capability to include lots of comments in your disk catalog, so that you can figure out that "NASTYLET.TXT" was sent to your mother-in-law rather than your lawyer, or whatever. It also lets you date things.

Until recently, though, I couldn't get Eureka! to work with

my big CompuPro System 8/16, nor would it catalog the system's hard disk. The Mendocino people kept trying, though, and eventually sent their stuff to Tony Pietsch; and as of an hour ago Noor Singh delivered a copy with the note that this time it works.

It's about time I changed over, and the ability to add comments and dates makes Eureka! nearly irresistible. Full discussion next month, or Real Soon Now if too much flows into Chaos Manor in the next few weeks; meanwhile, Mendocino Software deserves some applause for plugging away until they could make Eureka! work on my system. Thanks.

RAM Disk For The Z-100

Some weeks ago I got a letter from David James at the University of Kansas. Zenith offered the faculty and students at UK one of those deals you can't refuse, a Z-100 at a really good price, and Mr. James bought one with a lot of memory. When he went looking for a RAM Disk program, though, he couldn't find one.

I had my assistants send copies of his letter to half a dozen places known for their RAM Disks. We only got two answers:

Zenith recommends Standard Data of Fort Lauderdale, Florida. I've not used their boards, which come in 256/K Byte sizes, but I suppose their hardware and software must work or Zenith's people wouldn't have sent me Standard's address in reply to my inquiry.

I'd suppose that CompuPro's M/drive-H boards could be made to work, since they're IEEE-696 (S-100) standard; but I've never heard of an install program that would get M/drive-H running under ZDOS. Someone would have to hack up a BIOS for that, and I don't know of anyone who's done it.

One other source I know of is Macrotech out in the San Fernando Valley. They have a full one mega byte board for the Z-100. They've had it going for six months now with RAMDISK software.

Eat Your Heart Out

Speaking of Macrotech, they had an impressive board running at COMDEX Winter: an 8-bit Z-80 CPU coupled with an Intel iApx-20286 chip for 16/32 bit processing.

It was installed in a CompuPro boat anchor box much like mine. I admitted that I was impressed. To make sure there were no misunderstandings they opened the box, to show me that the board was wire-wrapped; production model sometime later this Summer or Fall.

The rest of the boards in the box were CompuPro. They claim that sometime before next Fall COMDEX they'll come over here, open my Dual Processor, remove the CompuPro 8085/8088 board, and insert theirs; after which my system will continue to operate on CP/M 8/16 as before, except that it will be faster, will be able to run Z-80 as well as 8080 software, and will accept 20286 commands. We'll see; my CP/M 8/16 isn't the common or garden variety, since Tony Pietsch did some work with the command processor, and enabled interrupts, and generally did a spit and polish job. On the other hand, I never throw anything away: I can certainly boot up the old standard CP/M 8/16 if I have to.

The New Moon Race

After I wrote my report on the AT&T machines, I put in calls to some of the micro industry leaders. Most were noncommittal at best.

Dr. William Godbout of CompuPro had a lot more to say. "The real impact is going to be on Japan, Inc. This is a big step forward in U.S. technology; a race between two big and highly competent United States outfits. Now maybe the U.S. electronics industry can get its act together instead of whining about tariffs and protectionism; we can give Japan, Inc. some real competition.

"What we have here is something like the race to the Moon. People have been wringing their hands about Japan's great steps forward, and their leap to the fifth-generation machines—but you can't count the United States out. The demise of the U.S. technology lead isn't anywhere near as imminent as the Chicken Littles with their 'sky is falling' have been saying."

"But what," I asked, "does this mean for companies like CompuPro?"

"Well, we're not going to take on IBM or AT&T nose to nose and toe to toe, obviously. But companies like that, while excellent, are pretty big spheres. When they're rammed as close together as you can get, there's still plenty of room for other companies.

"Just now, AT&T is going to impact on DEC, and the mid-range of IBM products."

"Sure," said I, "but I can see that as the prices on the 3B2 fall it's going to be direct competition with your Shirley (which is otherwise known as the CompuPro System 10)."

"That's why there's a 20, and a 30 in development. Right now you can get the 10 as a business system complete with software. When AT&T get into that market—and it will take them a while—we'll have something else. Meanwhile, they're raising the level of the competition, and I like that.

"The one thing I really envy is their ability to work directly with silicon. We get into chip design on a small scale, but they can do it massively. What they've done in silicon I can only envy."

I mentioned the huge numbers of people AT&T had brought to the smallest possible COMDEX. "They're probably training them for other shows," I mused.

"Sure," said Dr. G. "That's one of their strongest points, training their future managers. They've been running their 'breeder reactor' for years. When we expanded we could promote some people from inside, and you know they were good troops, but there weren't enough. We had to go outside for middle management. AT&T doesn't have to. They've been training their own for a long time."

He didn't sound worried, though. As Bill Godbout observes, there's a good bit of room in working with users, whether business people or hackers. It's true that until recently CompuPro hadn't much experience working with business users—CompuPro support used to consist of reading the spec sheets and sending circuit diagrams—but that's changed radically in the past two years. "We're putting a lot of emphasis on pre-testing," he said. "Which is why we shipped so many System 10s to test sites. I've got a lot of those units out, and we've got a lot of feedback on software and documentation."

Indeed. We even have one here at Chaos Manor, although I blush to confess that we've been slower in getting it set up and running than I'd like. That's not the Shirley's fault, it's mine: so much stuff has happened in the past couple of weeks that we've been running as fast as we can just to stay in the same place, and we've had little chance to work with either the CompuPro Shirley or the Sage IV; they both stare accusingly at me, while I try to get my novel done. Sigh.

Printer Optimizer

Last month I mentioned Applied Creative Technology's Printer Optimizer, which is a box full of memory that sits between the Golem (CompuPro 8/16) and the NEC 7710 Spinwriter. Shortly after that, ACT recalled the machine in order to add even more memory to it—

And I discovered that I was hooked. No sooner was the little jewel gone than I missed it terribly. It's amazing how you can get used to the idea that printing is something that happens nearly instantaneously (well, at 9600 baud, which is the speed at which the computer ships data into the Optimizer). Waiting for the machine to print at normal speed (1200 baud) was just no fun at all.

Ten days later it came back. The first time it showed up I'd had Alex install it, but he wouldn't be back up from UCSD for a couple of days, and I wanted that Optimizer *now*; so I tackled the installation myself.

I am no hardware genius. Like most Americans of my generation I learned to solder and install electrical switches and such, but when I was in school electronics meant vacuum tubes and hookup wire; not only didn't we have transistors, but printed circuit boards were pretty rare. Thus while I'm not afraid of the innards of my computers, I do tend to think of hardware jobs with a distinct sense of unease, not to say dismay. There was nothing for it, though, if I wanted my Optimizer—and I sure did—I was going to have to do it myself.

It turned out to be simple. Not as simple as it would have been had I wanted to connect it to a Centronics parallel port instead of through an RS-232 serial port; but simple enough. The ACT instructions are quite clear, with plenty of diagrams and examples, and a good explanation of the theory of what's going one. It took me considerably less than an hour to hook things up, and *mirable dictu* everything worked first time.

Now, with 256 K of memory in the Optimizer, I can pack a great part of an entire novel into it. I can do that as one long file, or as a series of linked files, or even file at a time if I want to fiddle with the last part while the beginning is printing out.

The Optimizer even has a way to program it so that the files aren't necessarily printed in the order you put them in: there's a way to shunt stuff off, as on a railway siding, so that something else can be printed first. It's not a feature I use very often, but it can be convenient, as for example when you don't have the fanfold tractor on because you want to print single sheets, but there's a convenient opportunity to load in a file that will need fanfold.

If you don't have a print buffer, you don't know what you're missing. They come in a variety of styles with various features, and I haven't much experience with any of them except the ACT Optimizer. I sure love this one, and it's hard to imagine one being easier to use. Given the wide variety of protocols and stop bits and other such stuff (the RS-232, means Revised Standard-232, is anything BUT standard; there is a bewildering complexity of ways to hook serial ports to computers), it would be difficult to write better hook up instructions.

Recommended.

Speeding Up Your PC

Another gadget I'd just got installed last month was the "Quickon" from Security Micro Systems. This is a little gizmo that installs rather simply in your IBM PC; when it's all aboard, all you'll see is a small switch on the back.

Throw the switch one way, and the PC behaves normally. Throw it the other way, and the memory tests are disabled: the PC comes on nearly instantly. Now I don't think you ought permanently to disable the memory tests; but I sure don't much care to wait for all that every time I have to turn the PC off to escape from some hang up—and with no true hardware reset on the machine, that happens more often than I like.

We've had the Quickon working for five weeks now, with zero trouble; and Jim Baen reports that he's had his almost a year. If you like waiting for the PC, you won't need this, but if you're as impatient as I am you'll find it nearly indispensable.

Diskmaker

New Generation Systems is a public benefactor.

Our Kaypro IV will, courtesy of a program called Uniform— itself a life saver—read a number of 5¼" disk formats, but there are machines it has never heard of. However, when we get a disk that the Kaypro can't read, we no longer despair; we take it to the Disk Maker.

I first heard about the Disk Maker at CP/M East when I stopped to talk with Leor Zolman. Leor was, naturally, demonstrating BDS C, the blindingly fast 8-bit C compiler he wrote while he was still an undergraduate at MIT; but he'd been so impressed by the Disk Maker that, although he owned no part of the company that makes it, he had one to show off at his BDS booth.

That was a pretty good recommendation by itself. I have considerable confidence in Leor's judgment. He introduced me to the box's inventor, and we arranged to get one shipped to Chaos Manor. The result has been as advertised. Disk Maker can read almost any conceivable 5¼" disk format.

The machine consists of one or two disk drives—mine has two, one 48 tracks per inch (TPI) like the IBM PC, the other 96 TPI like the Eagle 1600—and an S-100 buss disk controller card. You can install the Disk Maker card for your S-100 system and forget it's there until you need it; then, when you get a disk with a strange format, fire up the disk maker. Chances are very high that it will be able to read it, and you can PIP files to and from your normal system's disks.

We have the Disk Maker installed in the Zorro, the Zenith Z-100, who also runs 8 inch disks in addition to his normal 5¼s; thus we can move files from any 5¼ inch format to 8 inch IBM Standard, after which they can be brought in for Zeke and the Golem.

The Disk Maker will format disks, too; there are about fifty formats supported. It's thus nearly ideal for a small software house that tries to support a wide spectrum of customers.

It's easy to install, easy to use, and darned near unique. If you need one, you need it bad.

The Unshippable Sage

In my judgment, Sage Computers have about the same place in the world of the Motorola 68000 and follow-ons that CompuPro's boat anchor has in the Intel 8086 and beyond world: they're very probably the best systems you can get for software development; they certainly have a lot of bang for the buck.

The Sage is also useful as a general purpose computer: there's getting to be a lot of good software, including engineering applications stuff, for 68000 systems. Sage uses a number of Sage computers internally for everything from accounting to new systems design; and therein hangs a tale.

When I visited Sage at their Reno headquarters I was shown through the whole plant, including into the inner offices where new research is done. They have quite a lot of modern equipment, including some fascinating stuff for Computer Assisted Drafting, and for chip design. They also have the oddest computer I've ever seen in my life. I mean, I've seen plenty of desk *top* computers, but I never saw one bolted to the *side* of a desk before; yet there was a perfectly good Sage II in that situation. It was running, too. None of the Sage crew seemed to think that was odd at all. They were used to it. Finally I had to ask.

It turns out that in the early days of Sage, when they first began to ship machines, they got more orders than they could fill; so that whenever Bob Needham, one of the cofounders (with Rod Coleman) of Sage Computer would get a machine to help him with advanced system design, someone would see it and ship it off to a paying customer. Eventually Bob decided that enough was enough, and bolted a new Sage II, sans case and fan, onto the side of his desk. The disk drives and power supply were installed in a drawer.

No one has shipped that one. . . .

Raving About Calendar/1

Peter Flynn, our new (as of January) assistant sees a *lot* of software; alas, more than I do, since so much flows through Chaos Manor that I have to let Peter and Alex screen it unless it's something I'm particularly interested in. Thus he doesn't give very many rave reviews.

Here's one item he liked a lot.

"Calendar/1 puts date related information into a calendar format. It is easy to use. The manual is good, organized in a straightforward manner. The preface states that the manual assumes you know how to use the various CP/M functions such as PIP and COPY, and that you have and can use a text editor that can produce plain text files 'with no embedded control characters.'

"The text editor is used to create one or more files that are the sources for the date related information. This is the best approach I have ever seen for a calendar program; it is easy to input large numbers of notices, and it's very easy to update and modify into different calendars. This is by far the most useful and versatile program of its type I have ever seen. It is much better than the scheduler in **VALDOCS**.

"Calendars are composed of notices which are stored in calendar files. Each calendar file is composed of dates followed by notices pertaining to that date. The calendar files, which you create on a word processor, look like this:

% This is a comment.
@ 8/10/84
Meeting with Fred at 7:15 AM

@ 7/29
First Moon Landing, 1969

@ 8/10
Sally's Birthday

The order of the dates does not matter, and you can enter the same date more than once. They can be organized under headings such as birthdays, meetings, notices, social events, etc. Under each date is a notice or group of notices. They will be printed in the box for the corresponding date on the calendar. Lines beginning with % are comments and are ignored by the Calendar/1 program.

A new calendar file can be for a month, a year, or many years. If a date ends in a year, such as 5/16/84, then it will only be printed in that year; if only a month and day are given then it prints the notice for every year. (Years can range between 1583 and 9999 AD; if only two digits are given, the twentieth century is presumed.)

Calendar files can be separated or combined: you can have a file of birthdays and another of meetings, print a calendar for each, and combine those with others to make one master calendar incorporating many files. Calendar/1 comes with a number of pre-written calendar files containing holidays and historical dates of interest.

Calendars can be printed on screen or on your printer. You specify the length and width. If a notice won't fit, then what will fit is printed, a * is added, and the balance is printed as a note on an overflow page. The layout is very good considering the space you have to work with.

There are a number of other control features, all well documented.

Calendar/1 is useful for scheduling work; many people can

be given identical copies for job control; it is also useful for scheduling travel.

We expect to make a lot of use of Calendar/1 here at Chaos Manor. It's a well conceived and useful program.

We're Out of Space Again . . .

There's a ton of stuff on my list, and I'm out of space. At least let me mention the Infocom games, such as Sorcerer and Enchanter and the like. Not only do we at Chaos Manor love them, but I notice that my partner Larry Niven is hooked. For those few who don't know, Infocom games are script driven: there's no fancy graphics, no arcade action; only text adventures.

This kind of game grew out of the original Crowther and Woods Adventure of the Colossal Cave. The original Infocom implementers worked on Zork while at MIT; they later developed other software for role playing games. Some of the work they've done parsing and interpreting English is remarkable.

Enough. My taxes are due, after which I'm on the road for two weeks; meanwhile, I just opened a letter from Judy-Lynn del Rey, my long-suffering editor at Ballantine Books; she's expecting Larry and me to turn in *Footfall* Right Away: the letter said only, "Nag! Nag! Nag!"

I think that was a hint.

A Few Final Words

I'm out of space. This was originally intended to be a 70,000-word book; it's something over 100,000, and I've still not put into it everything I'd wanted to. I still have Computer Faire reports, book reports, and some 25 columns that weren't even touched.

There's nothing for it: we'll have to have another book. Lord alone knows what kind of cover Baen will put on *that* one. . . .

THE END

It really is. . . .

APPENDIX

Below are the addresses and telephone numbers of some of the hardware and software companies referred to in this book.

Applied Creative Technology Inc.
2156 West Northwest Hwy.,
　Suite 303
Dallas, TX 75220
(214) 556-2916

Borland International
4807 Scotts Valley Dr.
Scotts Valley, CA 95066
(408) 438-8400

Clear Systems
601 Ashland Ave., Suite A
Santa Monica, CA 90401
(213) 394-7740

Diser Company
385 East 800 South
Orem, UT 84058
(801) 227-2300

Hudson and Associates
POB 2957
Santa Clara, CA 95051
(408) 554-1316

MPI
4426 South Century Dr.
Salt Lake City, UT 84123
(801) 263-3081

New Generation Systems Inc.
1800 Michael Faraday Dr.,
　Suite 206
Reston, VA 22090
(703) 471-5598

Slicer Control/Computer
2543 Marshall St. N.E.
Minneapolis, MN 55418
(612) 788-9481

Soft Warehouse
P.O. Box 11174
Honolulu, HI 96828

Software Toolworks
15233 Ventura Blvd.
Sherman Oaks, CA 91403
(818) 986-4885

TNT Software
34069 Hainesville Rd.
Round Lake, IL 60073
(312) 223-0832

Workman and Associates
112 Marion Ave.
Pasadena, CA 91106
(818) 796-4401

INDEX

3B2/300, 311
8085/8088, 48, 114
  Compupro system, 69
  little bugs, 124
Accounting
  my problems, 12
  Pournelle Accounting
    Program, 13, 132
Accounting for Non-Accountants
  by John N. Myer, 12, 133
Ace Books, 67, 238
Ada, 221
  Augusta, 221
  Janus, 221
Adelle, 53
Adventure, 331
Alice, 149, 150
Alpha Omega Computer
  Systems
  See also: Small-C Plus
Altair, 2, 5
  the Nivens' old computer,
    149
Altos, 87
Americare service, 279
Ancient history
  IDM 650, 3, 189
  ILIAC, 3, 5, 226, 254
Anderson, Poul, 285
APL, 213
Apple, 298
  Lisa, 255
  Macintosh, 305, 317
Apple CP/M, 298
  See also: Gold Card &
    Applicard
Appledos, 298, 299, 300
Applicard, 299
Applied Creative Technology, 326

Printer Optimizer, 326
Archives keyboard, 149
Artificial Intelligence, 226, 238
  Eliza, 168
Ashton-Tate
  Vulcan (before dBase), 20
Asimov, Isaac, 285
AT&T, 308, 309, 310, 324
  3B2/300, 312
Attache, 73
  Adelle, 53
Augusta, 221
Aztec C II, 209

Baen, Jim, 67, 223, 238, 321
Bailey, Kirk, 208
Bascom, 26, 27, 119, 120, 126,
  127, 128
  speed, 178, 179
BASIC, 176, 177
  Bascom, 26, 27, 119, 120,
    126, 127, 128
  BASIC E, 24
  CB/80, 130, 131, 132, 140,
    141, 142, 175, 176, 178, 179
  CBASIC, 24, 25, 46
  Debbie, 121
  E-BASIC, 120
  MBASIC, 23, 185, 318
  first program, 9
  PBASIC, 319
  the great debate, 21
  the great debate continues,
    36
  the great basic compiler
    debate, 140, 210
BASIC E, 24
BASIC-80
  See: MBASIC

333

Index

Bdos errors
  Tony Pietsch's error traping, 168
BDS C, 30, 31, 32, 207
Benchmark, 177, 180
Benford, Dr. Gregory, 53
Billings, Roger, 92
Bilofsky, Walt, 167
Books
  Accounting for Non-Accountants, 132
  Brown's Instant BASIC, 8
  C Programming Guide, The, 218
  C Programming Language, The, 30, 216
  Computer Programming for the Complete Idiot, 196
  Flowers for Algernon, 226
  Footfall, 200, 331
  Forth Encyclopedia, 198
  Fundamentals of Accounting, 133
  Future Men of War, 200
  Greek Myths, 140
  Highland Clans and Tartans, 140
  Instant BASIC, 196
  Janissaries Two, 139, also 200
  King David's Spaceship, 22, 36
  Little Lisper, The, 214
  Managerial Revolution, The, 282
  Maturity, 225
  Mote in God's Eye, The, 287
  Oath of Fealty, 22, 36
  PL/1: Structured Programming, 36, 98
  Programming in Pascal, 45, 95, 161, 165, 173
  Science and Sanity, 38
  Software Tools, 29, 161
  Software Tools in Pascal, 160, 173
  Space Viking's Return, 146
  Starting Forth, 198
  Step Farther Out, A, 223
  Word Processing Buyer's Guide, 83

  WRITE, EDIT, AND PRINT: Word Processing With Personal Computers, 195
Borland International
  See also: Turbo Pascal
Brown's Instant BASIC
  recommendation, 8
Burgess, Eric, 110
Burnham, James, 282
Byte, viii

C, 30, 142, 207, 208, 209, 216, 217
  Aztec C ii, 209
  BDS C, 30, 142–143, 207, 209
  CW/C, 208
  Infosoft C, 208
  Kernighan & Ritchie, 30
  Q/C, 208
  Small-C, 208
  Small-C Plus, 208
  Supersoft C, 209
  the great language debate, 30
  Tiny-C One, 209
  Tiny-C Two, 209
  Whitesmith, 32, 142
C Programming Guide, The
  by Jack Purdom, 218
C Programming Language, The
  by Kernighan & Ritchie, 30, 216
C/80, 208
Cain, Ron, 208
Calculators
  TI-59, 4
Calendar programs
  Calendar/1, 329, 330
  Datebook, 39, 40
  Milestone, 40, 41
Calendar/1, 329, 330
Canon, Maggie, 99
Carousel, 203 (as Unicorn)
Carousel Systems, 166 See also: RATFOR
Carr, John, 12, 146
Cassette board
  Tarbell, 6
CB-80, 130, 131, 132, 140, 141, 142, 175, 176, 178, 179
  See also: CBASIC
  speed, 179

INDEX

CB-86 *See also:* CB-80
  speed, 178
CBASIC, 46 *See also:* CB-80
  first release, 24
  popularity against CB-80, 179
CBASIC86, 192, 193
Cbios, 169
CCS, 113, 114
CDOS, 274, 297
Chaos Manor, viii, ix, 17, 310, 331
  another day, 37
  typical Sunday afternoon, 22
Charly, 225
Christenson, Ward, 322
  Utilities, 91
Citizen's Advisory Council on National Space Policy, 37, 110
Clan and Crown: Janissaries II See: Janissaries II
Clark, Pamela, viii, 271
Clarke, Dr. Arthur C., 108, 112, 152
Clear Systems, 329 *See also:* Calendar/1
Cobol, 198
Code Works, The, 208 *See also:* Q/C *See also:* Small-C
Colbol, 215
Coleman, Rod, 49, 266, 308 *See also:* Sage
Colvin, Jim, 208
Comdex
  Spring 1983, 283
  Winter 1983, 272
  Spring 1984, 310
Communications *See also:* future trends
  serial/parallel, 300
Compal, 3, 7
Compatibility
  IBM, 223, 277
  PC-DOS vs MS-DOS, 302
  trends, 72
  UNIX, 89, 90
Compiler systems, 130
Compiling CBASIC *See:* CB-80
Compu-Plus, 137

Compupro, 48, 115
  10, 326
  8085/8088, 69, 114, 124, 125
  Colem, 326
  Z-80, 149
  Zeke II, 150, 259
Compupro 10, 224, 322, 325
Computer Power & Light
  See: Compal
Computer Programming for the Complete Idiot by Donald McCunn, 196
Computer System *See also:* future trends
  ideal system, 84
Computer systems
  overview, 64
  portable, 73
Concurrent CP/M, 278, 306
Consultants
  Proteus Engineering, 5
Cornucopia, 125 *See also:* Microproof
Corvus, 68
Corvus Concept, 68
CP/M, 90, 91, 275, 294, 295
  See also: Concurrent CP/M
  See also: ZCPM
CP/M +,
CP/M 3.0 *See:* CP/M +
Creator, The, 318
Cromemco *See also:* CDOS
  See also: Cromemco Z-2
Cromemco Z-2, 5, 17
  Ezekial, vii, 16, 17, 92, 146, 256, 259, 274, 279
Crowther & Woods, 331 *See also:* Adventure
CW/C, 208

Data base programs
  Creator, The, 318
  dBase II, 322
  Mimimum Data Base, 120
  Vulcan, 19
Datebook, 39, 40
Dbase II, 322
Dean, Samuel, 283
Debbie, 121
Del Rey, Judy-Lynn, 331

Destinies, 238
Diablo, 59
　1620, 7, 8, 18
　first printer, 7, 8
Dickenson, Dick, 137
Dickson, Gordon, 82, 274
Digital Research *See also:*
　　Concurrent CP/M *See
　　also:* CP/M *See also:* Gold
　　Card *See also:* CBASIC
　　See also: PL/1
　reception from IBM, 113
　Dijkstra, Edsger W., 186
Disk catalog
　Eureka!, 322
　Ward Christenson, 322
Disk drives
　overview, 61
Diskmaker, 327, 328
Dot matrix printers, 57, 58
　See also: impact printers
Drive
　iCom, 6, 7
Dvorak, John, 99

E-BASIC, 120
Eagle
　1600, 289
Ed-A-Sketch, 168
Edwards, Sam, 287
Eleanor, 290
Electric Pencil, 4, 115, 116, 322
　first use, 9
　problems, 11
Eliza, 168
EMACS, 117
　Final Word, 82, 81
　MINCE, 82
　Perfect Writer, 81
Epson
　QX-10, 288
Eubanks, Gordon, 46, 130 *See
　also:* Digital Research
　CBASIC, 46
Eureka!, 322
Execudata
　Joan Huges, 44
Ezekial, vii, viii, 9, 18, 92,
　108–9, 146, 256, 274, 279
　See also: Zeke II

FDOS, 8, 274
Films
　"Charly," 225
Final Word, 82
Flowers for Algernon, 226
Flynn, Peter, 329
Footfall
　novel by Niven and
　　Pournelle, 200, 331
Formatting programs
　Diskmaker, 327, 328
　Uniform, 327
Forth, 197, 214
Forth Encyclopedia
　by Mitch Derick & Linda
　　Baker, 198
Fortran, 162, 216
Foulger, Davis, 66
Frank, Richard, 48, 114, 125,
　260, 322 *See also:* Sorcim
Franklin, Ben, 322
Fundamentals, 245
Fundamentals of Accounting
　by Mackenzie, 13, 133
Future Men of War, 200
Future trends, 239, 255, 272,
　319

Galaxy Science Fiction, viii, 66,
　223
Games, 263
　Adventure, 311
　Inferno, 67, 263
　Mychess, 168
　Zork, 243, 244
Gerrold, David, 2, 274
Godbout, Dr. William, ix, 48,
　114, 151, 255, 267, 307,
　324 *See also:* Compupro
Gold Card, 300
Golden, Ellen Lewis, 242
Golem, 326
Graphics
　Ed-A-Sketch, 168
great software drought, the, 107
Greek Myths
　by Robert Graves, 140
Grieb, Bill, 150

Haldeman, Joe, 15

Heath *See:* Zenith
Heinlein, Dr. Robert, 107, 240
Helmers, Carl, 142, 192
Herbert, Frank, 15
Highland Clans and Tartans by Munro, 140
Holder, Wayne, 322, 47, 321
Home computers
 recommendations, 71, 72
Hudson, Jim, 267
Hyson, Dr. Michael, 318

IBM, 277, 308
 wrecked keyboard, 66, 138
IBM 650, 3, 189
IBM compatibility *See:* Compatibility
IBM-PC, 302
iCom, 67
ILIAC, 3, 5, 226, 254
Impact printers, 57, 58
Imsai
 Alice, 149, 150
Inferno
 computer game, 67, 263
Infocom, 331
Infosoft C., 208 *See also:* Small-C
Infosoft Systems Inc., 208 *See also:* Infosoft C
Infoworld, 99
Ink jet printers, 57
INMAC
 T-switch, 144, 145
Instant BASIC
 by Jerald R. Brown, 196
Intel
 8085/8088, 48
Interactive video disks, 264
Integrated software, 306 *See also:* Future trends
 Lotus 1-2-3, viii, 260, 363
 VisiOn, 260
Introduction to Pascal See: Pascal introduction package
Ithaca IA-1100 Memory-mapped video board, 145

Jackson, David, 87

James, David, 323
Janissaries II
 novel by Pournelle, 139, 200
Janus, 221
Japan, Inc., 324
Jet Propulsion Laboratory, 53, 110
Johnson, Wendell, 38
Journal *See:* Accounting

Kaypro, 267
 10, 64
 line of computers, 74
Kernighan, Brian, 203
Keyboards
 advice, 65
 Archives, 149
 early preferences, 7
 IBM, 66
 Memorex, 7
 QWERTY, 65
Killdall, Gary, ix, 294
King David's Spaceship
 novel by Pournelle, 22, 36

L-5 Society, 109 *See also:* Citizen's Advisory Council on National Space Policy
Lane, Eliot, 93
Languages *See:* BASIC *See:* C *See:* Forth *See:* Fortran *See:* Lisp *See:* Pascal *See:* PL/I
 CBASIC86, 192, 193
 comparisons, 180
Laser printers, 57
LASFS, 149
Lashley, Karl, 226, 227
LDOS, 94, 298
Lehman, Mike & Nancy, 45
 See also: Digital Research
 Pascal/MT+, 45
Lemmons, Phil, viii, 310
Levitical documentation
 thou shalt not..., 97
Lexi-Soft *See also:* Spellbinder
Ley, Willy, 223
Lifeboat Associates
 Whitesmith C. Compiler, 32

Index

Lisa, 255
Lisp, 33, 214
   muLisp-79, 33
   The great debate continues, 43
   The great language debate, 32–33
Little Lisper, The by Daniel P. Friedman, 214
Lobo
   LX-80 expansion interface, 93
   MAX-80, 94
   to the rescue, 93
Logical Systems *See also:* LDOS
Lotus 1-2-3, viii, 260, 303
LX-80 expansion interface, 93

Macintosh, 306, 318, 317
Maclean, Dan, 2, 3, 5, 7, 9, 36, 88, 94, 107, 108, 112, 125, 144, 145, 162, 261
Macrotek, 323
Macsyma, 118, 242
Magazines
   Byte, viii
   Destinies, 238
   Galaxy science fiction, viii, 67, 223
   Infoworld, 99
   onComputing, 271
   Popular Computing, 271
Magic Wand *See:* Peachtext
Managerial Revolution, The by James Burnham, 282
Math programs
   Macsyma, 118, 242
   muMath, 118
   muSimp, 118
"Maturity"
   story by Theodore Sturgeon, 225
Max-80, 94
MBASIC, 23, 185, 318
McCarthy, John, 33, 42, 214, 265
McCullouch, Mike, 111
McKee, D. W., 194
McQuestin, Paul, 322
Memorex
   first keyboard, 7
Memory boards
   Macrotek, 323
   Microsystems, 7
   Standard Data, 323
Memory drive *See:* Ram disk
Mendocino Software, 322 *See also:* Eureka!
Mick, Dr. Colin, 104, 113
Micropro *See also:*
   Wordmaster *See also:* Wordstar
Microproof, 108
Microsoft
   BASCOM, 26
   MBASIC, 23
   muLisp-79, 33
Microsystems, 7
Milestone, 46
Miller, Walter M., Jr., 285
Mimimum Data Base, 120, 210 *See also:* People's Data Base
Mince, 82, 118
Minsky, Marvin, 42, 212
MIT *See also:* EMACS
Modula-2, 219–220
   operating system, 309
Morgan, Chris, viii
Mote in God's Eye, The
   novel by Niven & Pournelle, 287
MS-DOS, 277, 302
muLisp-79
   Microsoft, 33
mu-Math, 118
muSimp, 118
Mychess, 168

Naiman, Arthur, 83
NASA
   JPL, 53, 110
   Saturn encounter, 53, 110
National Computer Convention
   1980, 274
   spring 1983, 253
NEC
   Spinwriter, 8, 58, 59
New Generation Systems, 327
   See also: Diskmaker

INDEX

NewWord, 80
Niven, Larry, 2, 10, 15, 52, 74, 115, 149, 263
Niven, Marilyn, 2, 52
North Star, 274, 275, 297, 294
Novels *See:* Books

Oath of Fealty novel by Niven & Pournelle, 22, 36
Omikron, 18
onComputing, 271
Operating systems, 215 *See also:* Future trends
  Apple CP/M, 299
  Appledos, 289–299
  CDOS, 274, 297
  Concurrent CP/M, 278, 306
  CP/M, 90, 91, 275, 294, 296
  CP/M +, 296
  explanation, 71
  FDOS, 274
  history, 292
  LDOS, 298
  Macintosh, 306
  Modula-2, 309
  MS-DOS, 277, 302
  North Star, 275, 297
  OS-1, 88
  PC-DOS, 277, 302
  TPM, 297
  UCSD Pascal (Apple), (also Apple P-system), 301
  UCSD Pascal (also P-system), 301
  UNIX, 297, 307
  ZCPR, 297
Organic Software
  Datebook, 39, 40
  Milestone, 40
OS-1, 88
Osborne, 264, 268, 276, 279
Osborne one, 109
Osborne, Dr. Adam, ix, 87, 96, 109, 253, 255
Otrona
  Attache, 73

P-System *See:* UCSD Pascal operating system
Palantir, 81

Parallel *See:* communications
Pascal, 29, 166, 173, 174, 175, 220
  implementation problems, 202
  M, 45, 200, 202
  MT+, 45, 200, 202
  Pascal Introduction Package, 161
  Pascal/M, 322
  RATFOR, 162–163
  The great debate continues, 45
  The great language debate, 28, 29
  Turbo, 192
  UCSD, 159
Pascal Introduction Package, 161, 166, 173, 200, 201
Pascal/M, 45, 159, 200, 322
Pascal/MT+, 45, 200
PBASIC, 319
PC-DOS, 277, 302
PC-Write, 105
PeachText, 81
People's Data Base, 120 *See also:* Mimimum Data Base
Perfect Writer, 81
Personal Computer Products *See also:* Applicard
"Personal Report for the Executive" from the Research Institute of America (RIA), 282
Peters, Dale, 198
Pie, 168
Pietsch, Tony (Anton), 5, 48, 52, 109, 114, 146, 286, 323
Piracy, 94
PL/I, 78, 192, 193
  The great debate continues, 45
PL/I: Structured Programming by Joan K. Huges, 36
Plauger, Bill, 162
Plauger, P. J., 32
Pocket Books, 238
Pope, Alexander
  quote from essay on criticism, 52

Popular Computing, 271
Portable computer systems
    See: Computer systems
Possony, Dr. Stefan T., 112
Pournelle Accounting Program, 13, 134
Pournelle's first law, 15, 56, 64
Pournelle's other law, 114
Pournelle's last law, 258
Pournelle, Alex, 137, 142, 159, 165, 200, 329 *See also:* Pascal Introduction Package
Pournelle, Roberta, (Mrs.), 244
Printer Optimizer, 326
Printers *See also:* Future trends
    See: Diablo *See:* Epson
    See: NEC
    impact, 57, 58
    ink jet (sprayer), 57
    laser, 57
Privacy, 101
    letter to *Infoworld*, 99
Programming in Pascal
    By Peter Grogono, 45, 161, 165, 173
Proteus Engineering, 5 *See also:* Tony Pietsch
    XMON, 8, 9
    XDIR,
Pseudo-Disk *See:* Ram disk

Q/C, 208 *See also:* Small-C, Small-C Plus, and CW/C
Quickon, 327
Quicksoft *See also:* PC-Write
Qume
    8" drives, 114

R&R Software, 221 *See also:* Janus
Radio Shack *See:* Tandy
Ram disk, 153, 172 *See also:* Memory boards
    Semidisk, 153
RATFOR, 162–163
    Carousel Systems (Unicorn Systems), 165
    Software Toolworks, The, 168

Ratliffe, Wayne, 322
Research Institute of America (RIA)
    "Personal Report for the Executive," 282
Roth, Richard, 208
RS-232 *See:* Communications
Rutkowski, Chris, 260

S-100 BUS, 87
    recommended system, 113
    Why I recommend it, 5
Sage, 329
    IV, 325
Sage Computer, 267
Sage IV, 325
Saturn encounter, 53, 110
Scanlon, John, 314
Science and Sanity
    by Alfred Count Korzybski, 38
SCUD *See:* UCSD
Security Micro Systems, 327
    See also: Quickon
Select, 81
Select Information Systems, 283
Semidisk, 153, 172
Serial *See:* Communications
Shake-Out, 279
Sherrer, Deborah, 165
Shirley *See:* Compupro 10
Shrayer, Michael, 322
Silverberg, Robert
    letter from, 53
    reply to letter, 54
Simon & Schuster *See:* Pocket Books
Singh, Noor, 323, 146
Slicer, 267
Small-C, 208 *See also:* Small-C Plus, Infosoft C, Q/C, and CW/C
Small-C Plus, 208 *See also:* Small-C, Infosoft C, Q/C, and CW/C
Software piracy *See:* Piracy
Software Systems *See also:* Digital Research
    CBASIC, 24, 25

INDEX

Software Tools by Kernighan & Plauger, 29, 161
Software Tools in Pascal by Kernighan & Plauger, 160, 173
Software Toolworks, The, 168
Sorcim, 123, 260 *See also:* Pascal/M *See also:* SuperCalc
Pascal/M, 45
Space Viking's Return, 146
Speech synthesis, 194
Spellbinder, 81, 82
Spellguard, 37, 38, 107, 108 140
Spelling checkers
  Microproof, 107, 108
  Spellguard, 37, 38, 107, 108, 140
  Word, The, 139
  Word Plus, The, 83, 322
Spinwriter, 59
Spreadsheets
  SuperCalc, 123, 260, 322
  VisiCalc, 322
Standard Data, 323
Starting Forth by Leo Brodie, 197
Step Farther Out, A by Pournelle, 223
Sturgeon, Theodore, 225
SuperCalc, 123, 260, 322
Supersoft Associates, 209 *See also:* Supersoft c
Supersoft C, 209
Superwriter, 260

T-switch, 154
Tandy, 276
  2000, 71, 275–76
  Model Two, 71
  TRS-80 Model I, 19, 71, 94, 276
Tandy 2000, 71, 275–76
Tarbell, 6
Tate, George, 145
Taxes *See:* Accounting
Technical Software Systems, 209 *See also:* Aztec C

Televideo
  950, 137
Terminals
  advice, 65
  Z-19, 137
Texas Instruments, 276
  TI-99, 301, 276
Text editors
  Electric Pencil, 4, 9, 11, 115–6, 322
  EMACS, 82, 117
  Final Word, 82
  Magic Wand (see also: Peachtext), 81
  MINCE, 82, 81, 118
  NewWord, 80, 81
  overview, 76
  Palantir, 81
  PC-Write, 164
  Peachtext, 81
  Perfect Writer, 81
  Pie, 168
  Select, 81
  Spellbinder, 81, 82
  Vedit, 82
  Word Processing Buyer's Guide, 83
  Wordmaster, 82, 115, 117
  Wordstar, 79, 80, 116, 117
  Write, 76, 83, 115, 116, 117
TI-59, 47
TI-99, 276, 301
Tiny-C Associates, 209 *See also:* Tiny-C One and Tiny-C Two
Tiny-C One, 209 *See also:* Tiny-C Two
Tiny-C Two, 209 *See also:* Tiny-C One
Tonkin, Bruce, 180, 318
TPM, 297
TRS-80 Model I, 18, 71, 276
  repair, 94
TRS-80, Model Two, 71
Turbo Pascal, 192
Twain, Mark, 147

UCSD Pascal, 202, 203
UCSD Pascal operating system, 300, 301

Unicorn Systems *See:* Carousel Systems
Uniform, 327
UNIX, 48, 89, 90, 297, 306, 312, 313
Unpleasant truths, 186
User friendliness, 286
Utilities, 91, 133, *See also:* Workman & Assoc.
  disk catalog, 322

Valdocs, 260
Van Vogt, A. E., 38
Van Zandt, James, 209
Vedit, 82
VisiCalc, 322
VisiOn, 260
Voice recognition, 264
Vulcan, 19, 20

Wade, Jeffrey, 199
Wallace, Bob, 105
Warp Drive, 153 *See:* Ram disk
WE 32000, 311
Whitesmith C Compiler, 32, 142
Wirth, Niklaus, 219, 309
Woodhead, Robert, 99
Word Plus, The, 83, 322 *See also:* Word, The
Word Processing Buyer's Guide
  by Arthur Naiman, 83
Word processor *See:* Text editor
Word, The, 140 *See also:* Word Plus, The
Wordmaster, 82, 117
WordStar, 79, 117
Workman & Associates, 161 *See also:* Pournelle Pascal Package *See also:* Write *See also:* BDS C *See also:* Minimum data base *See also:* Utilities
Workman, Barry, 91, 92, 120, 159–61, 165
World Science Fiction Convention Denver, 1982, 53
Write, 76, 83, 115
WRITE, EDIT, AND PRINT: Word Processing With Personal Computers by Donald McCunn, 195

XDIR, 172
Xerox, 205, 313 *See also:* Diablo
XMON, 8, 9

Z-19, 136
Z-80, 297
  Compupro, 151
  Zeke II, 150
Z-8000, 48, 49
ZCPR, 297
Zeke *See:* Ezekial
Zeke II, 150, 259 *See also:* Ezekial
Zenith *See also:* Software Toolworks, The *See also:* Z-19
Zilog
  Z-8000, 48, 49
Zolman, Leor, 90, 209, 216, 328
Zork, 42, 243, 244, 331